ALISON WEIR is the bestselling [...] the [...] bestselling historian overall) in the Un[...] 3 million books worldwide. She has published twenty history books, including her most recent non-fiction book, *Queens of the Crusades*, the second in her England's Medieval Queens quartet.

Alison is also the author of twelve historical novels, including the Tudor Rose trilogy which spans three generations of history's most iconic family – the Tudors. Her highly acclaimed Six Tudor Queens series about the wives of Henry VIII, all of which were *Sunday Times* bestsellers. *In the Shadow of Queens* is the complete short-story collection that accompanies this series.

Alison is a fellow of the Royal Society of Arts and an honorary life patron of Historic Royal Palaces.

Praise for the Six Tudor Queens series

'This series is a serious achievement'
The Times

'Weir is excellent on the little details that bring a world to life''
Guardian

'This brilliant series has brought Henry VIII's six wives as never before'
Tracy Borman

'Well researched and engrossing'
Good Housekeeping

'Lingers long after the last page is turned'
Elizabeth Fremantle

'Alison Weir makes history come alive as no one else'
Barbara Erskine

'Will change everyone's preconceptions'
Susan Ronald

Also by Alison Weir

The Six Tudor Queens series
Katherine of Aragon: The True Queen
Anne Boleyn: A King's Obsession
Jane Seymour: The Haunted Queen
Anna of Kleve: Queen of Secrets
Katheryn Howard: The Tainted Queen
Katharine Parr: The Sixth Wife
In the Shadow of Queens

The Tudor Rose trilogy
Elizabeth of York: The Last White Rose

Fiction
Innocent Traitor
The Lady Elizabeth
The Captive Queen
A Dangerous Inheritance
The Marriage Game

Quick Reads
Traitors of the Tower

Non-fiction
Britain's Royal Families: The Complete Genealogy
The Six Wives of Henry VIII
The Princes in the Tower
Lancaster and York: The Wars of the Roses
Children of England: The Heirs of King Henry VIII 1547–1558
Elizabeth the Queen
Eleanor of Aquitaine
Henry VIII: King and Court
Mary Queen of Scots and the Murder of Lord Darnley
Isabella: She-Wolf of France, Queen of England
Katherine Swynford: The Story of John of Gaunt and His Scandalous Duchess
The Lady in the Tower: The Fall of Anne Boleyn
Mary Boleyn: 'The Great and Infamous Whore'
Elizabeth of York: The First Tudor Queen
The Lost Tudor Princess
Queens of the Conquest
Queens of the Crusades

As co-author
The Ring and the Crown: A History of Royal Weddings, 1066–2011
A Tudor Christmas

ALISON WEIR

IN THE
SHADOW
OF
QUEENS

TALES FROM THE
TUDOR COURT

H

REVIEW

First published in this edition in Great Britain in 2021 by
HEADLINE REVIEW
An imprint of HEADLINE PUBLISHING GROUP

First published in paperback in 2022 by
HEADLINE REVIEW

1

Cataloguing in Publication Data is available from the British Library

ISBN 978 1 4722 8629 1

Typeset in Garamond MT by Avon DataSet Ltd, Alcester, Warwickshire

Printed and bound in Great Britain by Clays Ltd, Elcograf S.p.A.

HEADLINE PUBLISHING GROUP
An Hachette UK Company
Carmelite House
50 Victoria Embankment
London EC4Y 0DZ

www.headline.co.uk
www.hachette.co.uk

Dedicated in loving memory of
Elizabeth Weir
and
Eileen Latchford,
two great ladies.

Contents

Six Tudor Queens:
Telling New Stories

The idea of writing a series of six novels about the wives of Henry VIII came suddenly to me in 2014 as I was discussing another book proposal with my agent, and I was delighted when Headline commissioned the series. I was eager to revisit the stories of these long-dead queens and excited to have the freedom to explore their innermost thoughts and feelings through fiction. The project became even more exciting when the extensive new research I undertook offered a greater understanding of their lives.

The short stories that accompanied the six novels, now collected here for the first time, were written to offer different windows on six queens and life at the Tudor court. I was given *carte blanche* to choose the subjects. It was sometimes a hard choice, because there was such a rich supporting cast of characters. Writing each novel solely from the perspective of each queen has afforded new insights, but writing these short stories has brought even more depth and nuance to their tales. And being able to tell a story through another's perspective helps to bring the characters of the queens to life.

Fiction offers the scope to develop ideas that have no place in a history book, but which can help to illuminate motives and emotions, and solve mysteries. A historian uses such inventiveness at her peril, but a novelist has the power to get inside her subject's head, which can afford insights that would not be permissible to a historian, yet can also have a legitimate value of their own, although I believe that the fiction-alised version of the story must be compatible with what is known about the subject.

The intrigues that surrounded Henry VIII's queens and often wrecked their lives endlessly fascinate me. The setting for the series is a court dominated by an egocentric, suggestible king, in which factions fought each other with often bloody consequences. It was the duty of a queen to bear male heirs – and in that Henry's wives mostly failed spectacularly, and so exposed themselves to their enemies. Theirs are grim and tragic stories, played out in a lost world of splendour and brutality, a world dominated by religious change, in which there were few saints.

Henry's first wife, Katherine of Aragon, came to England in 1501 to marry Arthur, Prince of Wales, the heir to Henry VII, first sovereign of the Tudor dynasty. Katherine was a great prize in the European marriage market. Henry's throne was established on shaky ground, and winning the friendship of her parents, the mighty Spanish sovereigns, Ferdinand and Isabella, was a skilful diplomatic coup.

There was much public rejoicing when Katherine married Arthur in St Paul's Cathedral. Afterwards, the young couple were sent to Ludlow Castle on the Welsh border, so that Arthur, as Prince of Wales, could learn the art of kingship. But he was already mortally ill. Was his marriage to Katherine consummated? New evidence settles this long-debated question, which was to assume such importance in the years to come.

Tragically, Arthur died in 1502. The story *Arthur: Prince of the Roses* was written to introduce the Tudor dynasty and set the scene for his marriage to Katherine, and to showcase recent research on his health. It has often been claimed that he ailed only towards the end of his life, but it is clear that, having been a premature baby, he was delicate from birth.

Henry VII had no wish to lose Katherine's dowry or the Spanish alliance, so he decided to wed her to his surviving son, eleven-year-old Henry, now heir to the throne. She was five and a half years older, but that was not seen as an impediment in an age in which royal marriages were made for political or dynastic advantage. The potentially serious obstacle was the fact that Katharine had been Henry's brother's wife, but, after it became known that she was not pregnant with Arthur's child, the Pope issued a dispensation, and the betrothal took place.

A year later, however, Katherine's mother died, and the Spanish kingdoms were divided. Marrying her to Prince Henry did not now seem such an attractive proposition, but Henry VII still wanted her dowry. So he kept her in England, in increasing penury, until his death in 1509.

Henry VIII, a handsome, learned and athletic young man of eighteen, now ascended the throne with high ideals of glory. Like a knight errant of old, he rescued Katherine from poverty and married her, ignoring warnings that their union was forbidden in Scripture – and Katherine surrendered her heart unreservedly to her magnificent young husband. The early years of their marriage were a whirl of tournaments, pageants and revelry.

Yet there were clouds on the horizon almost from the beginning. Two of Katherine's children were stillborn. Three sons died soon after birth. There may have been two more abortive pregnancies. The only child to survive was Mary, born in 1516. By 1523, Henry and Katherine had to face the fact that there would be no more children.

When, in 1527, a French ambassador raised the question of the Princess Mary's legitimacy, Henry began to voice doubts that his marriage was lawful. When Katherine found out, she collapsed in grief.

Soon it became known that the King had fallen in love with her vivacious, accomplished and ambitious maid-of-honour, Anne Boleyn. Having spent years at the sophisticated French court, Anne was as poised and fashionable as 'a Frenchwoman born'. Henry was desperate to have her, but Anne kept saying no, and so he resolved upon marriage.

The Chateau of Briis is a fictional tale set in France in Anne's youth. 'Rarely, or ever, did any maid or wife leave that court chaste,' observed the sixteenth-century historian Brantôme, and King François I would recall 'how little virtuously Anne had always lived'. In 1536, a disillusioned Henry told the Imperial ambassador Chapuys that she had been 'corrupted' in France. At Briis-sous-Forges, south of Paris, there is an ancient tower called the Donjon Anne Boleyn. No one knows how it got its name, but legend has it that Anne spent part of her youth there. The many theories as to when, and why, have breathed life into this tale, which builds on all the elements cited above.

Spurred by his desire for Anne, and his need for a son, Henry VIII asked the Pope for an annulment of his marriage. But Rome had just been sacked by mercenary troops of the Holy Roman Emperor, Katherine's nephew. The Pope, now in thrall to the Emperor, kept deferring a decision on Henry's suit. When he finally sent a legate to England to try the King's case with Cardinal Wolsey, Katherine refused to acknowledge the court and made a dramatic plea on her knees before the King. That gave the Pope the pretext he needed to refer the case back to Rome, and an angry Henry took out his wrath on Wolsey, who fell from favour. In 1531, furious because Katherine was still insisting that they were lawfully married, Henry banished her and the Princess Mary from court.

The Pope kept the King waiting for seven years before he declared his marriage lawful. By then Henry had broken with Rome and declared himself Supreme Head of the Church of England. Thomas Cranmer, his new Archbishop of Canterbury, had annulled his union with Katherine and confirmed his marriage to Anne Boleyn; for, learning that Anne was pregnant, Henry had already married her. After she was proclaimed queen, Katherine was commanded (and refused) to call herself Princess Dowager of Wales, and her daughter Mary was declared a bastard.

Marriage to Anne broke the spell for Henry. He was unfaithful to her during her pregnancy and, when she complained, he brutally told her to shut her eyes to it as more worthy persons had done. In 1533, she bore him a daughter, the future Elizabeth I. A stillborn child, probably a son, followed in 1534.

Katherine's health was now declining fast, but, to the end, she insisted that she was Henry's true queen and fought bravely for her daughter's rights. Infuriated, Henry imprisoned her in one decaying house after another, determined to break her resistance. But he failed. When she was dying in 1536, she wrote to him: 'Lastly, I make this vow: that my eyes desire you above all things'. Then she defiantly signed herself 'Katherine the Queen'.

After her death, the findings of the autopsy were kept secret for a time, and Chapuys expressed doubts that she had died of natural causes. He reported that those who had performed the autopsy had 'found the corpse of the Queen and all the internal organs as normal as possible, except the heart, which had a black growth, all hideous to behold'. Modern medical opinion holds that this was probably a malignant tumour, but, for Chapuys and others, there was only one explanation: poison. And that gave me the idea for the second short story. What if rumour spoke truth?

On the day of Katherine's funeral Anne Boleyn miscarried a son. By then Henry had begun paying court to her maid-of-honour, Jane Seymour. Anne had made an enemy of the King's chief minister, Thomas Cromwell. In April 1536, realising that it would be his neck or hers, Cromwell (as he told Chapuys) 'thought up and plotted' a convincing case against her, laying before Henry evidence that she had betrayed him with five men, one her own brother, and had also planned to assassinate him. In May, Anne was arrested, imprisoned in the Tower of London and found guilty of treason. She faced death on the scaffold with great courage. In her final confession, she swore that she had never offended with her body against the King.

The Tower is Full of Ghosts Today is a story set in the present-day Tower of London. My company, Alison Weir Tours, runs historical tours and I have taken many guests around the Tower. The imaginary tour group in this story are following the 'Anne Boleyn Walk' that I devised, which takes in key locations that framed the final days of Anne's life. I hasten to say that what happens on this particular tour in no way reflects my guests' own experiences!

Anne Boleyn: A King's Obsession ended with her execution, so I wrote *The Grandmother's Tale* to relate the events that followed it, as seen through the reminiscences of Anne's grandmother, Margaret Butler, heiress of the Earl of Ormond. This enabled me to use the research I had done on Hever Castle and the impact Anne's fall had on her family.

Ten days after Anne was beheaded, Henry married Jane Seymour, who was pale in colouring and considered plain. But he was impressed by her virtue and her gentle, submissive character – so in contrast to Anne's. Jane had to tread a perilous path and showed courage on two occasions. After Henry had forced his unhappy daughter Mary to acknowledge that her mother's marriage was incestuous and unlawful, Jane persuaded him to receive her back into favour. And when he began to close down the monasteries, Jane knelt and pleaded with him to spare them. But he brushed her away, reminding her that the last Queen had died because she had meddled too much in politics. Jane never spoke out again.

In October 1537, after a long labour, she bore Henry his longed-for son and heir, Edward. But, as England celebrated, Jane died. Henry mourned her sincerely, yet the Privy Council humbly petitioned him to marry again for the comfort of his realm.

His daughter, the Lady Mary, appears in all six novels, but it was Jane Seymour who reconciled her to her father. Hence, I thought it appropriate to tell her story at this point, in *The Unhappiest Lady in Christendom*, which bridges the two-year gap between Jane's death and Henry's fourth marriage. There will be more to come about Mary in the future!

Anne Bassett, who appears in *The Curse of the Hungerfords*, was the stepdaughter of Henry VIII's bastard uncle, Arthur Plantagenet, Viscount Lisle, and served four of his queens. Early in 1540, and again in 1541–2, there was speculation that the King would marry her, which would have changed the course of history. While researching her life in depth for a short story to accompany *Anna of Kleve: Queen of Secrets*, I discovered that Anne later married into the Hungerford family and lived at Farleigh Castle, the scene of a brutal murder in 1518 – a gift to a novelist! The story is therefore told by two women, Anne herself, and Agnes Hungerford, who was convicted of the crime.

There was a long search for a fourth bride for the King. At 46, despite growing obese and infirm, Henry pressed his suit to the beautiful Christina of Denmark, only to be told by that young lady that, if she had two heads, one would be at his Majesty's disposal. At length he decided on a German princess, Anna of Cleves (or Kleve), whose beauty, Cromwell assured him, excelled that of Christina 'as the golden sun excelleth the silver moon'.

Henry sent Hans Holbein to Kleve to paint Anna's portrait. An ambassador vouched that it was a good likeness, but it probably showed her from the most flattering angle. Henry was enchanted and pressed ahead eagerly with the marriage negotiations. He was shocked to find

Anne so unlike what he had expected. It was the most disastrous of beginnings. But, in January 1540, the marriage went ahead. On the wedding night Henry pawed Anna's breasts and belly, but ventured no further, for by these tokens, he was to declare, she was no virgin. We might wonder what he meant by that.

Susanna Gilman (née Horenbout) was a talented painter from a family of Flemish artists who had settled in England and secured Henry VIII's patronage. He sent Susanna to Kleve to wait on Anna, his future bride, and settle some doubts in his mind about Anna's past. In *The King's Painter*, Susanna is a witness to the disaster that is Anna's marriage – but Anna will see her acts as a betrayal.

In the spring of 1540, the King's amorous eye lighted on pretty young Katheryn Howard. In July he found a pretext to have his marriage to Anna annulled. Anna consented with unflattering alacrity and was rewarded with a handsome settlement and the honour of being able to call herself the King's sister.

Immediately Henry married Katheryn Howard. She delighted in being queen and in the rich gifts showered on her by her besotted husband. The King could not stop proclaiming to the world what a jewel of virtuous womanhood he had found in her. But Katheryn had a past of which Henry knew nothing, and it came back increasingly to haunt her.

She had been brought up by her step-grandmother, the Dowager Duchess of Norfolk, who neglected her. At an early age she was corrupted by her music master. The girls in the dormitory she shared admitted young men late at night, and Katheryn became involved with the unscrupulous Francis Dereham. Soon they were sleeping together and calling each other husband and wife. But the Duchess found them together; Dereham was sent away and Katheryn was called to a higher destiny.

Several young women who had witnessed her amorous adventures were found places in her household – possibly as a result of blackmail. Unwisely, Katheryn appointed Dereham her secretary. She was then having an affair with Thomas Culpeper, a favourite of the King. During a royal progress to York she met secretly with him, even in her privy.

After the progress, Henry commanded that the whole realm give thanks for his happiness with Katheryn. Confronted with evidence about her past, he refused to believe it, but when indisputable proofs were laid before him, he broke down and called for a sword with which to slay her. Katheryn became hysterical under questioning and denied everything. At first it seemed that she was guilty only of misconduct before marriage, but then Culpeper was incriminated, and adultery in a queen was high treason.

Dereham and Culpeper were executed, and Katherine was sent to Syon Abbey under house arrest. An Act of Attainder depriving her of her life and possessions was passed and she was beheaded in February 1542.

Having written a biography, *The Lost Tudor Princess*, of Henry VIII's niece, Margaret Douglas, I could not resist writing a short story about her ill-fated (and ill-advised) love affairs, the second of which came to light at the time of Katheryn Howard's fall. *The Princess of Scotland* (the name by which Chapuys referred to Margaret) offers a different perspective on that. Margaret served five of Henry VIII's queens and played an important role in the life of the court. Beautiful and tempestuous, she followed her heart rather than her head and had a compulsive love of intrigue that saw her imprisoned in the Tower four times in the course of her long life.

A Man of God is a bonus addition to this collection because it was never published officially as a digital short story, but appeared in the Readers' Circle edition of the American paperback of *Katheryn Howard: The Tainted Queen*. As the novel is written solely from Katheryn's point of view, the reader never finds out who laid information against her or how the investigations into her offences began. This story fills the gap. It also enabled me, in writing from Cranmer's viewpoint, to show how the reformers at court regarded Katheryn Howard and why they were determined to destroy her.

The subject of *The Wicked Wife* is Anne Boleyn's sister-in-law, Jane, Lady Rochford, who served Katheryn Howard and (for reasons that are still not fully understood) abetted her affair with Culpeper and perished on the scaffold on the same day as her mistress. Here, I offer what I hope is a credible motive for her fatal intrigues. Her story casts a slightly different, and more chilling, perspective on the Boleyn family than I was able to portray in *Anne Boleyn: A King's Obsession*.

The tragedy of Katheryn Howard left Henry VIII old before his time and in no hurry to remarry. According to Chapuys, few ladies at court were aspiring to the honour. But in 1543, the King proposed marriage to Katharine Parr, a comely, intelligent, twice-widowed woman of thirty. She was reluctant to marry him because she was in love with Sir Thomas Seymour, Queen Jane's brother. But Henry could not be gainsaid. After she became queen, Katharine had to hide her feelings for Seymour, and her Protestant views, because the King was zealously burning Protestants for heresy.

She proved a loving stepmother to Henry's children. She was popular and, such was the King's trust in her that, when he invaded France in 1544, he appointed her regent of England in his absence. But, in 1545, the Catholic faction planted suspicions in his mind about Katharine's religious views, and he ordered that she be questioned. Fortunately, the warrant for her arrest was dropped in a gallery and found by one of her attendants. Reading it, Katharine became so hysterical that the King hastened to her, and she was able to deflect his suspicions.

Henry VIII died in January 1547, leaving Katharine a rich widow. His nine-year-old son, Edward VI, succeeded him, and Katharine retired to Chelsea. Almost immediately, Thomas Seymour renewed his suit, and they married secretly. The Privy Council was outraged, for any child borne by the Queen might have been the late King's, which could have prejudiced the succession. But the scandal died a natural death.

Katharine welcomed her stepdaughter Elizabeth into her household. She failed to see anything amiss in her husband romping openly with her. Sometimes she even joined in. In 1548, she discovered that she was pregnant, but her joy was shattered when she surprised Seymour and Elizabeth together. She had no choice but to send Elizabeth away. In August, having accused Seymour of giving her 'many shrewd taunts, Katharine bore a daughter, Mary, at Sudeley Castle, but died soon afterwards, probably of puerperal fever.

The Queen's Child tells the sad story of Mary Seymour through the eyes of her nurse, Bess Aglionby. There are several theories as to what became of Mary. In Victorian times, it was stated that she grew up and married a Sir Edward Bushel. My research for this short story proved that an impossibility. The truth is far more poignant.

For the final tale, *In This New Sepulchre*, I wanted to tell the fascinating – and sometimes macabre – story of what became of Katharine Parr's remains down the centuries. This found me fictionalising historical periods I had never written about before and fleshing out the obscure characters who peopled Katharine's afterlife. I very much enjoyed writing the final pages, in which I couldn't resist including myself. They seem a fitting end to the Six Tudor Queens series.

I hope you enjoy these stories of the people whose lives touched those of the six Tudor queens and that they bring something of their extraordinary world to life for you as never before.

Alison Weir, August 2021

KATHERINE OF ARAGON

Timeline

1485
- Battle of Bosworth. Henry Tudor defeats Richard III and becomes Henry VII, first sovereign of the royal House of Tudor (August)
- Birth of Katherine of Aragon, youngest daughter of Ferdinand and Isabella (December)

1486
- Birth of Arthur Tudor, Prince of Wales, eldest son of Henry VII (September)

1489
- Birth of Margaret Tudor, daughter of Henry VII

1491
- Birth of Henry, Duke of York, (Henry VIII) second son of Henry VII (June)

1496
- Birth of Mary Tudor, daughter of Henry VII

1501
- Marriage of Katherine of Aragon and Arthur Tudor, Prince of Wales (November)

1502
- Death of Arthur Tudor, Prince of Wales (April)

1503
- Betrothal of Katherine of Aragon to Henry, Prince of Wales
- Marriage of Margaret Tudor to James IV of Scotland

1509
- Death of Henry VII; accession of Henry VIII (April)
- Marriage and coronation of Katherine of Aragon and Henry VIII (June)

1513
- Death of James IV of Scotland

1514
- Marriage of Mary Tudor to Louis XII of France
- Marriage of Margaret Tudor to Archibald Douglas, Earl of Angus

1515

– Birth of Margaret Douglas, daughter of Margaret Tudor and Archibald Douglas

1516

– Birth of the Princess Mary, daughter of Henry VIII and Katherine of Aragon (February)

1519

– Election of Charles I of Spain as the Holy Roman Emperor Charles V
– Birth of Henry Fitzroy, bastard son of Henry VIII by Elizabeth Blount

1520

– The Field of Cloth of Gold: diplomatic summit meeting between Henry VIII and François I, King of France (June)

1522

– War breaks out between England and France; Anne Boleyn returns home to serve Katherine of Aragon, and makes her debut at the English court

1525

– Henry VIII starts paying court to Anne Boleyn

1527

– Henry VIII questions the validity of his marriage to Katherine of Aragon and asks Pope Clement VII for an annulment

1529

– Eustache Chapuys appointed Charles V's ambassador to England
– Cardinal Wolsey falls from favour; Sir Thomas More appointed Lord Chancellor

1531

– Katherine of Aragon banished from court
– Thomas Cromwell emerges as Henry VIII's chief minister

1532

– Death of William Warham, Archbishop of Canterbury, paving the way for the appointment of the radical Thomas Cranmer (August)
– Anne Boleyn becomes Henry VIII's mistress

1533

– Marriage of Henry VIII and Anne Boleyn (January)
– Jane Seymour leaves Katherine of Aragon's household to serve Anne Boleyn
– Cranmer pronounces the marriage of Henry VIII and Katherine of

Aragon incestuous and unlawful, and confirms the validity of Henry's marriage to Anne Boleyn (May)

– Coronation of Anne Boleyn (June)
– Birth of the Princess Elizabeth, daughter of Henry VIII and Anne Boleyn (September)

1534

– Pope Paul III pronounces the marriage of Henry VIII and Katherine of Aragon valid
– Parliament passes the Act of Supremacy, making Henry VIII Supreme Head of the Church of England, and the Act of Succession, naming the children of Queen Anne the King's lawful heirs

1535

– Executions of John Fisher, Bishop of Rochester, Sir Thomas More and several Carthusian monks
– Henry VIII begins courting Jane Seymour

1536

– Death of Katherine of Aragon (January)

ARThUR
PRINCE OF THE ROSES

For as long as he could remember Arthur had been surrounded by roses – red roses, white roses, and red and white ones topped by crowns. They were everywhere in his nursery – on the walls, on the ceiling, on the fireplaces and beds – and they appeared in books and the paintings that hung on the palace walls. The curtains concealing the paintings made them mysterious and a little frightening; once he had been too scared to look when the fabric was pulled aside, for fear of what he might see, but it was only the likeness of his father.

Father said that the roses were very important and Arthur should always remember what they stood for. He was the rose both red and white, the living emblem of the peaceful union of the royal houses of Lancaster and York. It was some time before Arthur understood that this meant the marriage of his parents and that Father was of the House of Lancaster – the red rose, he *must* get that right – and Mother was of the House of York, the white rose. Some years ago, the two royal houses had fought a long and nasty war, which must never be allowed to happen again, and the people of England had been overjoyed when a prince had been born to the King and Queen, a prince in whom the two royal bloodlines were made one.

This all took a lot of comprehending but it was clear to Arthur that he was a very special little boy indeed. Even his name proved that. His mother had told him the tales of Father's ancestor, a great hero-king called Arthur, who had once ruled this land and won great victories. Arthur had been named for that hero-king.

Father told him stories too – when he had time, for he was very busy – but his were of another time in King Arthur's life, when he had lived

9

in a far-off land called Brittany in the forest of Broceliande. Father had lived in Brittany too, before he became king, and he had not liked it very much, from the sound of it. There had been a wicked king called The Usurper on the throne then, who had tried to catch Father and kill him. But Father had raised a great army and fought a mighty battle at a place called Bosworth. There he had slain The Usurper and become king himself, so everything was all right in the end. Arthur had heard the story many times; he never tired of hearing it.

Father spoke often of his boyhood in Wales and spun tales of griffins, ancient battles and a prince called Cadwaladr, whose dragon badge he now had on his standard and the royal arms.

'On his death bed, Cadwaladr foretold that a Welsh king would restore the ancient royal line of Britain and that his descendants would rule the whole island,' the King said, his eyes afire. '*I* am that Welsh king, Arthur. I am the true successor of these ancient rulers; those who have ruled since were usurpers.' Arthur thought he understood this and nodded sagely. Father was sharp-witted – he would have noticed any lack of comprehension and disapproved. He was always watching Arthur and frowning, making him feel as if he had done something wrong or was lacking in some way.

Arthur found the Welsh stories fascinating, for he was the Prince of Wales himself. He could remember being taken on the King's state barge to Westminster and the sound of the trumpets as he was carried ashore to be brought to Father's presence. His most vivid memory was of being hoisted on to a horse and led into Westminster Hall, where the King dubbed him the Prince of Wales. Afterwards, he had sat alone in the King's huge chair of estate, his feet hardly reaching the edge of the seat, and presided over a feast. He thought he had been about three at the time.

'You will be a king one day,' Father often said. 'You will be the second Arthur. Remember that, as Englishmen rejoice over that name, other peoples and foreign princes quake for it is terrible to all nations.' That was why Arthur had to be the best at everything he did and surpass everyone else. As Father's son and heir, he must have no weaknesses: he must be strong and brave and clever. Arthur tried;

God alone knew how hard he tried. What Father did not seem to realise was that this was impossible for Arthur. But Father rarely made allowances for that. Arthur's reign must be long and glorious and, after that, Arthur's own son would ensure that the Welsh King's rightful blood continued to rule. He already knew who the mother of his son would be: for as long as he could remember he had been betrothed to the Spanish Infanta. Her name was Catalina, and she was a year older than he and supposed to be very pretty. Father had repeatedly told Arthur that this marriage was very important: Catalina's parents, the King and Queen of Spain, were great monarchs and their friendship was of enormous benefit to England. Most important of all, the Infanta would bring with her a dowry of two hundred thousand crowns. Father's eyes gleamed when he said this. Arthur did his best to look suitably impressed, but getting married meant nothing to him and it was ages and ages away in the future. He just hoped that, when she came to England, Catalina would share his interest in King Arthur and St George and toy soldiers.

As Arthur grew older he remained inspired by the legends of King Arthur and fired by the story of St George, England's patron saint. His child's mind was filled with heroes and dragons, wicked queens and princesses in distress, the mystery of the Holy Grail and swords held fast in stones or rising from lakes. He lapped up all the stirring tales of chivalry. When the court poets and ballad-makers and bards, vying to praise him, sang, 'Behold, the royal child Arthur arises, the second hope of our kingdom,' it thrilled him to learn that his coming had been foretold by the magician Merlin. It made him feel even more special.

He was proud that his birthplace was King Arthur's city of Winchester – although, of course, King Arthur had known it as Camelot. The huge round table at which he and his knights had sat long ago still hung in the great hall of the castle. One day, when he was king, Arthur promised himself he would have it taken down and used again as it was meant to be used.

'The King, your father, wanted you to be born at Winchester,'

Mother had told him, her gentle face softening at the memory. 'He knew it would be an auspicious place for the coming of a prince. It was just as well that I took to my chamber there in good time, for you arrived a month early.' There was a slight clouding of her face when she said that, soon banished by a bright smile. 'You were a fair babe! Everyone said so.'

Young as he was, Arthur suspected that Mother was not telling him everything. As always, she seemed detached; he could never get as close to her as he wanted to. She was beautiful in a plump, golden way, religious, gracious and kind, and she was indulgent to him, but he knew that she did not love him as she loved Harry. There was no doubting that Harry was her favourite of all her children. And who could blame her? Harry was everything that Arthur was not: energetic, boisterous and confident. Even though his brother was not yet two, Arthur could already see Harry would excel effortlessly at everything.

Arthur hated Harry, who seemed to know how to command attention instinctively, especially when their parents were talking to Arthur. He was greenly jealous of the time his younger brother spent with their mother. She had kept him with her from birth and even taught him his first lessons, whereas Arthur had been sent away to the gloomy old castle at Farnham with Lady Darcy for the first two years of his life. *He* had been taught by tutors.

'Why was I sent to Farnham?' he asked Mother, more than once.

'Because you were not strong when you were born and Bishop Courtenay offered to take charge of you there, where the air was healthy and there was less risk of you catching some disease.'

Arthur could barely remember being at Farnham but he was sure that he had missed Mother. He could not recall his sister Margaret's birth but seeing Mother with baby Harry, when he himself was five, had made him realise what he had missed. And then there was Elizabeth . . . They had all known what it was to be loved and nurtured by Mother, Queen though she was and burdened with many duties.

He, however, saw Father more often than he saw Mother. He understood that the King wished to be seen with his heir and to spend

12

time teaching him how to rule. For all Father's critical eye, Arthur knew that he was proud of him.

'In sending you to us, my son, God showed that He was pleased with my victory at Bosworth Field and with my marriage. You are the first prince of my line, the Tudor line.' And again Father had launched into a recitation of his Welsh ancestors, who had been princes of Wales in the distant past and the descendants of the mighty Cadwaladr. Arthur understood that his birth heralded a new Arthurian age of greatness, which would flower when he came to reign. Father's expectations were a heavy burden to bear, but there was one great compensation: being the heir was one thing that he had over Harry. Harry could never become king. That spoilt, bullish little boy would have to learn his place, and Arthur was going to make sure that he did.

He liked his sister Margaret, though. She was three years younger than Arthur, a merry child with rosy round cheeks and hair the colour of copper. He wished he could see her more often, for he loved her sunny nature and even her imperious manner. In her, it did not matter – unlike with Harry – because she was only a girl, and Arthur could order her about with impunity. Sometimes she stood up to him, or would run off complaining to her lady governess, but usually her sense of humour got the better of her, and the pair of them would end up laughing. It made Arthur realise that he did not laugh enough. He had to be serious with Father, of course, Mother was often absent both in body and in spirit and Harry was horrible and nothing to be funny about. So he thanked God for Margaret and her comical ways. But Margaret had her own nursery household and, soon after Harry was born she had been sent to join his at Eltham Palace. So Harry ended up enjoying Margaret's company and Arthur was left alone in isolated splendour in his own household. It was another score to hold against Harry.

Their grandmother, the Lady Margaret, was a loving presence in all the children's lives, but she was old and strict and she dressed like a nun. Father treated her with great respect and it was clear that she adored him, for he was her only son and he had won at Bosworth Field and become king. The Lady Margaret often asked Arthur about his health and she liked to see the work his tutors had set him. It was important, she said, to study hard. Learning was the greatest gift. She told him about the great colleges she was founding at Oxford and Cambridge and how poor scholars would benefit from them. She was very holy, his grandmother, and very stately. He was in awe of her. It did not make for closeness.

The person he loved best – although he hated to admit it even to himself, because he knew he should love God best and then his parents and then his siblings, even Harry, although that really was asking too much – was Lady Darcy, who ran his household. She had been with him from birth and he had overheard her mention that, years before, she had had charge of another prince and had given such satisfaction that the Queen had appointed her to look after her son.

Arthur felt safe in his nursery, where the ubiquitous roses rambled everywhere; he loved to loll on the crimson damask cushions reading or play with his model soldiers on the rich turkey carpets as his servants bustled around setting the table for meals or washing his linen in large pewter basins. And there, a constant presence, presiding capably over all, was Lady Darcy. Always she was deferential to him, yet she would also let him cuddle up to her motherly bosom when he needed it and she had an endless fund of the stories he loved. Yet there was one she would never tell.

'I want to hear about the prince you looked after before me!' he often demanded, but always she would shake her head.

'Ask the King your father,' she said, and changed the subject.

One day, when he had won praise for his lessons and was feeling bold, Arthur did ask the King.

'Sir, who was the prince Lady Darcy looked after before me?'

Father looked puzzled for a moment, then his angular face hardened.

'It was your uncle, the late King Edward.'

'But he was my grandfather.'

'No, Arthur, that was King Edward the Fourth, Mother's father. Lady Darcy had charge of his son, King Edward the Fifth.'

Arthur had not heard of Edward V. He waited to see what Father would say.

'He was Mother's brother.'

'But what happened to him?'

Father frowned. 'He died, poor boy, in the Tower. The Usurper had him and his brother murdered.'

Arthur was shocked. He had been taught that the King was the Lord's Anointed, set apart from mere mortals, appointed by divine right to rule. Truly The Usurper had been wicked to murder a king!

'How did they die?' he asked, curiosity triumphing over caution.

Father's mouth set in the tight line that Arthur knew all too well.

'There are various stories,' he said. 'Only a fool would believe most of them. Now, enough of this! Isn't it time for your archery practice? And I have my accounts to check.' Father was always checking his accounts. People laughed about it behind his back. Arthur had laughed himself when he heard that Father's pet monkey had ripped up an account book and eaten it.

As he took himself off to the butts, he remembered hearing talk of princes in the Tower. It occurred to him then that Father had been evasive because he didn't know what had happened to them. Maybe they weren't dead after all, but had escaped. Arthur liked to think so.

He was six when his life changed utterly. 'It is time that you learned how to govern your principality of Wales, my son,' Father told him. 'It will teach you how to be a king.'

Arthur was to be sent to live at Ludlow Castle on the Welsh Marches. The prospect of ruling Wales and being almost a king was enthralling. And it would mean he did not have Father watching his every move. But then he learned that Lady Darcy was not to go with him and suddenly he did not want to go to Ludlow at all. He even plucked up the courage to remonstrate with Father.

'But Arthur, you are too old now to be brought up by women,' Father said. 'Besides, Lady Darcy is going to Eltham to look after Harry.'

Not to be borne! But, of course, it had to be. Arthur had already learned that, once his mind was made up, Father was immovable and

15

anyway he was the King and had to be obeyed. He could not appeal to Mother after that, though he felt sure she wouldn't have sent Harry so far away.

Lady Darcy was more understanding. As they watched his household being packed up and his childhood things taken away, she hugged him and told him that he was a big boy now, and Harry needed her more than he did.

'Be a prince!' she told him, as they bade farewell. He was trying desperately not to cry and he sensed that she was too.

And so he came to Ludlow, the massive, forbidding castle so far to the west of London that, for all he knew, it might have been on the moon. For weeks he thought he would die of homesickness – for Lady Darcy, for Mother, for all the loved, familiar places – and even for Father.

But Father, as usual, had been careful and thought of everything. He had appointed Sir Richard Pole to be Arthur's chamberlain and head his household. Sir Richard turned out to be a merry fellow with a kind face. Arthur liked him at once. Gradually it began to dawn on him that it was a very grown-up thing to be in the company of men rather than being ruled by women in the nursery. And at Ludlow, as Father had explained, he had a very grown-up role, for he was to preside over the Council of the Marches, ruling Wales and the border with England in the King's name.

He soon discovered the Council was actually very boring. He had thought he would be giving orders himself. But no, he was quickly informed that he was far too young to do that. He was to be a figurehead until he was of an age to rule, which would not be until he turned sixteen. It seemed an interminable time away. For now, he would just sit on the Council in his great chair at the head of the board while Great-Uncle Jasper, who was Earl of Pembroke, and Bishop Alcock of Worcester governed for him with the other lords and gentlemen of the Council. He tried to take an interest in their endless discussions but often he found himself fighting off sleep.

However, he liked Great-Uncle Jasper very much. Great-Uncle's life had been full of soldiering and adventures and he had helped Father to become king. Arthur loved to hear his colourful stories of battles, escapes and secret plots: many a time they sat late after dinner as Jasper whiled away the evening with his riveting tales.

There were also young gentlemen on the Council who were eager to make a homesick young boy feel at home. Arthur's cousin, Maurice St John, was always kind to him; he, Anthony Willoughby and Gruffydd ap Rhys became his close friends.

Most of Arthur's time was spent with his tutor and chaplain, Master Rede. Master Rede had been headmaster of a famous school called Winchester College and made learning seem effortless. This was a great comfort to Arthur, who had heard of boys being beaten regularly for not knowing their lessons. For him, learning was the one thing at which he could excel. He had never been strong. He did not know why he was not like other boys, only that he had to work hard to do things they found easy, such as wrestling or swordsmanship or running. It bothered him immensely because the living embodiment of the union of Lancaster and York must be perfect in every way and the pretence was always kept up that he was. He had always felt that he was not meeting Father's expectations, even though Father prized him as his heir.

Gradually his homesickness was overtaken by his busy life at Ludlow. Lessons, council meetings, the sports and martial exercises that so drained him and playing host to visiting worthies filled his time. Lady Darcy's place was taken by two ladies who took it upon themselves to mother Arthur: his cousin Margaret, the wife of Sir Richard Pole, and his Great-Aunt Katherine, Jasper's wife. Both were kind to him and he could talk to them in a way he would never have talked to the men around him. These kinswomen understood his uncertainties, his frailty and the isolation imposed by his rank and they tried to help.

He was not an exile. Whenever his presence was required, he made the long journey to court and back, and every time he marvelled at how life there was going on without him. Margaret and Harry were growing up and Harry was smugly basking in their mother's attention. Mother was always delighted to see Arthur and interested to hear all about his life at Ludlow, but it was Father who commandeered his time, constantly wanting him at his side when receiving ambassadors and dignitaries, or at ceremonies at court or in the City of London. It was as if he was the King's son and Harry was the Queen's. He always went back to Ludlow with mixed feelings.

The years passed. He was seven, eight. When he was nearly nine his parents made a progress through the kingdom and visited him at Tickenhill Manor, his house near Bewdley, which Father was going to convert into a palace. Arthur preferred Tickenhill to Ludlow, for it was cosier, warmer and more welcoming and he stayed there as often as he was allowed. But he did not want to stay long on this occasion. Great-Uncle Jasper had laid on exciting entertainments at Ludlow and the next morning, before Father and Mother had arisen, Arthur was on his way there to make ready to welcome them and show them where he lived. Then it was down to the great hall for a sumptuous dinner and afterwards to the nearby dry quarry in the town. Today it was doing service as an amphitheatre in which a mystery play would be staged for the royal party's enjoyment.

Arthur watched his parents take their seats, acknowledging the crowd's stares and reverence with grace. He felt that he could always learn more about how to be a king from his father. As the play began, though, he couldn't resist giving it his full attention. It told the story of the Fall of Man and Arthur laughed out loud as the Serpent, deliciously wicked, ranted and writhed around the stage. Then God came with His thunderbolts – there always had to be thunderbolts in these plays – there was a great roll of thunder from behind the scenery and a shining angel appeared with a drawn sword to banish Adam and Eve – both suitably attired in a modest suit of leaves – from Eden. His laughter was forgotten as they walked slowly off the stage, leaving Arthur feeling chastened and overawed.

As he supped at the castle with his parents afterwards, Father seemed to be preoccupied.

'The pretender Warbeck may invade any day now,' he said to Great-Uncle Jasper, whose bushy brows met in a frown.

'Who is Warbeck, Sir?' Arthur asked.

'He is an arrogant and rather stupid young man who claims that he is Richard of York, the younger of the Princes in the Tower. It is ludicrous, of course.'

Arthur noticed the look of pain that briefly shadowed Mother's face.

'But why is he invading?' he asked.

'Because some foreign princes are misguided enough to support him!' Father grimaced. 'But fear not, my son. We are ready for this imposter: he will be routed.'

'But how can he claim to be Richard of York?' Arthur persisted. 'My uncle is dead.'

'He says he was spared by the men who murdered my brother, Edward the Fifth,' Mother said.

'It's a tissue of lies,' Father interrupted. 'Why spare the younger brother when you have been sent to kill the two people standing in The Usurper's way?'

Again Mother looked as if she was about to cry. Arthur had the treacherous thought: *What if Warbeck is telling the truth?*

He looked at the Queen. How must it feel, having mourned her brothers for years, to be given hope that one of them was alive? And then to realise that, even it were true, it could bring no happiness, because if Richard of York lived, he must be the true King.

Of course, Father was right. And he would vanquish the pretender. Arthur had no doubt about that. When his parents departed for Shrewsbury the next day, he said farewell to them without a qualm.

The pretender was caught. He publicly confessed that he was not Richard of York, but was really the son of the comptroller of Tournai, and was placed under house arrest at Westminster, carefully watched. Hearing the news from Great-Uncle Jasper, Arthur felt that Father had been incredibly lenient. Had it been up to him, he rather thought he would have had the wretch executed, not only for his treason but also for causing Mother distress.

Arthur was nearly eleven now. He was old enough at last to be betrothed formally to the Spanish Infanta, Catalina, though he had given little thought to his marriage in the past few years. He was summoned to

Woodstock Palace near Oxford for the ceremony, for which Father and Mother were coming up from London.

Father was fussing over every detail. Everything had been arranged to impress the Spanish envoys and the noble guests.

'You've grown since I last saw you, my son,' he said. 'You're taller than your age would warrant. That gown looks too short now.'

Arthur looked down at the white satin suit that had been made for him in the spring. He stuck out a leg. It was true, the gown was hanging well above his skinny ankles. Father was already calling for the tailor. Then he complained that the table set for the betrothal feast was not looking suitably festive and servants were sent scurrying into the nearby woods to gather some greenery.

At last, when all was ready, Arthur stood in the great chamber before the Archbishop of Canterbury with the Spanish ambassador, Dr de Puebla, a misshapen little man with swarthy features and a large nose, who was acting as proxy. He felt rather silly when he took the doctor's hand in his and solemnly betrothed himself to the Infanta, but the King and Queen looked on, beaming. Afterwards Dr de Puebla congratulated him.

'The Infanta is a lucky young lady! I have never seen a prince of such remarkable beauty and grace,' he enthused. Arthur was old enough to recognise flattery when he heard it, but it was pleasing to be praised so warmly.

'I have heard that the Infanta is very beautiful,' he said courteously. 'I have been working hard on my Latin so that we can converse easily when she comes to England.'

'I have heard that your Highness is very accomplished in the Latin tongue,' the little man enthused.

'We hope that the Infanta will come to England before long,' Father said, almost rubbing his hands in satisfaction at having secured such a prize for his son. 'We are planning even more splendid celebrations to welcome her!'

It was still a matter of indifference to Arthur whether she came sooner rather than later. In truth, he hoped it was the latter, for Dr Rede had told him, using mostly Latin terms, what marriage entailed (which had left both of them pink with embarrassment) and Arthur knew for a certainty that he was not yet ready for it. The part of him that was to be impressed into service was by no means able to accomplish such an important duty and all he could do was pray that it would not be required to do so for a year or so.

He was four months shy of thirteen when he was married, again by proxy, in a ceremony in the chapel at Tickenhill. The manor house was now a splendid palace surrounded by a vast hunting park and it was here that Arthur was at his happiest. Duty regularly obliged him to be at Ludlow, or sometimes at court, but he was older now and adept at making his will known. These days, when he expressed a wish in a certain tone of voice, people hastened to obey; and so he was often at Tickenhill.

Being a married man made little difference to his life. Dr Rede had retired earlier that year and in his place was the blind friar, Father André, but his lessons continued as before. Arthur loved to immerse himself in books. He devoured the ancient classics, history and philosophy. He saw how his friends, Maurice, Anthony and Gruffydd, loved to joust and run at the ring and wrestle, but he had not grown any stronger as he grew older. He still could not sustain the energy for such pursuits. He suspected that the young men thought it unusual for a prince to be studious, reserved and thoughtful. But he needed to excel at something.

Father André, at least, was very impressed. 'Your Highness seems to have committed to memory all the best Latin and Greek authors!' he marvelled.

That summer they were joined in the schoolroom by Dr Thomas Linacre, who had been Father's physician and was a great scholar. It was stimulating to hear him speak of his time in Italy and of great modern thinkers such as Erasmus of Rotterdam. Arthur was thrilled when Dr Linacre presented him with his own translation of a Greek text and he found that it was dedicated to himself.

He was not able to forget his marriage completely, however. His tutors ensured that he wrote to the Infanta regularly, in Latin, and said all the right things.

'There are certain sentiments that a gentleman should express to his wife,' Father André said – he who would never know what it was to have a wife. 'It is your duty to love each other. Begin, *Most illustrious and most excellent lady, my dearest spouse, I wish you much health, with my hearty commendations . . .*'

He continued to dictate as Arthur wrote in his cursive Italian hand. '*I have read the most sweet letters of Your Highness, from which I have easily perceived your most entire love to me. Truly, these letters, traced by your own hand, have so delighted me that I fancied I beheld Your Highness and conversed with and embraced my dearest wife. I cannot tell you what an earnest desire I feel to see Your Highness . . .*'

He wished it all meant something to him, but the prospect of living with the Infanta, pretty though she was said to be, did not move him at all – especially the part of him that, according to the jests his gentlemen made, should be the most moved. In fact it was rarely moved at all. Surely by now something should be happening to him?

He thought he might speak to Dr Linacre, but when they were face to face he lost his courage and gabbled that he wanted to ask about a Latin text he had been translating. He didn't think that Dr Linacre had noticed anything amiss.

Father André was still dictating. '*How vexatious to me is this procrastination about your coming,*' Arthur dutifully wrote. In fact he was heartily relieved that there had been endless delays in thrashing out the final arrangements for the Infanta's departure for England. Father André made him write of his ardent love for her, as he sat there wondering what that really meant. '*I cherish your sweet remembrance night and day. Let your coming to me be hastened, that the love conceived between us and the wished-for joys may reap their proper fruit.*' How that would be achieved he had no idea, he thought despairingly.

Father Andre read the letter and nodded approvingly.

'Very proper, very proper,' he observed, handing it back to Arthur to be sealed.

Whenever Arthur went to court these days the talk was of his wedding. He did his best to look happy about it, but sometimes he felt that events were spinning away out of his control. He also felt like an outsider in his family. *He* was there in Ludlow, most of the time – and *they* were all here together, or near each other, in the palaces on the Thames. And there was Harry, ruling the roost in the nursery at Eltham – Harry was eight now and *he* had not been uprooted and sent away – with Margaret and the baby Mary, who was three and Harry's shadow in all things. There was Mother, doting on them all. And here was Arthur, isolated because he would be king one day. Even so, he knew that Harry would have given much to change places with him.

Just now Harry was full of Perkin Warbeck, who had escaped from the Palace of Westminster.

'They're hunting him down!' he told Arthur with some relish, one night at supper. 'He can't avoid capture.'

'He is a fool,' Father said. 'He was treated well. He had every comfort.'

'Except his liberty,' Mother chimed in.

'*And* he wasn't allowed to lie with his wife!' Harry piped up.

Father frowned. 'We could not have him siring children to take up his cause. He was lucky that he escaped a traitor's death.'

Arthur was still puzzled about that. 'Why did you show him such mercy, Sir?'

'Because he was a fool and others had used him for their own purposes. But I will be merciful no longer. He will be treated like any other felon.'

Mother winced. Surely she did not still wonder if Warbeck was her brother? She had seen him daily; she must have known who he really was. But, being Mother, she said nothing. It was often hard to know what she was thinking.

Harry reported the news with glee when Warbeck was taken; he was in the Tower, in a cell without a window.

Arthur knew that he was not the only young man held in the Tower. He did not like to think of Mother's cousin, the Earl of Warwick, who had been imprisoned there from childhood on Father's orders.

'It is necessary, believe me,' Father had said, when Arthur had once asked what Warwick had done wrong. 'He is of the old royal blood and

could easily be set up as a figurehead by those who want to depose me.'
Arthur was aware that there were any number of wicked people who
might plot against his family, for there yet lived several heirs of the
House of York who coveted the throne. Some had backed Perkin
Warbeck. Arthur understood why Father had had to treat Warwick so
harshly. Yet it did trouble him. What must it be like to be cut off from
all your friends, shut up in a prison without exercise or diversions, and
deprived of any education? Small wonder that people said Warwick
could not tell a goose from a capon.

That autumn, back in Ludlow, Arthur was not completely surprised
to hear that Warbeck and Warwick had been discovered plotting
treachery together, and were both to be executed. You could hardly
blame the hapless Warwick for seizing his chance of overthrowing the
man who had robbed him of his life, but it had been such a stupid plot.
How did those two idiots even think they could have escaped, let alone
taken the Tower and raised a rebellion? But, stupid or not, what they
had done was treason by any definition, and they deserved to die for it.

Soon after the executions, Arthur was summoned back to court, and
was with the King when he gave audience to the Spanish ambassador.
They were discussing the wedding, yet again, but Father seemed even
more bullish and satisfied than usual.

'Your Excellency will no doubt be gratified to report to the Sovereigns
that it has pleased God that not a doubtful drop of royal blood remains
in this kingdom, except the true blood of myself and the Queen and,
above all, that of Prince Arthur,' he said.

'Their Majesties will be reassured to hear that,' Dr de Puebla said, in
his usual unctuous manner. 'Now we will proceed to the arrangements
for the marriage.' He beamed at Arthur. It rather sounded to Arthur as
if a barrier to the marriage had been removed. He glanced sharply at
Father, but Father had gone on to speak of the celebrations he had
ordered for the Infanta's reception, and looked as if nothing in the
world was amiss. Arthur thought no more of it.

It was the year 1500. A new century was about to begin. People spoke
of a golden age to come under King Arthur and Queen Catalina. Arthur

24

knew Father was not liked; the taxes he imposed were too burdensome. But he had brought peace to a kingdom torn by civil war; his treasury was full; and he had triumphed in securing the Spanish alliance. In January, Arthur was told that the Infanta would be coming in September, when he had had his fourteenth birthday. He prayed that he would be ready for marriage by then.

But that spring he began to feel unwell, as if he was going down with a fever. He found himself sweating, even though the weather was not warm, and then he began coughing. Dr Linacre diagnosed an ague. There was nothing to worry about, he said.

By the summer, Arthur had lost weight. He had always been lean and lanky, which his growth spurt had exacerbated, but there was no denying that he was shrinking inside his clothes – and that he still felt ill. When he visited court, he made little of his ailment. It was just an ague, he said dismissively. But Mother kept looking at him anxiously, and Father unexpectedly pressed a hand to his forehead and said, 'My boy, you are burning up.'

'It's nothing,' Arthur said. 'Dr Linacre told me not to worry.' But Father and Mother still looked concerned.

Father took him aside. 'Arthur,' he said, 'the Infanta will be here in a few weeks, and soon it will be time for you to do your duty as a husband. You know what I'm talking about?'

Arthur nodded, blushing furiously, to his mortification. 'Yes, Sir.'

'We do not want you overexerting yourself, especially in view of this continuing ague. I think it best if you consummate your marriage but live apart from the Infanta after that – for a couple of years at least.'

Arthur could think of nothing he'd like better – apart from the bit about consummating the marriage. If he still felt as he did now, he would just not be up to it.

'Yes, Sir,' he said again.

Father gave him a curious look. 'I was expecting a protest.'

'Not at all, Sir,' Arthur replied.

'We must not overtax your strength,' Father said. 'It is dangerous for young people to overexert themselves in the marriage bed. The Infanta's brother, the heir to Spain, did that, and died.'

Arthur had heard that. He was sure that the Infanta, of all people, would understand.

As the weeks passed, his cough worsened. He was still losing weight. But he would not give in to this wretched ague; he *would not* let it get the better of him. He decided that he would never complain and would make little of it. He could not risk anyone suggesting that he was not fit to be his father's heir, for he could not bear the thought of being passed over for Harry.

Fortunately no such idea seemed ever to have occurred to Father. He was too busy telling everyone that no expense was to be spared for the wedding of his heir, though the Infanta's departure kept being delayed for one reason or another. Arthur began to think that she would never come, but in the March after he turned fourteen, in the year of Grace 1501, word came from Spain that she was at last on her way.

Overjoyed, the King lavished fourteen thousand pounds on jewels for the happy couple. But there were storms at sea, and the Infanta's fleet was forced to return to Spain. It was not until October that Arthur heard she had finally set foot in England, at Plymouth.

Arthur was then at Ludlow. His symptoms were worse rather than better. Lately he had suffered pains in his chest and, when he coughed, there were sometimes spots of blood on his kerchief. But he kept on pretending that all was well and washed out the blood in secret.

He wondered wretchedly if he was dying. He had heard of people coughing blood and dying soon afterwards. In truth, he was feeling so awful these days that he hardly cared – well, not for himself. It was his parents who would grieve for him. It would be ironic if he expired just as he was about to be married, after thirteen years of negotiations. He looked in his mirror and saw a poor, thin travesty of the Prince he had been not so long ago. A fine bridegroom for the Infanta! He prayed that his changed appearance had not struck too many others.

It was vital to carry on as normal. He could not let Father or Mother or anyone else down. However bad he was feeling, he would defy this thing, whatever it was.

Even at Ludlow he received reports of the Infanta's rapturous welcome by the people of Plymouth, and of the jousts and feasts the King had hosted in the Tower of London to mark her coming. Then came the summons to court and the inexorable journey through the golden autumn countryside towards his marriage.

They were deep in Hampshire when a royal messenger halted Arthur's procession and announced that the King wished his dearest son to meet with him at Easthampstead, near Woking, whence they would ride together to greet the Infanta.

As his party neared Easthampstead, Arthur was filled with an encroaching sense of dread. He was not ready for this. He would as soon meet his bride as wed Harry. But Father, when he joined him, was as excited as if he were going to his own wedding.

'We must see the Princess!' he kept saying. 'By all reports she will lay this night at Dogmersfield.'

'I thought we were to receive her in London, Sir,' Arthur said.

'That was the plan,' Father replied, 'but I want to see my son's bride and be reassured that she is as fit a mate for you as I was led to believe.'

Arthur leaned forward in his saddle. 'Does your Grace have reason to believe she is not?'

'Not at all,' Father said. 'But if I have learned one valuable lesson in life, it is to trust no one. *Caveat emptor!*'

Dogmersfield was in darkness when they approached. The cold night air made Arthur cough and, as he strove in vain to suppress it, Father looked at him anxiously.

'I just caught my breath,' he said weakly. ''Tis nothing, Sir.'

Father nodded. He dismounted, and Arthur followed suit, then followed the King into the Bishop's Palace. There they were greeted by Dr de Puebla and two outlandishly dressed Spaniards: the Infanta's chamberlain, who was expansively welcoming, and a fearsome dame with olive skin and a sharp nose, who introduced herself as the Infanta's duenna, Doña Elvira. By her manner, you might have thought that he and Father were ruffians come to ravish her charge.

'I wish to see the Princess!' Father said, pleasantly enough, as Arthur took a deep breath and braced himself, but the duenna bristled and gabbled something in rapid Spanish with tones of outrage.

Dr de Puebla turned to Father. 'I regret, Sire, that the protocol of my country demands that the Infanta must remain veiled until she is married. She may receive no man.'

Father's gaunt face darkened with suspicion and Arthur began to wonder if his bride really was deformed or ugly.

'Tell this woman,' Father commanded, in a tone that would brook no argument, 'that the King will see the Princess even if she is in her bed.'

There was more incomprehensible gabbling, then Doña Elvira flounced resentfully off up the stairs.

'Well?' Father snapped.

'The Infanta is being made ready to receive Your Graces,' Dr de Puebla told him.

Presently a pretty young Spanish girl came hastening down the stairs, curtseyed, and bade the King and the Prince follow her. At the entrance to the Infanta's apartments, a herald announced them, and there, standing before them, her head bowed, was a diminutive girl in crimson velvet with an embroidered veil of white lawn covering her person down to the waist. Tendrils of red-gold hair curled to her hips, glinting in the candlelight. As the King approached, she knelt gracefully before him. Arthur's heart was in his mouth. This was the moment he had been dreading.

'Welcome to England, Your Highness,' Father said, then raised the Infanta to her feet. With both hands, he lifted the veil.

THE
BLACKENED
HEART

Her father always accounted himself a gentleman, but it had not been that long since Margery's family had been master craftsmen. The creative streak still survived in her brother William, who was a broiderer and freeman of Canterbury, much to their father's disgust. But Thomas Otwell's pretensions belied his true status: he was not a man of property, but held Brockley Hall and manor under lease from Bayham Abbey.

It was here that Margery had grown up with her brothers, John and the errant William, and her sister Elizabeth. William had run away and got himself apprenticed when Margery was just six, but John was their father in miniature and looked set to build on Thomas's reputation. Careful investments over the years had made for a comfortable life and Thomas, who lived his life on the periphery of the royal court, hoping to attract patronage, supplemented his income by dabbling discreetly in trade.

Margery, John and Elizabeth were close. They all had the same copper-coloured hair, green eyes and heart-shaped faces, and were near in age. Margery had been born just before the turn of the sixteenth century, John just after and Elizabeth a year after that. As children, they did everything together and Father even allowed the girls to share some of John's lessons, so that they grew up able to read and do sums.

It pleased Father's vanity to be on social terms with the local gentry. He was genial company and well liked, and when word spread of his generous hospitality, he was often invited to the houses of men of rank. And that was how he learned that Lady Peche of Lullingstone Castle was looking for a young gentlewoman to wait on her. So, at the age of fourteen, Margery found herself travelling the sixteen miles through the leafy lanes of Kent to Lullingstone to take up the post, miserable at being parted from John and Elizabeth and leaving the home she loved.

As she approached the great red-brick gatehouse she was shrinking inside. It was much grander than Brockley Hall, which was really just a manor house with a superior name, chosen by Father, of course. The carter who was conveying her and her bags drove up the long drive. There were gardens to the left and a fine big house ahead of them. Inside, Margery was led by the steward through panelled chambers and a gallery around two wings of the house, the windows of which overlooked an enclosed courtyard. Everything smelt of beeswax, dried flowers and careful tending.

Lady Peche welcomed her with a smile. She had well-bred features and was beautifully attired in good black velvet with exquisitely embroidered sleeves, and a gable hood with a voluminous veil. Her fingers were laden with rings.

'Mistress Otwell, I am very pleased to see you,' she said. 'My dear, you are very pretty. Your hair is a most unusual colour.'

Margery had tried to confine her unruly copper tresses under a cap. She dimpled at her new employer's praise.

'I look forward to serving you, Madam,' she said, as respectfully as she could.

'You are to be my chamberer,' Lady Peche said. 'You will make my bed, change the sheets when needful, wash my body linen, help me dress and look after my clothes. I have two maids who will instruct you further in your duties.'

And that was Margery's life for the next seven years. It was a happy household, well run and provided for, and Joan and Bess, the maids, were a jolly pair, always laughing or singing. Lady Peche was a kindly mistress, easy-going and generous with praise. Margery soon got over her homesickness and learned the household routines.

She grew to love Lullingstone, its lovely grounds on the River Darent and its vast deer park graced with ancient oak trees and wildflowers. Near the castle, which was supposed to have been built originally by a brother of William the Conqueror, there was a pretty Norman church dedicated to St Botolph, where the household regularly attended

Mass. Margery loved the rich colours in the stained-glass windows and the rood screen with its carved and painted roses for King Henry and pomegranates for Queen Katherine. Sir John Peche had built it in honour of the King's visit two years before she joined the household. People still talked of the marvellous jousts that had been held on a tournament ground laid out especially in King Henry's honour. Margery wished she could have been there and seen him; he seemed to have dazzled everyone with his prowess in the lists, his good looks and his hearty manner.

On her days off, a groom would escort her to Brockley and back so that she could see her family. Every time she went home, John had shot up in height and filled out with muscle and she suspected that, with his angelic good looks, he was popular with the ladies. Soon he would marry and they would lose that special closeness they had enjoyed as siblings.

But that would be compensated for, because Margery was now half in love with Sir John Peche. It was in no way reciprocated, she was sure, because Sir John was far too important to take much notice of a lowly chamberer, although he had sometimes said a friendly word to her. He was a man of great reputation, Sheriff of Kent, Knight of the Body to the King and the monarch's lord deputy of Calais; but first and foremost he was a courtier and he was often absent at Richmond or Greenwich or Eltham or the other royal palaces. The King loved him for his loyalty and his heroic reputation in the tiltyard.

When Margery first came to Lullingstone, Sir John was forty and still a handsome man with heavy-lidded eyes, full, sensual lips and a noble nose. His wavy hair was cut at chin-length and he was powerfully built, as became a champion jouster. He and his wife, who came of the ancient Scrope family, seemed happy enough together. Margery never saw them display anything other than kindness and courtesy towards each other. It had been an arranged marriage, of course, but a successful one in terms of partnership, yet there was no evidence of any passion between them.

Margery knew it was wrong to have feelings for a married man, especially one whose wife was so good to her, but she could not help it and no one would ever know. She cherished her youthful passion in her heart, hugging it joyfully to herself, lost in a fantasy world in which Sir John wore her favour in a tournament and declared himself her knight, swearing undying love . . . Her inexperienced knowledge of men prevented her from conjuring up much beyond that.

When Sir John was absent from Lullingstone, the world seemed a greyer place. When he returned, it was as if the sun came out. Margery thrilled to see him dismounting from his horse, wearing his customarily colourful court clothes and his great gold collar of linked SSs. A year after Margery joined his household, he was among the escort that attended the King's sister, the Princess Mary, over the sea to marry the King of France, and was away for weeks. The next year he went to court to participate in the revels, taking with him a suit of green velvet gored with yellow satin, which Margery had lovingly pressed. The year following he was at Greenwich for the jousts held to celebrate the birth of a daughter, another Princess Mary, to the King, and on this occasion Margery ironed an outfit of black and blue, in velvet and satin. As she wondered how much it must cost to keep up such courtly finery, she was imagining how debonair Sir John would look in it.

When the master was at home, he and Lady Peche entertained often. Their guests were mostly local lords and gentlemen, among them Margery's own father on occasion, and sometimes richly dressed courtiers would visit. Margery was allowed to be present with Joan and Bess in the great hall when feasts were held, although some way down the board from the high table where Sir John and Lady Peche sat with their guests. She revelled in the rich food, the music and the dancing that followed dinner.

It was on one of these evenings that a young man bowed before her and invited her to dance. She glanced at Lady Peche, who nodded approval, and allowed the young man to take her hand and lead her to the floor, where they joined a circle of dancers in a lively brawl. Her partner was rather attractive, Margery thought, sneaking glances at his high cheekbones, long dark hair and Roman nose. He was tall and graceful too, and well dressed in green satin. She knew who he was; his father was tonight's honoured guest, a man rising high at court and, like Sir John, in good favour with the King.

After the dance ended he asked for another, and another, but Margery caught Lady Peche frowning at her and knew she must not accept a third dance. The young man took it in good part and went back to his place. He did not dance with anyone else, but sat there looking at her with his intense dark eyes.

After dinner the next day, he came upon her as she was gathering flowers on the river bank. It was an overcast summer afternoon, with a hint of rain in the air, but she had been grateful to escape the teeming household. Her thoughts were in turmoil: she could not stop thinking about the handsome young man and yet she knew that her heart truly lay with the unsuspecting Sir John. But then, suddenly, he was there, and all became clear.

As they sat on the bank and talked, she was amazed to hear that he was only sixteen. He looked so much older. If she told him she had recently turned twenty, would he still be seeking her out? But he was so attentive that she concluded that it did not matter and anyway, he would be going home tomorrow, and who knew when she would see him again? It was no good wishing for what could not be. She was below him in rank and not well-dowered, and ambitious families like his looked to marriage to bring them wealth and land. She must enjoy their tryst while it lasted.

She took him to the field by the wayside where there stood the ruins of the old church. Long disused, it had been claimed by briars and nettles and they had to pick their way through these to get inside. It was a place that fascinated her, though there was not much to see, just crumbling walls of flint and thin old bricks covered in lichen and damp patches, and the remains of traceried windows.

'In the castle they have a collection of things that have been found here,' she told him, aware that they were alone together in this deserted place, and not wanting him to think that she had brought him here for any purpose other than showing him something that intrigued her.

'What have they found?' he asked, looking up at the jagged edges of the remaining roof timbers silhouetted against the lowering sky.

'Small pieces of coloured stones, some coins and pieces of pottery.'

He turned to her. 'You are so beautiful, Margery.' And he held out his arms.

What impulse seized her she never knew, but suddenly they were kissing as if their lives depended on it, and her need, her sinful need – oh *now* she knew what the priests warned against – was overwhelming. Had she been but half-alive before? She only knew that she must have this completeness, this sweetness, this joy . . .

How long they lay on the mossy earth, where he had spread his cloak, she could not tell. It was as if they had been lost in time, lost in a wonder of which she had never dreamed. There was no shame in it, no embarrassment, just glory and ecstasy. And then there descended a great calm and a deep contentment.

'Will you be missed?' he asked at length, sitting up and reaching for his shirt.

'No, I am free in the afternoons. They know I like to go out walking.' She pulled on her shift.

'That's a relief!' He smiled and continued his dressing.

She wondered, shocked, what had happened to the passionate lover of minutes before. He seemed diffident, distant even, whereas she wanted to go on speaking words of love, even if desire had been sated. Yet some instinct warned her not to be too forward. Father and Lady Peche had both said that men did not respect girls who were like that.

They stood up, and she smoothed down her hair, pulling out tiny twigs, and tied on her cap. They walked back towards the house and she showed him St Botolph's Church. He took her hand as they walked around the empty building and admired the window installed by Sir John Peche, which showed St John the Baptist and St George slaying a fierce-looking dragon.

In the church Margery became aware, for the first time, of a sense of having committed a sin. But she did not regret it. After all, no one would know, only *him*, and he was unlikely to say anything. And if he came back, she knew for a surety that she would commit the sin all over again if he so much as beckoned her. Having tasted the wonderful delights of love, she knew herself to be a changed person. The old

Margery would have thought of her honour; the new one did not care.

He did come back. It transpired that his father had some business to discuss with Sir John Peche, and so there was another convivial evening and he brought his son with him. During the dancing Margery was again sought out and propositioned, and that night, when the whole castle was abed, she and her lover stole out of doors using a hidden key and ended up lying together once more in the leafy gloom of the abandoned church, with the moonlight flooding the broken roof over their heads and owls hooting in the darkness. This time he was more ardent than before, overwhelming her with his vigour and determined passion, and she was lost, irrevocably lost.

After he had left the next day, promising to see her again soon, she went about her duties in a dream. She could think of nothing but him. She longed to see him again. She was counting down the hours and minutes until that blessed day came.

And then, perforce, she had to wake up when it dawned on her that she had not seen her courses for two months. She counted frantically on her fingers and calculated, but the result was the same each time. The impossible had happened. She was with child.

She had heard of servants being cast off for immoral behaviour and she felt very much that she had let down Lady Peche, for misconduct on the part of the maidservant always reflected badly on the mistress. She could not bring herself to confess what had happened to that kind, blameless woman.

What was she to do? She had heard old wives' tales about how unwanted babies were got rid of, but could not summon up the courage to try. That would be a far worse sin than the ones she had already committed.

Should she try to get a message to *him*? She knew where he lived, but it was some way off and she did not know how she could send to him without incurring suspicion. All she could do was pray that he would visit again. But God was evidently not in a receptive mood.

She agonised for weeks and weeks, until one morning she could bear the constriction no longer and had to unlace her stomacher a little. Soon she would start to show and then there would be a reckoning.

There came a day when she was alone in the bedchamber, brushing her mistress's velvet gown and her tears were dripping down on the rich material, causing dark blotches. At that, she began crying hopelessly and that was how Sir John, come to seek out his wife, found her. Once she would have given her soul to have his arms around her and his kind voice gentling her, and to sense that there was more to his purpose than consoling a damsel in distress, but falling in love had spoiled all that for her. Even so, she took comfort in it.

'Tell me what ails you,' Sir John was insisting again, squeezing her tightly. 'You must tell me, sweeting.'

And so she told him and he did not judge her harshly or censure her. He had thought as much, he said. Poor little wench!

'Who is responsible?' he asked and she told him.

'Hmm, that could be difficult,' he said. 'His father will not take kindly to his son being accused of fornication. I will get a discreet message to the young man himself, and suggest that he must look to his child when the time comes.'

'Thank you, Sir, oh, thank you!' Margery wept.

Sir John took care of everything. They were to say he had found her in a faint and that she had confessed to feeling unwell for some time with a malady in her stomach and that the best thing was for her to go to the nuns at Lillechurch Priory, where she could be nursed back to health. She was immensely grateful to Sir John, whom she now regarded as her saviour rather than her hero. Lady Peche and the maids were all sympathy and they sent her on her way with little gifts and good wishes for a speedy recovery.

And so she came to Lillechurch, an ancient community of nuns, once ruled by the daughter of King Stephen. It was a poor house and the number of sisters seeking their vocation there had dwindled over the years, so that the three nuns who remained had a hard life of toil and making ends meet and welcomed the substantial sum Sir John generously provided to pay for their guest and buy their discretion.

But, following the lead of Prioress Anchoretta Ungerthorpe, they were cold to Margery, and disapproving. The guest house was meanly furnished, the food plain and of poor quality. The months she spent

38

there were miserable ones, enlivened only by letters from her concerned family and from her friends at Lullingstone. There was talk of the priory being closed down, which accounted in part for the nuns' sharpness, for they were all worried about their futures.

Margery was utterly relieved when her labour began, for it heralded the end of her exile. The baby, delivered by Sister Godliff, was a healthy boy with a fluff of dark hair, and she called him after the father he favoured in looks. But even as she took joy in him and was filled with the strong, protective love of a new mother, she fretted constantly about what would become of him. She had heard nothing from her lover and was sure he had abandoned her.

But no. As Prioress Anchoretta, Sister Godliff, Sister Anne and Sister Elizabeth were beginning to drop heavy hints about her leaving Lillechurch and taking her bastard with her, for Sir John's money had all but run out, a carter arrived with a plump, rosy-cheeked wet-nurse on board. She carried with her a sealed note signed with his spiky writing, which informed Margery that the child was to be put out to nurse on his family's estate with Mistress Lemon, who came very highly recommended.

She had no choice. She had to give up her babe to this stranger and watch as he was carried off to an unknown home to be brought up as someone else's child. God grant that one day he would know how much she loved him and would understand that, in letting him go, she had done the best for him. Forever after, she knew, her heart and her empty arms, would ache for him.

It was only after she had dried her tears and packed her belongings that she looked again at the note he had sent and realised that it contained no word of love or endearment.

When she returned to Lullingstone, her wan appearance was in keeping with the state of one who had suffered a long illness, but no one commented very much because they were all preoccupied with their fears for the master. Margery had been away for just five months, but in that time Sir John had lost flesh to an alarming extent and looked an unhealthy shade of yellow. Within two weeks of her arrival, he was confined to bed – a sad wreck of the man he had once been. The doctors, it seemed, could do nothing for him, although they tried remedy after remedy.

Lady Peche herself took charge of the nursing, but as the weeks passed she grew exhausted and came to rely heavily on Margery's tender skills. Margery would have done anything for Sir John, who had saved her from shame and dismissal, and he loved to have her tend him and read to him. Many was the evening she would sit by him and chat, telling him of what was going on in the household and gossiping of the world beyond Lullingstone's gates.

'You're a good girl, Margery,' he often said, patting her hand weakly.

His friends did not forget him. As soon as he was able to sit in his chair, they beat a path to his door and did their best to cheer him, trying to hide their dismay at his altered appearance.

After one such visit he said to Margery, 'I hear that the Queen needs two new chamberers. Would you like me to recommend you?'

She stared at him. 'But Sir, I'm needed here.'

'It is no life for you,' he said, vehemently. 'You are young. You should not be cooped up with a dying man.'

'Don't say that!' she cried.

He reached for her hand. 'I am resigned to it, Margery. I have had a good life, all that a man could want. Although, if things had been otherwise, I would be wishing myself young again.' He looked at her intensely. She understood what he was trying to say.

'Go to the court,' he instructed. 'Live and be happy. My word carries some weight. The place may well be yours if you want it.'

Margery bit her lip. It seemed so selfish to say yes, but the prospect of serving the Queen was too good to forego. It would distract her from her grief at losing her child and it would be pleasing to Sir John. It seemed churlish to turn down his generous offer. She thanked him warmly, her heart full.

'What of Lady Peche?'

'I will speak to her,' he promised. 'She will understand that this is a piece of fortune too good to pass over.'

'You said there were two places, Sir? Would you consider recommending my sister Elizabeth as well? She has done praiseworthy service with Mistress Roper at Well Hall.'

Sir John's yellow face creased in a smile. 'Of course I will. Anything for you, Margery.'

Thomas Otwell was delighted to hear that his daughters were going to court to wait on the Queen. He did not complain at the cost of fitting them out with the requisite clothing to befit them for royal service. Thus it was that they arrived at Richmond Palace in fine black gowns of good cloth and matching gable hoods.

Margery was trembling when they were ushered into the presence of Queen Katherine, who was waiting for them in her privy chamber, her ladies and maids ranged around her, sewing. One was strumming a lute.

There was no need to worry. The Queen warmly welcomed them with a gracious smile. She was a stout little woman, gorgeously dressed, with a plump oval face that looked sad in repose – and small wonder, for all her sons had died at birth. Her nose was straight with an upward tilt at the bottom, her chin firm and determined. She spoke with a marked Spanish accent.

Their duties were much as Margery's had been at Lullingstone, but on a grander scale. Margery loved serving the Queen. She soon found out why Katherine was much beloved of all who attended on her: she was a kind mistress, devout and fair.

Margery loved being at court too. She had never seen houses of such splendour as the royal palaces, never witnessed such lavish feasting and revelry. Caught up in the teeming bustle of the royal household, she was able to rise above her sense of loss, laying it away in her heart as a private, tender sorrow, never to be probed.

Meeting the King was an overwhelming experience. The Queen presented Margery to him when he whirled into her chamber one day, a magnificent, godlike figure in cloth of gold, glittering with jewels. As Margery fell quaking to her knees, he raised her up and considered her with his piercing blue eyes.

'I have heard good reports of you, Mistress Margery,' he said, his voice surprisingly high in pitch for so manly a gentleman. 'I trust you are enjoying being at court.'

'Oh, yes, Your Majesty,' Margery answered, her voice hoarse.

'There is no need to be afraid of me,' he laughed, 'as the ladies here will tell you!'

There was a ripple of feminine giggling. The Queen smiled. Margery relaxed and joined in the merriment. Within weeks she was almost as comfortable in his presence as she was in the Queen's, although she remained in awe of him.

One day she was hastening across a courtyard on an errand for the Queen when she saw, coming towards her, a young gallant in gaudy-coloured clothing. It was *him*!

There was no escape. He stopped when he saw her.

'Margery? What do you here?'

'I am chamberer to the Queen, Sir,' she told him, blushing, her breath coming fast and irregular.

'And I am an usher to the King,' he said. There was an awkward pause. 'I am sorry for what happened. Our son is doing well.'

'I rejoice to hear it!' she said fervently.

'Well, I must be on my way,' he told her. 'I will give you news of the child whenever I have it.'

And that was the beginning of a rather strained friendship – strained because, for her, it could never be enough. She knew her love for him was hopeless and that she was not worthy of more. But every encounter, every tense conversation, twisted the knife.

She saw yet more of him when his sister came to court two years later as maid-of-honour to the Queen. His sister was elegant, charming and witty, and people – especially men – noticed her. No one noticed Margery, even though she was much prettier; it was as if they knew she would not be interested.

In October of that same year, 1522, Margery received a letter from Lady Peche, informing her that Sir John had died. He had rallied unexpectedly some months ago and had gone to Ireland on the King's business. But it had proved too much for him and his decline had been inexorable. Enclosed with the letter were eleven pounds. He had left that sum to her in his will. It had been at the top of his list of bequests. It was more money than she had ever dreamed of owning and she locked it in the coffer she kept under her bed, with the coins she had saved from her wages. It would assure her of a comfortable old age.

She knew she would never marry. *He* had spoiled her for that. When he got married, her heart broke all over again. As the years passed, she almost rejoiced when no children were born to his wife. Only she had given him a son. The boy was doing well: he was being properly tutored and showing great promise. She knew she had done the right thing in giving him up.

She had been at court six years when her brother John visited her at York Place. He had filled out now and become a handsome man with a commanding presence. The Queen gave Margery an afternoon's leave, so she and John walked along the Strand and into the City, where they wandered around St Paul's Cathedral, looking at the monuments and catching up on their news. It was so good to be with John again. He embraced her warmly when they parted at the palace entrance and promised to come to London again soon.

She never saw him again. Two days later, she learned what had happened. That night, near his lodgings, he had accidentally kicked a dog, whose owner had exploded with rage and stabbed him.

She thought she would never stop crying. She only ceased when *he* came and told her that the killer had been arrested and would almost certainly be hanged. That was some comfort. It meant she could go on living.

But then *he* came again, his face overcast, and said that the King had pardoned the wretch.

'Why?' she almost screamed. 'How can he pardon a murderer?'

'Because the man genuinely believed that John had kicked his dog deliberately and so he had sought revenge.'

'But that is no justification for murder!'

'The King issues pardons all the time. He likes to be seen to be merciful.'

Margery began to hate the King. Her anger against him festered. When the Queen found her and Elizabeth weeping one day and asked what was wrong, they could not tell her, for they dared not be seen to be criticising the King. So they let her think they were weeping for their brother and for the death of Lord Willoughby, whose wife was one of the Queen's closest friends.

Margery's hatred of the King deepened when it became known that he had approached the Pope for a divorce from his blameless Queen. She loved her gentle mistress and hated to see her discarded so shabbily just because she had not borne a son. And she inwardly raged against the King even more when it became obvious that his true motive was not some scruple of conscience about his marriage being invalid, but his lust to marry Mistress Anne Boleyn.

Margery's loyalties were with the Queen from the first. She hated to see Katherine bearing her sorrows so cheerfully and maintaining her dignity while Mistress Anne queened it over the court and vented her spite on the Princess Mary. She applauded the Queen's insistence that she was the King's true wife, and her courageous stand for her rights.

He, of course, sided with the Boleyns, as did all who chased favour and preferment. It was the end of their friendship. After he had defended Mistress Anne and said the Queen had no right to her title, Margery refused to speak to him. After that his mother sent her reports on her son's progress.

It went on for years, for neither King nor Queen would give way. A court was convened in London, but it ended with the case being referred back to the Pope for a decision – a decision that seemed never to be forthcoming. Margery watched as the Queen fought her solitary battle, maintaining her position and provoking the King's increasing anger, until the day came when he resolved to brook her defiance no more, and banished her from court.

Margery went with her, first to the More, then to Easthampstead, Eltham and Ampthill. She was present when the Queen was informed that her marriage had been declared invalid and, as the King was now married to Anne Boleyn, she must not call herself queen but princess dowager of Wales, the title she had borne long ago as widow to Prince Arthur, the King's elder brother. Bravely the Queen declared that she was the King's true wife and would be addressed by no other title. Inwardly Margery applauded, and her anger against the King burned white hot. How dare he put this good lady through all this suffering!

For her defiance, the Queen was banished to Buckden, a damp house in the Fens, with a pitifully reduced household. Fortunately Margery and Elizabeth were of its number. Margery hoped that the Queen would be left in peace, but in vain. Shortly before Christmas the Duke of Suffolk, a crony of the King's, arrived with a force of soldiers and said that everyone had to swear an oath acknowledging the King's new marriage as lawful, or lose their positions. Margery, and almost all the rest, refused.

Dismissed! After thirteen years in the Queen's service, she could not credit it. And dismissed without a pension. Thank goodness she had her horde of coins.

Elizabeth was dismissed too. As they and the other ladies sat weeping in the gatehouse, pending their eviction from the premises, the Duke of Suffolk strode in.

'Two of you may remain,' he said. 'The Princess Dowager is asking for Eliza Darrell and Margery Otwell.'

Margery slumped in relief. Then she looked at Elizabeth.

'Don't fret,' her sister said. 'I've had enough of this sad situation. I want to go home.'

The presence chamber had been stripped of all its royal trappings. Where there had once been two hundred and fifty maids-of-honour, there were now three. But the Queen, who looked tired and drawn, was delighted to see them. She embraced and kissed them all.

'For your faithfulness I am advancing you to maid-of-honour,' she told Margery.

'But Madam, I am thirty-four – hardly a maid!' Margery protested, weeping and deeply touched.

'It is the rank that counts, not the condition!' the Queen assured her.

The other maids were Eliza Darrell and two Spanish ladies, Blanche and Isabel de Vargas, who had come to England with the Queen. From now on, in the absence of any great ladies, the four of them were Katherine's daily companions and friends.

As the months passed, they suffered increasing privations, deliberately inflicted on them. They were moved to Kimbolton Castle, which became a gilded prison for the Queen. Margery cared little for her own comfort, but wept for her beloved mistress, seeing her suffer under the strain of her unending troubles. Early in 1535, Katherine took to her bed with a bad cough and an ague and they took turns in dabbing her burning brow with damp cloths, shaking their heads at each other at how her feet and legs had swelled with dropsy. The doctors themselves seemed worried.

The Spanish ambassador, Messire Chapuys, managed to write to the Queen occasionally, despite all correspondence being banned. Margery knew how much these letters meant to Katherine, but at the same time dreaded what news each would bring. Chapuys warned the Queen repeatedly that Anne Boleyn wanted her dead. She had issued threats and never ceased urging the King to have Katherine and her daughter put to the sword. Chapuys feared she might resort to poison. There had been an attempt to poison the Bishop of Rochester, one of the Queen's staunchest advocates and the finger of suspicion had pointed at the Boleyns – but, of course, no one could touch them.

Margery and the others resolved to be watchful. They decided to oversee the preparation of the Queen's food themselves. They had a cooking pot set up over the fire in her room, but none of them could cook and at first the meals they produced were mostly unpalatable. But Katherine was so grateful to them for trying and soon, through trial and error, their skills began to improve, as did their mistress's health.

That December the Queen turned fifty.

There was a weekly market in Kimbolton and the Queen's maids were allowed to go there to buy food for her. Mostly Eliza went, but on the morning of the birthday Margery accompanied her, both carrying large baskets. The Queen had asked for some broth – she ate very little these days – so Eliza went to look for vegetables and whatever meat was available in this winter season. Margery wandered among the stalls, looking at cheeses and nuts and loaves of bread. Suddenly she had the feeling she was being followed. She turned and looked around her. A few paces behind stood a youth in a heavy hooded cloak. She had noticed him earlier by a stall selling honey cakes. He looked up. He was his father to the life.

A wave of faintness smote her. She clapped her hand to her mouth, gasping. He came quickly towards her and led her to the market cross, where he made her sit on the step. Then he sat down beside her, looking at her tenderly.

'I knew it was you,' he said. 'Father described you so exactly. I did not mean to startle you.'

'It's all right,' she breathed, her eyes drinking him in. His face – his nose, his cheekbones – there was no mistaking whose son he was. She had no words to express the magnitude of her feelings, for he was still in every way a stranger despite being her own flesh and blood.

'I have been plucking up courage to seek you out for ages,' he said, his boyish eagerness touching. 'I knew you were at Kimbolton and I was on my way to the castle when I saw you. I wanted to buy a gift for you.'

Tears filled her eyes. He had grown into a lovely young man. He must be, what, sixteen? And yet he seemed so mature. He had sought her of his own volition. It overwhelmed her.

'You knew me?' she asked.

'Father said you had hair of an unusual colour. I noticed it. I was sure it was you.'

They talked for a while, of trivialities, which seemed strange when there was so much more to say. He said he was enjoying being away from his tutor.

'You are a scholar?'

'I want to go to university one day, if Father agrees.'

She thought of her savings. If they could buy him a place, or support him, she would give them to him in an instant. It was the least she could do for him.

'You are shopping?' he asked, interrupting her thoughts.

'Yes. It's the Queen's birthday. She has asked for some broth.'

His expression was unreadable. She realised, too late, that she should not have referred to the Queen openly by her title. *He* would never have approved and no doubt his son was of the same opinion. But the youth said nothing.

She rose. Eliza would be looking for her and she did not want to answer any awkward questions.

'I must hasten,' she said reluctantly, for the time with him had been all too short. 'I just have to buy some herbs. The herb garden at the castle is pitifully neglected.'

He followed her. The herbalist had a fragrant display of wares, both fresh and dried.

'Rosemary would give the broth a nice flavour,' Margery said, rubbing some between her fingers. 'I'll get some, and a few sprigs of this marjoram.'

'Allow me to give the Queen a gift on her birthday,' her son said, digging into his pocket and handing over a coin to the herbalist. 'I have a great admiration for her.'

'That's very kind,' Margery said, surprised, 'but I wouldn't refer to her by that title in public. You never know who is listening.'

'Oh, of course.'

Just then Margery espied Eliza coming towards them.

'I must go,' she said.

He laid the herbs in her basket. 'For the Queen,' he said. 'And I will come again, I promise.'

'I'll make it for your Grace,' said Margery, busying herself at the cooking pot, while Blanche laid out the cold meats and bread for the rest of them.

The Queen took a few sips of the broth then laid down her spoon. Margery wondered if she had overdone the herbs. It had been such a nice gesture on her son's part and she was bursting to tell her mistress why her food was so unusually flavoursome.

But the Queen was quite obviously too unwell to eat. That afternoon, she had a bad attack of breathlessness and stomach cramps, but mercifully they passed and in the evening she was able to sit by the fire and do some embroidery. A week later, when Christmas came, she joined in their modest festivities and even ate some of the goose that Eliza's parents had sent.

On St Stephen's Day, Margery made a stew of the leftovers, adding more of the herbs. The Queen ate a little of it sitting in her chair, swathed in shawls, but suddenly she hissed that she could not breathe and seemed to be trying desperately to draw in air. Margery and Eliza thumped her back until, to their relief, she got her breath back. She was coughing and complaining of pain, so they helped her to bed and called the doctors. But they could do little to relieve her.

As the days dragged by, the pain grew worse. Eliza sponged her mistress's brow and tried to divert her by reading aloud; Margery made her herbal cordials, infused with the dried leaves, grateful for her son's bounty. She wished she could see him again.

'That will soothe your Grace's throat,' she said. But the poor Queen was failing. They could all see it.

On the afternoon of New Year's Day, the first day of the year of our Lord, 1536, the Spanish ambassador came unexpectedly to visit the Queen. Margery and the others rejoiced to see him. They went scurrying to take his cloak and bring him some ale. His very presence was a tonic to their mistress.

He stayed a few days, until another unexpected visitor arrived. It was Lady Willoughby. She had heard that Katherine was weakening daily, and forced her way into the castle so that the Queen would have her oldest friend with her at the end.

Lady Willoughby was unimpressed by the cooking arrangements. She announced that she was taking over. Margery and the other maids found themselves hurrying to the kitchens to beg the ingredients she demanded for what turned out to be a surprisingly good stew.

One meal was enough effort for Lady Willoughby. Again Margery and Blanche were delegated to do the cooking and Margery was instructed to continue making the herbal cordial, for Lady Willoughby thought it beneficial to their mistress.

But the Queen grew weaker still and her symptoms more alarming. Constantly she complained of palpitations and breathing problems.

'I am dying,' she said one morning. 'I must make my will.'

It took nearly all her strength and afterwards she had to rest. Lady Willoughby ordered Margery to bring her some cordial and they raised her up so that she could sip it. She could take very little and signed to them to lay her down to sleep.

It was market day, so Margery seized the opportunity to walk into the town. She was hoping that her son would be there waiting for her. She had not forgotten the wish he had expressed to go to university, and before she left she took from her casket three-quarters of her savings. The rest she must keep, because God alone knew what might happen after the good Queen died, as she surely would soon.

There was no sign of him in the market. She went on past St Andrew's Church and down to the river, where she often liked to walk. She never knew who, or what, struck her head and caused her to tumble into the freezing water, then held her down until the bubbles ceased to rise. And it was not until two hundred years later that, when walking through nearby woods, a farmer found the remains of a skeleton that no one could ever identify, with fragments of carved wood lying beside it.

The wax chandler looked anxiously at the Bishop of Llandaff, the late Queen's confessor.

'My lord, we found the corpse of the Queen and all the internal organs as normal as possible, except the heart. It had a black growth, hideous to behold, which clung closely to the outside. When I washed it in water, it did not change colour, and when I cut into the middle, I found it to be the same colour.'

The Bishop frowned. They were alone in the Queen's empty chamber, and the door was closed, but still he looked over his shoulder.

'What does this suggest to you?' he asked nervously.

The chandler lowered his voice.

'Poison,' he said.

Author's Note

The story of this novella has been constructed imaginatively from fragments. Katherine of Aragon did have a servant called Margaret 'Margery' Otwell. She had joined her household by April 1521, when Sir John Peche of Lullingstone Castle (d. 1522) left Margaret a bequest of £11 in his will, describing her as 'one of the Queen's chamberers'. In April 1529, Margaret Atwell and two other chamberers were given gowns of tawny damask lined with tawny velvet.

Margery remained in the Queen's service until December 1533, when she was dismissed for refusing to swear an oath recognising Henry VIII's marriage to Anne Boleyn. Most of Katherine's female English attendants also refused to swear and were likewise dismissed. Katherine protested that she would not accept replacements, and would sleep in her clothes and lock her door, so the Duke of Suffolk said that two maids could remain. I have conjectured that Margery was one of them, the other being Eliza Darrell.

An Elizabeth Otwell was dismissed at that time. Possibly she was Margery's sister.

In her will of January 1536, Katherine of Aragon left bequests to Eliza Darrell (£200); Blanche and Isabel de Vargas (who had accompanied her from Spain in 1501, and were left £100 and £40 respectively); and 'Mrs Margery' (who got £40). Margery Otwell then disappears from the historical record.

In 1526, one Thomas Otwell and John Otwell were leasing the manor of Brockley in west Greenwich from Bayham Abbey, near Frant, Sussex. I have made them father and son and related them to Margery and Elizabeth Otwell. William Atwell (or Otwell), broiderer, is recorded as a freeman of Canterbury between 1515 and 1543. I have made him their brother.

In October 1526 the King granted a pardon for the death of John Atwell (or Otwell) to Robert Hilton of St Clement Danes, *alias* of Burton, co. Westmorland, *alias* of Berwick-on-Tweed. Upon this I have built my tale of the death of Margery's brother.

Many details are authentic, such as the descriptions of Sir John Peche's clothing and of the church and ruins at Lullingstone. I am not, at this stage, going to reveal the identity of Margery's lover, but he may have had a bastard son. The findings of the autopsy are exactly as I have recounted them.

The rest is speculation – or is it?

ANNE BOLEYN

Timeline

1499?
- Birth of Mary Boleyn

1501?
- Birth of Anne Boleyn

1503
- Birth of George Boleyn

1509
- Accession of Henry VIII
- Marriage and coronation of Katherine of Aragon and Henry VIII

1514
- Marriage of Mary Tudor to Louis XII of France

1515
- Anne Boleyn arrives at the French court to serve Mary Tudor and later joins the household of Queen Claude, wife of King François I

1520
- Marriage of Mary Boleyn and William Carey
- The Field of Cloth of Gold: diplomatic summit meeting between Henry VIII and François I

1522
- War breaks out between England and France; Anne Boleyn returns home to serve Katherine of Aragon, and makes her debut at the English court

1524
- Marriage of George Boleyn and Jane Parker

1525
- Anne's father, Sir Thomas Boleyn, created Viscount Rochford
- Henry VIII starts paying court to Anne Boleyn

1527
- Henry VIII questions the validity of his marriage to Katherine of Aragon and asks the Pope for an annulment
- Jane Seymour goes to court as maid-of-honour to Katherine of Aragon

1528
- Death of William Carey

1529

- Thomas Boleyn created Earl of Wiltshire; George Boleyn becomes Viscount Rochford

1531

- Katherine of Aragon banished from court; Jane Seymour remains in her household
- Thomas Cromwell emerges as Henry VIII's chief minister

1532

- Death of William Warham, Archbishop of Canterbury, paving the way for the appointment of the radical Thomas Cranmer (August)
- Anne Boleyn becomes Henry VIII's mistress
- Anne Boleyn created Lady Marquess of Pembroke

1533

- Marriage of Henry VIII and Anne Boleyn
- Jane Seymour leaves Katherine of Aragon's household to serve Anne Boleyn
- Cranmer pronounces the marriage of Henry VIII and Katherine of Aragon incestuous and unlawful, and confirms the validity of Henry's marriage to Anne Boleyn (May)
- Coronation of Anne Boleyn (June)
- Birth of the Princess Elizabeth, daughter of Henry VIII and Anne Boleyn (September)

1534

- The Pope pronounces the marriage of Henry VIII and Katherine of Aragon valid (March)
- Marriage of Mary Boleyn and William Stafford
- Parliament passes the Act of Supremacy, making Henry VIII Supreme Head of the Church of England, and the Act of Succession, making the children of Queen Anne the King's lawful heirs

1535

- Executions of John Fisher, Bishop of Rochester, Sir Thomas More and several Carthusian monks
- Henry VIII begins courting Jane Seymour

1536

- Death of Katherine of Aragon (January)
- Anne Boleyn arrested and imprisoned in the Tower of London (May)
- Anne Boleyn executed for treason (19 May)

THE CHATEAU OF BRIIS

Introduction

At Briis-sous-Forges, south of Paris, there is an ancient tower called the Donjon Anne Boleyn. No one knows how the tower got its name. Legend has it that Henry VIII's second wife spent part of her youth there and the many theories as to when, and why, have breathed life into this tale.

The du Moulin family owned the chateau. All its members mentioned in this story really lived. The ruined chapel in the woods exists, but it is at Brantôme in the Dordogne. The love affair really happened, in another place, another time. The rest is conjecture . . .

1515

Freedom at last – if only for one magical evening! Anne Boleyn could hardly contain herself. Dressed up in wine-coloured satin, with her long dark hair loose, she was attending a great ball at the French court, presided over by King François and Queen Claude, her virtuous mistress. It was a heady experience – and a rare one, for the Queen usually shunned court entertainments.

The palace of the Louvre was packed with lords and ladies, and the dancing had begun, led by the King and his latest mistress, on whom he was casting lascivious looks. Anne looked away in disgust, remembering what he had done to her sister Mary, and resolving to make herself scarce if he showed any sign of coming in her direction.

She was longing for one of the flamboyantly attired gallants to ask her to dance. It was rare for her to be enjoying the opportunity of meeting them. Some were looking at her with overt interest. She knew she was attractive to the men, but it was the game of love she enjoyed. At heart – and at just fourteen years old – she was indifferent to them. She smiled at the sight of one of her fellow maids-of-honour simpering at her dancing partner. What a fool she was making of herself!

It was not long before a well-built young man with pleasing features and long wavy hair was bowing before Anne.

'May I have the pleasure of your hand in the dance, mademoiselle?'

She looked up into warm eyes above a wide nose and smiling mouth, but the things she really noticed were his hands, which were large and shapely, and his sheer physical presence. He exuded masculinity, for all the glamour of his apricot damask gown and heavily embroidered doublet and bases.

She had never thought to feel so attracted to a man, and as they danced and he asked her about herself, she began to feel very special indeed. It was easy to sparkle in response to such flattering interest and overt admiration.

His name, he told her, was Philippe du Moulin, and he was seigneur of a place called Grigny, not far south of Paris.

'But it is quite isolated, as it is far from any road. My family own many estates in the area, most of them richer and more interesting. When I am not at court, I prefer to visit them in their fine chateaux rather than going home.'

'And what do you do at court?' Anne asked, twirling under his arm.

'Mostly wait for the King to notice me!' he laughed. 'Seriously, you may have seen me serving him at table. It hardly covers me with glory!'

Philippe was a good dancer. As they performed the steps, Anne was conscious of the nearness of his body and the scent of him, a blend of herbs and lavender oil. Where had she smelt that before? On King Henry of England, she remembered, when she had danced with him at Tournai. But the King had had only his crown to recommend him; Philippe du Moulin had so much more.

He stayed with her all night, until the dancing broke up in the small hours. They talked and laughed, sipped wine and returned to the floor many times. It was as if she had known him always. She cared not a fig for the frowns of Madame d'Aumont, the *Dame d'Honneur*, who was watching them with pursed lips. And then Philippe took her hand and said it was hot and could they walk in the gardens, and she forgot about what had happened to Mary after being lured out of a court ball, and ran with him through galleries and deserted chambers. From behind closed doors came muffled sounds, giggles and gasps, letting them know that they were not the only couple seeking privacy.

Philippe looked at Anne and grinned. Then they were outdoors in the sharp night air, a mantle of moonlight cloaking the lawns and terraces before them. They walked, holding hands, and talked, discovering a common interest in art and music and poetry.

He did not try to kiss her, as she had anticipated, even under cover of the shadows beneath the trees, but he put his cloak around her, saying he'd noticed that she was shivering. Something inside her was powerfully moved by that. Then they walked back to the great hall, where Philippe fetched a platter of sugar comfits for them both.

They did not have time to eat many.

'The King is leaving,' Philippe said, rising to his feet with the rest of the company. 'I must go with him. Mademoiselle Anne, it has been a pleasure!' His eyes were warm as his hands enclosed hers. 'Please say you will allow your humble suitor to pay his addresses when you come to court!'

Anne knew well how to play this game of love, for she had practised it often enough at the court of Brabant, when she had served the Regent of the Netherlands. But those early flirtations had meant nothing. This was somewhat different and unexpected, and she wanted it to go on. And Philippe had called himself her suitor, which allowed her to think that his thoughts were running in the same direction as her own.

Well, she must bide her time and see what transpired. But, oh God, after he had pressed his lips to her hand and left, she could not still her wildly beating heart! How long would it be before she saw him again?

Queen Claude was kind, but very strict, and this now filled Anne with dismay. With so little freedom, and constant chaperonage, how was she going to see Philippe? Had he been looking for her, asking after her whereabouts? Was he still interested in her? Had she misread the situation? Not knowing the answers to any of these questions was so frustrating!

A month after the ball, when the land was basking in the June sunshine, the Queen announced that the King was leaving with an army for Italy, where he was to uphold the cause of his ally, Venice, against Spanish pretensions to power. He was holding a great feast on the eve of his departure, and Claude was to grace it with her presence. Anne was overjoyed to learn that she was one of the maids chosen to attend her.

When they gathered in her great chamber, ready in their finery, the little Queen entered, richly clothed in cloth of gold, and, like a flock of swans in their white gowns, they all sank to the floor in their curtseys.

Being Claude, their mistress had to deliver a well-meant homily to which few paid attention, for they were fidgeting to be off to the feast. Anne sighed as she was exhorted to guard her chastity and reminded that the court was a sinful place and they had best beware putting their reputations at risk. It called to mind the wan face of her sister Mary – a far more salutary lesson than any high-minded words. Even Claude's vigilance had not been able to protect Mary from the lust of King François. But Claude had been newly wed then and had yet to understand her power, while Mary hadn't been strong enough to stop François getting her alone and taking advantage. Outraged for her sister as she had been, Anne was sure that she herself would have fought back!

The trumpets sounded and they followed the Queen into the magnificent hall where the long tables were laid, and Anne saw the assembled throng of lords and gentlemen. She cast her eyes around eagerly, searching for that one face among the host of gorgeously dressed young lords, who were all eyeing the Queen's retinue appreciatively.

'Mademoiselle Anne!' Claude hissed. 'A virtuous lady keeps custody of her eyes. She does not boldly stare at gentlemen!'

Anne felt herself blushing, as her companions smothered titters and ranged themselves behind the Queen's chair. The rebuke stung. A girl could look at a man and still be virtuous, surely?

Another fanfare of trumpets announced the King, and everyone stood as François entered and proceeded to the dais, a vision of satyric, virile manhood in crimson satin slashed with silver. But still Anne could only feel hatred for him, for dishonouring her sister. She would not look at him, the beast, as she and her fellows moved to their seats at a lower table, and the first course was brought in.

And there, wonder of wonders, was Philippe, serving the King his choices from the many succulent dishes that had been placed before him, and standing respectfully back behind the royal chair. It was then that his eye met Anne's, and a slight smile illumined his handsome face. After that they exchanged glances often, Anne's eyes darting from his to the Queen, whose gaze was often on her and the other maids. Would Claude never relax her vigilance?

It seemed that the meal would drag on for ever, but at last the King signalled that the dancing should begin, and the cloths were drawn up and the trestles carried away. Anne and the other maids hastened to see if the Queen needed anything. They attended her to the stool chamber, and when they returned François was already at the centre of the floor, partnering a buxom beauty in the midst of a throng of dancers. Claude stiffened, sat down in her chair and bade two of her ladies wait behind her. Poor lady, with her limp she could not hope to outshine her rival on the dance floor, so she must needs look on, as if nothing was amiss.

Anne now sidled away, which was easily done in the press of people, and there was Philippe, waiting for her.

'Mademoiselle Anne! I have been looking for you.' His gaze was warm.

'I have been serving the Queen, Sir.'

'Sir?' he echoed, smiling. 'I thought we knew each other better than that.'

'Philippe,' Anne corrected herself, loving the sound of his name on her tongue. 'We should not talk here. The Queen is a kind mistress, but a strict one. She watches us all the time. To hear her, you would think that all men were savages!'

'Oh, we are, we are!' Philippe assured her, with a wicked grin.

'Then can you be savage elsewhere?' Anne riposted.

'Is that an invitation?' he asked, taking her hand.

'It is nothing of the kind!' she protested, laughing, as he led her through a door into a gallery thronged with courtiers, and then through another into a lofty room lined with books. It was dark and – praise God – deserted.

'This is the King's library,' Philippe explained, lighting two candles. 'Be seated.' He indicated one of the chairs at the table in the centre, and took the one opposite himself. 'His gentlemen are allowed the use of this room. Not that I come here often, but it will serve tonight.'

Anne had never seen so many books in one place, and normally she would have been eager to explore them, but for now her whole focus was on Philippe. They talked, and again they were so natural with each other.

He told her about his family. His father, who had been dead for seven years, had been the youngest of four brothers, and the surviving ones evidently took a protective interest in his orphaned sons, Philippe and his brother Pierre, who was seigneur of a place called Faronville. They were a landed family, well established, with an impressive history. *Oncle* Philippe, the late seigneur of Fontenay, had been a notable soldier and chamberlain to the old King Louis. Philippe spoke proudly of how his uncle, in the heat of a battle at Fornoue, in Italy, had saved the life of Louis' predecessor, King Charles. *Oncle* Jacques was seigneur of Briis, and clearly much admired and loved by his nephew. *Oncle* Antoine was seigneur of Vaugrigneuse.

Hearing all these titles, Anne was remembering Father expressing his hope that she would find a good – which meant noble and wealthy – husband at the French court. Well, he would surely be more than satisfied with Philippe. In her family and at court, marriage, often as not, had little to do with love. It was more a matter of suitability and money. But Philippe was suitable in every way! He had a title and land; he came from a good family; he was a rising man at court; and he was twenty-four years old and handsome. If he had not seemed devastatingly handsome at the start, he certainly did now, and Anne suddenly understood what people meant when they spoke of beauty being in the eye of the beholder. Her father, surely, could never object to such a match.

Slow down! she admonished herself. They had spent only two evenings together, and of course no word had been said of love or marriage! Yet a gentleman like him, of good family, would surely never have monopolised the time of a respectable young lady unless he had honourable intentions. And she could only think that Philippe's thoughts were tending that way, for a gentleman bent only upon seduction would hardly bother to discourse on his family's genealogy and estates.

'What of your mother?' she asked.

'She died six years ago,' he said, 'but my aunt at Briis is like a mother to me. I hope you will meet her one day.'

That sealed it. His intentions were honourable. Anne's heart was ready to burst with joy.

She told him about her family, and it was clear that he was highly impressed. Then they talked about her life in the Queen's household, and he laughed when she pulled a face at Claude's strictness.

'At least you will be in safe hands while I'm away,' he said.

'Away?' she echoed, dismayed.

'Yes, Anne. I march with the King tomorrow. Did you not realise?'

She must not let him see that the prospect, revealed to her so suddenly, had made her distraught.

'Of course, I should have guessed,' she said, as lightly as she could, her voice sounding hoarse and wobbly.

'Beside the King, family honour demands it of me. I have a long tradition to uphold!' His eyes were searching hers. He reached across and took her hand in his warm, shapely one. 'Do I detect that you will be sorry to see me go?'

She could not answer for a moment. She was searching for the right thing to say.

'Should I be?' she asked.

His eyes were still on her, ardent, quizzical. 'I hope so,' he murmured.

She was the first to look away. 'I must get back. The Queen will be angry if she misses me.' She stood up, and in an instant Philippe had skirted the table and was there by her side.

'I will miss *you*, Anne,' he said, 'and, if God spares me, I will seek you out as soon as I return.'

'Don't say that!' she cried. 'It is tempting fate.' And then, as he smiled at her, she realised that she had given herself away – and that it did not matter. Impulsively, remembering how knights had competed for favours at the tournaments at Mechlin, she took a ring from her finger and gave it to him.

'For luck,' she said.

It fitted his little finger. He raised her hand and kissed it. 'I will wear it with honour,' he said, 'and count the days until my return.'

Anne gazed into her mirror. For once, she thought, she looked beautiful. Definitely she was growing up and becoming more attractive with it. There was a glow to her plain, narrow features, a sparkle that brought her eyes to life – and it was all down to Philippe. She missed him dreadfully and worried about him all the time; but she felt loved, and that carried her through day after anxious, empty day. She went often to the royal library. It was the place where she felt closest to Philippe.

Time passed, and the long weeks of waiting for news and for Philippe's return turned into months. Where was he? Was he safe? If only she knew.

Autumn found the bells of Paris ringing out triumphantly. King François had won a great victory at Marignano, and made himself King of Milan. In one fell swoop he had achieved what King Louis had fought and negotiated for over many years. The people were wild with joy.

The Queen's court was at Amboise. Anne, stitching a silk flower on to a sleeve, or trying hard to focus on the words in her book, could only hope that Philippe was among the triumphant French forces. News crossed the Alps all too slowly. François had been in Milan, he was at Bologna – but that was weeks ago, so where was he now? Why had Philippe not written? Had he forgotten her? Had his letters gone astray? Or, worse, was he among the fallen?

Anne was out on the terrace, braving the chill winds to look out across the Loire and beyond to where, in the invisible distance, her love might be, when a letter was brought to her. It was from Philippe, dated weeks before, crumpled and stained, and it contained everything she wanted to hear. He had acquitted himself well in the battle; the King himself had praised his courage; he was missing her and longing to see her; he would hasten back to court as soon as he could.

She wished she could reply, but he had given no forwarding address, so he must be on the march home. Her mind, at last, was at rest, her heart full of joy. She could dream of a future in which Philippe loomed large.

1516

In January it was announced that King François was to make a slow, triumphal progress through Provence on his way north, and the Queen declared her intention of travelling south to join him. Anne's heart leapt. In a few days she might be reunited with Philippe!

Two weeks later they were in Sisteron, high up in the mountains of Provence, where the King was waiting to be reunited with his women-folk, his court gathered around him. As the chariot Anne shared with nine other maids ascended the steep hill to the fortress high above, she strove to see Philippe in the throng, but in vain.

When she alighted, suddenly there he was, sketching a courtly bow, his eyes as warm and admiring as ever.

'Mademoiselle Anne!' he murmured. 'You rival Venus for beauty! How I have yearned to see you.'

Her heart almost stopped. He was more captivating than she remembered, having gained a new assurance from his successes in the field of battle.

'Meet me after the feast, on the ramparts outside the tower, if you can slip away,' he said, and left her standing there in a whirl of emotions. She could not wait for the evening's celebrations. She would wear her most beautiful gown, the one of plum damask bordered with black velvet, and her hair loose, interlaced with jewels.

All through the feast she could not stop looking in Philippe's direction. Every time her eyes lighted on him, they locked with his.

It was dark when she stole away from the festivities and emerged, cloaked and hooded, from the tower, slipping past the impassive guards who must have been pretending not to see her. She could hear the sea, hundreds of feet below, as she crossed to one of the great fortified walls and waited there in its shadow, out of sight. Philippe came after her, and then, at long last, she was in his arms, and everything changed between them. Nothing in nearly fifteen years on Earth had prepared her for the depths of feeling that overwhelmed her, or the unsuspected physical response of her body. And when Philippe kissed her, and surprised her by thrusting his tongue in her mouth, she thought she might die of the joy.

'Anne, you have bewitched me!' he breathed, letting her lips go and gazing at her. 'You are more lovely than I remembered, if that could be possible. I have held you in my heart all these months. You have no idea how I have wanted you.'

How could it be, she thought, that two strangers could meet just three times and feel this way about each other? Could it be love, the love of which the poets wrote? Could one really fall in love so quickly?

She should not be alone with Philippe like this, she knew. Anyone might come out and see them, and that could have dire consequences. She could see why the rules of the game of love existed. They were to stop silly girls making fools of themselves, and to keep them chaste until they were wed. She dared not imagine how Father would react if he heard that his daughter had been dismissed for misconduct. He had been furious with Mary for turning down her place in Claude's household, 'on a whim', as he had written in one of his rare letters, and he had added that he trusted Anne, at least, not to disgrace him.

'I should go,' she said. 'I dare not stay. The Queen is ever vigilant and protective of the honour of those who serve her. And I would not lose my honour for all the riches in the world.'

'Your honour is safe with me, Anne,' Philippe said. 'My intentions are true.' She thrilled to hear those words.

He relinquished her slowly. 'May I see you again?'

'Yes,' Anne whispered, wishing she could stay in this enchanted moment. 'Now I *must* go. Farewell.' And she ran on slippered feet back to the tower.

* * *

They were nearing Marseilles, with four thousand soldiers and two thousand children wearing white going before them, when Claude, who had been acknowledging the cheers of the crowds along the wayside, turned to Anne, who was seated behind her in the litter, ready to carry her train, and smiled.

'I meant to say, Mademoiselle Anne: the King tells me that a young man has spoken for you.'

Anne was astonished. For a moment she wondered who it was, and then she realised, with a great uprush of happiness, that it must have been Philippe.

'We will talk of this later,' the Queen said, nodding graciously to the people. 'The King and I approve. You are most fortunate.'

Anne was giddy with excitement. A young man speaking for her could mean only one thing: that he wanted to wed her. Not so long ago she would have shied from the idea of marriage, which had seemed far less exciting than being at court, being admired and enjoying all the pleasures that life had to offer. But now, by some almost magical process, her priorities had changed.

She could not wait for the Queen to summon her. She watched the King, in his suit of silver velvet, receive the keys of the ancient port; like everyone else she was deafened by the booms of cannon fire. She sat impatiently watching the jousts that had been laid on in the King's honour, only paying attention when it was Philippe's turn to enter the lists and he bowed in the saddle before her, craving her favour, as the other maids-of-honour looked on enviously and giggled. Then she suffered agonies praying that he would not be hurt. But he emerged victorious, to hearty cheering, and then she could relax and bask in the knowledge that people were looking at her, this gallant knight's chosen lady.

That evening he sought her out in the dance.

'I have spoken of you to the King,' he told her, his hand closing on hers. She knew what he meant, and that he could not say more until the King had signified his approval. She wanted to shout out her joy.

'I know,' she told him, gazing into his shining eyes. 'The Queen wants to see me.'

'Does she not approve of me? His Majesty was most encouraging.'

'He approves! They both do. The Queen told me!' she cried, and he swung her around exultantly.

'Is there somewhere we can be private, Anne?' he urged. 'I need to speak to you.'

'Not now,' she said, aware of the Queen's eyes on her. But as soon as Claude's attention was elsewhere, she let Philippe lead her out to a balcony, where the cool air was a balm after the sweaty heat of the banqueting chamber.

He took her hand and raised it to his lips. 'It's love, isn't it?' he said, his eyes dark wells of desire. 'Please marry me.'

The world exploded in an outburst of stars. 'It is love,' she managed to say, 'and I will marry you.'

'Oh, my darling,' he said, as his lips sought hers.

The Queen smiled. Her grey eyes were kind, her smile wiser than her seventeen years might merit. 'Philippe du Moulin wishes to marry you. My lord the King and I approve and wish to give you our blessings.'

Anne was nearly shaking with happiness. 'Thank you, Madame.'

Claude smiled. 'He is an honourable man. It is a most fitting match. It wants only his family's approval and that of your father, before you can proceed to a betrothal. I dare say that neither will object, for you seem so well suited in every respect. The King has told Philippe that he must write to your father to ask for your hand.'

Anne nearly cried with joy. That afternoon, she attended the Queen into the town centre of Marseilles, where a battle of oranges was staged, in which the King and the court gallants enjoyed boisterous merriment in pelting each other with fruit. Philippe was in the thick of the combat, joining in with gusto, and when Anne found him afterwards, all splattered with yellow stains and pith, she could not help laughing. Soon they were in each other's arms, kissing in sight of all the court, and Philippe told her that he had sent a letter to her father by fast courier.

As often as they could, they spent time together, as the court made its slow, triumphant way north. It was at Lyon, where François fell in love with the city and insisted on lingering there for three months, that Philippe came to Anne as she was trailing the Queen around the Roman forum of Trajan, high on a hill, with all of Lyon and the broad confluence of the two great rivers, the Rhône and the Saone, spread out below them.

His smile was broad. 'I've had a letter. My *Oncle* Jacques and my aunt have invited us to visit them at their castle at Briis. They want to meet you as soon as it can be arranged after we get back.'

'And I should so like to meet them,' Anne enthused. It was really happening – this was tangible proof of it. To have found such happiness, in fulfilment of all her hopes, was the greatest of blessings.

The Queen had her back to them. She was admiring the carving on a fallen pillar. Anne moved forward to the parapet to admire the breathtaking view.

Philippe bent and brushed her lips with his. She squeezed his hand.

'You have made me the happiest man alive,' he smiled, his eyes warm, and kissed her again, lingeringly this time.

It was on a beautiful May day that Anne and Philippe set out from Amboise and took the road north towards Briis. They were accompanied by two knights, two grooms and two manservants, sufficient number to attend on a young man who had just been appointed cup-bearer to the King, as well as Anne's French maid, Gabrielle, who had been recommended by one of the Queen's ladies, and an elderly widowed noblewoman who had been appointed by Claude to act as chaperone until they reached Briis. Having been assured of Philippe's honourable purpose in taking Anne home to meet his family, and of Sir Thomas Boleyn's approval, gladly given in an unusually ebullient letter, Claude had granted her maid-of-honour leave of absence without demur, stipulating only that she take with her the dowager and a young lady of good character to preserve the proprieties.

The prospect of such freedom – and of being with Philippe for days on end – was heady. Their duties at court, and Claude's strict rules, had of necessity kept them apart for much of the time, and their meetings had been the sweeter for that, but never enough for either of them.

Now they could be together as never before – and, God willing, as they would be hereafter. Anne was beside herself with anticipation.

No time limit had been set to the visit, so they deliberately took a leisurely way towards Blois, where they paused to admire the royal chateau and visit the market, and thence to Orléans. Then, staying overnight at inns and the guest houses of abbeys and convents, they joined the steady stream of travellers making for Paris.

One noontide they sat by a river eating bread and ripe cheese they had purchased from a farm. It was a beautiful, mysterious spot, shaded by woodland, with trees overhanging the banks and gnarled branches and roots emerging like sea monsters from the water. After they had eaten, and washed down the food with a flagon of sour rustic wine, the dowager fell asleep, snoring noisily, and their attendants, smothering chuckles, obligingly moved a little way off, sensing that Anne and Philippe wanted to seize this opportunity of being private together, so that they could steal kisses and whisper words of love.

They set off, hand-in-hand, to explore the sun-dappled woods. Ahead of them, through the dense foliage, Anne glimpsed grey stone walls. She ran ahead and stopped.

The ruined chapel rose stark and eerie from dense undergrowth. There was no roof, just arcades of pointed windows, and trees growing where once holy souls had knelt and prayed.

'I wonder what this place was,' said Philippe, coming up behind her.

'I don't know. There's something haunting about it.'

'It's beautiful. Look at its reflection in the water, and at the carving on the stonework.' He put his arms around her waist, nuzzling her neck. 'And it's very secluded!'

She turned to him, and his mouth closed on hers, and then he was kissing her with a new fervour, and she found herself responding urgently. Now he was drawing her down to the ground, the tall grasses making a soft bed beneath them, and they were lying entwined, and it was the most beautiful, irresistible feeling she had ever known. Truly there was magic in this strange place.

Then Philippe moved his hands down to her hips and pulled her closer against him, and she could feel something hard pressing against her, and the feeling was warm and pleasurable, and then suddenly she felt the beginnings of an explosion of pleasure, and drew back, shocked at her body's response. At once she understood what priests and giggling girls meant by the point of no return. And she had nearly been there, risking disgrace and ruin! What would the Queen and her father say if they could see her lying here wantonly like this?

She scrambled to her feet, feeling her cheeks aflame.

'What's wrong?' Philippe asked.

'We shouldn't have gone so far,' Anne said, her heart pounding furiously.

'*Ma chère*, we have done nothing we should not have done. There is nothing immoral in embracing and kissing.'

'But lying together! I have heard it is a sin.'

He laughed. 'Lying together does not mean just lying down, my sweet Anne!'

'But I felt something – something I shouldn't.' The blush had now spread down to her breast, she noticed, as she lowered her eyes. 'That was wrong.'

'It is natural,' he assured her, smiling. 'I cannot stop myself feeling desire for you.'

He had misunderstood her drift. It was best to say no more about the desire she herself had felt. The conversation was straying into forbidden territory.

'We should go back,' she said, leading the way out of the ruins, but her steps were light. She might have drawn back at the crucial moment, but she was exhilarated to have discovered within herself a capacity for bodily pleasure of which she had never dreamed. Where would it have led her had she let Dame Nature take her course? The possibilities were thrilling.

Past the turn-off for Chartres, they arrived at a little fortified town called Gometz-la-Ville, then rode on across a broad green plain, travelling ever upwards. On the crest of a hill they halted their horses, so that Philippe could show Anne the view, which encompassed a vast and beautiful valley.

'Not far to go now,' he said, taking her hand and kissing it. 'Look yonder, down the hill. There is Briis.'

As they began to descend, a small village fully came into view, its houses clustered around a great chateau dominated by a tall square tower and surrounded by strong walls bisected by turrets and drawbridges.

'My family have lived here for seven hundred years,' Philippe told Anne, 'but the castle was rebuilt in the reign of our great King, Philippe-Auguste. This was around 1200.'

'My father's castle of Hever was built in the twelve hundreds,' Anne said. 'It is smaller than this, more like a manor house, but it is beautiful.'

'My family own much of the land in these parts and several chateaux,' Philippe told her. 'We will ride over to see mine at Grigny. It is not thirty miles distant. That will be our home, *ma chère*, but of course we will be at court often.'

'Until we have children,' Anne said.

'Yes! Six strong sons and six lovely daughters!' Philippe laughed.

'You go too fast!' she told him. 'I'd like to wait a while.'

'Children come when God sends them,' he said.

'Well, I don't much relish the prospect of being stuck out in the country rearing them while you're having all the fun at court! It's what my mother does, and her life is so dull.'

'Then we will be careful, Anne. There are ways to prevent children coming. You may leave that to me.'

She longed for the day when they would be formally betrothed. It would be soon, she knew, as soon as his family had met and approved of her. Then they would set a date for the wedding. She had always envisaged herself marrying in springtime, but that was now months away! She could not wait that long. They could be married at Christmas.

'That is a fine church yonder in Briis,' she said, pointing, thinking of a quiet wedding here, with Philippe's family. Maybe her own family would be able to be present. Father might, if his duties permitted. Her brother George would certainly come. Mary might not, which was a relief, because no doubt she would be jealous.

As they rode into Briis and bade farewell to the dowager, Anne was happily making plans.

* * *

Jacques du Moulin, Seigneur of Briis, and his enormously fat and charming wife Antoinette were a warm and hospitable couple. They kissed Anne heartily as they arrived, welcomed her into their chateau, embraced Philippe, and led them both up the turret stairs to the hall, where they had servants running with wine and sweet cakes.

Tante Antoinette, as Philippe called her, looked Anne up and down approvingly.

'Nephew, you have chosen well for yourself,' she declared. 'Your dear father and mother would be proud.' She turned to Anne. 'Since they died, we have tried to fill their places. It was the least we could do for the dear boy. Now, Mademoiselle Anne, you must stay as long as you wish. Philippe regards Briis as his second home anyway.' She smiled at him. There was clearly much affection between the three of them.

Oncle Jacques wanted to know all about the new King and affairs at court, and a happy hour was given over to gossip and the exchange of news.

'And when are you two to be betrothed?' *Tante* Antoinette asked. 'I do love a wedding!'

'As soon as we have agreed a settlement,' Philippe said, smiling at Anne. 'Maybe while we are here.'

'Oh, that would be wonderful!' cried *Tante* Antoinette.

'Anne, I hear that your father is a good servant of the King of England and serves him as ambassador,' *Oncle* Jacques said. 'I trust he has given his blessing?'

'Oh, yes!' Anne said.

'And you are content to live in France? You will not pine for England?'

'Not at all,' she assured him. 'I love it here.'

'Anne is a rising star at court,' Philippe said proudly. 'Queen Claude thinks very highly of her.'

'Then you do come highly recommended!' *Tante* Antoinette exclaimed. 'And you are very becoming, *ma chère.*'

Anne basked in the older woman's warmth. This was not courtly flattery; it was genuine.

'Philippe, we must talk,' the old man said. 'Come down to the courtroom.'

Tante Antoinette stood up. 'Let me show you to your room, mademoiselle.'

She heaved her bulky form up the narrow spiral stairs, Anne and her maid following, and led them to a bedchamber on the third floor. Dark floral tapestry hangings adorned the bed and the walls, flowers scented the air, and there was a small table with a chair by the empty hearth, and a pallet bed for Gabrielle. The view from the window was spectacular; below were the roofs of Briis, and beyond them acres and acres of verdant rolling countryside sweeping into the distance.

'The men will be discussing the financial arrangements,' *Tante* Antoinette said, getting her breath back. Anne knew they would all be in order. Father was well-off and could afford a good dowry.

'This is a lovely room,' she said. 'Thank you for making me so welcome.'

'Bless you, child,' *Tante* Antoinette replied, and hugged her.

When, at the sound of a hunting horn, Anne emerged later, washed and refreshed and ready for dinner, Philippe was coming down from the floor above. He drew her into his arms and kissed her lingeringly, until she fended him off, giggling, and ran down to the first floor, where the table was laid for four.

'It's good to be camping out on the top floor!' Philippe jested. 'Methinks I am in one of the store rooms.'

'Nonsense!' his aunt reproved. 'We've made it very comfortable! And with your young legs, getting up there won't be a problem. Mademoiselle Anne, those stairs finish me. I thank God that I rarely have to go up beyond the second floor. Now, do be seated.'

'I will write to your father,' Philippe told Anne, 'to ask him to approve the jointure I can settle on you. I intend to be most generous.' His eyes were warm. She appreciated his sensitivity in not mentioning the dowry he would receive with her.

'I am sure he will reply quickly,' she smiled.

Dinner was lavish, clearly in Anne's honour. There were two great roasted joints of meat, turnips in honey, salmon in mustard sauce, a spinach tart, eggs in what tasted like a custard sauce, and some delicious cheeses, all washed down with good wine. Anne's head was swimming by the time the old couple rose and said they were off to bed.

'Douse those candles when you go up, Philippe,' *Oncle* Jacques instructed. 'God give you both a good night.'

When they had gone, Anne and Philippe looked at one another.

'I can't believe they have left us alone,' she marvelled.

'They are showing us that they trust us,' he said, taking her in his arms and burying his face in her hair. 'Besides, they probably think that we are lovers already.'

Anne was amazed. Certainly they did do things differently in France!

She longed for them to be betrothed, for the contract to be signed, the formal promises made before witnesses, and the ring given. Then all would be assured. Philippe had promised to buy Anne a ring with the stone of her choice as soon as everything was agreed. She rather fancied a sapphire, or a ruby. But what matter rings and contracts when they were here by themselves, embracing and kissing, and her feelings were overwhelming her?

They sat on a cushioned settle by the hearth, holding each other. Philippe began to caress her. His touch was so light. It aroused all her senses.

'I love you!' he whispered, and then he gripped her powerfully, and she could feel the urgency of his need. How easy it would be to surrender, was her last coherent thought, because she wanted him just as much. Nothing else mattered. His fingers, his lips were at the low neckline of her bodice, awakening divine sensations, and she wanted him to go on, she wanted to feel again that burgeoning rush of pleasure and let it build to its conclusion . . .

He was lifting her skirt and his hand was on her calf. Some deep-seated protective instinct warned her that it must go no further. Somehow she remembered that she was no serving wench to be tumbled at will. Gently, and with some reluctance, she guided Philippe's hand away.

'Let me touch you!' he pleaded. 'I ask only to touch you.'

'It would be wrong,' she whispered.

'You want me to!'

'Yes! But we must wait.'

'We will soon be married,' he protested. 'What harm can it do? I'm not asking for your virginity. There are other ways that lovers can give pleasure. Let me show you!' His hand was stealing down her stomacher; it found her nipple and began playing with it. The sensation was so glorious that she almost weakened.

'No, Philippe.' Even to herself she sounded half-hearted.

With an enormous effort she pulled away and sat up. Her skirts and her hair were disordered. This could not be her, Anne Boleyn, knight's daughter and granddaughter of the Duke of Norfolk, surely? Anne Boleyn did not do such things!

'We should go to bed,' she said, rising with a great effort of will. Oh, for the day when they could go to bed, lawfully, together!

Philippe looked up at her and caught her hand. 'I respect your wishes,' he said. 'I cannot help wanting you. I pray you will think on what I have said and take pity on me. It might be months until our wedding. How can I wait so long? How can you wait?'

'It will be but a short time,' she replied, knowing it would be an eternity, however long it was. 'Now good night, dear heart.' She took a candle and crossed to the stairs.

'*Je t'adore*, Anne,' Philippe called softly after her, his voice heavy with yearning.

The next day he showed her around the castle, and they climbed to the very top of the stairs. They emerged on to the roof, which was surrounded by crenellations and had four turrets, one at each corner.

'They used these for look-outs in the old days, when the times were dangerous,' Philippe explained, his arm tight about Anne as the wind whipped at their hair.

'Briis was built for defence. Look at those walls – they are three feet thick.'

'Hever was built for defence too,' she told him, 'but its fortifications were never tested. I should hate to think I was living in a place where blood was spilt.'

'But you will be living in Grigny soon,' he said, his smile mischievous, 'and all sorts of dastardly deeds were committed there, and ghosts drag their chains along the battlements, and spectres wail in the chimneys where they were walled up!'

Anne buffeted him playfully, as he pretended to recoil in horror. 'My brother used to try to frighten me with such tales, but he never succeeded!' she told him.

They descended the stairs to the ground floor, where Philippe led her into the courtroom. On the wall there was a painting of a crucifix crossing a dagger.

'This is where my uncle receives his vassals,' Philippe said. 'King Louis XI granted the seigneurs of Briis the right to dispense justice and the prerogative of the gallows.'

'You mean *Oncle* Jacques can sentence his tenants to death?' Anne was astonished.

'They are not his tenants, Anne. They are his serfs, bound to him and to the land. That is the way of things in France.'

'It is not in England,' she said. 'There are no serfs now, just free men, tenants and yeomen.'

'You will have to accustom yourself to a different way of life, *ma chère*. But do not fret, I will be here to guide you.' He bent and kissed her, tenderly, in the way she loved.

'See that door in the wall?' he said, breaking away. 'In times of war the peasants would seek shelter in this room, and that door afforded them a means of escape. It also gave the garrison a way out during a siege, so that they could mount an unexpected attack on the enemy – and when we were boys Pierre and I used it to mount surprise attacks on each other!'

Anne was growing bored with this talk of fighting. It was a lovely, sunny day and she wanted to be out of doors enjoying it. 'Let us walk around the village,' she suggested. 'I should like to see the church.'

Hand in hand they walked across the drawbridge and down into Briis. The church of St Denis was very ancient, with strong walls, round stone arches and a separate bell tower, and as soon as Anne entered she was enveloped in a hushed atmosphere redolent of centuries of prayer.

She knelt down with Philippe on the cold flagstones, and they bent their heads in silence for a while. Then Anne raised her eyes to the altar. It seemed strange that she might be married here, in this unremarkable little church; it would be so different from what she had imagined her wedding would be like. But it did not matter at all. If it joined her in holy wedlock with Philippe, that was all she asked for. And, no doubt, at Christmas St Denis's could be made festive with holly and bay and mistletoe, if such things grew in these parts.

She looked at Philippe and reached for his hand, imagining herself arriving at church in her wedding finery, and his eyes lighting up at the sight of her.

He bent forward and kissed her, and they stood up. They wandered around and he pointed out the tombs of his ancestors and told her all their stories.

On the walk back to the chateau, through the silent village in which not a soul was abroad, for it was near the supper hour, he was thoughtful.

'I should like to have a splendid wedding at court,' he said.

'I would not want that,' Anne said.

'But why?'

'Because King François will be there, and I don't want him to be.'

'But it would be a great honour for the King to attend. Why don't you want him to honour us?'

'Do not ask me,' Anne told him, realising she had said too much. The rape of Mary must never be spoken of, for it was *her* reputation that would be stained, not the King's.

Philippe stared at her. 'Tell me he has not made advances to you!'

'Never, of course!' Anne could feel her cheeks burning. She was appalled to realise that her evasion had led Philippe to think that her aversion to François was on her own account.

'There's no of course about it. His appetites are legendary!'

She was indignant, unable to believe that they were having this conversation. 'What do you take me for? I have but seen his way with women. He is the King, and what he wants he must have.'

'I'm sorry, I'm sorry!' Philippe held up his hands in mock surrender. 'I did not mean to sound as if I thought ill of you. As for the King, he only takes what is freely given – and there are many willing to donate!'

'Not so!' Anne cried before she could stop herself. 'He forces himself on women, even when it is against their will.'

Philippe frowned. 'Is that so?' He paused. 'Is it the reason why your sister was so eager to leave court?'

They were nearly back at the drawbridge. Anne hastened her pace, horrified with herself for having virtually given away what should have remained a secret. Truly, she did not know how to answer. She could either lie, and say she had been referring to someone else – or she must trust Philippe with the truth.

'It was,' she said, unable to meet his eye. 'He left her no choice in the matter. I wish you had not pressed me!'

'I am sorry,' he said, 'but don't you think I have a right to know?'

She rounded on him. 'Why? I had nothing to do with it. I had to comfort her afterwards. She was distraught, shocked. No man, even the King, should be allowed to force a woman like that.'

Philippe looked shocked too. 'Anne, I must tell you. The King was bragging of it. He did not mention a name, but he said to his gentlemen that he had enjoyed riding an English mare, especially one who was not broken in.'

'How vile of him!' she cried, horrified. 'Was he not content with violating her, that he must needs slander her too – and by implication all of us English ladies? And you – do you now think the worse of me because I am sister to one who has been defiled?'

'No, no, no, *ma chère*! How could I think that?' In one bound Philippe was at her side and clasping her to him. 'I love you! I am very sorry for your sister. The King has done her a great wrong, one that would be difficult to avenge. Does your father know of this?'

'I doubt it! Apparently Mary told him only that she went home to escape the King's attentions, but I know that Father is displeased with her. He probably thought she should have stayed, stood her ground and taken advantage of the place he had secured for her in the Queen's household. He is very ambitious.'

'I wish you had felt you could tell me about this,' Philippe said.

'You should have trusted me, especially since we are to be betrothed.'

'I could not bring myself even to think of it and, as it did not happen to me, it did not occur to me that I should have told you. It was not my secret to share.'

'No, of course,' he said. But she thought his voice seemed to lack conviction.

They were back at the entrance to the tower now.

'I must go and tidy myself for dinner,' Anne said, and sped up the stairs, trying not to cry. Why did she feel as if she had done something wrong? Did Philippe really think her deceitful? Worse still, did he think that Mary was a loose trollop who had not put up a fight when she should have done, or even encouraged the King and regretted it later, and that her sister was cut from the same cloth?

Staring at her blotchy face in her mirror, Anne pulled herself up. This was silly. Philippe loved her; she had ample evidence of that. He would never think of her in those ways. She was letting her imagination run away with her.

Tante Antoinette helped herself to a second portion of beef in red wine and tucked in with relish.

'Anne, our families may be related!' she said.

Anne was surprised. 'How could that be?'

'Jacques' father, the late King's chamberlain, was married to a lady called Marie de Boulan de la Rochette. With her name being similar to Boleyn, it occurred to me today that there may be a distant connection.'

'It's possible,' Anne said, thinking it unlikely. 'The founder of my family was a Norman knight who came to England with William the Conqueror and settled in Norfolk. I suppose he could have had kinsfolk in Normandy or France.'

'It would be nice to think that we are blood kin,' *Tante* Antoinette said. 'Your family is of noble descent, I hear.'

'My father is grandson to the Earl of Ormond and my mother is daughter to the Duke of Norfolk. Both my parents are descended from King Edward I.'

The old couple looked suitably impressed, but Anne was watching Philippe, who seemed – perhaps she was imagining things again – a little withdrawn tonight. The thought came unbidden that descent and titles counted for nothing against virtue and honesty. But that's ridiculous! she told herself, trying to elicit a smile from her lover. I *am* virtuous, and I am honest. Mary's secret was not mine to divulge. And when it comes to match-making, family counts above all else!

Philippe roused himself. 'Shall we ride to Grigny tomorrow?'

'I would love that,' Anne told him.

'We must be up early,' he said.

'I will have some food packed for you,' said *Tante* Antoinette. 'God knows if that lazy, misbegotten steward you employ there will have anything ready for you. Anne, you will have your work cut out, pulling the servants into shape!'

It sounded so normal, so reassuring, as if nothing could threaten the prospect of her marriage to Philippe. And when Philippe laughed, and – or so it seemed to her – the mood lightened, she could have cried for joy.

Again the old couple retired early to bed; again Philippe took her into his arms, and this time, when he ventured to caress her breasts and her thighs, she did not refuse him, but when he wanted to go further, and have her touch him intimately, she would not.

He chuckled at that, and let it go. It was only a matter of time, he seemed to be implying. Well, he could think again. She was of a sterner mettle than her sister would ever be.

The old chateau at Grigny wore an air of neglect. Philippe was apologetic.

'I am never here,' he excused himself, as Anne eyed the cobwebs and the grime with dismay. 'It needs a woman's touch.'

'It has one,' she retorted, glaring at the lazy slattern of a steward's wife. 'Mistress, I hope you will ensure that this place is clean and well ordered by the time I come here.'

The woman bobbed a resentful curtsey.

'Her idea of clean and mine are probably very different things,' Anne muttered as they moved into the next chamber, which smelt damp. What a pity they could not live at Briis! No wonder Philippe was always there.

On the ride back Anne spoke of the improvements she wanted to make at Grigny. 'It needs some bright hangings and cushions, and fresh rush matting on the floors, like they have at court. We can make it a cheerful place.'

Philippe shrugged. 'We will hardly be there. Is it worth it?'

'It will be our home, your seat as the seigneur!' Anne cried.

'Wouldn't you rather be at court?'

'To speak the truth, I'd prefer to live at Briis. I love it there. But of course it is not yours.'

'I wish it was. I think my uncle and aunt would like nothing better than to have us live with them, but it's not practical, and they are further from Paris.'

'I am growing to love them,' Anne said, resolving not to let her disappointment show.

Philippe smiled. 'Who could not?'

As day followed day, Anne could not rid herself of the impression that Philippe was distancing himself from her. Sometimes when they were together he seemed distracted, and he did not initiate love play as often as before. She shrank from the thought that his ardour might be diminishing, for she now loved him so much that her very life depended on it, and she was longing to be his wife and give rein to the desires that she was only with difficulty holding in check.

He still wanted her, that much was clear. Three days ago they had climbed the hill behind Briis and sat together watching the sunset, with not a soul in sight, and he had pulled up her skirts and exposed her, and she had not stopped him. Instead she had arched in pleasure as his expert fingers taught her how exquisite desire could be when brought to its shattering fulfilment. She had known, as she lay on the grass, breathless and quivering with joy, that it was for this moment that she had been born. He must love her, to give her such a gift.

And then he was unlacing the points of his hose, and she was seeing for the first time what happened to a man when his passion was aroused, and timidly she laid her hand on him and did what he asked, grasping and squeezing hard until she felt him convulse again and again and her fingers were covered in something wet and warm.

She had thought he would let flow his feelings for her after such magnificent intimacy, but he'd simply kissed her, tidied his clothes and helped her up.

'Come, or we'll be late for supper,' he said, grinning, and they set off down the hill.

At table, she had felt like a Jezebel, and that it must be writ large on her face what she had done. But the du Moulins were acting as if nothing was amiss, and Philippe chatted amiably, never betraying by look or gesture any hint of the great passion he had shared with Anne. It was as if nothing had happened.

There had as yet been no word from Father about the jointure, and Philippe had said no more of the wedding. When his aunt and uncle brought up the subject, eagerly making plans, he merely smiled and nodded. Had they noticed anything amiss? She thought not, for surely they would not raise the subject, and they would be uncomfortable in her presence, if they knew that Philippe was cooling towards her. They were honest people, and too kind to deceive her easily. So maybe she was imagining it all, and should learn to understand Philippe better.

Anne was praying that Father would write soon because, once the financial settlements were agreed, her betrothal could go ahead, and all would be well. So when Philippe said that they must return to court, and that he had sent for the dowager to accompany them, she could have wept because any letter from Father would be sent to Briis, of course, which would mean another agonising delay while it was forwarded on to wherever the court was.

Her mirror told her that she was losing weight. Her skin looked more sallow than ever, and her eyes were dark pools of anxiety. But Philippe did not seem to notice. By night, he was still an ardent lover; by day, he was a different person. She wondered if this was the way of men – that, once they had taken their pleasure, they retreated. She was still a virgin – on that she would not budge – but since that time on the hill she had allowed Philippe to come as close as she dared let him. These last two nights she had waited for Gabrielle to fall asleep and then stolen up to his chamber, where she had let him undress her completely and do – almost – what he would with her. Letting him love her like this brought them close. She needed it, as she needed air to breathe and food to eat. In bed he was hers, and she could reassure herself that he always would be.

On the night before they were due to depart, as they lay together in the darkness, all desire sated, Philippe spoke.

'We don't need to get a betrothal ring, Anne, do we?'

It was as if he had slapped her. She could not speak.

'After all, we are almost as good as wed,' he went on.

'Am I not worthy of one?' she whispered. 'I have never heard of a betrothal without a ring.'

'I am still waiting to hear from your father about your jointure. Then we can discuss our betrothal.' He spoke as if it was a transaction at market.

Her spirits sank. It was as plain as day. Love, it was agonisingly clear, no longer drove him. Thanks to her foolishness, he had had as much of her as he needed, and clearly did not think it worth pursuing marriage for what little she had left to give him.

And yet, she could not bring herself to believe that his feelings for her had died. How could a man lie with a woman and show himself so ardent if he did not love her?

She turned her back to him and tried to sleep, but the tears came unchecked, and soon her pillow was saturated.

'Anne?' he said, pulling her round to face him. 'What's wrong?'

'Nothing,' she lied. 'I am just sad at the thought of leaving here. I have grown to love this place, and your aunt and uncle.'

'I think they have grown to love you,' he said, and his voice was wistful. 'Try to sleep now. We have a long ride ahead of us.'

In the morning *Tante* Antoinette was ready with great panniers of food for the journey.

'God bless you, my lamb,' she said, hugging Anne. 'Come back and see us soon. I will write to you, and I hope you will write back.'

'Oh, I will!' Anne promised. 'Thank you for everything.'

'The next time we see you, you will be a bride!' *Oncle* Jacques said, beaming.

Anne was choked. Maybe all *would* come well in the end. God send she was just imagining that something was wrong.

Their little party rode away, up the hill and over its crest, leaving Briis behind, a poignant memory that she knew she would always cherish in her heart. The long journey back to Amboise passed uneventfully, but at the inns and guest houses, and even when they stopped again by the ruined chapel, Philippe did not contrive to see Anne alone. And when they were back at court it would be difficult, she knew.

As they neared Amboise she grew desperate. She had wanted the idyll at Briis to go on for ever. She did not want to return to normal life. She needed Philippe to tell her that he loved her – he had not said it for some days now – and to speak of marriage. But he did neither. Their conversation had become general; they did not touch on their feelings or the future. At Amboise he insisted on escorting her to the door to the Queen's apartments, and there he bowed formally and kissed her hand.

'I will see you soon, Anne,' he told her, then pressed the ring she had given him – in another age – into her hand and walked away, leaving her in pieces in the gallery.

How was she to hold herself together in the presence of the Queen? What was she to say when Claude and her maids and ladies asked her about her forthcoming marriage? And what, above all, would Father say? Would he come storming across the Channel, like an avenging angel, and demand that Philippe honour his promises?

Yet there had been no promises. They had not been formally betrothed. He had asked her to marry him, it was true, but there had been no vows and no witnesses to make them binding. No one, not even Father, could hold Philippe to anything.

A letter arrived from Hever. Father was wondering why he had not heard from Philippe. What was going on? He demanded to be told.

She would not cry. She had her pride, the pride of ranks of noble ancestors. She would not let Philippe treat her like this. She would seek him out at the earliest opportunity and end it. But for now she must remember her duty to the Queen. With a heart like lead, she opened the door.

Her moment came when Claude, who was pregnant again, was sleeping one afternoon. Anne was not the only maid-of-honour to snatch an hour away from her duties. At least two others had disappeared, no doubt for clandestine meetings with their sweethearts. Once, that would have been her. The memory almost choked her. It had been a week now, with no word from Philippe – the worst week of her life. She had spent it fending off all conversation and trying desperately not to cry.

This was her last card to play. Maybe the prospect of losing her would make Philippe wake up and realise that he loved her after all. But for that ploy to work, she must be strong and show him that she meant what she said.

She found him in the gardens, watching a game of tennis. When he saw her, a look of dismay fleetingly shadowed his face, but then he recovered himself and bowed.

'Anne,' he said.

'Tell me!' she said. 'Was it the thought of my being sister to a whore that killed your love for me? Was it that I concealed her shame from you? Or was it that my father didn't offer you enough for me?'

Philippe had the grace to blench.

'Don't answer the last question!' Anne snapped. 'You never wrote to him about the jointure, did you? He wrote to me, asking why he had not heard from you. I told him that I am no longer interested in marrying you, and that you are not worthy. I came to tell you that, and that I do not want anything more to do with you!'

Philippe had flushed an angry red, but before he had a chance to answer, Anne walked away, holding her head high.

* * *

90

Her proud resolution soon wavered. Even before she had reached Claude's apartments, she was realising that she had lost her love irrevocably, and that, thanks to her determination to be the one to finish it, there was now no chance of putting things right. That broke her. Ignoring the stares of the Queen's attendants, and Claude calling after her, she fled up to the dorter and collapsed on her bed, crying hopelessly. Of course, they came after her. Claude demanded to know what was wrong, but Anne could not speak, nor stem the tears. She wept for so long that her nose began to bleed, sending her fellow maids running for cloths, water and powdered eggshell, which someone said worked well as a cure. It was an eternity before the bleeding stopped, leaving Anne with an unsightly scab blocking one nostril. She could not have felt more wretched.

How she stumbled through the days that followed she never knew. She felt like banging her head against the wall to stop the misery. The Queen, thinking she was ill, gave her leave to rest, but that way lay madness. She did not want leisure to think about Philippe and what could have been. It was torment to remember the love they had shared. It had been the most magical time of her life.

Claude, while kind, rarely noticed how her maids were feeling, but Anne's misery was too great to ignore. One day, as she was kneeling at Claude's feet, stitching a torn hem, the Queen reached down a hand and lifted her chin.

'What is the matter, mademoiselle?'

Anne felt the ready tears welling.

'Madame, I have broken with Philippe du Moulin,' she whispered. 'I cannot speak of my reasons, the matter is too raw. I told him I did not wish to marry him, but I do! I do! I love him, God help me – but he no longer loves me.'

Claude's eyes were full of concern. 'He has not done anything dishonourable?'

'Apart from growing cold towards me, no, Madame,' Anne said, knowing that Claude would have viewed much of Philippe's behaviour as dishonourable. But she too had been taken in.

'I am sorry to hear this,' the Queen said. 'He is a very stupid young man if he lets you go. Maybe he will come to his senses.'

It was what Anne wanted to hear. She was living on hope, if little else. But as the days passed, that hope began to die a lingering death.

And then, at a court masque, she was sitting in her place watching the dancing, trying to remember what it had felt like to enjoy herself, and looking enviously at the happy, laughing couples weaving about the floor in their fantastical costumes, when two feet planted themselves before her and she looked up to see Philippe standing there. Her heart lurched.

'Hello, Anne,' he said, looking nervous, but as handsome as ever. 'How are you?'

She could not speak. This was the moment she had longed for!

'I am well,' she replied, aware that her voice sounded hoarse.

'What have you been doing?' he asked.

She could not help herself. 'Missing you,' she said. He needed to know that.

There was a pause.

'I have missed you too,' he said. Could it be true? Her hopes began to revive.

'This isn't easy for me either,' Philippe went on, sitting down beside her and looking straight ahead. 'We were happy together, and I wanted us to go on like that, but things became complicated.'

'Was it because of my sister? Or the fact that I did not tell you what happened to her?'

'No. Anne, it was because I realised I did not want to be married.'

She was appalled. 'But Philippe, you asked me to marry you! Did you think you could have me any other way? I am a knight's daughter, a maid-of-honour to the Queen, and an honest woman.'

'I am sorry, Anne.' He looked at her then, and for her it was like seeing a stranger. But he was still Philippe, the man she had loved – and still did. 'Do you want the truth?' he went on. 'Forgive me, but I realised I did not love you enough to marry you.'

His words struck her like a dagger.

'I see it now,' she flared. 'You wanted only one thing, and I would not give it to you! Or rather, I gave you too much for you to want more!'

'No, Anne.' He hung his head. 'I do not think I am the marrying kind.'

She was not convinced. 'But what of your property? Who will inherit Briis if you do not marry?'

'My brother Pierre. Anne, do not think unkindly of me. My love for you was genuine.'

'Was?' It was as if a stone had lodged in her chest.

He swallowed. 'It still is. But I cannot offer you anything.'

It was an opening. She might not lose him after all. 'Yes, you can. You can still be my knight. We can see each other, and I might even permit you a few favours.' She spoke lightly, but her heart was heavy. She would keep him hers on any terms. The realisation depressed her. But what price pride, when her happiness was at stake?

Philippe was silent for a long moment.

'We will speak no more of marriage,' Anne said. 'No doubt my father or the Queen will arrange one for me in due course. But until then, I intend to enjoy myself.'

'Very well,' he said, 'let us be friends. Will you dance with me?'

He led her into the throng and they touched hands and whirled around. When the music stopped, he fetched her some wine and they drank together. But he was not the Philippe she had known. There was no spark there, no warmth. It was a travesty of what they had shared.

But when the evening drew to a close he took her hand and kissed it formally, and asked if he might wear her favour at the coming jousts.

'Yes,' she said, fretting because everything felt so odd. This was not how she had envisaged their reconciliation.

One of his friends brought her a note. It sounded so unlike him – it was almost incoherent.

I am sorry, I cannot love you as you deserve. I feel such hatred for myself. I am playing a sad song on my lute. When it is finished, I will be gone. Farewell. Forget me and be happy.

She grabbed his friend's sleeve. 'Go to his lodging,' she gasped, trying to steady her breathing. 'Bid him come to see me without delay. Hurry!'

She waited in the gallery for what seemed like an eternity, praying that her summons was not too late, and hoping that she had read the wrong meaning into the note. And then Philippe appeared, wearing a truculent look.

'What did you mean by this?' she cried, flapping the note in his face.

'What I said,' he told her. 'I am leaving the court for a while. It's no use, Anne. It is over between us.'

Anne braced her hand against the wall for support. She could feel the hot tears welling.

'Then go!' she cried. 'I never want to see you again. You're despicable!'

Without a word he turned and disappeared from view. Only then did she break down.

1520

It was evening when Anne emerged from the cloth-of-gold pavilion that had been erected for the Queen and her ladies in a great field in the Vale of Ardres. Tomorrow the kings of France and England would meet. The preparations had been going on for months.

Wearily she made her way through the crowded encampment to the servery, hoping there would be something left for supper. They were still busy, so she took her place in the queue, trying to see what was in the great cauldrons. Some sort of fish stew. It smelt good.

Her eye lighted on the gentlemen milling about and laughing ahead of her. One was Philippe du Moulin. She looked away. The sight of him no longer moved her, although for two years she had hated seeing him about the court, and avoided coming face-to-face with him. How silly she had been back then. Thank Heaven she had had the sense not to confide in anyone, for the court was a hotbed of gossip, and reputations could be ruined overnight. None save Philippe knew of her near fall from grace, or the wounds to her pride, and he had behaved so dishonourably that it was a fair certainty that he had not talked.

She could feel his eyes on her. She fixed hers on the cauldrons. Philippe would find her very different now, for at nineteen she was no longer the naïve girl he had known. Her mirror showed her the same dark-haired woman with the same high cheekbones and pointed chin, and yet there was a knowing quality to her gaze these days, for she had learned that the way a lady used her eyes, to invite conversation or convey a promise of hidden passion, had the power to command the allegiance of many a man.

She was aware of Philippe being served, of his pausing and turning in her direction. She looked away and was grateful to see another maid-of-honour smiling at her. 'A busy day!' she observed.

'Indeed!' the girl said. 'And it will be busier still tomorrow.'

When Anne turned back to be served, Philippe had gone.

She was dressed almost like a queen. Her French gown was of black velvet with great slashed sleeves, a low bodice and strings of pearls draped from shoulder to shoulder. She wore a gold-braided French hood. Standing in her place among the throng of Claude's attendants, she looked around her at the crowds of courtiers. All were waiting expectantly.

Word had yet to arrive that the English King was approaching. King François was waiting in his pavilion, the most sumptuous of them all. He must be chafing at the delay.

There was an excited buzz of expectancy. Horses' hooves could be heard in the distance. King Henry was coming.

The Tower is Full of Ghosts Today

'Welcome back, everyone!' Jo counted heads as her group gathered in the clearing at the bottom of the greensward that sloped down from the White Tower. The sun was shining down mercilessly, and she wanted to be on the move so that she could get them into the shade. Some tour guests were still emerging from the Medieval Palace Shop. During the lunch break she'd seen others watching re-enactors in Stuart costume giving a lively performance of Colonel Blood stealing the crown jewels, and had hoped that it wouldn't go on too long and delay their return. She had the costumed guide-lecturer booked for two o'clock, and it was now a quarter to. Always allow more time than you need: that was her mantra.

She finished the head count. They were all here, even the nice couple who were habitually late for everything.

'Thank you for being so prompt!' she smiled. 'Any moment now our guide for the Anne Boleyn walk will be here.' It was going to be the highlight of the day, the treat they were all waiting for. It seemed that everyone who came to the Tower of London wanted to hear about Anne Boleyn. It had been a piece of luck, finding a guide who came complete with an authentic Tudor costume and could expertly lead the group around the sites connected with the celebrated Queen's imprisonment and execution. Jo was looking forward to meeting her; she had come very well recommended.

'I can't wait!' said one of the women in the group. They were all passionately interested in everything Tudor.

'It should be good,' Jo said. 'You'll get the truth from the guide-lecturers here, not the film version!'

'Anne Boleyn's my heroine,' said a young guest, opening a locket to reveal a portrait of Anne – the famous one from the National Portrait Gallery. Jo, a historian herself, knew Anne's face as well as she knew her own: it was long, thin and vivacious, just like that of her daughter, Queen Elizabeth I.

'The guide's here,' she said, seeing a lady in Tudor dress advancing towards them. 'She's early too. And what a gown!' It was an exact replica, in sumptuous black velvet, of the elegant attire Anne wore in her portrait. Even the French hood – no easy thing to get right – was perfect.

'Historic Royal Palaces are very fussy about authenticity,' Jo said. 'Just look at that!' The woman even had a look of Anne. Certainly she had the right colouring: dark hair and dark eyes.

'Hello, good sirs, ladies,' the guide greeted them. Jo smiled. Groups loved it when guides got into character. This was going to be good, as she had promised. Even the French accent sounded right. Hats off to HRP!

'I am Anne the Queen,' the guide continued, 'and I am going to show you the places where I spent my last days.' She turned to face the White Tower. 'To our right is the site of the Queen's Lodgings, where I was imprisoned. You'll have to use your imagination, as those foundations are all that remain, but my apartments were splendid. They were done up at great cost for my coronation. But before we walk around and see them more closely, we will walk to Traitors' Gate, although it was called the Water Gate in my day.' Holding her hand aloft, her fur over-sleeve trailing down her skirt, she led the way through the archway that led to the Outer Ward.

'This is Water Lane,' she said, 'and before you is Traitors' Gate. I did not enter the Tower here, whatever the sign says!' The group laughed, rapt. They were hanging on her every word. 'You have to see it, though, because later on many so-called traitors were brought into the Tower this way, including the poor men who were falsely accused with me, and my great friend, poor Archbishop Cranmer, whose only crime was his love of the true religion. But Queen Mary remembered that he had divorced her mother, Katherine of Aragon, so that King Henry could marry me, and she had him burned at the stake. There were no burnings in my time as queen. I was a great friend to the Gospel, and the King heeded me.'

She had really done her homework. It was great, Jo thought, when you got someone who was highly knowledgeable.

As the guide went on to speak about the other illustrious or notorious prisoners who had come through Traitors' Gate, Jo saw another group approaching. This was going to be a scrum, she thought, given the narrowness of Water Lane. As the two groups seemed to merge, she found herself staring at a young woman in that group. Never had she seen such a gaunt, haunted face. Yet what really struck her was the uncanny resemblance to Anne Boleyn's portrait: the high cheekbones, the small mouth, the black eyes, dark hair and whitish pallor. And although the girl was with a group, she did not seem to be a part of it. They were all listening to one of the Yeomen Warders, but she seemed to be fixated on Traitors' Gate, oblivious to all else, and in her eyes there was an expression of pure misery. But there was nothing unusual about her in other ways: she wore jeans and a sweater, and carried a camera.

Jo kept staring at her until she realised that her own group was moving on. They walked a little way until their guide paused by a dark arch beneath the Byward Tower.

'Through here is the former Court Gate, the postern opening on to the River Thames. It was the royal entrance to the Tower in my day, and this is where I entered on the second day of May in the year of Our Lord 1536. And it was here, on the cobbles, that I sank to my knees and protested my innocence of the terrible crimes of which I was accused.' Her words evoked for the group the poignant scene on that long-ago evening and the agony of the doomed Queen. They were entranced.

They retraced their steps along Water Lane, walking, their guide told them, in Anne Boleyn's footsteps. 'This was where the Constable of the Tower led me to my lodgings.' Again they paused at the Medieval Palace Shop.

'On this site,' the guide said, 'stood the King's Hall, the great hall of the Tower. It was here, on the fifteenth day of May, 1536, that I was tried and condemned to be burned or beheaded at the King's pleasure.

It was only later that I realised that my husband the King must have sent for the headsman – the famous Sword of Calais – before my trial. This swordsman was renowned for his skill in cutting off heads.' She paused, and the hubbub all around them might have ceased. The guests were waiting eagerly for her to go on.

'When the sentence was read out, I lifted my eyes to Heaven and protested my innocence – but it did me no good! The King was set on marrying that wench Seymour!'

'Didn't Thomas Cromwell play a large part in bringing down Anne Boleyn?' a guest asked.

'Cromwell!' The guide's eyes flashed. 'Oh yes! He hated me, for he feared I would ruin him. So he pre-empted me. He was a man without scruples.'

'Not if you read Hilary Mantel!' muttered one of the group.

The guide smiled at him as she led them up the steps to where the ground sloped towards the White Tower. She pointed at it. 'It was there, in what I knew as Caesar's Tower, that the little Princes were murdered, fifty years before I became queen. King Richard, the usurper, had them shut up there because they had a better claim to the throne than he did. And we all know what happens to inconvenient royal personages!'

'He didn't murder them,' a man said firmly.

'Who truly knows?' The guide looked piercingly at him. 'In my day most people thought that he did. On dark nights they say you can see their little faces at a window in that keep.' Everyone looked up, their eyes focused on the windows high above, as if trying to see or imagine the boys' pale, anxious faces looking out.

'I guess you have many ghosts here at the Tower,' a lady from Kansas said.

'People see what they want to see,' the guide said. She looked at the man who had spoken in defence of Richard III. 'And they believe what they want to believe. Sometimes it is hard to tell what is truth and what is legend. This place is full of legends.'

They had skirted the White Tower and come to a stop by the wide steps that descended past the Bloody Tower.

'Look down,' the guide instructed, 'and you will see the remains of the Coldharbour Gate. That was the only way into the Inmost Ward where the royal palace was, where I was confined. On the nineteenth day of May, 1536, I walked through that gate to my execution. I was escorted by the Constable, his Lieutenant and a guard of two hundred yeomen warders. Four young ladies attended me. I was trying to be resolute and brave, but I was distracted by their weeping.'

The group they had passed earlier came to a halt next to them. Again Jo saw the pale young woman with dark hair and eyes. There was something stark and unsettling about her. Jo was still struck by the uncanny resemblance to Anne Boleyn. The girl was staring at the broken masonry of the great gate. Her pallor was almost unearthly.

Jo realised that her own group was again moving on.

'What's that building there, with the sentries in front?' a man asked.

'It's the Queen's House, the residence of the Governor of the Tower,' the guide said. 'In my day it was the Lieutenant's Lodging.'

'I read that Anne was imprisoned there,' a guest told her.

'No, it was too dilapidated for that. I was lodged in the Queen's apartments.'

The guide turned, her long skirts sweeping behind her. For the umpteenth time Jo found herself admiring that beautiful and very authentic-looking French hood. She resolved to give the woman a good tip, because she knew her stuff so well.

The guide waved a hand dismissively at the new glass memorial on Tower Green, in front of the Chapel Royal of St Peter ad Vincula. 'For a long time people have mistakenly thought that Queen Anne died on that spot,' she said, 'but it was over there that the scaffold was set up, before the old House of Ordnance, facing Caesar's Tower.' She led them to a place just in front of the entrance to the Waterloo Barracks, where people were queuing to see the Crown Jewels.

'It was here, on the tournament ground, where there was space to accommodate a large crowd. They wanted everything above-board, so that justice was seen to be done. The public were allowed in. Over a thousand came to watch.'

Once more the group were engrossed, straining to hear. The guide looked from face to face, her gaze intent. When she spoke, her voice wavered. 'I walked to the scaffold with my head held high.' She paused, as if for effect. It was clear she was living the experience in her head, as good re-enactors should.

'I wore a grey gown, a red kirtle, and a short ermine cape. I declared I had been a good wife, and praised the King's gentleness to me. You understand that I did not want to risk my family suffering any more than they had already, which they might have done if I had questioned King Henry's justice. I myself took off my hood and bandaged my eyes, for my maids were too distressed to help. Then I knelt in the straw and covered my feet with my skirts, for modesty. There was no block. They distracted me . . .'

The other group had caught up with them. Jo looked for the pale girl, but there was no sign of her. Then she noticed her at the back. She was trembling visibly, and on her face was an expression of utter fear. Yet no one was taking any notice of the poor girl. Just then, a man moved in front of her, and when Jo looked again, the girl had disappeared from sight. Jo looked here and there for her, but she had gone. Where was she? *Who* was she? There was no time to speculate because their guide was leading them towards the Chapel Royal.

Jo sat in the pews with the group. She heard not a word that the guide was saying. She could not get that haunted face out of her head; she kept seeing those terrified eyes, that unearthly white face. She felt chilled, despite the warmth of the day. Was she just being fanciful, or had she really seen a ghost? Was Anne Boleyn condemned to walk the place where she had died, even in the guise of a tourist? Yet reason dictated that she be rational. How could a historian like herself tell anyone that she thought she had seen the ghost of Anne Boleyn? Imagine the reaction! She would never live it down. And yet . . . And yet, there had been something uncanny about the pale girl from the first. It was as if she had been surrounded by silence in a teeming world.

She pulled herself together at the sound of clapping. The group were showing their appreciation of what had been a great tour, and it was time to express her own thanks. She pressed a note into the guide's hand as they walked out of the chapel. 'You were amazing!' she said.

'I noticed you were a little distracted at the end,' the woman told her, still in that lilting French accent. 'I saw her too. I have seen her several times. She is a very sad lady. I do not know what she is looking for.'

Jo was astonished. 'It sounds a silly question, but is she real?'

'She is real to those who see her,' the guide said, with a slight smile. 'Now I must go.' She turned to the group. 'Thank you all. I have enjoyed showing you around. You have been wonderful company.' To more clapping she walked back into the chapel.

'In ten minutes, everyone, please be back at the meeting point,' Jo cried, then hurriedly made her way there. As the tour leader, she wanted to reach it first, hastening past the Medieval Palace Shop, she was still thinking about the pale girl and what the guide had said.

At the meeting point a lady in rather drab Tudor dress was looking at her watch and frowning. Seeing the logo on Jo's badge, she hurried over and shook her hand. 'Jo Maddox? I'm so sorry I was late. I don't blame you for going ahead without me. I missed my train.'

'I'm sorry, I think there's been a mix up,' Jo said, confused.

'No, dear. I'm Sue. You booked me for the Anne Boleyn walk.'

Alison Weir's Anne Boleyn Walk
at the Tower of London

The main entrance to the Tower of London is via the Middle Tower. Before you go through, walk on towards the River Thames. You will pass the Middle Tower and, beyond it, the Byward Tower. In front of the Byward Tower you will see the Queen's Stairs leading up to the postern gate, which was the Court Gate in the fifteenth and sixteenth centuries. This is where Anne Boleyn entered the Tower after her arrest on 2nd May 1536.

Retrace your steps and enter the Tower by the main entrance. Walk ahead along Water Lane (the Outer Ward) and pass under the Byward Tower. To your right, you will see a short passage leading to its postern gate (the former Court Gate).

Continue along Water Lane. On the left, you will see the Bloody Tower and an archway leading into the Inner Ward of the Tower. Walk through the archway and up the long flight of shallow stairs to Tower Green.

At the top, on your right, you will see the White Tower and, before it, the ruins of the massive Coldharbour Gate. This led to the Inmost Ward, where the Queen's Lodgings – where Anne was held prisoner – were located. Anne walked through this gate on her way to her execution.

Ahead of you, you will see the Chapel Royal of St Peter ad Vincula, where Anne is buried. You can only go inside if you join a tour led by a Yeoman Warder; these run through the day and people gather outside the Chapel. The Warders will tell you when the next one runs. Inside the Chapel, go to the chancel beyond the altar rails. Anne was buried here – but probably not beneath the Victorian memorial plaque that bears her name. She almost certainly lies under that dedicated to Jane, Lady Rochford, which is usually hidden by the altar frontal. Anne's brother George lies somewhere nearby.

Outside the Chapel, you will see the so-called scaffold site on Tower Green. Only two of the people listed on the memorial were actually beheaded on or near this spot: William, Lord Hastings, in 1483, and Margaret Pole, Countess of Salisbury, in 1541. Tower Green used to cover a much larger area than it does today and served as the Chapel's burial ground. Somewhere in this area, the four men executed for committing adultery with Anne are buried. The precise location is unknown.

To the right of the Chapel (as you face it) stand the Waterloo Barracks, built in the nineteenth century on the site of the old House of Ordnance. On 19th May 1536, Anne was beheaded on a scaffold erected outside the House of Ordnance, facing 'Caesar's Tower', as the White Tower was then known; it was thought that Julius Caesar had built it. The House of Ordnance stood slightly further back, in front of what was then the tournament ground; the likeliest site of the scaffold is in front of the main door to the Waterloo Barracks.

Continue walking in the same direction, keeping the White Tower to your right, then walk around it in the direction of the River Thames. You will see on your right the remains of the Wardrobe Tower, then, a little further along, the foundations of the Queen's Lodging, where Anne was held during her imprisonment.

Continue towards the river until you come to some stairs leading down on your right. Walk down them, and you will find the Medieval Palace Shop. In Anne's day, you would have been standing in the Inmost Ward, with the Tower palace between you and the river. The shop stands on the site of the great hall, or King's Hall, where Anne was tried and condemned to death on 15th May 1536.

You may like to retrace your steps a little and go up the stairs to the wall walk that links that palace to other towers. Follow it (going away from the palace) to the Martin Tower. Here, you can see the name 'Boullen' roughly carved into the stonework beneath a rose, such as appeared on Anne's falcon badge. This was possibly the work of George

Boleyn, who, according to tradition, was imprisoned here. Anne's falcon badge – minus its crown and sceptre – is the subject of another carving in the wall of a first-floor cell in the thirteenth-century Beauchamp Tower, which you will find on the opposite side of Tower Green, to the left of the Chapel. It was this carving that perhaps gave rise to the ancient, but erroneous, tradition that Anne herself was imprisoned in the Beauchamp Tower.

That brings your walk to an end, but there is a lot more to see in the Tower. Enjoy your visit!

JANE SEYMOUR

Timeline

1508

- Birth of Jane Seymour
- Birth of Thomas Seymour

1527

- Henry VIII questions the validity of his marriage to Katherine of Aragon and asks the Pope for an annulment
- Jane Seymour goes to court as maid-of-honour to Katherine of Aragon

1531

- Katherine of Aragon banished from court; Jane Seymour remains in her household

1533

- Marriage of Henry VIII and Anne Boleyn
- Jane Seymour leaves Katherine of Aragon's household to serve Anne Boleyn
- Cranmer pronounces the marriage of Henry VIII and Katherine of Aragon incestuous and unlawful, and confirms the validity of Henry's marriage to Anne Boleyn (May)
- Coronation of Anne Boleyn (June)
- Birth of the Princess Elizabeth, daughter of Henry VIII and Anne Boleyn (September)

1534

- Parliament passes the Act of Supremacy, making Henry VIII Supreme Head of the Church of England, and the Act of Succession, making the children of Queen Anne the King's lawful heirs

1535

- Henry VIII begins courting Jane Seymour

1536

- Death of Katherine of Aragon (January)
- Fall of Anne Boleyn, arrest and imprisonment at the Tower of London
- Anne Boleyn executed for treason (19 May)
- Marriage of Henry VIII and Jane Seymour (30 May)

- Jane Seymour proclaimed queen of England (4 June)
- Parliament passes a new Act of Succession settling the succession on the children of Henry VIII and Jane Seymour
- Katherine of Aragon's daughter, the Lady Mary, acknowledges her mother's marriage incestuous and unlawful and is reconciled to Henry VIII

1537

- Birth of Prince Edward, son of Henry VIII and Jane Seymour
- Death of Jane Seymour (24 October)

THE GRANDMOTHER'S TALE

I can just about get around these days, and thank the good Lord for that, as I believe I really would go mad were I to be confined to that chair by the fire. They think I'm mad anyway, the servants who attend me; Thomas saw to that. There aren't many of them left now – not like in the glory days when William and I first came to this place. It was heaving with servants then, and everything was new. Of course, his father had not long completed his building works – completed them and then departed to his rest. I never met old Sir Geoffrey. He died long before William and I wed. Oh, I was young then, and beautiful. The young do not realise how short a time beauty lasts.

They are all gone now, those I loved best. Three children – of all my ten – have been spared to me. Bitter Anne, sanctimonious James and pious William. I never see any of them these days, for they are all far away. How hard life has touched us all.

Archbishop Cranmer came today, wearing his mournful face and the air of one doing a heavy duty. I know him well; he was once our family chaplain. I offered him dinner and, after some browbeating the servants resentfully placed a meal of sorts before us as we sat at the board in the hall, for I had insisted on keeping some ceremony. Surrounding us were the tangible benefits of Thomas's riches: the fine tapestries, the Turkey carpet, the fine silver-gilt plate. All that, and he left me just a pittance of four hundred marks a year out of *my* estates!

Well, much good did his wealth do him in the end. *We brought nothing into this world, and we can take nothing out of it.*

'I'm sorry to intrude on your grief so soon, my lady,' the Archbishop said. 'I felt it my duty to come and explain to you what will happen now.'

'I've suffered so much grief these past years that I'm numbed to it,' I told him.

His eyes glittered with tears. He's doing this for *her*, I realised.

'The position is this,' he said gently, mastering himself, 'that your late son's co-heirs are your granddaughter Mistress Stafford and the Crown.'

The Crown. Of course. But it should have all gone to my grandson George or, failing him, to Anne and Mary, or Anne's daughter, Elizabeth. Five years old now, if my memory serves me, which it often doesn't. But George and Anne are no more, their share of their father's wealth confiscated by an Act of Attainder passed after . . . No, I will not think of it now, although God knows their appalling fate haunts my nightmares. Poor Elizabeth. That one so young should suffer the stain of bastardy and being declared unfit to inherit, on top of the loss of her mother. It makes me want to weep.

'The late Earl of Wiltshire's property is to be divided,' Cranmer said, taking a sip of pottage. Neither of us had much appetite, and I don't eat much these days anyway.

'So who gets what?' I asked, wondering what was to become of me and hoping I could stay here at Hever. Mary's in Calais, and if the castle came to her, she would not turn me out. She has a soft heart.

'Hever Castle, the manor of Seal and Blickling Hall are to revert to the Crown,' the Archbishop said. The news gave me a turn, and I felt my old heart miss a beat. I had feared the worst, and here it was. I was to be turned out of my home – the home I have lived in for thirty-three years.

'The Crown may not wait to take what is rightfully its property,' his Grace of Canterbury continued, 'which is why I am here. Fortuitously, the King has granted me full jurisdiction and authority over many churches, villages and parishes in Kent, including Hever Castle. I intend to save some of the late Earl's goods for your ladyship and Mistress Stafford, while there is still time.'

'Bless you!' I said. And then it happened again, that thing that visits me from time to time and so distresses me, and which twenty years ago gave Thomas grounds for declaring me insane, just so that he could appropriate my estates and live off my wealth. It was happening, and there I was, staring at the Archbishop and seeing his portly form surrounded by a glow of flames. It was only a momentary impression, but it so horrified me that I gasped.

'Madam, are you all right?' Cranmer asked, all concern, looking quite like himself again, to my relief.

I could barely speak, for I had seen such visions before, and knew that they were portents. 'It was the shock,' I croaked.

He patted my hand. 'Do not worry, my lady. My men are here to remove any possessions you wish to keep. They can be stored at my house at Knole until your granddaughter comes home and decides what to do with them. She is in Calais, is she not?'

'Aye, my lord. But what is to become of me? Where do *I* go?'

Cranmer's mouth set in a grim line. 'If I have anything to do with it, you will stay here, my lady. Do not fret.'

I spent the afternoon heaving myself around the house, showing my kind visitor what to take and what to leave. A nasty fall last winter did my aching bones no good, and I am now horribly lame and have to use a stick to get about.

All the time, my vision was preying on my mind. I hardly dared look at Cranmer in case I saw it again, and I was inwardly praying that I was wrong, and that this good man would not have to die so horribly. I could not forget that I had not been wrong those other times.

It was an effort going through everything, but worth it, and by supper time the carts lined up beyond the drawbridge are full of furnishings, hangings, plate, clothing and jewellery. The castle looks horribly bare. All that remains are the necessities of my daily life, a few sticks of furniture, and some tapestries that we felt it politic to leave, lest the King should accuse us of robbing him of his rich pickings. When the Archbishop says goodbye, I kiss him out of gratitude and because of what might lie in store for him, when the knowledge that he had eased an old woman's last years might cheer his heart.

Of course, he had done it for her. He had loved her from the first, and it was clear that he still grieved for her. But he dared not say so.

* * *

119

Cranmer's kindness yesterday came not a moment too soon. Today, I've just received a letter from Lord Cromwell, informing me that the King's officers will soon be visiting me. He's common scum, Cromwell, for all that he's the King's chief minister. His father was a blacksmith. He thinks he can barge in upon my grief, even though my son died only two weeks ago and is barely cold in his grave. If I could foresee some dire fate for Cromwell, it wouldn't bother me one bit.

I order that a message be sent to Thomas's man of business, John Tebold, to come over from Seal to see me. He's with me inside an hour, but is staring around him in dismay.

'Where is everything?' he wants to know. I tell him.

He shakes his head, frowning. 'I wish my lord of Canterbury had stayed his hand. There could be trouble. Do you have Lord Cromwell's letter?'

I hand it to him and he reads it, looking perplexed. 'I'll have to tell him,' he says, clearly worried. He sits down at the table, calls for ink and paper, and begins to write. 'They're taking Seal too,' he says. 'My instructions were to keep everything in place until the King's pleasure is known. I've got Sir Thomas Willoughby at Seal right now, taking an inventory. He's one of the King's chief justices. What on earth is he going to say about this?'

'He's our neighbour at Chiddingstone, and a good friend – and I think you'll find that Archbishop Cranmer has the authority to do what he did, granted by the King himself.' I relate what Cranmer said.

'I think I'd better ask Willoughby to come over here now,' Tebold says, and calls for a messenger.

Sir Thomas arrives by supper time, a portly and urbane man of vast experience, and again I stir those lazy servants to prepare a passable dinner for us, over which I repeat what the Archbishop said.

'I myself will write to Lord Cromwell this evening and assure him that I will aid Master Tebold in taking possession of Hever,' Sir Thomas replies. 'I shall not mention the removal of your goods.'

'Am I to be turned out?' I ask, dismayed. 'Where will I go?'

'Not at all!' Willoughby smiles. 'His Grace the King is aware that you have been unable to manage your affairs these past twenty years.

He has graciously said that you may live out your days here.'

Never have I felt such relief. 'God bless his Grace!' I cry, from my heart.

The men are smiling. And now the servants are approaching with platters of roasted meat and boiled fish, jugs of fragrant sauce and ewers of wine. They haven't done us so badly after all.

'I think I have cause for celebration,' I say, pouring the wine. 'Will you join me in a toast, sirs?'

They raise their goblets. 'To your ladyship's long and happy life!'

Long, I doubt. I'm sixty-nine, well past my grand climacteric. As for happy, no one could suffer the losses I've had and be happy. And my elation at my reprieve is tinged with sadness, for when I go, there will be no more Boleyns at Hever. I'd have liked to see Mary here with her children, and I suppose that fool varlet of a husband of hers, but fate – or the King – has decreed otherwise.

'You've been living in these parts a long time,' Sir Thomas observes.

'About half my life,' I tell them. 'Before that, I lived in Norfolk, but I was born in Ireland, in Kilkenny Castle.' In my mind I can see the great stronghold, set in the lush greenness of the land of my childhood. 'My father was the Earl of Ormond, and I and my sister were his co-heiresses.'

'A great inheritance indeed,' Willoughby says.

'We Butlers have an ancient lineage,' I boast. 'We are descended from King Edward the First. My father was one of the wealthiest nobles in the realm. He inherited a great fortune, and was lord of seventy-two English manors. He sat in Parliament as premier baron of England too! But before he came into his inheritance, he had no money. The Boleyns were the saving of him. His debts were paid with their help, and they were repaid in the lands I got as dowry. It's largely on my account that my husband's family became so wealthy.'

The two men are listening with polite interest.

'But you don't want to hear an old woman's reminiscences,' I say.

'Nay, go on,' urges Tebold.

'Pray do!' Sir Thomas smiles. 'We would entertain your ladyship to your comfort, and you must have many memories to recount.'

I do. There's not much point in talking about the future these days, so the past is where my mind often dwells. And although there is much of it that I cannot bear to revisit, it heartens me to return to the days when I was young and full of hope. Like the day William first brought me to Hever Castle, and I fell in love with it.

There is no place I would rather be than Hever, and I knew that when I was eighteen and came here as a bride, riding across the drawbridge with William and seeing for the first time the fine new house within the ancient walls of the castle. Even today I can still recapture that thrill whenever I see sunlight streaming through the leaded windows onto the magnificent panelling, or make my painful way through the herb garden, conjuring up the scents of long ago. Hever is a little jewel of a castle, its mellow stone walls drowsing in a leafy valley. It holds for me the echo of that distant summer, lost in time, when William and I were lovers in Sir Geoffrey's grand bedchamber, and all around us was magic and joy.

Now, as I creak along the long gallery that Thomas built, I can hardly bear to look at the portraits hanging there. *Hers* has gone, of course. It's in the attic. But there are Thomas and Elizabeth, all decked out in their brave finery, and neither evokes happy memories. How they do stare, tight lipped, keeping secrets now never to be told, for he lies beyond the gatehouse in St Peter's Church, far from her. She, of course, had to be buried with her Howard forebears at Lambeth.

But I digress, as I am wont to do these days. I tell my listeners how I love this house, and that I find beauty here, and an inner peace of sorts, and quietness in abundance. Yet there remains the taint of dark deeds, of treason or bloody retribution, and the shadow of a queenly wraith. I see *her* from time to time, and I wish I didn't, but I don't say that. Nor do I tell my guests of my awful gift, or of how I kept seeing a sword over her head. The gift is a curse, and it's got me into trouble several times. In one of his unkind moods, Thomas once called me a witch. But witches practise their craft willingly. My visions come unbidden, and I have never been able to control them.

Oh, I am rambling! So I tell Willoughby and Tebold how the Boleyns' fortunes improved over the years, and how they rose to prominence by acquiring wealth through good marriages, and by their own cleverness and acumen. Again and again, the family has demonstrated its solid loyalty to the Crown. My William was knighted by King Richard III, although after the Battle of Bosworth he prudently switched his allegiance to the new King, Henry VII, and never looked back. Soon we were dividing our time between Blickling Hall in Norfolk and Hever Castle, so that William could be near to the court when need be. And the old King showed his trust in him by making him responsible for keeping the peace, delivering prisoners to the assizes, and for the beacons that would herald the approach of the King's enemies. William was also made a baron of the Exchequer. I was so proud of him.

Most of the time we lived at Blickling Hall, a handsome gabled manor house of moulded brick and tile, surrounded by a moat and yew hedges. William also owned a house at Mulbarton by Norwich, and a mansion in Norwich itself, on the River Wensum, very convenient for entertaining our many friends in the city. My husband was lord of a good number of manors in Norfolk and Kent, which afforded a substantial income. We lived well, and in comfort.

These were the years in which we prospered and loved and conceived our children. Eight of the ten survived childhood, yet even now, I feel a great lump in my throat at the recollection of those two small waxen bodies lying in their coffins, their still faces lit by candles, and those tiny graves in Blickling Church. Part of my heart lies there too. The rest of it, broken beyond repair, lies in Norwich Cathedral, where my dear lord was laid to rest thirty-four years ago. A short illness, which no one thought dangerous – and he was gone.

Thomas inherited everything, to his great satisfaction. Numb with grief, I allowed myself and my possessions to be bundled up alongside my grandchildren and trundled south to Hever with him and Elizabeth, Thomas declaring that James could have Blickling, as it was imperative that he himself be near to the court from now on. Preferment was his god, and I don't recall his ever doing anything without a degree of self-interest. It was why he begrudged me the two hundred marks annually that his father had left me. That rankled, for years.

He was even more discountenanced when my father died ten years later – to my great heaviness – and left me half of his extensive wealth and property, amounting to thirty-six manors and two great houses in Essex, Rochford Hall and New Hall. All Thomas got from his grandfather was a hunting horn of ivory and gold, which had been in our family for generations. That really infuriated him for, as a widow, I had the right to do what I liked with my inheritance.

But he browbeat and pressed me into letting him take control of it, saying it would stand him in good stead for claiming the earldom of Ormond. Now *that* was a sore issue for years! And because I wanted him to have the earldom, I let him do it, and he immediately sold New Hall to the King, who turned it into a magnificent palace. I was put out by that, I admit, and yet I thought the sacrifice would be worth it. But Ormond was appropriated by my father's cousin, Piers Butler, who had the effrontery to assume the title. Thomas was confident that he could wrest it from Piers. It took him years, and of course, in the end, he triumphed. It was all down to *her*. Besotted as he was, the King granted the earldom of Ormond, and that of Wiltshire, to Thomas.

But I digress again. My earlier tale is not finished. It was my misfortune foolishly to mention seeing that vision of young Anne with a sword over her head. And my son, my own son, made it an excuse to deprive me of my income, getting his lawyer to declare me insane and incapable of managing my affairs. And so he grew fat on *my* wealth.

'You have not mentioned your granddaughter,' Sir Thomas ventures, refilling his goblet.

'Mary?' I ask, although I suspect he does not mean her. 'She's a foolish girl. Fancy marrying that landless clod Stafford – and for love!'

'But did not your ladyship marry for love?'

'No, my marriage was arranged for advantage, as marriages should be. Love came afterwards, and I was lucky, but it's a fool who marries for love. It is love that has brought this family low. Both my grand-daughters have suffered for love. Look at Mary, exiled from court and skulking in Calais with that landless dolt. And remember Anne . . .'

There is an embarrassed silence. No one dares to speak of her these days, in case they say the wrong thing. It could be dangerous, in some quarters, to say the wrong thing.

'A bad business,' Sir Thomas says at length.

'And because of it, we Boleyns have lost Hever,' I sniff, pleating the tablecloth unthinkingly. 'You know, she was as much her mother's daughter as her father's, and her mother was no better than she should have been, for all that she was a Howard and granddaughter to the Duke of Norfolk. But it was a grand marriage, and Thomas was fortunate. Had her father not fought for Richard the Third at Bosworth and been down on his luck afterwards, he would not have looked at my son as a possible husband. But he did, and we all rejoiced.'

I take a spoonful of syllabub.

'It was only later that I became aware that Elizabeth was cuckolding my son.' I knew what had been going on with the steward while Thomas was at court. 'That a noblewoman should stoop so low!'

The men regard me with interest.

'There were rumours,' Willoughby says.

'Especially after Master Skelton wrote that poem comparing her to Cressida!' I tell him. 'Thomas was furious, but he cared little for Elizabeth by then, and was content to leave her to her indiscretions. It was his pride that was hurt, that people should know. Fortunately, the children were all growing up. There was no question of them not being his. And Anne was Elizabeth's child, as is Mary, and every bit her father's too; Mary inherited none of his ambition.'

'Then you accept Anne's guilt,' Willoughby says.

'I make no comment!' I declare, and take myself off to bed, bidding them both good night.

In the morning, I feel up to taking a short walk. Hever has glorious gardens, set in the beautiful, undulating Kentish countryside. But everywhere there are reminders of those who are now gone into the hereafter. I see my grandchildren playing on the grass, Thomas waiting on the drawbridge to welcome the King, Anne peering elusively through a window – she knew well how to play Henry and tie him in knots – and Elizabeth with a trug full of the flowers she loved. It is hard to believe that they are all gone now, and that I, who by the law of Nature should have died first, am still here.

I know what they say about Thomas, that he was complicit in destroying his children. God alone knows what it cost him to sit in judgement on them and declare them both guilty – and of the most disgusting crimes. But Elizabeth was ill; he had to think of her. He really didn't have a choice. Had he refused, he might have been brought down with Anne and George, and then where would Elizabeth have been?

He came home a broken man. They were both broken, paralysed with grief and horror. I remember Elizabeth sitting in her chair, rocking in her misery, and her hysterical cries when word came that the dread sentence had been carried out. Thomas uttered no word of protest or sorrow, but you had only to look at him to know that he was suffering. They were never the same afterwards, either of them.

There is no doubt in my mind that the tragedy hastened Elizabeth's death. Not two years afterwards – two years in which grief and illness destroyed her, and the last vestiges of her marriage – she died in London.

Thomas rallied, for a time. He had lost his office of Lord Privy Seal to Lord Cromwell, but managed to retain his place on the King's Council. It was good to see ambition surfacing in him again. He was determined to claw his way back into royal favour, and it didn't take much, for I believe that the King genuinely liked him – and found him useful. Thomas smiled bravely and made himself courteous to that pallid little bitch who stole Anne's husband and her crown. He even attended the christening of the prince she managed to bear. How different everything would have been had Anne achieved that. No one could have touched her then.

But she had failed in that one crucial thing, and so she had been brought down.

I am in no doubt that they concocted a case against her. The granddaughter I knew had her faults, but she was not that much of a monster – and nor was George. As to what was said about them – no one in their right mind would credit it. But I must stop myself here, or I'll end up going over and over it all in my mind and torturing myself by wondering what it was like for her at the end, flesh of my flesh. They didn't even give her a proper burial. I can't forgive that, nor the King for marrying again only eleven days after her death. And I can't forgive George's unspeakable wife, for it was she who claimed that he and Anne committed incest. The word is bitter gall on my tongue.

Thomas would do nothing for her when she was widowed and left destitute, and can anyone blame him? I have never forgotten him exploding with rage when the King asked him to provide for her. His pen jabbed the page as he asked Cromwell to inform the King that he did so only for his Highness's pleasure. But he made sure that that filthy whore (for such she was) didn't get her hands on the widow's jointure settled on her at her marriage. And I'm determined she won't have it in my lifetime either! What galls me is that she was welcomed back to court to serve the Seymour woman. I have no doubt that it was a reward for services rendered in bringing down her husband and her Queen.

Slowly, I make my way along the path to the castle. The sun has gone in and I'm getting cold. I'm remembering how tenacious Thomas was. He kept in with Cromwell and others with influence, and was soon being well entertained at court. There was even a rumour that he would wed the King's niece, Lady Margaret Douglas, which would have been the greatest honour and restored him to an even higher eminence than he had enjoyed before. But he was ailing. Although he was my son, I never liked him, but he died like a good Christian man.

George being dead, there is no heir male, and Piers Butler gets the earldom of Ormond at last, much to my annoyance. His victory eats at me, although I suppose I should be past such things, with death just around the corner, but my blood – my noble blood – cries out for reparation. Unfortunately, even God seems to be deaf to my entreaties.

I've had more visions over the years, but kept them to myself. I saw my grandson George doing something so abominable to his wife that I can't bear to think about it. But there's another vision that comes increasingly these days. I see a young woman with red hair wearing a crown, and I wonder who it could be. Not my Elizabeth, surely – the grandchild I've never seen. How can a bastard be crowned queen?

I hope Henry's being a good father to her and sees that she is well cared for. She needs stability after losing her mother so tragically, poor mite. I wish I could see her and be a proper grandmother to her. But she is far beyond my reach.

I never saw Anne either after she married the King. I was left here at Hever while almost everyone else entrenched themselves at court to bask in her glory. Only Mary was here – Mary, who was supposed to stay out of sight as far as possible. And I knew why. Before Anne had become his obsession, Mary had borne the King a child, which was passed off as her first husband's. That was a compliant man, if ever there was one. You have only to look at Katherine to see whose child she is.

It wasn't just the fact that Mary bore a bastard child, more that she was a walking reminder of the unlawfulness of Anne's marriage. For Anne was forbidden to Henry. Katherine's existence rendered their union incestuous. It was the unspoken truth between us all, and I suspect it was the grounds upon which the King disinherited Elizabeth. No wonder Anne flew into a rage when Mary married William Stafford in secret and turned up at court pregnant, drawing undue attention to herself when Anne wanted her kept in the background!

I remember Mary coming back here, in floods of tears.

'I have been banished from the court, my lady!' she wailed to me, running around the house like a whirlwind, gathering up her belongings. 'Father says we can't stay here, so we're going to William's people.' William was just standing there looking awkward. And so they went. Later I heard that they had gone to Calais, where William was serving as a soldier in the garrison. Later still I gave thanks for it, for, being abroad, Mary did not have to live through the scandal – or the dangers – of Anne's fall. What grieves me is she and Anne never were reconciled.

Mary is the only one left to me now, my silly, sweet grandchild. Her, and her two children, Harry and Kate. I have missed them cruelly these past four years. But now there is no more risk of royal displeasure, and Mary can return whenever she wants to.

The months pass so quickly now that I am old. It seems that no sooner are the servants pulling down the Christmas greenery – or what passes for it nowadays – they are putting it up again. And now another Christmas is approaching, and Mary is coming home.

I am so happy to see the little procession trotting into the courtyard. I'm even happy to see that fool Stafford, with his big wide grin and gangly frame.

'My lady!' Mary cries, and runs into my arms. Her children are dancing about her, glad to be home. I hug and kiss them all, feeling life seeping back into my ancient bones. Now the servants will no longer be able to tyrannise me!

Mary is looking about her in wonder. 'I had forgot how lovely Hever is,' she breathes. A shadow clouds her pretty face. 'It seems so strange and empty now that they are all gone – Father, Mother, George . . . and Anne.' Her eyes gleam with tears. 'I feel quite an orphan!'

'You have me, child,' I assure her.

'Thank the good Lord for that,' she says, taking my arm, and leads the way into the entrance hall.

They have returned to England in the train of the new Queen, another Anne.

'What is she like?' I ask over supper in the evening, as we tuck into dishes of suckling pig and herring.

Mary hesitates. 'Very pleasant, it seems, but – very unlike any of the King's other wives. She's no beauty.'

'I daresay he knew what he was doing when he chose her,' Stafford offers. 'But it's an odd choice.'

'Who can fathom the minds of kings?' I ask.

'Aye.' Mary's response is heartfelt. I see Stafford wince.

'Will is to go to court,' Mary tells me. 'He will be serving his Grace as one of the Gentleman Pensioners, keeping watch in the King's presence chamber. They are but fifty in number, and there is much demand when a vacancy arises. But Will was recommended by Sir Anthony Browne, whom we met in Calais.'

'You are a lucky fellow, Will,' I tell him. I find myself quite liking him, despite myself. He's amiable and straightforward, and he clearly worships Mary.

'Will you go to court with him?' I want to know.

'I think not. There is nothing for me there now. Besides, I have to take possession of my inheritance. I need to find a good lawyer.' She frowns. 'I'm surprised but pleased to see you still here at Hever, my lady.'

'I'll be here till I die,' I say. 'The King has sanctioned it.'

'Then, God willing, you will be here for many years yet!' she smiles.

In the morning, I walk with Mary to Hever Church, leaning on her arm. We stand for a time by Thomas's tomb, staring down at the fine memorial brass showing him wearing his Garter insignia. Masses are being said for his soul here, by the King's order.

Mary whispers, 'I wish I could weep for him, but he was a stern father.'

'And an unkind one,' I add.

'Anne was his favourite by far. I always knew that.'

'He never bothered to hide it,' I say, tart.

'Nevertheless, I will say a prayer for him,' she murmurs, and sinks to her knees on the flagstones.

Christmas has come and gone – the merriest Christmas I've had in years. Will has departed for the court with Katherine, who is to serve the new Queen. Harry has been returned, protesting, to his tutors, and Mary is trying to make sense of her father's will. Nothing is clear, and it looks as if she has a long legal battle ahead.

And I – I am confined at last to my bed. These old legs of mine have finally given up on me. And so I lie here, with Mary sitting untiringly at my side as I wait for my soul to be harvested. I shall be glad to leave this world. William awaits me in the next, and Anne too, and all those who have gone before me.

The visions are coming more frequently now. It's Hever I see, but not the Hever I know. The castle is decayed and all but ruinous.

Sheep graze where the gardens should be. Then – and maybe I am dreaming – I see a man in strange dark attire, with a pugnacious face and a moustache, very upright and correct. And then my vision of the castle returns once more, only this time it is surrounded by crowds of people all trying to get in, and the gardens are restored, but looking so different, and more lovely than ever; and there is a lake, something we never had.

In my dream, I drift through the courtyard, noticing that the mullioned windows have been replaced. Our kitchen has been transformed into a fine hall, the deep well hidden under a wooden floor. Fine wood carvings abound everywhere, and there are portraits on the walls. I recognise the King, and Anne and Mary on either side of the fireplace. In our great hall, a fire crackles in the large fireplace and tapestries grace the walls. The tables are set side by side, and laid as if for a sumptuous banquet, but the dais has gone and there is no high table for us persons of rank. On the wall hangs a little painting of the hall as I know it. How very strange!

The steward's office, where Elizabeth kept her not-so-secret trysts, is transformed into a library. There is new panelling in Thomas's long gallery, and still, life-size figures acting out some kind of pageant.

Mary is gently shaking my shoulder. 'My lady! Wake up. Here is some broth for you.'

But I am gone. Why should I tarry for broth, when I can fly on wings across the glorious gardens of Hever? On, on I go, into the distance, my spirit soaring ever northwards to Norwich, towards the shining, waiting arms of William, my dearest love.

THE UNHAPPIEST LADY IN CHRISTENDOM

Oh, what lamentations were made for the death of my dear stepmother! Even at a distance of twenty years, I can still feel the reverberations from her loss. And although I and many others who knew her were stricken by the heart-rending sight of her body lying lifeless on the bed, her struggle over, no one took it more heavily than the King my father. I don't remember ever seeing him so affected by anything. As soon as the Queen had breathed her last he stumbled from the room, tears streaming down his face, and withdrew to his apartments, refusing to see anyone.

My father could not bear anything to do with death, so I was not surprised to hear that, on the following morning, he had departed early for Windsor. I imagine he could not bear to stay in the same house as the cold corpse of the woman he had so loved. Locked in grief, he left us all to deal with the morbid aftermath. My lord of Norfolk was to be in charge of the funeral arrangements, with instructions that everything was to be done with the greatest magnificence. I was to be chief mourner – I, for whom Queen Jane had done more than anyone. She could never have filled the shoes of my dear, sainted mother – no one could – but she had done her very best to restore me to my rightful place in my father's affections, and for that I shall always be grateful.

We ladies who had loved her took turns to keep watch over her body. She looked peaceful, almost as if she were sleeping, but when I touched her hand it was cold, and after some hours her face took on a purplish-grey hue. That morning the wax chandlers came and did their work on her. When we returned, dressed in the mourning habits that had hurriedly been made for us, she was lying on a bier covered with a rich pall of gold cloth, and dressed in a robe of gold tissue and some of her jewels, with the Queen's crown on her head. Her fair hair lay loose like a cape of pale gold, her face was painted in an attempt to give a semblance of life, and there was a strong smell of herbs and spices in the bedchamber.

We followed in procession as the bier was reverently carried to the presence chamber, where her body would lie in state for a week. Tapers were lit around it, and a black-draped altar was set to the side and furnished with a jewelled crucifix, holy images and censers of gold.

As Masses were sung night and day for Queen Jane's soul, we ladies kept vigil, ensuring that there were always some watching over her. The officers of the Royal Wardrobe gave us white kerchiefs for our heads and shoulders, to signify that our good mistress had died in childbed. We knelt there through all the services and Masses, lamenting and weeping, while I tried to ignore a raging toothache and the stiffness in my knees.

I had plenty of leisure to mourn my loss, and think back on the blows life had dealt me. My childhood had been so happy. The only one of six children to survive, I was cosseted and loved by my parents, both of whom I adored, and brought up to be courteous, decorous, learned and merry – merry, that is, until my father was led astray by Anne Boleyn. How I hated her, the source of all my mother's woes and mine. Through those dreadful years, I could barely bring myself to utter her name, and never, ever would I acknowledge her as queen. How could I, when my mother was my father's true, lawful wife? But Father had been seized with a temporary madness, so in thrall was he to his enchantress, and so my mother and I endured humiliation upon humiliation.

For four long, terrible years of exile from court we were kept cruelly apart, and I was often ill. Declared a bastard, to my shame and horror, I was made to wait upon my half-sister, the babe Elizabeth, although I would never call her princess, which riled Anne Boleyn still further. In spite of all, I came to love Elizabeth, since I was never likely to have babes of my own to cherish. For what prince would want me, disinherited and demeaned as I was? And I would not take any lesser man, for all the Lady Anne had threatened to marry me to some varlet. I did not put it past her to bring that to pass!

When my mother became gravely ill, I was desperate to see her. When she died it was as if the sun had fallen out of the sky and I was adrift in a black void of grief. And then Anne Boleyn's wickedness was revealed, by a great stroke of providence and the perspicacity of Lord Cromwell – how she had betrayed my father with a string of lovers and plotted to kill him. She paid for it with her head. It was as if my mother had been vindicated, although there was no reversing of my bastardy. Instead, Elizabeth and I were now bastards together, and I did my best to take the place of the mother she had lost – even though I could not, and still cannot, believe that she is truly my sister. She has a look of Mark Smeaton, the lowly musician who confessed to adultery with that whore Boleyn.

The Lady Anne did repent of her cruelty to me at the last. She went on her knees to my friend, Lady Kingston, wife of the Constable of the Tower, and begged my forgiveness by proxy. Lady Kingston recited her message, word for word, kneeling before me in turn, but I did not know how I should feel. Jesus exhorted us to forgive seventy times seven, but it was a struggle. How can you forgive the person who ruined your life and robbed you of your future?

We took it in turns to rest from our vigils by the Queen's bier. I could not stop thinking of the poor babe who was now motherless and, as soon as I was free for a short time, I would hasten to his nursery to see that he was thriving, and watch him as he lay in his cradle swaddled up snugly and making little snuffling noises as he slept. All I could think of was how tragic it was that he would never know his mother.

One night, as I emerged from the presence chamber, swaying with weariness, I saw someone waiting for me. It was Lord Cromwell, who had turned out to be an unlikely friend in my great troubles. I had never trusted him, but last year, when the King my father demanded I sign that dreadful declaration acknowledging that his marriage to my beloved mother had been incestuous and unlawful, and I had shrunk, horrified, from doing so, Lord Cromwell had given me wise counsel and tried to protect me from my father's wrath. It had been a hard lesson in pragmatism, and I cannot bear even now to recall that I did sign, in the end – and I doubt I will ever forgive myself. But I can see that my father wanted to ensure an undisputed succession for his children by Queen Jane.

Cromwell looked anxious. He lowered his voice. 'Madam, I am worried about the King. I hear that he is keeping himself too close and secret,' he confided. 'Bishop Tunstall has tried to rally him, but in vain. He has taken his loss very hard.'

'And no wonder,' I said, feeling tears welling again. 'We all miss the Queen terribly. It is a great tragedy.'

'Almighty God has taken to Himself a most blessed and virtuous lady,' said Archbishop Cranmer, joining us. 'But consider what He has given to us, to the comfort of us all – our most noble Prince, to whom God hath ordained your Highness to be a mother. God gave us that noble lady, and God has taken her away, as pleased Him.'

I did not want Cranmer's comfort. How could I? It was he who broke my mother's marriage, and for that I could never like or approve of him. (And in the end I punished him as he deserved, the great heretic.)

I turned back to Lord Cromwell. 'Maybe it is best to leave the King's Grace in peace for now.'

He regarded me sadly. 'And maybe we should not. Some of his councillors think he should be urged to marry again for the sake of his realm. He has his son at last, after waiting all these long years, but the Prince is but an infant and might at any time succumb to some childhood ailment.'

I was shocked. 'But the Queen is not yet buried! For decency's sake, my lord, let it alone for now.'

'Some feel that the matter is pressing, my lady.'

We left it there, and I took myself off to bed, shaking my head. But a few days later, Cromwell was waiting again as I emerged from the presence chamber to seek a clove for my worsening toothache. 'I have word from Windsor,' he said. 'The King is now taking his loss reasonably. A deputation of councillors has visited him and laid their concerns before him. He is, of course, little disposed to marry again, but he has framed his mind to be impartial to whatever they think best. His tender zeal towards his subjects has overcome his sad disposition.'

'I pray he will not be manoeuvred into a fourth marriage too soon,' I said, severe.

'Has your ladyship ever known the King to do anything he does not want to do?' Cromwell asked with a wry smile.

'Of your charity, pray for the soul of the Queen!' Lancaster Herald cried, as the court assembled in silence to pay its respects. After a week, we were relieved when the funeral obsequies began, for not all the spices in the world could mask the stink from the body, and we were glad to see it coffined and moved to a catafalque set up in the Chapel Royal, where we were to keep vigil beside it for a further week.

I had done what I could. I paid for Masses to be sung for Jane's soul, and took charge of her household, which would shortly be disbanded. I distributed her jewels, as she had directed, to those she had favoured with bequests, and delivered the rest – the Queen's jewels, those same ones that my dear mother had been forced to surrender to that witch Boleyn – to the Master of the Jewel House.

It was as well that etiquette precluded kings from attending the funerals of their consorts, for I do not think my father could have borne it. Lord Cromwell told me that he was in good health and as merry as a widower might be, which probably wasn't saying much, but he was at least attending to state business again.

There was a great public outpouring of grief. By order of the Lord Mayor, twelve hundred Masses were sung in the City of London for the Queen's soul, and a solemn service was held in St Paul's. That day, my stepmother's coffin was carried with great solemnity to Windsor, where my father had decreed that she should be buried. Riding on a palfrey caparisoned in black velvet, I followed the hearse, which was drawn by six horses similarly trapped. On the coffin lay a wooden effigy of the Queen in her robes of state, with false fair hair loose under a rich crown of gold, a sceptre of gold in her right hand, rings set with precious stones on her fingers, and a jewelled necklace around the neck.

Behind me rode twenty-nine mourning ladies, one for every year of the late Queen's life, and in their wake two hundred poor men, all wearing Jane's badge and bearing aloft lighted torches. At Colnbrook, Eton and Windsor, the poor men went ahead and lined the streets. Behind them stood the sorrowing crowds, hats in hands, watching silently as we processed past them.

And so we came to the steps of St George's Chapel within the precincts of Windsor Castle. I watched as the coffin was received by the Dean and College, and walked behind as it was carried inside by six pallbearers. Archbishop Cranmer received it there, standing in the chancel, and led the congregation in prayer, after which the body lay in state before the high altar. I sat there all night, keeping watch over it, feeling my grief like a heavy burden. Without my stepmother, the world seemed an empty place, and I had no idea of what would happen now.

The next day, masses and dirges were sung, and we laid velvet palls upon the coffin. Upon them was set the effigy of the Queen. The next day, my stepmother was finally laid to rest with all the pomp and majesty that could be. There were many pensive hearts in that concourse of mourners. Her brothers looked especially stricken, and no wonder, for she had been the source of their advancement and prosperity. Yet there was no doubt that they would now enjoy enormous influence as uncles to the Prince. The prospect perturbed me not a little for, while Jane had been a devout Catholic, Edward and Thomas Seymour were known to hold radical views about religion.

I watched, weeping, as the coffin was lowered into a vault in the middle of the choir, before the high altar. The officers of the Queen's household broke their staves of office over it, symbolising the termination of their allegiance and service. It was all so final. I heard that, on that day, the bells in London tolled for six hours, and there were Masses and dirges sung in every parish church.

Jane had been our Queen for such a short time – seventeen months in all – but the people had taken her to their hearts, just as they had my sainted mother. She had given England a prince, which my poor mother had been unable to do, and for that we were all profoundly grateful, since it warded off the prospect of civil war. And I was grateful in other ways, and especially for her attempt to halt the wicked closure of the monasteries, even if she had not succeeded. I heard that my father was very abrupt with her. That's as may be, but he loved her truly, I am sure – more truly than he ever loved that witch Boleyn.

After the funeral, my father came out of seclusion and took up the reins of everyday life once more, but the joy had gone out of him and he had put on an alarming amount of weight, for grief and the sores on his legs had prevented him from taking his usual exercise. He sat alone, brooding and wearing deepest black, when he and my stepmother should have been rejoicing in their child. It was as if a pall lay over the court.

'I must marry again,' Father sighed. 'I have one son, and I must ensure the succession by siring others.'

We were at supper in his chamber. He had sent for me to join him, saying that he needed some female company to lighten his spirits. Lord Cromwell had been invited too, and he looked up eagerly when Father raised the matter of his marriage.

'There are great advantages to be gained by a foreign alliance, Sir,' he said.

'I'm not so old,' Father said. 'I'm only forty-six, and I must be the most eligible catch in Christendom.'

I smiled, but I was wondering if, with two dead wives and two divorces behind him, the princesses of Europe would agree with him.

'Indeed, Sir. There should be many ladies who would be delighted to be honoured by your hand, but I have been looking into the matter, and the problem is that, just now, there are very few suitable brides available. Some are of the Protestant persuasion, and others not politically desirable.'

Father waved a dismissive hand. 'Well, look around, look around. I'll rely on your judgement, Crum.' It was a name that made Cromwell cringe, but probably it was less demeaning than being called the King's pet dog Thomas.

* * *

141

That November, I went home to Hunsdon, where I hoped that a quiet and peaceful life in the country would help to heal my sorrow. I took Elizabeth with me and looked after her, for Lady Bryan, who had been my lady governess and Elizabeth's in turn, had been transferred to the Prince's household. Elizabeth was unhappy about that. I think she felt the loss of Lady Bryan far more painfully than that of her mother, for Lady Bryan had cared for her daily in the most loving yet firm way. But she was a resilient child, sharp witted, intelligent and very self contained. I did my best to fend off awkward questions about her mother and her own reduced status, wishing to spare her the brutal truth. Even if she was not my blood sister, I loved her as one.

We spent our days enjoying simple pleasures and good food. Our table was replete with partridges, larks, pheasants, good cheeses, cherries, apples, quinces and pears, all washed down with wine and – once – a good bottle of sack. But my tooth was bothering me again, so much so that, in the end, my father sent a surgeon to draw it out. It was a painful procedure, yet the relief was blissful.

I distracted myself from my grief by ordering new clothes – embroidered partlets, caps of silver and gilt, gloves of Spanish leather and a kirtle of cloth of silver, among other fripperies. Then, of course, Elizabeth must have new clothes too, so I set the seamstress to work again, making pretty things for her. In the afternoons I played the virginals while Elizabeth danced, and in the evenings I gambled at cards with my ladies. I did not forget my devotions or my charities, but sent money to poor beggars and the prisons, and tokens of thanks to the late Queen's servants. And I acquired two more godchildren, standing sponsor at the font for each. It was the next best thing to having children of my own.

There was talk that my father was looking for a bride in France to counterbalance the extensive power of the Emperor. It hurt me to hear that he had said he did not want another Spanish bride like my mother; being her child and half-Spanish myself, I have always hated the French. But King François had marriageable daughters, and it was said that there were other beautiful ladies of high rank available in France.

My father liked to keep his intentions hidden, and it was in character that, even as he considered a French marriage, his ambassadors abroad were told to report on other likely brides. Rumours were rife, even at Hunsdon, but soon we learned that my father was interested in a cousin of mine, the young Duchess of Milan, niece to the Emperor, as our future queen.

Messire Chapuys, the Imperial ambassador, wrote regularly, keeping me informed of what was happening at court. He was one of my truest and most devoted friends – and I suspect he wished he could have been more to me. Yet he never went beyond the bounds of what was proper, for he served my cousin, the Holy Roman Emperor Charles, and was bound to protect my interests. I loved him dearly for his faithfulness, but he was in holy orders and of an age with my father – and far below me in rank. There could never have been anything between us – and yet, when I tried to imagine the husband I might one day have, he had many of the qualities of Messire Chapuys, and even looked like him a little.

Chapuys wrote that the Duchess of Milan was sixteen years old, very tall and of excellent beauty. By all reports, she was softly spoken and had a gentle face. Young as she was, she was already a widow, her elderly husband having died, and she was still in mourning. Apparently my father was entranced by reports of her loveliness. No doubt he saw her youth as an advantage, anticipating that her character could be the more easily moulded to suit him.

But then, mercurial as ever, he changed his mind. Chapuys informed me that he was now seeking a big wife, since he himself was big in person. I inferred from this that he had put on more weight, which rather concerned me, as it could not be doing his health any good.

The big wife he had in mind was another widow, a French noble-woman called Marie de Guise. She was mature and sensible and – more importantly – had borne two sons. But, after receiving advance warning of my father's imminent proposal, she hastily married her other suitor, the King of Scots.

My father shrugged off his disappointment and sent his painter, Master Holbein, to Brussels to paint the portrait of the Duchess of

Milan. With thoughts of marriage in mind, he discarded his mourning garments. By then, Queen Jane had been dead for five months. When my father summoned us to visit him to celebrate Easter at court, I asked his permission to wear a new gown of white taffeta edged with velvet, which seemed appropriate for one who had just discarded her black weeds, and for the joyful feast of our Lord's arising. Elizabeth had a new gown too, and twirled about vainly in it. At four and a half, she was pretty and confident – far more so than I had been at that age. I kept a vigilant watch on her, lest she turn out to be too like her mother. That was not to be borne!

I was dismayed to find my father looking more aged than when I had last seen him, and suffering constant pain from an abscess in his leg. Soon he was forced to submit to the advice of the barber surgeons and have it lanced, which relieved the agony, but did not cure him. I know it galled him to have the sporting activities he loved curtailed: no longer could he ride in the lists, but was obliged to sit and watch younger, fitter men doing what he had once done better. Increasing immobility was making him fat, and his once splendid red-gold hair was thinning. Yet he still dressed sumptuously, setting a new fashion for short full-cut gowns with built-up shoulders and bulky sleeves. Soon every man at court was wearing one, which meant that his increasing girth no longer looked conspicuous.

Pain and advancing infirmity made my father's temper highly unpredictable. I was not the only one to suffer the fearful lash of his tongue, and poor Cromwell got bawled at every week. You could hear the King shouting, calling him a knave and other, less-flattering names that I would blush to repeat. Sometimes he even hit him on the head, pounding him soundly. After one of these outbursts, I saw Cromwell emerge from the chamber with rumpled hair, shaking with fright, but smiling bravely. We were all learning to tiptoe around my father's sensibilities, for in certain moods he could be dangerous.

He was in such a mood when he heard that my mother's old chaplain, Father Forrest, was still speaking out in her favour from his prison. Immediately, my father gave orders that the old man be taken to Smithfield and there roasted in chains over a fire. Father Forrest was a dear, kind soul, very upright and devout, and he had loved my mother devotedly, so I was devastated to hear of his unimaginable sufferings. Sometimes I thought my father was the most cruel man in all the world.

Summer came, and with it the King's spirits seemed to revive. He ordered that Prince Edward be brought to Hampton Court, so that all his children could be together. Attended by his vast retinue, Edward arrived, gorgeously dressed in cloth of gold, and cradled in the arms of Lady Bryan.

My little brother was eight months old and thriving. He had a solemn heart-shaped face, steady blue eyes and a pointed chin that gave him an elfin look. He was the goodliest babe that ever I set eyes on. I never wearied of looking at him. I would sit watching him take suck from his wet-nurse, Mother Jack, and took pleasure in seeing my father proudly carrying him around in his arms, showing him off to the courtiers, and holding him up at a window, so that the crowds below could see their future King.

I loved to cuddle Edward and feel his sturdy little body on my lap. He had a loving nature then – before the Protestant heretics got at him – and always came joyfully to me, an earnest, fond expression on his face. When I asked my minstrels to play for him, he could not sit still, and leapt in my arms, as if he would dance. Truly, I felt no resentment towards this child who now took precedence over me. I had never wanted to be queen of England. All I wished for was a husband and children, and a peaceful existence.

That summer, France and Spain signed a truce that left England dangerously isolated. Since my father had broken with the Pope and declared himself Supreme Head of the Church of England, he had been vulnerable to the hostility of Catholic princes. Yet still he hoped to marry the Duchess of Milan. I was at court when her portrait arrived, a magnificent full-length study that showed a demure young woman with an enigmatic smile and inviting eyes – rather bold, I thought.

But Father was captivated, and immediately dispatched an embassy to Brussels bearing his proposal of marriage. Back came the young

Duchess's answer. She was perturbed that the King had so speedily been rid of his previous three queens, the first by poison, the second innocently put to death, and the third lost for lack of keeping in her childbed. If she had two heads, she said, one should be at his Grace's service!

In short, she turned my father down. I think, for all his spluttering at her impudence, he felt secretly relieved, having heard with his own disbelieving ears the evidence of her pertness and disrespect.

'His Grace is now inclined to heed my advice and seek a bride among the Protestant princesses of Germany,' Cromwell told me, as we strolled together in a garden filled with the scent of late roses. 'I think he would be willing to set aside his religious scruples if it meant making an alliance that could tip the balance of power in Europe in England's favour once more.'

'But – a Protestant queen?' I had long deplored the fact that some states in Germany had embraced the Lutheran faith. They were permanent thorns in the Emperor's side – and threats to the unity of Christendom.

'The princesses I have in mind have been brought up by their mother as strict Catholics,' Cromwell replied, smiling. 'It is their brother who has turned Lutheran. I speak of the children of the Duke of Cleves, who has a liberal, enlightened approach to religion. Duke John has two unmarried daughters, Anna and Amalia. He has hastened to offer the hand of Anna, the elder, to the King. He is sensible of the fact that it would be a brilliant match for her.'

'I trust she is no giddy sixteen year old like the Duchess of Milan,' I said, unhappy at the prospect of seeing my father married to the princess of a small German duchy. Heavens, I had no idea of where it even was!

'She is twenty-three,' Cromwell supplied.

'It will seem strange having a stepmother only a year my senior.'

Cromwell picked a rose and handed it to me, an unusually chivalrous gesture in a man who was normally so hard headed. 'You may never have her for a stepmother. These negotiations take time – and I fear that the King's Highness is lukewarm in the matter.'

* * *

That summer, I saw her. Queen Jane. Her apartments had been left untouched since her death, and I wanted to retrieve a book I had lent her. I ascended the stairs to her lodging, the one that had originally been built for my mother, and pushed open the door. No one was there, and the rooms had an abandoned air. They smelt musty and empty. I found the book and left, but as I turned on the staircase, I saw a glimmer above me in the dusky twilight – and I swear to this day that it was my late stepmother, carrying a lighted candle in her hand and wearing a white night-robe that trailed on the ground. It was her to the life, except that her face appeared luminous. As I stared, too startled to feel frightened, she glided past me on the stairs and out to the Inner Court. When I chased after her, she had disappeared.

I pondered much upon what I had seen. Was it a warning against my father's proposed marriage? My stepmother was a devout Catholic; she would not have wanted to see a queen with Protestant connections taking her place. She had hated Anne Boleyn's reforming zeal.

Or had she come to let me know that she was watching over me? On reflection, I preferred that explanation. If only my own dear mother had manifested herself in such a way! But her blessed soul was with God and the angels – she was waiting for me in Heaven.

Later that summer, I took Elizabeth back to Hunsdon. Without a queen in residence, the court was a male preserve, and my father thought it best that we depart, on that account and because the country air was better for us.

Lady Bryan wrote to me regularly and reported that the Prince was growing fast. He had stood alone and grown four teeth before his first birthday, and when I read that, I grieved afresh for Queen Jane, knowing how much joy and pride she would have taken in her son. When Edward was weaned, Mother Jack was dismissed, and in her stead Mrs Sybil Penne was appointed chief nurse under Lady Bryan.

It was of little consequence to me, for by then I was feeling somewhat distraught. Dark matters were afoot, and I was deeply worried for my beloved old governess, Lady Salisbury. She was of the old Plantagenet royal blood and a dear friend of my mother, and when I was a child the two of them had hoped that I might marry Lady Salisbury's son Reginald, which still seems to me to have been an excellent idea. Yet my father would have none of it. He distrusted his Plantagenet kinsfolk, fearing they would plot to seize his throne. He would not see that, by marrying me into the old royal House – which had been displaced by his own dynasty when my grandsire, King Henry VII, had won the Battle of Bosworth – he would have united the two royal lines. So Reginald had entered the Church, and was now a cardinal, and – unfortunately for me – my father's enemy, while I was still only the Lady Mary, the unhappiest lady in Christendom.

I adored Lady Salisbury. When it became clear that I would never have a brother, I was sent to Ludlow Castle to learn how to be the Princess of Wales, as my father's sole heir. Lady Salisbury came with me and took charge of my household, easing the separation from my mother and ensuring that I was kept happy, healthy and well diverted with my lessons. Against all the odds, those two years at Ludlow were happy ones.

Then, at eleven years old, I returned to court to find Anne Boleyn flaunting herself. Lady Salisbury did not like or approve of Anne, and so she was dismissed. In her place was a Boleyn aunt, who was instructed by that woman to beat me for the cursed bastard I was. She did her best for me though, concealing her sympathy under a brusque manner and rough tongue, and protected me from the worst of her niece's vindictiveness. How I missed Lady Salisbury in those bleak years when I was deprived of my mother's company. And how overjoyed I was when, with the advent of the good Queen Jane, she was welcomed back to court. It was heartening to hear the people cheering when she arrived, and to be folded in those loving arms again.

But now the taint of treason had infected the Pole family, and my beloved Lady Salisbury was in peril. Two years earlier, safely in Italy, Cardinal Pole had written a tract damning my father's marriage to Anne Boleyn, and in such insulting terms that it was as well for him that he was out of reach in Rome. Had my father been able to arrest Reginald, he would surely have had his head, for my father was no respecter of cardinals, as the execution of the venerable Cardinal

Fisher had shown. Fisher, like the respected Sir Thomas More, had been among the few who had upheld my mother's marriage. That was why they had to die.

My father had exploded with rage on reading Reginald's treatise. Hearing that made me uneasy, especially when I learned from Chapuys that Lady Salisbury had felt bound to distance herself from her beloved son, and had written a stern letter castigating him for his treacherous disloyalty.

My father was never one to forgive and forget. Obsessively suspicious of his Plantagenet kinsfolk, he had convinced himself that the Poles were a pack of traitors. They had clearly been watched and, in August I was shocked to hear that Reginald's younger brother Geoffrey had been imprisoned in the Tower for aiding and abetting him. I was even more appalled when, in December, the oldest brother, Lord Montagu, and a cousin, the Marquess of Exeter, had been executed for having plotted to assassinate the King. It was hard to believe that the Marquess, a kindly, good man of principle who had supported my mother and Queen Jane, could have been guilty of such a horrible crime. In fact, I did not believe it.

I could not bear to think of how my dear Lady Salisbury was bearing the loss of her sons – one dead, one in prison and one in exile. Her grief must have been terrible, for they were everything to her. I prayed for them all, and for the sons of the executed lords, two little boys who remained prisoners in the Tower with the rest of their family, and with no hope of release, given my father's temper. It seemed that he was determined to eliminate or neutralise every remaining member of the House of Plantagenet.

The Christmas of 1538 was approaching, but I could take little pleasure in the preparations. Brooding on the recent grim events, I helped Elizabeth to make a cambric shirt to send as a New Year gift for Edward. I was secretly relieved that we had not been invited to court, as I knew I would find it hard to conceal my dismay over the fate of my kinsfolk. So we kept the Yuletide season as merrily as we could at Hunsdon.

In the new year of 1539, I received the most unwelcome news. The

Duke of Cleves had proposed a double alliance. My father should marry his daughter, and I should marry his son, the abominable Protestant William. Dear God, I prayed, deliver me from such a fate!

The Duke had asked to be sent my portrait. Cromwell informed me that he had protested against that, since the Duke's envoy could well testify to my beauty, my grace and my excellent virtues, which were in such number that, bastard though I was, it could not be doubted that any man would hesitate to hurry me to the altar. I knew he was flattering me, but I also think he meant to be kind. It was my father who saved me from my unwanted suitor, though. He had realised that my marriage to William of Cleves would preclude any that he himself might wish to make with Anna or Amalia, which would make him my brother-in-law as well as my father. Such a union would be incestuous, and my father would not risk that. His first two marriages had been annulled on the grounds that they were incestuous – though of course my mother's wasn't, not at all. But my father never would admit that he had been wrong.

Soon afterwards came awful news from Rome – the thing I had been dreading for some years now. Aghast at the executions of Montagu and Exeter, the Pope had excommunicated my father.

I prayed for him as I had never prayed before. What must it feel like to be cut off from God and Christian fellowship and the sacraments of the Church? How dreadful to know that your soul is in mortal peril. But, of course, my father was adamant that the sentence of the Bishop of Rome – as he liked to call the Pope – had no force in England. It would make no difference. Yet it was clear from Chapuys' tactfully worded letters that France and the Empire were now hostile towards him. Daily, the prospect of an alliance with Cleves grew more attractive. Its Duke could be counted upon to remain friendly in the face of the Papal anathema.

As the March winds shrilled around Hunsdon, there came another letter from Chapuys. Lady Salisbury's house had been searched by the King's officers. They had found a banner embroidered with the royal arms of England, as used by the sovereign alone. It looked damningly as if my dear old governess had been scheming to seize the crown.

'It's ludicrous!' I cried to my dear friend and lady-in-waiting, Susan Clarencieux. 'Lady Salisbury is sixty-six, far too old to be plotting rebellion! There is not a disloyal bone in her body.' Yet she had been sent to the Tower all the same. I wept when I read how rigorous her imprisonment was, how she was being kept in a cold cell without adequate food or clothing. I despaired of my father. Where was his humanity? Clearly he wanted her out of the way like the rest of her kinsfolk. That was made plain in May, when Parliament passed an Act of Attainder against her, depriving her of her life, title, estates and goods.

'No!' I wailed, when the news came. 'Not dear Lady Salisbury!' Surely my father would not have her head?

I waited, tremulous, for news. I heard that he had seized all her property, but there was no word of his ordering her execution. As the weeks went by, I began to relax, anticipating that he would leave her to languish in prison, or even release her. I prayed that that day would come soon.

That he took her so-called treason seriously was evident in the new security measures he put in place to safeguard the Prince. Edward now had a greater household than before, and no effort or expense was spared to protect the most precious jewel in England's crown. I think everyone realised that, the sooner Edward was provided with a brother, the better.

The coldness between England and the two allies, France and the Empire, grew, to my distress. Like my mother, I had always wished to see England and the Empire bound in eternal amity. But when the Emperor and King Francis signed a new treaty pledging not to make any fresh alliances without the consent of the other, my father finally resolved to press ahead with the Cleves marriage. He sent envoys to Germany, followed by Master Holbein with instructions to paint the likenesses of the princesses Anna and Amalia for his inspection. Then he would decide which young lady pleased him the more.

Cromwell wrote to me. He seemed eager for the alliance. 'Every man praises the beauty of the Lady Anna. She excels the Duchess of Milan as the golden sun excels the silver moon.'

Chapuys wrote, with a touch of his wry wit, that my father already fancied himself in love with the lady. He had even said he would take the Lady Anna without a dowry if her portrait pleased him. And please him it did.

I own that portrait today. It's a little miniature in a carved ivory frame, which opens to reveal Anna smiling demurely. Her complexion is clear, her gaze steady, her face delicately attractive. Her Dutch head-dress conceals her hair. It's a good likeness – to a point. And the whole world knows that, when my father saw it, he made up his mind at once that he wanted to marry Anna.

I had very mixed feelings. I wanted to see him happy and contented again, as he had been with Queen Jane. And yet I feared that the Protestant cause would be greatly advanced if Anna of Cleves became Queen. Brought up a Catholic she might have been, but her brother, who now ruled Cleves, was a Lutheran, and might have infected her with his heresies. God forbid, she could turn out to be another Anne Boleyn, which was what the reformers were all hoping for.

Elizabeth, at six, was most curious about her future stepmother. 'Do you think she will invite me to court and let me wear pretty gowns and dance?' she asked hopefully.

'I'm not sure that she likes dancing,' I said. By all reports, Anna had had a very strict upbringing. Apparently even music was frowned upon at the court of Cleves. I was praying she would not be a dragon, frowning on frivolous pleasures. I did so enjoy dancing and music and gambling. After all, what other pleasures did I have?

'I will make her like it!' Elizabeth declared, tossing back her long red hair and skipping a few dance steps. What a wilful and enchanting child she was!

I was staying at Hertford Castle in October, when word reached me that the marriage treaty was signed. We heard that the ambassadors from Cleves had been royally entertained by the King. Truth to tell, I was more concerned about my dwindling funds. Christmas loomed ahead, the money my father had given me had run out, and I realised I had not the wherewithal to buy gifts or keep the season properly. Again, Cromwell came to my rescue and persuaded the King to make good the deficit. He himself sent me a beautiful horse as a gift. It set me wondering whether Cromwell, like Chapuys, had deeper feelings for me than he could ever admit to. Why else would he have been such a friend to me in my troubles?

Chapuys reported that great preparations had been set in train for the reception of the Princess Anna. No doubt I would soon be summoned to court to meet my new stepmother. Fervently I prayed that she would be as kind and well disposed to me as Queen Jane.

There had been much jostling for places in the new Queen's household. My father was planning a Christmas wedding at Greenwich, to be followed by twelve days of festivities and Anna's coronation on Candlemas Day. I was gratified to hear that he was in exuberant spirits, and that his leg was troubling him less. He sounded impatient to meet his bride!

We all waited expectantly. It had been two years since the death of Queen Jane. Now England was ready for its new Queen and the benefits she would bring. Setting aside my reservations, I resolved to welcome her warmly and make a friend of her, if I could. She would have need of it, I was sure.

ANNA OF KLEVE

Timeline

1515
- Birth of Anna of Kleve, daughter of Johann III, Duke of Kleve (22 September)

1519
- Election of Charles I as the Holy Roman Emperor Charles V

1527
- Anna precontracted to François, Marquis of Pont-à-Mousson, eldest son of Antoine, Duke of Lorraine.

1536
- Execution of Henry VIII's second wife, Anne Boleyn
- Marriage of Henry VIII and Jane Seymour

1535
- Revocation of the betrothal between Anna of Kleve and François, Marquis of Pont-à-Mousson

1537
- Birth of Prince Edward, son of Henry VIII and Jane Seymour
- Death of Jane Seymour (24 October)

1539
- Henry VIII opens negotiations for a marriage with Anna of Kleve (January)
- Hans Holbein sent to Kleve to paint portraits of the princesses Anna and Amalia (August)
- Wilhelm V, Duke of Kleve, signs Anna's marriage treaty (4 September)
- Henry VIII signs the marriage treaty (4 October)
- Katheryn Howard appointed a maid-of-honour to Anna of Kleve
- Anna sails to England (27 December)

1540
- Marriage of Henry VIII and Anna of Kleve (6 January)
- Henry VIII begins courting Katheryn Howard (April)
- The Privy Council begins looking for grounds for an annulment (May)
- Thomas Cromwell arrested (10 June)

- Anna's marriage formally annulled by Act of Parliament (12 July)
- Execution of Cromwell (28 July)
- Marriage of Henry VIII and Katheryn Howard (28 July)

1541
- Fall of Katheryn Howard, followed by rumours of Anna's restoration (November)

1542
- Execution of Katheryn Howard

1547
- Death of Henry VIII (28 January) and accession of Edward VI

1553
- Death of Edward VI (6 July); Lady Jane Grey proclaimed queen, deposed after nine days; accession of Mary I

1557
- Death of Anna of Kleve (16 July)

THE CURSE
OF THE
HUNGERFORDS

Anne Bassett, 1557

Every time I go to Vespers, she is there, standing in the twilight shadows by the chapel door, seemingly oblivious to my presence. A moment later, she is gone. It still chills me to my bones.

Who had she been? I pondered it for a long time. I asked Walter as soon as he was home from court, but his face took on that tight-lipped look I have come to know well, and I knew I would get nothing out of him.

I asked the servants too. They knew nothing. Some regarded me as if I were mad; some looked fearful. Walter said I must not spread such stories. People are superstitious; they will believe anything. When I pressed him to tell me what he thought I had seen, he said it was merely something I had imagined.

I can't imagine Walter seeing a ghost. He has not the imagination. The famous Knight of Farleigh is a soldier, a sporting man, a practical soul, far more at ease fighting a long battle to get his lands back than with speculation about the supernatural. One skeleton in his closet is enough, and he doesn't like to talk about that.

I see little of Walter these days, which suits me well. Apart from rare forays home to perform the necessary act of getting me with child, he spends most of his time in London, at Hungerford Inn, his magnificent mansion by the Thames, which is so convenient for the court and Parliament. Earlier this year, he rode north to fight the Scots, and now he is made sheriff of Wiltshire, so I suspect he will be at home more often. We rub along well enough together – and I have as much of his company as I want. But, oh, I do miss the court!

Queen Mary danced at our wedding! I shall never forget it. We had the privilege of being married in her own Chapel Royal at Richmond, and all day the Queen was very pleasant, commanding that everyone join in the mirth and pastime. It had pleased her to be able to offer me, her favourite gentlewoman, to a man whose family had stood up for the Catholic religion – and suffered for it. It was to mark our marriage that she knighted Walter and reversed the Act of Attainder against his father, restoring all his confiscated estates – not to Walter, but to me! He wasn't at all happy with that, or about having to pay five thousand pounds to buy them back.

Nevertheless, it meant that he was able to bring me here to Somerset; and here I have remained these three years since, bearing his children while he makes his way in the world.

I am praying that this pregnancy will result in a healthy child – a son and heir, if God wills. It's what Walter wants, more than anything. I married late – I was thirty-three, still comely, people said, yet probably too old to be embarking on motherhood. How my empty arms yearn for my two little girls, each cruelly snatched from me soon after birth. It comforts me to go to the chapel and pray for their souls, knowing that their tiny bodies are at rest in the crypt beneath my feet. And so I see her, every evening.

Maybe I am becoming fanciful in my pregnant state. Each sunset, as I go to the chapel, I find myself looking for her. I look for details. What she is wearing, some clue to her identity. But she fades away if I look at her directly. I can just glimpse the blur of a hood, or a widow's wimple, and those sad eyes, staring at something – or someone – I cannot see. I have wondered if she has been sent to warn me of some danger, but she seems unaware of my presence. Maybe, as Walter said, she exists only in my head.

Walter comes from an old west country family, the Hungerfords. Farleigh Hungerford is their seat, and lies in the glorious valley of the river Frome, not far from Bath. It's a peaceful place, for all its stout defences, a pretty, stately castle. As I stand in the inner court, I am in a courtyard house with high towers at each corner, surmounted by conical roofs. There's a horrible legend attached to one of them. It's known as the Redcap Tower because of its red roof. But the word redcap has another, more sinister meaning that folks in these parts relish relating. I had not known that a redcap was an evil, bloodthirsty goblin who likes to lurk in ancient buildings.

Our old seamstress told me she'd seen one. 'Mistress, they be short, squat old men. They have fangs, and claws and red, fiery eyes! They wear iron boots and red caps, and they carry pikeshafts. They do love to throw stones at unsuspecting humans, and if they kill them, they rinse their cap in the blood.'

I shuddered, but I was sceptical. Such stories are only for the credulous, and I had had the benefit of a French education.

But the old lady was bent on making sure I knew how to protect myself. 'Mistress, you can drive them redcaps away if you recite Scripture or hold up a crucifix. Then you'll see 'em yell out and vanish in flames!'

I thanked her for her advice, and went on my way, thinking what nonsense she had spilled forth. And yet, whenever I've had occasion since to go up into the Redcap Tower, I make sure I do so in the hours of daylight.

There's another tower here, the Lady Tower, and the terrible, dark deeds that gave it its name aren't just silly legends. They really happened, and not that long ago. But I don't think I could face recounting them now. It might affright the child in my belly. They say unborn babes take fear from their mother.

It's hard to credit that this peaceful house was the scene of such cruelty and wickedness. People hereabouts say there is a curse on the Hungerfords, that they will be unlucky in their marriages. If that means the pain of losing children, then yes, my marriage has been unlucky. But not as unlucky as my mother-in-law's.

It is time for prayers. Even though seeing the phantom lady still strikes me with fear, I love the chapel. It contains several tombs of Walter's ancestors, and the most vivid wall paintings, among which St George looms largest. I never tire of looking at him.

As I make my way there, through the rich rooms of the castle, I can't help but think – as I always do – of the great tragedy that befell this family. All this, and more, Walter's father threw away. And for what?

Agnes, 1506–1517

When Agnes married John Cotell of Somerset, she thought she was marrying a gentleman. It never occurred to her to wonder – not at first, anyway – what he was doing in Canterbury. He was well spoken, well dressed and well supplied with money, and he rented a comfortable lodging. He was good to look at too. He seemed never to be idle, and had found a hundred different ways of earning a living. He could turn his hand to anything – buying, selling, supplying; building, painting, repairing; you named it, he could do it.

It upset the town guildsmen of course, for he trespassed on their jealously guarded territory. Therefore some of his work was done after dark, and sometimes after midnight. That prompted a string of complaints from neighbours, angry at having their sleep disturbed by the banging of a hammer, or the unloading of a cart. Agnes was sure they complained to the guilds too, but of course they had no proof that John was stealing work from them. The people who got angrier than most were the Maryons, who lived right next door.

'Shut that noise!' Master Robert Maryon would bellow out of his window, driven beyond the need to keep his voice down. 'Don't you understand that a man has to be up fresh and alert each morning to do an honest job?' There was just the slightest stress on the word 'honest'. Of course, Maryon was a master carpenter by trade. His resentment ran deep.

Then his wife, Kate, would be hammering at the Cotells' door, nightcap askew, curls tousled, hissing at John to desist and let decent folk sleep! More often than not, the hissing turned to bawling, and then other neighbours would be shouting at *her* to hush her mouth. Her sister Edith would chime in, and sometimes the arguments got physical – and nasty.

Agnes never knew she had a temper on her till then. The daughter of a wealthy mercer, she had been daintily raised in all the ladylike virtues, in the hope that she would make a good marriage. Her parents still thought she had. They did not know the half of it. For John Cotell's fists did not rain down exclusively on his irate neighbours; they pummelled his wife whenever he felt she had offended him. And he was an easy man to offend. It did not take long, though, for Agnes to retaliate. Rage and resentment would build in her until she exploded in wrath, lashing out and raining blows on her despicable spouse.

Of course, there were complaints. The Cotells and the Maryons were twice fined for being common scolds, and Agnes was lucky to escape the ducking stool or the bridle. When the exasperated city authorities bound them over to keep the peace, both families were forced to call an uneasy truce, but their anger still simmered.

Three years later, Archbishop Warham carried out a visitation of the clergy and people of Canterbury in St Alphege's Church. By then, John had been chosen as warden of the fraternity of St John the Baptist at Barham, and become puffed up with self-importance. He was outraged, therefore, when the Archbishop accused him of appropriating forty marks belonging to the brotherhood of St John's Chapel.

'I took nothing!' he protested hotly. 'I'll wager I know who made that complaint against me!' It made no difference. He was ordered to render an account, and spent the evening grumbling as he did so. Agnes kept well out of the way.

Nothing was found to be amiss with the accounts, and the complaint was dismissed. But John's resentment against his neighbours festered. They were watching his every move, he was sure of it, and waiting for an opportunity to make life difficult for him. The craft guilds were powerful; they could prevent a man from working if he was not one of their members.

It was time, he decided, to go back to Somerset. Not Dunster, where he had grown up, but Bath, at the other end of the shire. Agnes wondered about this. By now, she knew that John had not been what he seemed when she married him, and suspected there was a good reason why he did not want to go home. Had he been up to some mischief in Dunster? Or was she overreacting? If it was true that he had no family there now, there was nothing to go back for. Bath was a big place – there would be plenty of work there. She was content to leave; she was not close to her parents, and it was uncomfortable living in Canterbury, where all their neighbours hated them.

Armed with a letter of recommendation from a fellow member of the fraternity of St John the Baptist, John made his preparations. He terminated his lease, packed up their belongings, made Agnes sew their savings into his doublet, and, in the middle of the night, loaded everything onto the big cart and rode away. As a parting gesture, he thrust a lighted taper into the thatch of the Maryons' cottage. They had not gone far when, turning around, they saw flames leaping up and heard shouts. John drove on, grinning.

In Bath, they found lodgings and John was soon acting as a middle-man for a wealthy merchant. The pattern of their lives was set for the next seven years.

As those years passed, Agnes grew more discontented. She lacked for nothing materially, yet she still felt a yearning for something more in life – for love, for adventure – for she knew not what! And she was conscious that time was running out. She was well into her thirties now, middle-aged by anyone's reckoning, and she lived in dread of finding another faint line on her face or another grey hair in her nut-brown tresses. Yet she knew, from the whistles that followed her when she ventured out of doors, that some still found her comely. Her figure was yet youthful because, for reasons of His own, God had never sent her children; her cheeks were rosy and her lips cherry red.

John barely seemed to notice her these days – apart from when he wanted food or sex. He lived his own life away from the home, and filled it with friends and business acquaintances – and probably lewd women too, for all Agnes knew.

It was through one of John's acquaintances that he learned that Sir Edward Hungerford of Farleigh Castle needed a steward.

'You could do that,' Agnes said encouragingly.

'Of course I could, woman!' His tone was nasty.

166

She ignored that. 'Think of it! Living in a castle. There would probably be a fine lodging for us. And the wages . . .'

'Would not be as much as I earn now. But there would be prestige, and patronage. I could become an influential man. Sir Edward, I hear, is much at court, when he is not fighting the French. You never know where it could lead, wife!'

So there they were, living in Farleigh Hungerford Castle in more comfort than they had ever known, warm and cosy with winter setting in, and Agnes felt like a lady. And it was not just because of their opulent surroundings.

Anne, 1521–1533

I have some memories of my father. He died when I was seven, and I can still conjure up the sense of loss I felt. Not that I was close to him. He was an old man when I was born, an old, respected man of high importance in the West Country, but burdened by his many duties as sheriff of Cornwall and Devon, and by the demands of a young and boisterous family. Yet he was a solid, reassuring presence in our lives, in control of everything, and protective of his children.

There were seven of us. I was the third-born, after Philippa and John. John was Father's pride and joy, the son and heir he had craved throughout the thirty years of his first marriage, which had produced four daughters and a boy who died at birth. Once started, it seemed my mother could not stop, for two other sons – George and James – followed and then two more daughters.

Ours was a busy household, ruled capably by Mother, the former Honor Grenville. When she married Father in 1515, she was twenty, with – I have heard – the competence of a woman twice her age. Right into old age and infirmity she looked deceptively fragile and delicate, and was always exquisitely dressed, as a lady should be, but there was a forcefulness in her, and determination as hard as steel. Yes, she was proud, as some have levelled at her, and certainly she could show a haughty demeanour; if there was hypocrisy in her, you might rather call it tact. Defend her I will from the jibes of her enemies, for she was always a wonderful mother, utterly devoted to our interests, and indefatigable in working for our advancement in the world.

I never saw my lady idle. Always she was busy, writing endless letters to her many connections at court; working in her still room, where her amazing knowledge of physic came into its own; on her knees in chapel (no doubt seeking God's cooperation in her plans for her children); ordering the servants, or tending her many dogs. She loved to ride out with her bow, or dance, or lose herself in a book. Whatever I achieve in life, I will never have the vitality of my mother.

So there we all were, a big merry household: seven children, and my older half-sisters, Jane and Thomasine. The other two, Anne and Margery, were married – Anne to a Courtenay, a relation of the Earl of Devon, as my mother liked to remind people – and living in Cornwall. My oldest sister Philippa's life would take a similar course.

I was closer to my younger sisters, Kat and Mary. Mary was the fairest maiden you could hope to see, Kat much plainer, but the kindest and most winning of us all. Our worlds were bounded by each other.

The time of our childhood was divided among my father's three houses. Above the porch of each was a shield on which was blazoned the crest of Bassett, a silver unicorn's head. The principal seat was the manor house at Tehidy on the north coast of Cornwall, which has been in Bassett hands since the time of the Normans. We children ran free in the grounds, exploring the woodland around the North Cliffs, clambering around the ancient earthwork hidden away there.

Umberleigh – Mother's dower house – is even older than Tehidy, for it stands on the site of a palace built by a Saxon king on the west bank of the River Taw, by the old bridge. Nearby lies a pretty village of thatched cottages with an inn that was then said to be haunted. I used to run past it whenever I was on errands for Mother, taking food or physic to sick tenants – terrified lest I might see the spectre!

The third house, Heanton Court, stands at Heanton Punchardon, also in the north part of Devon. Many of my Bassett ancestors lie in the church there.

These places marked the parameters of my early years, when the world seemed constant, safe and secure. Until, in the wintry frost of January, in the year of our Lord 1528, Father died.

He left us all well provided for, with good marriage portions for me and my sisters. Since my brother John, the heir, was but ten years old, Mother and our kindly cousin, John Worth, Sewer to King Henry VIII, made him their ward.

When a decent year had passed, Mother hied off to London to look for a new husband, and that was how Arthur came into our lives. He saw her at court, and was smitten. Being Mother, she took care to let him chase her until she caught him, and really, she could not have netted a much bigger fish. For Arthur Plantagenet was the bastard son of King Edward IV, and therefore uncle to King Henry, who liked him well and afforded him great prominence at court.

Arthur was in his fifties when he wed my mother. As I was to see for myself, he bore a strong resemblance to the King, and was of a similar great height and broad build. He had held many high offices, including those of Vice-Admiral of England, Privy Councillor and Lord Warden of the Cinque Ports, as well as the title Viscount Lisle, which he had in right of his first wife. He had three daughters of his own, Frances, for whom my brother John would soon conceive a certain liking, and Elizabeth and Bridget, who were both married.

Marriage to Arthur Plantagenet raised my mother, and indeed us, to the highest ranks of society. It was great good fortune, and doubly so for me, because I liked him well. He was a good and fair stepfather to us. In his household, no distinction was made between children and stepchildren. He was a kitten of a man, for all his great size and near-royal status, friendly, hearty, gentle and easy-going.

Mother soon dominated him. It was in her nature; she could not help it. He happily bowed to her rule, and left most decisions to her discretion. If he opposed her, even in the smallest domestic matter, she would fiercely protest and incessantly nag him until he bowed to her supremacy. Dear man, he was too gentle to stand up to her. And yet, there was great love between them, and I am sure he relied on her completely.

It was thanks to her that, three years into their marriage, Arthur purchased Master Worth's share in my brother John's wardship and marriage; the plan was that John would wed Frances Plantagenet when he was older, and John was very happy with that.

By then, of course, we were all living in Arthur's house in London, and the great matter of the King's marriage was the burning topic of the day. Mother, of course, sided with the King, who wanted to divorce Queen Katherine and marry her maid-of-honour, Anne Boleyn.

'His Grace needs a son!' she declared. 'Can't the Queen see that? She ought to stand aside for a younger woman who can give him one. And many doctors have told him that his marriage is invalid. It's about time the Pope stopped prevaricating and declared it so.' I had a strong feeling that Mother alone, given five minutes with his Holiness, would have sorted out the whole dragging business.

Arthur nodded. He always agreed with her – and it was politic to support his nephew, the King.

There was high excitement when Mother was selected as one of the six ladies who would accompany the Lady Anne to Calais in the autumn of 1532. The King was taking his sweetheart there to meet the French King, plainly hoping for support from that quarter. I looked on with envy as Mother supervised her packing, watching the rich gowns poured like molten gold and silver into the chests, the hoods encrusted with pearls, the soft slippers, the furs and the jewels. How I wished I could go with her!

When she returned, full of her experiences, Kat, Mary and I thrilled to hear her tell us how she had danced with two kings, and how charmingly the Lady Anne had condescended to befriend her.

'What is the King like?' we wanted to know.

'Tall, magnificent and very handsome!' she enthused. 'His eyes are so blue, and he has such a kingly manner. And *she* is exquisite! Not beautiful in the accepted way, but there is something special about her. She is so elegant in her dress, so regal in her carriage. She will make a fine queen!'

'When his Grace is free to marry her!' Arthur put in.

'It will not be long now,' Mother declared. 'You'll see.'

She was right.

The following March, Arthur was appointed Lord Deputy of Calais, and had to hasten back across the English Channel to take up his duties. It was a high and prestigious honour, yet it threw Mother into an agony of joy and sorrow. Joy, because she was delighted at his advancement; sorrow, because she did not want to move so far from the court. But, of course, she had no choice but to join him there, and I and my younger sisters went too. My brothers were left at Arthur's house in Hampshire with their tutors; and Mother gave Jane and Thomasine, both still unmarried, permission to stay at Umberleigh.

For those who do not know it, Calais is an English enclave on the north-west edge of France, just across the Channel. King Edward III captured it two hundred years ago, and it has been a closely guarded territory ever since, surrounded by stout walls and defences. We lived in the Staple Inn, in the middle of the town. It was a fine house, suitable for receiving those of the highest rank, yet Mother, naturally, would have preferred to lodge in the Exchequer Palace, where kings and queens stayed on their rare visits to Calais. She felt that Arthur, as the King's deputy, should have been allowed the use of it, but no matter how she pressed him, he would not ask for that particular favour. It was one of the few issues over which he defied her.

We had a good life in Calais, a bustling, noisy town with a great harbour, where we liked to watch the ships. We lived in some splendour, and Arthur entertained often. At twelve, I was quite observant of my elders, and I became aware that he was somewhat indolent in the exercise of his vice-regal obligations. It was Mother who ruled Calais – at least, until Master Cromwell, the King's Principal Secretary, sent a tactful letter to Arthur, hinting that he should not let his wife tell him what to do when it came to state affairs. I remember Mother spluttering in rage when she read it, and Arthur trying to placate her. I'm not sure that she ever did entirely desist from instructing him, and certainly he had not the will to control her.

Not a month after we moved to Calais came the sensational news that the Lady Anne Boleyn was queen! The King, it transpired, had married her in secret. Soon afterwards, we heard that Queen Katherine had been divorced. Now, Mother was more discontented than ever with being exiled to Calais. She was desperate to be at court, for the court was at the centre of her world. Accordingly, she dashed off a volley of letters to her friends there, hoping not to be forgotten, and praying that, by their means, she could ingratiate herself with the new Queen.

Agnes, 1518

Agnes watched John as he ate. How she hated him. He had beaten her again last night, for rebuking him when he came to bed drunk. Her arms and back, which had sustained the worst of the blows, were sore today. Almost, she was glad of the attack. It salved her conscience. Tit for tat.

Sir Edward Hungerford, who was far more of a gentleman than John would ever be, had been more than kind to her. Much more than kind. She revelled in the stolen hours in his bed, luxuriating in his muscular, soldierly body, and his cultivated sweet talk. From the moment he had first looked at her and their eyes had met, she had known for a certainty that he wanted her.

Edward warned her that he would often be away at court, but she would be in his heart and thoughts when he was gone from her. Except that he wasn't gone from her very often. It seemed that his duties as sheriff of Wiltshire, Somerset and Dorset were suddenly very pressing. Temptation stalked her daily. She would feast her eyes on his tall, noble figure clad in black velvet, cloth of silver and sleeves of crimson, cloth of gold, green tinsel and yellow satin . . . fine attire that John could never aspire to. She could not get enough of Sir Edward.

If John knew what had been going on almost under his nose for the past two months, he did not care. He was enjoying the prestige of his new role, and Agnes suspected he had his sights on the bailiff's wife, a lazy slut like an overblown rose. It mattered not a whit to her. Why bother about the steward when you can have the master?

They had to be careful, of course. Sir Edward was married, to a member of the powerful Zouche family; he wanted no scandal. Yet Lady Hungerford was rarely to be seen. She spent her days in her tower room, endlessly embroidering, or in the chapel, at her devotions, and when she did emerge it was only long enough to eat dinner or take short walks in her garden for the sake of her health. Agnes doubted she was sickly, for she looked rosy enough; she was sure that my lady had long ago learned to feign incapacity to avoid her husband's embraces, and that it had become a habit. Witness the evidence: there was but one son of the marriage, and Sir Edward was a lusty man.

Neither parent had much control over young Walter, who was fifteen, bullish and headstrong. The lad was left very much to his despairing tutors and the temptations of the great outdoors, and Agnes had only ever seen him with a scowl on his face. It was not surprising that he was resentful. In place of the love he should have had, all he got were reprimands from his father and helpless shrugs from his mother. Agnes tried to talk to Edward about Walter, but he silenced her with a kiss and rolled her over on her back.

'Don't concern yourself with that young scamp, darling,' he murmured, kissing her into forgetfulness.

Agnes tried to be kind to Walter, but it was clear that he resented her. She suspected he had some inkling of what was going on between her and his father. After a while, she gave up trying with him, knowing she would get nowhere.

She really had eyes for no one but Edward. Desire was a constant flame in her, consuming her, like a kind of madness. It was a madness he shared in equal measure. Sometimes their passion was so violent it scared her, yet it excited her too. She had never dreamed that lovers could cross such boundaries.

And then, suddenly, when the snow was thawing in January, Lady Hungerford died. There was no warning, no sign of illness. One day, her maid walked into the tower room and found her dead on the floor.

There was no mark on her body, save a bloodshot eye and a blue hue around the lips.

'It must have been an apoplexy,' Edward told his household, who were crowding the doorway and stairs, agog. He closed his eyes, clapped his hand to his mouth, and sighed deeply, then made a visible effort to control himself. 'Move her to her bedchamber,' he ordered. 'My dear lady must be honourably laid out.'

On the night after the burial, even before the funeral hatchments had been removed from their places of honour on the walls, Edward and Agnes lay together again.

'My dear love,' Edward murmured, caressing her cheek, 'I think you know what must happen now.'

'What do you mean?' Agnes spoke more sharply than she intended. She thought he was going to say they must part – at least until he was out of mourning.

He pulled her against his hard, bare chest. 'I want us to be together. I want to marry you!'

He had given voice to an idea that had been germinating and flowering in Agnes's mind ever since she had seen Lady Hungerford lying cold on the rushes. She was not of equal rank to Edward, but that need not matter. They loved each other, and were surely meant to be united. She had begun to weave a fantasy, seeing herself presiding at the high table, being deferred to as my lady, and enjoying the Hungerford wealth. Marriage to Edward would bring her all the status, luxury and comfort she had ever desired, and it would give her an entry to the court. She might even meet the King himself.

John had no place in this fantasy.

For answer, she twined her arms around Edward's neck and kissed him soundly. 'I want nothing more than to be your wife,' she told him. 'But there is one obstacle. There is John.'

She had been exercising her mind on how to go about dissolving a marriage, and had a plan ready hatched. If John was amenable – and Edward might make it worth his while – they could go to a priest and say they had never consummated their marriage. That would be grounds enough, she was sure. It seemed the perfect solution.

She outlined her plan to Edward, and was dismayed to see him frown. 'Even if John agreed, our marriage would be invalid, founded upon a lie. Sweetheart, I have to think about safeguarding the family inheritance. Should – God forfend – Walter die, I would need a lawful heir to succeed me in his place. And *John* would know that no child born of our marriage was lawful. It would give him power over us. I would not put it past him to make demands.'

Agnes knew he had good reason to be concerned. She knew John. 'So, what are we to do?'

Edward placed his hand on her breast and began to knead it. 'I would do anything for you, my love,' he murmured. 'You can have no idea of how much I have already done to smooth the way for us.'

Her eyes met his, understanding dawning. To her surprise, she was not horrified or repelled, but aroused.

'To what lengths would *you* go to ensure that we can be together?' he whispered, as he mounted her.

From the darkest abyss of her mind, the idea came to her.

For two months, she pondered how to go about it. And then Dame Fortune favoured her. Out riding one day, she had come upon two men punching and robbing a man who was lying prone and moaning on the dirt track. The two archers who were escorting her had seized and bound them, and dragged them at the horse's tail back to the castle, with their victim riding pillion.

'My lord shall hear of your offence,' Agnes told them when they arrived, and went off to find Sir Edward.

'My love,' she said, winding her arms about his neck, 'I pray you, offer them their freedom in return for their performing one task for me in the strictest secrecy. Say that, if they speak a word of it, they shall, for a certainty, be hanged for their assault on that poor gentleman – and for libel!'

Their eyes met in understanding. By now, she knew, Edward would have jumped out of a window for her, so she was not surprised when he agreed to do as she asked.

* * *

The men stood before her. Despite the July heat, Agnes shivered inwardly, aware that she was about to cross a line and that there would be no returning. Yet John had to go. He had to pay for what he had done to her. And she must be free to attain her destiny.

William Mathew and William Inges were watching her apprehensively. They were not common thugs, but yeomen of Edward's manor of Heytesbury in Wiltshire. Both, she had learned, gratified, had a reputation for violence.

'My husband, Master Cotell is the steward here,' she told them. 'He is an evil man, a bane on this household, and he has threatened to kill me. I have no redress in law, so I need your help. I want you to ensure that he threatens me no more.' She fixed her gaze on them, at once – she hoped – appealing and challenging.

'You want him dead?' Mathew asked.

'If that is the best remedy, yes,' she replied. 'If you do this for me, and swear to keep it a secret, my lord will let you go free immediately.'

They looked at each other and nodded.

'We'll do it,' said Inges.

'Good,' Agnes said, knowing that the line had been crossed.

The bell chimed midnight. John had not come to bed. It was still hot, and the curtains were drawn to let in the gentle breeze. In the moonlight, Agnes got up, pulled on a night robe and tiptoed down the spiral stairs to the bailey. Opposite, she could see lights in the kitchen windows.

As she made her way across the cobbles, she could smell roasting meat. The cook must be preparing ahead. They would have cold cuts tomorrow.

She paused. A voice in her head was telling her to go back to bed. If Mathew and Inges were about their business, she should not be visible anywhere nearby. But, as she turned around, she saw she was not alone in the bailey. A dark figure was standing in the shadows below the Redcap Tower.

No! It could not be! Had one wickedness begotten another? Had the redcap sensed blood? Atavistic fear engulfed her, and she ran back to the stairs. Lifting the door latch, she looked behind her fearfully, only to see that the figure had disappeared. She could not see it anywhere.

Back in bed, she tried to still her racing heart. Had the men done as she had commanded? Had the dark deed really raised the dreadful redcap? If not, who had been standing in the shadows – and had they seen her?

In the morning, John's side of the bed remained empty. Dared she hope that he would trouble her no more, and that the path to happiness lay open before her?

She got up, determined to act as if all was normal, and made her way to the kitchens, where the servants were busy preparing breakfast. The warm smell of new-baked bread filled the room.

'Have you seen my husband?' Agnes asked the cook.

'No, mistress,' he said. No one else had, either.

'He did not come to bed last night,' she elaborated. 'Perchance he was detained somewhere on Sir Edward's business.'

'What's this?' a kitchen wench asked, bending down to pick up something from the floor. It was part of a necktie, ragged at one end, as if it had been ripped in half. Agnes recognized it at once.

'It's my husband's,' she said.

'He were here last night,' a scullion told her. 'I saw him near the bakehouse.'

'That's strange,' she answered. 'When was that?'

'About ten o'clock,' he replied.

'Then he must be around somewhere,' she said. 'I'll go and look for him.'

She searched, and when, of course, she could not find John, everyone else hastened to look for him. It was soon clear that he had simply disappeared.

There was a lot of speculation about the necktie. Had he ripped it himself? Or had there been some sort of scuffle, or even violence done? But there was no indication that a struggle of any sort had taken place. The bailiff's wife was weeping, Agnes saw, to her satisfaction.

By now, Sir Edward had been informed of the mysterious absence of his steward, and had ordered a wider search of the countryside round-abouts. As soon as the horsemen had ridden off, he saw Agnes alone.

'I have been told that the deed is done,' he told her. 'I will let it be known that the robbers promised to pay compensation to the poor wretch they ambushed, who was well enough to go home this morning. In truth, it will come from me. They have been sworn again to secrecy, in no uncertain terms, and offered positions here, in the stables, so that I can keep an eye on them. But I am sure they will not talk.'

Agnes found that she was trembling. 'How do we explain John's disappearance?'

He smiled at her. 'Easily. If people ask, you can testify to his wanderlust, his discontent at being here, the coldness between you. You can say you think he'd been planning for some time to leave.'

She let him take her in his arms. 'What did they do with . . . it?'

'I know not. They just said that no one would find any trace of it. Sweetheart, you must not fear. No one will point a finger at you, even if they had cause to. They would have me to reckon with. I am sheriff hereabouts, and responsible for law and order. I will protect you from calumny. And when we are married, no person will dare to spread wicked slanders about my Lady Hungerford.'

Anne, 1533–1536

Arthur continued to struggle with his responsibilities. He was honest and conscientious, but clearly not competent. You could sense the exasperation in Master Cromwell's letters, in which he complained about Arthur pestering the King with trifles and dispensing favours to all who begged them, and that people were laughing about his Majesty's deputy being dominated by his wife. We all feared that Arthur might be relieved of his office, and I think Mother would have been delighted if he had, yet still a stream of orders arrived from London. It was obvious, though, that nothing too demanding was being asked of him. Heaven knows what would have befallen Calais if the French had decided to invade!

Mother was preoccupied with what was happening at court, and at Umberleigh, where my stepsister Jane's high-handedness had upset the servants. Jane, in turn, complained that, when she and Thomasine had arrived, they had found the priest's whore living in the house and ruling it extravagantly. It was the whore's fault that the servants were shirking their duties and defrauding Mother. Jane had kicked her out and set about imposing decent standards on the household. You could see why the servants were complaining.

We heard regularly from John. He and his tutor sent Mother regular reports on the progress of his education. He was fifteen now, struggling with Latin, but otherwise doing well; and he was clearly impatient to come into control of his inheritance. Mother was grateful for the support given him by Master Husee, Arthur's man in London, who was well known about the court and marvellous at dealing with the many practical tasks involved in looking after the Lisle interests in England.

With John's future assured, and Philippa soon to be wed, Mother began to nurture ambitions for me, Kat and Mary. We must be found places at court, preferably as maids-of-honour in Queen Anne's household. It was the most prestigious career to which any young lady could aspire – and the best way to secure a good husband.

With her usual zest and determination, Mother set to work, calling in favours and urging her friends to make representations on her behalf. None of it had the desired effect. She wrote directly, appealing to the Queen, but was rejected, to her mortification. Her Grace had a superfluity of maids-of-honour.

Mother then remembered that Anne Boleyn had been educated at the French court, which had lent her such polish and so many accomplishments that she had shone like a star when she came to the English court. That was the way to get us noticed, Mother decided. We too should have French accomplishments, so that we, in our turn, could cause a stir at court.

And so, in the November after the Princess Elizabeth was born, I was sent to Pont-Rémy near Abbeville, to be schooled in the household of the Sire de Riou, a great friend of my stepfather, and a renowned soldier who had distinguished himself in serving the French King. Mary was dispatched to the tutelage of his sister, the wife of the Sire de Bours, not far away. We were to learn French, and be taught to play the lute and virginals, as well as manners, deportment, dancing, embroidery and anything else that would get us noticed and befit us for serving at court.

I missed Kat, who had stayed at home because a possible marriage was in the offing, and Mary too, but I had a happy time at Pont-Rémy. For all her aristocratic pedigree and patrician looks, Madame, the Sire de Riou's second wife, treated me as tenderly as if I had been her daughter. Small wonder, as she had but one child living, a daughter from her first marriage. I flourished in her care and under her instruction. Soon, I was writing letters in French to Mother, demonstrating my prowess and asking her to send me new attire, for I was growing fast. She, in turn, constantly exhorted me to please my loving hosts and keep myself a good and honest maiden.

I had been at Pont-Rémy for a few months when I learned that, through the good offices of Master Husee, John had entered Lincoln's Inn to study law, and that Mother's hopes of a marriage for Kat had fallen through. There was news of Thomasine too – startling news, for she had run away early one morning from Umberleigh to her sister Margery's house. Mother thought an elopement had gone wrong, but I wondered if Thomasine had merely tried to escape the domineering Jane. Jane was furious, blaming the servants, of course, but even she could not complain when Thomasine fell ill and had to remain with Margery.

By August 1535, I was settled in the Riou household. To my joy, John paid me a visit, charming Madame with his good looks, newly moulded into manliness. Two months later, Madame gave birth to her first baby by the Sire de Riou, a girl who she named in my honour. In the spring, she took me with her when she made the long journey to visit her daughter at Vendôme. Young Madame de Langey was expecting her first child, and Madame wanted to be there for the confinement. We visited many of her friends and relatives on the way, and coming back, and I was touched by their kindness.

'It is good to see you so merry, Anne,' Madame declared. 'I rejoice that you are esteemed by all my kinsfolk. You are such a good girl, and you deserve to be cherished.' Her words brought a tear to my eye. I knew myself truly happy then.

I returned to the sad news that Thomasine had died on her way back to Umberleigh. It had happened on the Friday before Palm Sunday. Poor, gentle Thomasine, who had not lived to know the fulfilment of marriage and children: I missed her more than I could have imagined, and wished I had made more of a friend of her.

Hers was not the only death that touched us that year. Easter had not long passed when there was other, even more shocking, news from England. Queen Anne had been arrested!

Agnes, 1519–1522

Agnes had hated being called 'the widow Cotell', but it was a small price to pay for staying on in her lodging at Farleigh Hungerford Castle. The two Williams had stayed too, giving no trouble, although she would have preferred not to have to see them every day, living reminders of her crime. But she had greater matters to occupy her now; and she was the widow Cotell no more. In the dark days of January, soon after Christmas, she and Edward had been quietly married.

Tongues had wagged, she was sure of it. Walter was going around looking like thunder and would barely speak to her. People were still talking about John's disappearance, and no doubt they thought it scandalous that she had remarried before a decent year of mourning was out. She did not care. She was my Lady Hungerford now, and mistress of the castle. Let one word of gossip come to her ears, and there would be trouble!

She was beginning to feel invincible. She had done the deed – and got away with it. No one would dare accuse Edward of murder, or his lady.

Life was good. They had gone up to court several times, and the King himself had congratulated her on her marriage. This year, they would be going to France for the great meeting of the kings of England and France. Edward was having a silk tent made for them, with carpets and a tester bed for their comfort. They could lie there and take joy in each other – and in their good fortune. Sometimes, Agnes reflected, you had to make your luck in this world.

Anne, 1536–1537

Each piece of news was more astonishing than the last. The Queen had been imprisoned in the Tower. Five men were being held there with her. It was said they had been her lovers, and had conspired with her to murder the King.

Then we heard that her brother was one of those men. Her *brother*? It was unbelievable.

When the sweet May blossom was out, they were all put on trial and condemned to death. A week later, Mother wrote to say that Queen Anne had been beheaded – with a sword, a last courtesy accorded by her husband.

And then – as if that were not sensation enough – the King married again, almost immediately. Even Mother had never heard of Mistress Jane Seymour, or Queen Jane, as we must now call her. A jumped-up nobody, by all accounts. Yet people were clamouring to serve that nobody. When Master Husee told Mother that two of her own nieces had been appointed maids-of-honour, she was more determined than ever to find us places in her household.

I was instantly summoned back to Calais to be ready for my preferment. I was fifteen, and Mother was delighted with me.

'I am pleased to find you so polished, Anne – and grown into such a beauty. I always knew you had a good wit, but you have mastered the art of conversation adroitly. You shall be the first of my daughters in line for a position at court. It will not be long coming, I am sure of it. If only we were not stuck out here in Calais!'

Nine months later, Mother was beside herself with frustration, still desperately trying to secure places for me and Kat in the Queen's household. Letter after letter had gone flying over the Channel, exhorting, wheedling and begging anyone with any influence to assist. Master Husee had done his very best, making up to the Queen's ladies and beseeching them for their help. He had bribed a gentleman of the King's Privy Chamber to approach the Duchess of Suffolk, and Mother was almost speechless with elation when that lady hinted she might put in a good word for us. She and Arthur both wrote effusive letters to the Duchess, thanking her most lavishly, and trusting she would do them good service.

To me, Mother confided that she had reservations about the Duchess, who was only eighteen years old and might not handle the matter properly; but Master Husee had insisted that, despite her youth, she was clever, wise and discreet.

Success came in the most unexpected circumstances. We had shared in the general rejoicing in the news that Queen Jane was with child, and soon Mother learned from one of her correspondents that the Queen had developed a craving for quails. There are more quail in the marshlands surrounding Calais than we knew what to do with, and they were often served at our table. Mother seized this golden opportunity to win favour with the Queen by sending her a generous supply. Arthur was sent out daily to snare the birds, which were sent by fast messenger. And what joy it was to Mother to hear how much the Queen had enjoyed them.

Master Husee wrote excitedly from the court. He had spoken of my beauty and accomplishments to Sir John Wallop, who had mentioned them to the King himself – and the King had promised to speak to the Queen for me. You may imagine the excitement in the Staple Inn when that letter arrived!

Maybe the King did speak for me; or maybe it was the quails. But one day, having eaten some of the birds at dinner, Queen Jane summoned Master Husee and said that, as a token of her gratitude to Lady Lisle, she would accept one of her daughters as a maid-of-honour. However, she wished to see two of us before deciding who it should be. Mother was commanded to ship us over from Calais, suitably dressed for court. Above all, we were to show ourselves sober, wise, discreet, and lowly. We must be obedient, and willing to be governed and ruled by my Lady Rutland and my Lady Sussex, our cousin, and serve God and be virtuous, and be sober of tongue, for that was much regarded at court. The sister not chosen by the Queen would be offered a place in the household of the Duchess of Suffolk. Once the choice was made, the Queen would provide wages and food only, not apparel.

Mother was ecstatic. I have never seen her so happy and triumphant. As Mary was still at Bours, it was decided that Kat and I should go to court. Kat had not had the advantage of being brought up in a noble French household, yet she had benefited from our mother's vigorous training; even so, it was drilled into us, hourly, how we were to behave. Tiresome as that was, we both so quaked at the prospect of not being chosen that we were ready to become nuns if need be, to satisfy our mother.

No expense was spared in decking us out for royal service. Arthur was not a poor man, but even he shook his head at the enormous cost. We were to bring two changes of clothes, one of satin, the other of damask. Mother thought that two gowns were not enough, so we both had six, all in the French fashion, which, she told us, was all the rage at court.

It was September when, our stomachs knotted with apprehension, we arrived at Hampton Court, a place of such magnificence that I could never have even dreamed it up. Two of the Queen's ladies-of-honour received us, Lady Sussex, whose mother was my mother's sister, and Lady Rutland. They were most welcoming to us, and very kind.

'Her Grace has taken to her chamber to await the birth of her child,' Lady Sussex told us, 'but she will receive you tomorrow.'

That night, we were much gratified to be feasted by three officers of the court, as well as Lady Dudley (who was married to Arthur's stepson) and another lady. Afterwards, I slept on a pallet bed in Lady Sussex's chamber, while Kat was accommodated with Lady Rutland.

Before I retired, I stared at myself in her ladyship's mirror. A pretty young creature stared back at me, fair and well-made; there was nothing here to complain of, or put the Queen off. I did so want to be chosen, even though I knew that Kat was as eager as I, and would be crushingly disappointed to be rejected.

The next day, we were brought before Queen Jane, who sat in a cushioned chair in a stuffy room; the weather was unseasonably hot, yet a fire burned and the windows were tightly shut. She looked pale; she was no beauty, but pleasing enough. By the size of her belly, it was clear that the birth of her child was imminent.

She talked amiably with us for a short while, asking after our mother and Lord Lisle, and if our crossing had been calm, all the while looking us up and down appraisingly, giving nothing away. Then she asked us to wait outside. We stood in the antechamber, barely daring to hope, with our hearts in our mouths.

'Truly, I won't mind if you are chosen,' Kat whispered.

'I hope *you* are,' I said, trying to mean it. 'Maybe she will choose us both.'

At last, after a seemingly endless interval, Lady Rutland emerged, smiling at me. 'Mistress Anne, the Queen has chosen you. You will be sworn to her service this afternoon.'

I hardly dared look at Kat, but when I did, she was smiling bravely at me.

Lady Rutland spoke kindly. 'You must write to your mother, Mistress Anne, and ask her to look to your wardrobe. Your attire does not meet the Queen's standards. She has graciously agreed that you can wear out your French gowns, but that French hood will have to go. Her Grace has banned them at court, so we all wear the gable, and English gowns.'

All that expense! And all for nothing!

Lady Rutland put an arm around Kat's shoulders. 'You can stay with me, child. The Duchess of Suffolk is in the country, soon to be confined. You may remain with me until she returns to court.' Kat looked immensely relieved. She might not be serving the Queen, but it was still an honour to serve the Countess of Rutland – and Mother would see it that way too.

The Queen smiled at me. 'Welcome to my service, Mistress Bassett.' She extended her hand for me to kiss.

'Oh, your Grace, thank you!' I breathed. 'I will do my utmost to please you.'

'I am sure you will,' she said, 'but you must obtain two new gable hoods and two good gowns of black velvet and black satin. Lift your skirt a little. No, that linen shift is too coarse. You need fine lawn. In the meantime, suitable clothing will be lent to you.' She indicated my girdle. 'How many pearls does that have?'

'A hundred and twenty, I think, Madam,' I faltered, much dismayed.

The Queen sighed. 'Not enough, I fear. Write to your mother and ask for another girdle. And tell her that, if you do not appear at court in the proper clothes, you will not be allowed to attend the christening.'

'Yes, Madam.' I could just imagine Mother's reaction – and the cost!

Suddenly, the Queen smiled again, and it was as if the sun had come out. 'I hope you will be very happy at court,' she said.

I had only been in waiting for one day when her Grace looked at me and frowned.

'Mistress Anne,' she said, 'you may not wear your French gown here.'

I did not like to remind her that she had said yesterday that I might wear it out.

The previous evening, I had dashed off a letter to Mother, begging her to send me the correct attire, dreading to think of the outlay, and what she and Arthur might say. Now I had to write to her again, informing her that I must have English gowns. Fortunately, for now, Lady Sussex came to my rescue and lent me a suitable one of crimson damask and a gable hood of velvet to wear in the Queen's presence. The gable hood did not become me nearly as well as the French hood.

Lady Sussex was very good and loving to me and Kat, as was Lady Rutland. In my next letter to Mother, I told her I was sure I had them to thank for my position.

Lady Rutland had long been married to the King's cousin, and was therefore a veteran of the court, and highly respected, but Lady Sussex had only been there for a year. The Earl of Sussex had married her back in January, and now she was expecting their first child.

I got on well with the Queen's other ladies and maids, and soon began to feel at home at court. There was a great sense of privilege in being there. Queen Jane was not as waspish as she had at first seemed, but proved to be an essentially gentle and devout lady who, I soon realised, felt obliged to be on her dignity. Like me, she was but a knight's daughter, and I imagined how I would feel were I to be raised, with little notice, to a throne, and had to wield authority over ladies of much higher birth.

I saw the King almost daily. The Queen was not supposed to receive men in her chamber during her confinement, but evidently that rule did not apply to her husband. He came often to cheer and hearten her, for she was a timid soul, afraid of the plague that was abroad in London, and of the coming birth.

When I was first presented to this huge, glittering, god-like man, he raised me to my feet and looked piercingly into my eyes. 'Mistress Anne, I have been told that you behave yourself so well that everybody praises you!'

I felt myself blushing. 'My lady mother would be pleased to hear that, Sir,' I murmured. 'You will know what she is like.'

He roared with laughter. 'I see you are witty too,' he grinned, and passed on, leaving me aghast that I had dared to joke familiarly with the King. Looking back, though, I do think that the high regard he always showed me stemmed from that moment.

I knew he liked me in another way too, for Mistress Astley, another of the Queen's maids, told me that the King had said that I was the fairest of my mother's daughters. But that he had any feelings other than liking for me at that time I would refute, for it was plain that he was devoted to Queen Jane.

Mother, meanwhile, having concluded that the Duchess of Suffolk was no longer interested in employing Kat, was doing her best to have Kat preferred to the service of the Lady Mary, the King's daughter by Queen Katherine. But the Lady Mary had her full complement of maids, so Kat stayed with Lady Rutland, of whom she had grown fond, and was often at Belvoir Castle, the Earl of Rutland's country seat. It was an arrangement that suited Kat very well, and she was contented with her lot.

So was I, especially when the Queen bore a son that October. Everyone went wild with joy, and we saw the King cradling the babe with tears streaming down his face, so overjoyed was he to have a son at last. It was a wonderful time to be at court, with all the celebrations going on.

Mother had sent me the clothing I needed, not without a few tart remarks about having to provide twice for me, and I wore one of the new gowns to Prince Edward's christening in the Chapel Royal. With my first quarter's wages, I ordered another for the Queen's churching. But I never wore it. A little over a week after the christening, my good mistress died.

All rejoicing ceased. The court was plunged into black, and I found myself kneeling and weeping with the other maids and ladies, keeping vigil beside the Queen's bier. For two weeks, we took turns to keep watch over her, and then we rode, in four chariots, in a great procession to Windsor, behind her coffin. When she was lowered into the vault in the chapel, my service came to an end.

What would I do now?

Agnes, 1522

Agnes had been married to Edward for nearly three years when she began seriously to worry about his health. Since the summer, he had lost weight and, by December, he was as weak as a kitten, with an alarming pallor. Unable to eat without pain, he called for his lawyer, while Agnes wrung her hands and sobbed uncontrollably in her bedchamber.

An hour later, Edward summoned her to his bedside and reached for her hand. His was skeletal. 'My love,' he said, looking at her with those dreadful, sunken eyes, 'I think it is God's will that we should part. I have made a new will, leaving my estates and houses to Walter, and everything else to you. I have also named you my sole executrix.'

Agnes threw herself over his wasted body, weeping and wailing. 'Don't leave me!' she cried piteously.

He stroked her hair. 'If my prayers are heard, I will not, my darling.'

Six weeks later, Agnes stood at her window, dressed in the deepest mourning, watching through a blur of tears as the funeral cortege wended its way to the chapel, where her dear love was to be entombed for all eternity. Walking behind it was Walter – Sir Walter now. He had been icily civil to her since his father's death, when he wasn't angrily complaining about his father's will, and she trembled when it occurred to her that he might turn her out. But she was a wealthy woman now; all the movables in this castle and Edward's other houses were hers, and could be sold to provide her with a roof over her head. She did not think that Walter would like that. If she stayed here, they stayed.

Before the week was out, the fear of Walter throwing her out became the least of her worries. It was nowhere near as terrifying as the summons from Westminster that arrived just as she had plucked up courage to read the letters of condolence that had been piling up.

She saw, from the expression on Walter's face, when he took evident pleasure in telling her there was a summons for her, and that soldiers were waiting below, that he knew what it was about.

Trembling, she stood before the justices in the Court of the King's Bench in Westminster Hall, a guard on either side – the same guards who had ridden beside her litter all the way from Wiltshire.

'Agnes Hungerford, you are accused of procuring the death of your husband, John Cotell. What say you, guilty, or not guilty?'

'Who has accused me?' she cried. 'Is it my stepson? He hates me . . .'

'Just make your plea, Madam,' she was told.

'Not guilty,' she faltered. There was no way anyone could testify to what she had done. Even so, the order was given for her to be imprisoned in the Tower of London, pending an investigation. Had she been of lesser rank, she would have been cast into the common jail.

She was not badly housed in the Tower. She was allowed to keep her maid with her. It was explained to her that prisoners could send out for choice food and comforts, if they could afford it, and for possessions to ease their confinement. She wrote to Walter, asking, then begging, him to send what was hers, but there was no reply. She sold the jewels she had on her, entrusting them to the Constable, only to learn that he had obtained a poor price for them. As the months went by, the food served to her and her maid deteriorated in both quality and quantity, and their gowns became frayed and stinking.

She had a lot of leisure to think. She was sure it was Walter who was responsible for her ordeal. Whoever it was had waited until she no longer had Edward's protection to lay accusations against her. And who had a better motive than Walter? He stood to gain handsomely if she was convicted. Why would Mathew and Inges have talked? They had too much to lose.

Obsessively, she kept going over the events of July, four years ago. There *could* be no evidence against her. She had been too careful, had not been anywhere in the vicinity when the murder was carried out. She didn't even know *how* it had been carried out – and there was no body. Hadn't she heard somewhere that a body had to be found before someone could be hanged for murder?

And hadn't she heard also that women who murdered their husbands were guilty of petty treason, a far worse crime than murder. Hanging was too good for them. Their punishment was to be burned alive.

She felt faint at the thought. Terror gripped her. No! There could be nothing to connect her to John's death.

But what if Walter, or anyone else, gave false testimony against her? And what if the two Williams were tortured to extract confessions?

Wait! she admonished herself. As far as she knew, no one had accused them of anything; and if someone had been keeping their knowledge of her role in the murder to themselves all these years, they would have known who actually carried it out.

So she was safe – she prayed. All she had to do was sit it out here, and wait to be released. Because they had nothing on her. Nothing at all.

Anne, 1537–1539

As the other maids were packing, ready to leave for their homes, and I was standing there forlorn, wondering when Master Husee would next be at court, so that I could ask him to arrange my passage to Calais, Lady Sussex came to my rescue.

'Anne, don't leave!' she said. 'I can find you a place in my household until your mother decides what is to be done with you.'

Gratitude filled my heart. I could not have wished for a kinder offer. Thus it was that I found myself at Woodham Walter Hall in Essex, where life resumed in a grand, but quieter, manner.

We heard that the King had taken his loss grievously and shut himself away at Windsor. Nevertheless, as Christmas approached, I had a surprise, in the form of a letter from Lord Cromwell. The King had granted me a stipend at court. I could visit at any time, and lodgings would be provided for me; and I should have a place with the new Queen, when the time came. So the rumours were true: his Grace was thinking of marrying again.

Lady Sussex raised her eyebrows when she read the letter. 'This is a signal mark of favour, Anne. The King's Grace is a good lord to you. Your mother will be pleased to hear that your future is assured.'

I was pleased too, if not a trifle amazed, that the King should be so kind to me.

In the new year of 1538, my brother John, now twenty and a qualified man of law, married Frances Plantagenet, Arthur's daughter, and my mother rejoiced that royal blood would be mingled with Bassett and Grenville blood. Soon afterwards, she had even more cause for celebration, when John found a place in the household of Lord Cromwell. It would be – so we all hoped – a stepping stone to royal service itself.

I did not attend John's wedding, for the winter weather was rough and the Channel perilous. I was itching to go to court, but stayed at Woodham Walter until my good mistress bore her child in March. It was a puny boy who survived just long enough to be baptised. My lady was in great grief, so I stayed on until April to comfort her, and then she firmly commanded me to go to court. At Easter, I made my way to Whitehall, and was glad to see my sister Kat there, in the train of Lady Rutland.

The King had put off his mourning garments, and seemed quite cheerful whenever I saw him. Once, he tipped my chin up and told me it was good to see me back at court, and I thanked him for granting me a place there, and for my stipend. But there was no familiarity between us then.

I whiled away that April playing cards with Kat and Lady Rutland. Once or twice, the Lady Mary joined us. There was much gossip about a new marriage for the King, and speculation as to which princess he would choose, but Lady Rutland had her own opinion. 'I think his Grace will wed closer to home,' she said one day, when the Lady Mary wasn't present. 'Have you seen how merrily he keeps company with Mistress Skipwith?'

'But I saw him flirting with Mistress Shelton,' I said, surprised.

'He has flirted with her for years,' my lady said, shaking her head, 'and bedded her too, in Queen Anne's time. They are old friends. Mark my words, Mistress Skipwith will be the one.'

After that, I watched the King whenever I could, to see if Lady Rutland spoke truth. I had never taken much notice of Margaret Skipwith before, but now I did, and when I learned that she too had a stipend and a lodging at court, I felt a slight pang of jealousy, for I'd thought the King had favoured me alone. I also wondered why his affections had lighted on her, rather than me, for – though it sounds vain – I knew myself to be the more beautiful.

So I watched them, saw him partnering her in the dance, walking with her in the spring sunshine and sitting by her side amidst a crowd of gentlemen sharing an amusing story. Of course, rumour was rampant.

The affair lasted for many months, and the longer it went on, the more likely it seemed that a royal wedding was in the offing. Until, at Christmas, the King asked me to dance.

One dance led to another, and I could see Margaret Skipwith's flushed, resentful face, as she stood at the side of the hall, by herself. But the King had eyes for me alone. A week later, he invited me to sit beside him at one of the Yuletide feasts, and was most attentive.

'I have always liked you, Mistress Anne,' he said, helping me to a choice morsel from his own plate. 'I trust you will look upon me as your servant.'

I took his meaning, but he mistook my amazement for reluctance.

'I would serve you alone,' he murmured, taking my hand beneath the tablecloth.

It was so unexpected. Could I love him? I asked myself, rapidly trying to collect my thoughts. He was the King, and he had always been good to me, but I knew there was a cruel side to him. He was a man too, a man who was no longer young and who was growing stout. Yet I hesitated no longer.

'Pardon me, your Grace, for not answering immediately,' I gabbled. 'I was overwhelmed by the honour. I would love nothing more than to have you serve me.'

Too late, I recognised the *double-entendre* in what I had said, and felt my cheeks grow hot. But the King was rocking with mirth.

'I take it you mean in the courtly fashion,' he grinned. Suddenly, I was laughing too, and from that moment, everything was easy between us.

Henry – for thus I was now permitted to call him in private – spared no effort to make me feel cherished. He laid on private banquets, over which I presided like a queen; he took me hunting with him; he visited me of an evening after Vespers, and we talked and talked, quite intimately. I know things about Henry Tudor that I have never revealed to a living soul.

There was more to it, of course. The midnight hour would find me in his arms as we exchanged increasingly urgent kisses and caresses. Yet, to my surprise, he did not press me to bed with him. It left me wondering if he was capable of lovemaking, with his increasing bulk and his bad legs. Had he asked me, I would have put him off, for I was not that far from forgetting myself, or my honour. My maid was always in the outer chamber, within earshot, and never once did I overstep the bounds of modesty.

Did I love him? Yes, I did, although I was not *in love* with him. I have never been in love with anyone, so do not know what it feels like. I loved his presence, his masculinity, his power. I loved what he could give me, and if he had given me a crown, I know I would have loved him all my life for it.

Of course, people were talking about us. I first realised which way they thought the wind was blowing when the Imperial ambassador, Messire Chapuys, came with one of his gentlemen and brought me gifts of venison and wine, saying they hoped I would be a friend to the Emperor. I was stunned that they thought I had that kind of influence, stunned, too, to be treated with the deference that belonged to a queen.

I never abused that influence. I asked only for small favours. Mother would have expected more of me, but Mother was in Calais and didn't know what was going on. I certainly did not tell her, and if she heard gossip, she never mentioned it in her letters. I'm sure she didn't hear anything, for her ambition would have been uncontrollable, and she would have bombarded me with orders and advice. But she was preoccupied with my sister Mary's growing infatuation with Gabriel de Bours, the son of the Sire de Bours, and with trying once more to place an unwilling Kat in the service of the equally unwilling Duchess of Suffolk.

The banquets and feasts continued, and the King even took me with him when he travelled down to Dover to inspect the fortifications. While we were there, he asked me to be his wholly, but I thank God I resisted. I'm sure Henry respected me for that. I wonder now if he ever thought it worth winning me by marriage.

You can imagine how gratified I was to hear that Margaret Skipwith had got married. She had remained at court, on good terms with the King, and I had fretted a little that there was still some love between them; so when, that April, I heard the news of her sudden marriage, I was jubilant. She had done well for herself, for her new husband was Lord Tailboys – the reward, I suppose, for being the King's mistress.

The following month, I had more cause for rejoicing, when news arrived from Calais that Frances had borne John a healthy daughter, whom they had called Honor, after Mother. I prayed that God would send them joy of their goodly babe, and that, next time, He would send them a son.

Languishing in the Tower, Agnes had convinced herself that Walter was to blame for her predicament. No one had had a better motive. It was jealousy that was behind it, she was sure, jealousy because his father had left her all his goods. If she were to be found guilty, they would be restored to him.

Had it been Walter lurking in the shadow of the Redcap Tower on that fateful night? She could not be sure. Even if he had seen her, she had been doing nothing wrong. She could say she had been hungry and making her way to the kitchens to get something to eat, but had thought better of it, being mindful of the sin of gluttony. Yes, that sounded plausible.

She got a nasty shock when, in August, after seven months in the Tower, she was summoned to appear before the justices at the Ilchester assizes.

'You have been indicted for murder, my lady,' the Constable told her. She felt faint hearing that.

The journey down to Somerset was nightmarish, enclosed as she was in an old litter with drawn leather curtains in the summer heat. Worse than that was the fear and dread that threatened to overwhelm her. Worst of all was being thrown in the common gaol, then arriving in court and seeing William Mathew and William Inges standing at the bar, staring hopelessly at her. She knew then that they had all been discovered. But where was the proof that she had been involved? There might be hope yet.

When the jury was seated, the crier proclaimed, 'If any can give evidence, or can say anything against the prisoners, let him come now!' No one came forward.

One of the justices read out the indictment, which asserted that the two Williams had murdered John Cotell by the procurement and abetting of Agnes Hungerford, which gave her a nasty jolt.

'On that day,' the justice continued, 'William Mathew and William Inges took a certain linen scarf, which they put round the neck of the aforesaid John Cotell and, with the aforesaid linen scarf, did feloniously throttle, suffocate and strangle him, so that the aforesaid John Cotell immediately died. They then and there put the body of the same John into a fire in the furnace of the kitchen in the castle of Farleigh, which did burn and consume it.'

There were gasps from the packed public benches. Agnes felt sick, remembering, with horrifying clarity, the smell of roasting meat that had assailed her as she made her way to the kitchens that night. She could smell it now, and feared she would vomit. Oh, God, what had she done? She had not meant it to be like that. She could only pray that John had been dead when they put him in the oven. Agnes clapped her kerchief to her mouth, hoping to stem the nausea.

The justice was regarding her sternly. 'And this was carried out with the knowledge and, indeed, at the behest of Agnes Hungerford, who gave comfort and aid to the actual murderers after the deed was done.'

Agnes felt herself sway, and feared she would faint.

The justices conferred amongst themselves. 'We find,' said the leading judge, 'that we are not competent to try this case. We are referring it to the Court of King's Bench at Westminster. Mathew and Inges, you will be tried for murder; Lady Hungerford, you will be tried for petty treason.'

Already, as she was led away, shaking uncontrollably, Agnes could feel the heat of the flames.

Anne, 1539–1542

Early in August, I was one of ten young ladies whom the King invited to Portsmouth, where we toured his magnificent new warship, the *Henry Grace à Dieu*. It irked me that Margaret Skipwith – or my Lady Tailboys, as she now was – was among the party, yet there was no sign that the King's love for me had diminished in any way, and he paid her no more attention than he did the others, while I was by his side the whole day, basking in the good cheer he made us. At the end of it, he gave us all bountiful gifts, and mine was the most costly.

It had been nine months since he had become my servant, and I was wondering what would happen in the future. Would he tire of me? I could not credit that, given how loving he was towards me. So what, then? Marriage and a crown? I was beginning to believe it, and I know that others were too.

My hopes suddenly came crashing down when, early in October, it was cried throughout the court that the King was to marry the Princess Anna of Cleves.

I should have known that negotiations for a marriage were afoot. The ambassadors of Cleves had been at court sometime earlier, yet I had taken no notice of them. I had heard the gossip about his Grace fancying first one princess, and then another. I had given it little credence, because I had been busy reminding myself that he had already married two commoners. So I was utterly crushed when the news hit me.

What made it worse was that I wasn't well. I had been troubled by recurring agues for some time, and the King, who was always devising remedies of his own, ordered me to go and stay with my cousin, Lady Denny, at her house at Westminster.

'There are fair walks and good open air there,' he told me. 'My physician says there is nothing better for your disease than walking.' So I went to Westminster, wondering how long I would be away from him.

Within a week, I was feeling a great deal better, but then came that note from Kat, telling me the news.

I remember sitting down, feeling dizzy with shock, and writing to my mother, telling her I trusted to God we should have a new queen shortly. It dawned on me that I had already been promised a place in the Queen's household, and I shrank from it, for how could I bring myself to serve the woman who had displaced me?

When I saw the King again, I was crestfallen to find him very formal towards me, smiling graciously and bowing, but moving on within moments, and I knew then that it was all over between us. I stood there, stunned, then saw that people were watching me. I would not give them the satisfaction of seeing my discomposure, so I put on a smile and walked away. My dreams in the dust, I went about the court with a merry face, wondering whether to go back to Woodham Walter or to Calais. Soon, I realised I had no choice, because I was informed by the Earl of Rutland, the new Queen's chamberlain, that I had been appointed a maid-of-honour.

'You are very lucky, Mistress Anne,' he said. 'There has been great competition for places, but his Majesty reserved this one for you. Your lady mother sued for one for your sister Katherine, but every post is taken.'

How I wished I could have given Kat my place.

On her way to England that winter, the Princess of Cleves was delayed by storms at Calais, where Arthur and my mother received her with lavish ceremony. Mother wrote, telling me all about the celebrations, little realising that every mention of the Princess brought me pain. My future mistress, she said, was gentle and easy to please. Having heard reports of her notable virtues and excellent beauty, she was pleased to let me know that the Princess did not disappoint. I wish I could have taken pleasure in reading that, but I was so resentful, so jealous of this foreigner I had come to regard as a rival.

It was no secret that the King was impatient to receive his bride. Whenever I saw him about the court, he always greeted me kindly, but I could tell that he was holding himself aloof. I could not say anything to him, or ask why he had forsaken me, because he was the King, and it was not for me to question him – and because he was no longer free to love me.

Mother had always taken pride in the favour his Grace had shown me, little dreaming of the form that favour had taken, and now, more determined than ever to secure a maid-of-honour's post for Kat, she urged me to approach him, not realising how difficult that would be for me. She even sent a jar of his favourite quince marmalade and some damson conserve, which she herself had made, to sweeten him.

A few days before Christmas, I came upon his Grace in a gallery, talking to some councillors, and stood patiently, waiting for him to notice me. Presently, he came over and raised me from my curtsey. It was no more than a courteous gesture, monarch to subject. Had he forgotten what we had been to each other? I wondered.

I gave him the conserves. 'They are from my mother,' I told him.

'Now that is a gift I like wondrous well.' He gave me a warm smile. 'Pray give her ladyship hearty thanks for it!'

I was so captivated by that smile, so full of hope that all would again be as it was before, that I dared not ask for a place for my sister, for fear of how he would take it.

Mother was not pleased! She said I had no need to fear losing the King's favour. He understood that people sought advancement. I must seek him out again, without delay, and put in a good word for Kat.

I caught up with him on Christmas Eve, as he was leaving the chapel; I was praying he would not think I was chasing him. 'Your Grace, Sir . . .'

He turned, and there was that smile again. I could see that he was in a high good mood. 'What can I do for you, Mistress Anne?'

'Sir, my lady mother beseeches your Grace to look kindly on her request for a post for my sister Katherine in the Queen's household.'

He took it in good part. 'I will think on it,' he said, amiably enough, 'if you will tell your mother that I so liked the conserves she sent me that I command her to make me more.'

'I will, Sir, and I am hoping she might bring them herself when she comes to England in the Queen's train.'

'It is better if she sends them,' he said. 'Lord Lisle is needed in Calais.' I took that to mean that Mother must stay with him. How disappointed she would be! And how sad I was, that I would not be seeing her at court.

'I have a New Year's gift for you, Anne,' the King said, addressing me familiarly as he used to, and my heart leapt. It seemed that the old easiness between us was flowering anew. But my conscience was pricking me. What was I thinking? He was to be married; his bride would soon be in England, when the wind that had delayed her was favourable. I could not be a partner in adultery.

'I thank your Grace,' I said, drawing away a little. 'I am most bounden to you above all creatures.'

'By then the Queen will have arrived, God willing,' he said, and bowed before walking away, leaving me in a turmoil.

I first saw the Princess Anne on the downs beyond Rochester, when she was received by the Duke of Norfolk, Archbishop Cranmer and many other lords and gentlemen. I was among the great company of ladies who were to wait upon her. When it was my turn to be presented, I was shocked to see that she was so unlike what we had been led to believe. How could Mother have written that her beauty did not disappoint? Her nose was long, her chin pointed and her face narrow; it was a face, I thought, that the King could never love, for it was so unlike the faces of the ladies, including me, whom he had favoured. Worse still, there was about the Princess a faint, sickly-sweet smell of unwashed body linen and sweat. When she spoke, it was with a guttural voice, and soon I realised that she knew very little English.

Those were my first impressions, and I admit now that I was ready to think the worst of her, and in no frame of mind to search for the best. Later, I came to realise that she had a kind, docile nature, and an innate willingness to please. I know she tried hard to learn our language and customs. Yet I was resentful of her, for she had taken my King away from me. I simmered all the way through the great state reception on Blackheath, when his Grace formally welcomed her to the kingdom, and I found it hard to keep smiling and cheerful when I attired her first for her wedding and, later that day, for her bridal night. She would be experiencing the pleasure I had been denied.

But, as the world knows, I was wrong. Within days, the talk at court was of little else but the King's marriage. I felt a glimmer of sympathy for the future Queen, isolated in her rooms and by her inability to speak English – although that was probably a blessing. If she knew what was being said, she gave no sign of it.

Mother was still pressing for a place for Kat, having now resorted to begging the Chancellor of Cleves to intercede with the King on her behalf – only to be told by that gentleman that patience must be had!

Undeterred, she asked Lady Rutland to move his Grace in the matter. Lady Rutland looked distressed when she told me that Mother had sent her gifts of wine and barrels of herring as inducements.

'I had to tell her that the King's pleasure is that no more maids shall be taken in until such time as some of those now with the Queen's Grace are promoted or married. I said she might approach Mother Lowe, who can do as much good in this matter as anyone here.' Mother Lowe was the German mistress of the maids. 'To tell the truth, I am loath to lose Kat. I have grown very fond of her.'

Mother agreed to approach Mother Lowe. In the meantime, she wrote to me, urging me to press the King again, and once more I sought him out, this time as he came from the tennis play after watching a match. He seemed pleased to see me, and I fondly imagined that he was remembering what had been between us and comparing it to his barren existence with the Queen.

He heard me out patiently and sighed. 'Anne, many have spoken to me on your sister's behalf. As I told them all, I will not grant a place for your sister, for there is no place; and if there was, I would fill it with someone fair and meet for the position.'

The insult to Kat – dear, sweet, plain Kat – stung, and my anger flared brighter than my disappointment. I made my curtsey and departed in a huff, hoping he realised he had offended me. Then I sought out Kat, and told her it was useless to pursue the matter further, as there were no places.

'It is no matter,' she said. 'Mother wanted it more than I did. I am for Belvoir Castle today, with my Lord and Lady Rutland.' And she went on happily with her packing.

When I thought later about what the King had said, it occurred to me that he was probably tired of being bombarded with these incessant requests, and had meant to put a stop to them, once and for all. But it had been an unkind way to do it.

Mother, though, would not be deterred. My heart sank when Lady Rutland told me that Mother Lowe had received a large bribe from my lady, for I knew what the answer would be.

And then, out of the blue, the King summoned me. It was a fine March day, and he invited me to walk with him in his privy garden – an honour not accorded to everyone. Needless to say, it threw me into confusion, especially when he began speaking in earnest.

'I have missed you, Anne,' he said, and my heart soared. All my resentment was forgotten. 'You understood, of course, why I could no longer be your servant. But now . . . This so-called marriage. It is no marriage.' He was looking at me pleadingly.

My thoughts were racing in several different directions, and at the end of one of them there was a crown.

'I await proofs from Cleves,' Henry said. 'If there are none, I will have the marriage annulled.' I wondered, my heart racing, if I had taken his meaning aright.

We had reached the gate, and he led me along the path to the stables. There, in the cobbled courtyard, stood a grey palfrey equipped with a fine saddle and bridle.

'For you,' the King said. He was smiling eagerly at me, waiting for my reaction, and I could only stand there and wonder what this princely gift betokened. I could not credit that he was expecting me to become his mistress, for his talk of divorce had led me to think he was looking forward to a time when he was free to wed.

'I am astonished,' I murmured. 'Your Grace is too kind.'

'It is a measure of my esteem,' he said, and kissed my hand. I was sure then that I knew what was in his mind.

It all came to nothing. Within a month, as the world knows, he was pursuing Katheryn Howard, one of my fellow maids-of-honour, and my crazy hopes were extinguished.

I understood how the Queen felt, abandoned and humiliated. The courtiers had deserted her chambers to flock to the new favourite. Even Mother ceased pressing for a place for Kat. That was a sure sign of how the wind was blowing.

I cursed Henry for his fickleness. I wondered bitterly if he had it in him to love someone truly. Twice he had led me on, then forsaken me. I could only thank God that he had been discreet in his renewed pursuit of me, relieved that few could know of my mortification.

I soon learned that there was another reason why he had distanced himself.

Just days later, I was delighted to hear that Arthur had been recalled to England. Mother and my sister Mary would be following. The news could not have come at a better time. I could not wait to see them all. I had visions of us all retreating to the peace of Devon, where my battered heart could heal, my spirits braced by Mother's down-to-earth support. She would be ecstatic that her exile was at an end.

Arthur had not yet arrived when Master Husee came banging on my door at court. His pleasant face looked unusually troubled.

'Mistress Anne,' he said urgently, 'my Lord Lisle has been arrested on suspicion of treason, and has been taken to the Tower.'

'What? When? What has he done?' I cried, panicking.

'As far as I can tell, he is accused of plotting to sell Calais to the French.'

I was horrified. 'But he would never do that! He is loyal to the King.'

Master Husee shrugged despairingly. 'I know he has had dealings with the French, but I never heard or suspected that there was anything remotely treasonable going on. My lady wrote a hasty letter saying he was questioned about a secret betrothal between your sister Mary and the new seigneur of Bours. Such closeness to a subject of the French King could be open to misinterpretation.'

It seemed trivial to me, a family matter and nothing more. I knew Arthur too well to believe anything else.

I had another shock, very soon afterwards, when I learned that Mother and my sisters had also been arrested, and were being held under house arrest in Calais. Master Husee learned that Mother had been seen disposing of papers in the privy, which sounded ominous. My brother John, greatly alarmed, hastened over to Calais and carried away Frances and their daughter to England.

I don't know how I got through those dark days. Hourly, I expected to hear of my stepfather's execution. The Council summoned me for questioning, but I could tell them nothing, and they let me go. Tainted by treason as I was, some of my friends deserted me, among them Lady Sussex, who I dared to upbraid for her faithlessness. Later, we were reconciled, after a fashion, but things were never the same between us again.

I had relied on my mother and stepfather for many of the luxuries I enjoyed, the clothes I wore, and a handsome allowance. I could look for none of those now, and as time wore on, I began to run out of money. But I was more worried about Mother. The few letters I received from her were incoherent, and I was scared that she had gone mad.

My true friends rallied around me. Many ladies-in-waiting were protective of me, and my fellow maids kind. The Queen herself was sympathetic. They all seemed to think that the worst consequence of the tragedy that had befallen my family was that I now had no chance of making a good marriage. But I cared nothing for that. I was reeling from the news that our household at the Staple Inn had been broken up, and that the Crown had seized all the plate, jewels, clothes and papers found there.

Malicious tongues had it that Mother was the real traitor, having plotted to marry her daughter to a Frenchman who was bent on seizing Calais. There was a story that Arthur had tried to enlist the Pope's support in surrendering Calais to the French. Speculation got wilder and wilder. It was even being said that Mother had taken a Catholic priest, the aptly named Sir Gregory Sweet-Lips, as a lover, and that he was her intermediary with the Pope.

In the end, of course, the scandal died down, and it became clear to me that there was not enough evidence to support the charges of treason; had there been, Arthur would have suffered for it. Nevertheless, he remained in the Tower, and Mother and Mary were kept under house arrest in Calais.

This horrible affair left my heart bruised and my nerves shattered, but there was one consolation. The King.

He sent for me at the height of the madness, and was kind. 'I have a great liking for you, Mistress Anne, as you are aware,' he said. 'I know you were not involved in this bad business, and I am sorry for your trouble. Rest assured, your place at court is secure.'

I thanked him, from my heart, miserably aware that his was given elsewhere.

* * *

One reason why the fuss abated was that there were three other, juicier, scandals. One was the arrest of Lord Cromwell in June; the second was the attainder of his colleague, Lord Hungerford, for treason, sodomy and sorcery. And the third was the matter of the Queen.

I was not sorry to take my leave of her, standing in line with all her other servants, on the day her household was disbanded. I had never warmed to her, and I still believed that, but for her coming, the King would have married me. It was an irrational dislike, because she had had no say in the matter, but it had been on her account that he had abandoned me.

I felt even more resentful of Katheryn Howard. Had she not fluttered her bright blue eyes at the King, and conducted herself provocatively towards him, luring him into her snares, it might have been me whom he married that summer – on the very day that the heads of Thomas Cromwell and Walter Hungerford fell. And I was commanded to serve her as maid-of-honour. Kat was very envious. Once again, she was passed over. All she was offered was a post in the household of the Lady Anne of Cleves.

But when news of our brother John's death reached us, that all seemed trivial. He was just twenty-three, far too young to be struck down by a wasting illness no physician could diagnose. Our thoughts were at Umberleigh, with Frances, whom he had left pregnant, and her two fatherless little girls.

Little Arthur, who was named after my stepfather, was born there in October 1541, the month before the fall of Queen Katheryn. For the third time in four years, I was present at the disbanding of a royal household. This time it was Sir Thomas Wriothesley who ordered us all to repair to our families or friends. Afterwards, though, he took me aside and informed me that I might remain at court in my old lodgings, even though there was no queen to serve.

'His Majesty is conscious of the calamity that has befallen your family,' he explained. 'He will provide for you at his own expense, and arrange a suitable marriage for you.'

Again, I was struck by Henry's kindness to me, even in the midst of his sorrow – for it was no secret how badly the affair of the Queen had shaken him. He was out hunting daily, from November until after Christmas, doubtless trying to divert his ill humour, and it was bruited about the court that he was neglecting state affairs. Yet he did not forget me or mine. Early in the New Year of 1542, when Arthur had been in the Tower for twenty months, his arms were restored to their place in the chapel of the Garter knights at Windsor. Rumour had it that it was a sign that he would soon be freed. How I prayed for it, and especially for my mother, who had been permitted to write to me only infrequently. All her letters had betrayed the incoherence that had alarmed me in the first place. It seemed that she was no less confused with the passing of time. I feared that the strain had permanently robbed her of her wits.

At the end of January, the King invited me and dozens of other ladies to a lavish supper and banquet, the first he had hosted in months. He had never been merry since first hearing of the Queen's misconduct, but he was on good form that evening, when the tables were laden with gold and silver plate, fine Venetian glass and a delicious variety of dishes, and he made us all great and hearty cheer. I had a place of honour on his left hand, while Elizabeth Wyatt, whom Sir Thomas Wyatt had repudiated for her adultery, was on his right, being of higher rank. For all her reputation, she was a pretty, likeable creature, and his Grace showed her the greatest regard. To be fair, he did divide his attention between us and the other guests, but I sensed his preference for Lady Wyatt, probably because he thought her easy game.

Listening to him paying us compliments, and seeing him smile at our witty remarks, it was hard to believe that, earlier that day, Parliament had drawn up an Act of Attainder against the Queen. No wonder the gossips were busy, for it was widely believed that the King would not be long without a wife, if only because of the great desire he had for more sons. Lady Wyatt was soon discounted, for it was out of the question for him to marry a lady of such a notoriety; but there were many who looked covertly, or hopefully, at me.

Yes, the King did seek my company in those difficult weeks, but what the inquisitive courtiers did not know was that he wept on my shoulder when we were private, bewailing the misfortunes that had befallen him. I may have been the only person, apart from his fool and confidant, Will Somers, who knew that Henry now shied from the prospect of marriage. He had been too deeply hurt. Small wonder that Parliament passed an Act declaring it treason if a woman with a past did not declare it when the King made plain his interest in wedding her.

Well, I had no past, but this time I was not hoping for a proposal. Twice bitten, three times shy. And yet, I think now that, if I had played my cards aright, I could have had him then. It was me he had turned to in his grief, me to whom he showed the greatest favour. Had he promised to find a husband for me? He never did, so was he reserving me for himself? I shall never know. Maybe he shrank from marrying another young maid-of-honour.

It was during one of these harrowing, emotional evenings that I was emboldened by Henry's favour to speak up on Arthur's behalf.

'Is it true that your Grace means to release him? He is a good man who would not hurt a fly, still less commit treason.'

The King nodded thoughtfully. 'For all the Council's searching, no evidence has been found to support the allegations. We had to be sure, Anne. But you are right. Lord Lisle is harmless, and yes, I do believe him to be loyal. I will pardon and release him, and your mother and sister.'

I was so overcome with relief that, rather than kneeling to express my gratitude, as I should have done, I flung my arms around Henry and kissed him. 'Thank you, Sir! Thank you!'

He looked startled, then kissed me back, on my cheek, and patted my hand. It was the last time he kissed me.

In March that year, Arthur was to be set free. I made my way, with my maid, to the Tower of London to greet him when he emerged. I had planned to take him for a celebratory dinner at the Swan in Gray's Inn Lane, where the City guildsmen eat. I waited, and I waited, listening to the bell of All Hallows chiming the hours. At length, I ventured to the gatehouse and spoke to the guards on duty. Where was my Lord Lisle? I was sure he was due for release today. After they had consulted their papers and confirmed that was indeed the case, one hastened away to find out what was happening.

He came back with a grave face. 'Mistress,' he said, his voice cracking, 'I have bad news. I am afraid that Lord Lisle collapsed at the sudden rapture of learning of his pardon. He lies in his chamber, very sore sick from the pain in his chest.'

I was so distressed that they let me in to see him. I stayed two days, watching over him, before he suffered severe and fatal pangs and died. I followed the coffin when it was buried in the chapel of St Peter ad Vincula in the Tower.

The worst of it was that, as Mary wrote to me, being liberated had lifted Mother's spirits, and she had rejoiced to learn that Arthur was also to be freed, thinking soon to be reunited with her husband; but the news of his death plunged her back into a stupor, and after that she barely knew where she was or who we were. It was pitiful to see, Mary said, and not the homecoming Mother had dreamed of. Mary took her down to Tehidy, where she could benefit from the bracing air and be looked after. And there she has stayed ever since.

Agnes, 1522

Agnes knew that her only hope was to plead not guilty. She was sure there was no proof to convict her. She had not even been present when the murder was carried out, and if her co-accused testified against her, saying she had incited them to do the killing, she would deny it. It was the word of a lady against common thieves.

But when she was brought into Westminster Hall, she was surprised to hear Mathew and Inges plead not guilty too. So they had not betrayed her; she was fairly certain of that. It must have been Walter. Alarmingly, the court seemed to be in possession of damning depositions by someone who seemed to have a very good idea of what had taken place. How could they have known? Was it just clever guesswork – or had there been a witness to the killing? One thing remained certain: no one could have witnessed her part in it.

'William Mathew and William Inges, the court finds you guilty of murder,' the presiding judge declared, at the end of the day. 'Agnes Hungerford, we find you not guilty of petty treason, but guilty of inciting and abetting the murder. Accordingly, you are all three sentenced to hang.'

The spectre of the flames receded. She was not to burn, to her profound relief. Yet she was still to die, and hanging was no easy death, as she had seen for herself on one or two occasions. Agnes began to tremble. This time, it was not on account of something that might happen to her, but because of what would of a certainty happen to her – unless she could make a successful plea for mercy.

The judge ruled that, because Agnes was now a convicted felon, all her possessions were forfeit to the Crown. It was then that she noticed Walter among the spectators, looking smug with triumph, and knew, without any doubt, that she had him to thank for her present trouble. He would get his hands at last on his father's goods; and he had exacted a cruel vengeance.

Anne, 1542–1554

I stayed on at court, where I had the King's special favour and many friends. In 1543, when I was twenty-two, I was again appointed maid-of-honour, this time to Henry's sixth wife, Katharine Parr, and I served that gracious lady for three years and more. I grew close to the Lady Mary, and we often partnered each other at cards or on the virginals and lute. I remember giving her some embroidered gloves one New Year.

Even now, I cannot bear to recall how affected I was by the King's death in 1547. He had been the lodestar of my life, and when he was gone, the world seemed an empty, troubled sea in which I was cast adrift. I was granted an allowance for mourning attire, and went about the court like a wraith, feeling as if I no longer had any place there.

Queen Katharine retired to Chelsea. Kat was still with the Lady Anne of Cleves, and stayed with her even after her own marriage later that year. I went to the wedding at the church at Hever, and was glad to see my sister a happy bride. I was godmother to her son Henry the following autumn.

I had received an annuity for my service to Queen Katharine. It kept me in relative comfort, enabling me to rent a house in London when it became clear that there was no place for me at court under the new King, Henry's son, Edward. During the six years of his reign, I visited Mother at Tehidy a few times, and was sad to see her still out of her wits. She hardly knew me, and spent her days sitting in her chair by the fire, mumbling incoherently and wringing her hands. It was a long way to go for such poor reward, and eventually I made the journey just once a year, to salve my conscience. She had been a good mother, and it was the least I owed her.

The Lady Mary did not forget me. When she became queen in 1553, she invited me to be one of her chamberers at her coronation, an unexpected and touching honour. The next day, she knighted Kat's husband and named me a lady of her Privy Chamber, which meant that I was in constant attendance at court.

I know Queen Mary to be a resolute, warm-hearted lady. I'm aware that she has earned criticism for being too stout in religion and for reviving the heresy laws, yet she has never shown me anything but kindness. It was she who chose a husband for me. At the advanced age of thirty-three, I found myself at the church door, exchanging vows with Sir Walter Hungerford.

I knew, of course, about his father's execution, thirteen years before. People had talked of little else. My Walter, the present Lord Hungerford, had survived the scandal and the shame. He had campaigned tirelessly for the restoration of his family estates until, finally, Queen Mary had reversed his father's attainder and restored him in blood.

It was from Walter that I learned the full story of his father's crimes. That wicked man had locked up his wife, my husband's stepmother, in the Lady Tower at Farleigh Hungerford, and tried to starve her. But for a priest who smuggled her food, thanks to the covert efforts of local tenants, he might have succeeded.

'She thought he was trying to poison her,' Walter confided. 'And I could do nothing to help because I feared him.'

'But why was he so cruel to her?' I asked. I was then well into my first pregnancy, and we were lying in bed with the curtains drawn, holding hands, as we did in our early months together.

'Her father had been beheaded, having rebelled against King Henry,' Walter told me. 'My father wanted to demonstrate how much he despised his in-laws. My stepmother smuggled out a letter to Thomas Cromwell, begging him to help her seek a divorce. And I am fairly certain that she accused my father of sodomy.'

That alone would have been enough to bring Lord Hungerford to the block.

'Cromwell ignored her,' Walter went on. 'Maybe he was protecting him. They were friends, you know, as well as colleagues. It was my father's association with Cromwell that proved his downfall. When Cromwell was arrested, so I believe, my stepmother's letter came to light and was investigated. It was found that my father employed a priest who went about calling King Henry a heretic. He also kept in our household a shady doctor who gave me the shivers; Father had him cast the King's horoscope to find out when he would die. Then came the evidence of unnatural acts and abominable vices. He was accused of committing buggery with some of the servants. In the end, he was condemned for treason, witchcraft and sodomy. My stepmother remarried, and lives still.'

Walter fell silent. It had been a terrible time for him, and after that night, we did not speak of it. But, before we went to sleep, he confided something else to me.

'I think that my father's character was shaped in his youth. His stepmother was accused of murdering her first husband here in this castle, and his father may have been complicit. I don't know much about it. Father would never talk about it. When I was a child, I heard the servants gossiping about a body being burned in the kitchen oven. They said it was my step-grandmother's first husband, whom she had murdered so that she could marry my grandfather.'

'What happened to her?' I asked.

211

'She was hanged,' he said, and I thought immediately of the spectre by the chapel door.

Agnes, 1523

On a cold February day, Agnes walked from the Tower to Holborn, with William Mathew stumbling behind her and guards marching on either side, through streets crowded with angry citizens baying for her blood. William Inges wasn't there; he had claimed benefit of clergy to save his neck, although Agnes found it hard to believe that he was ever in holy orders.

At Holborn, the cart was waiting for them, and they climbed up and sat down on the two rough coffins that had been set there. There could not have been a starker reminder of their imminent fate, but there was nowhere else to sit. Agnes's maid was with them, she who had loyally attended her mistress during the long months in the Tower. Her presence lent Agnes some shred of dignity, but few would have recognised the once-proud Lady Hungerford in the wretched, dirty creature in the cart.

The appeal to the King had failed. There was no earthly help to be had now. Agnes tried to pray, but the words would not come, for she was too consumed by terror. Every step, every turn of the wheels, was bringing her closer to the gallows. Her life was now measured in minutes.

Too soon, Tyburn came into view, and Agnes stared transfixed as she saw the gallows and the throng of people around it, waiting to see her die. The cart drew to a halt and the executioner leapt up and fixed the noose around Agnes's neck before moving on to William. Agnes was trembling so much, she thought she would die of fear before the rope got her. Already she had lost control of her bladder.

A priest was saying prayers, but she was beyond hearing him. The cart pulled away.

Anne, 1557

The child came too soon, in a gush of blood and mess. They would not let me see him.

I had known this pregnancy would end in tragedy. Before I took to my chamber, I had seen the ghost by the chapel, and knew for certain that it was Agnes, for she no longer looked serene, but agitated, and the weal around her neck was clearly visible before she faded. Worse still she had beckoned me. It struck a chill into my heart.

I have been haunted by her fate, imagining how it was for her at the end. This castle is indeed cursed, I am certain: the Hungerfords will never know joy in their marriages. And I fear I have become an inconvenience to Walter . . .

I can feel my strength ebbing. My body seems light and insubstantial.

Walter is at court. I know why; I am no fool. There is a lady there whom he is pursuing; I recognise the signs, for she is not the first. He was meant to come back in time for the birth, but of course it was premature.

As I drift towards sleep, it seems he is here with me now, and that we are alone together for once. He is embracing me, and I am choking, gasping for air, as Agnes must have done in her final moments. Everything goes black.

Author's Note

The lives of Anne Bassett and Agnes Hungerford are well documented in contemporary sources, notably the *Lisle Letters* and *Letters and Papers of the Reign of Henry VIII*. 'Lady Agnes Hungerford' by W. J. Hardy (*Antiquary Magazine*, 2, 1880) and *The Tudor Murder Files* by James Moore (2016) illuminate Agnes's story. Although it's often stated that her origins are unknown, I found traces of her and her first husband in Canterbury. I am indebted to Elizabeth Norton for the information on Margaret Skipwith.

When I read *The Tudor Murder Files* recently, I was so captivated by its brief, but riveting, account of murder and executions in the aristocratic Hungerford family that I began reading more on the subject and resolved to write that story one day.

Just a week later, I was pondering on which subjects to choose for the two e-shorts to complement my novel *Anna of Kleve*. For one, I settled on Anne Bassett, who might have become one of Henry VIII's wives had fate not decreed otherwise – or so contemporary speculation had it. I knew a lot about Anne's time at Henry's court, but little about her later life. Imagine my surprise when I discovered that she married a Hungerford, and that I could weave those grim stories into my e-short.

William Inges was hanged six months after Agnes. Some have seen Agnes's ghost at the entrance to the chapel in Farleigh Hungerford Castle. There is no evidence that Anne Bassett was strangled.

THE
KING'S
PAINTER

1539

A ray of October sun shone through the greenish glass in the mullioned window and illuminated the King's face. Seated before him, sketching his familiar features, Susanna reflected on how he had put on weight and aged these past three years. She knew his face and form better than most, having taken his likeness several times in the past sixteen years. It grieved her to see the sagging of that noble profile, the heavy jowls, the wreck of his athletic body, which was now encased in fat.

At first, she had been awestruck having the King as a sitter, but over the years she had relaxed into an easy, pleasant relationship with him. It went no further. The natural distance of monarch and subject lay between them, and he had never given any sign that he had found her homely Flemish features attractive. It was better that way. She did not need complications in her professional life.

'Mistress Gilman, I want this miniature to be small, two inches in height at most,' the King said.

'Would your Grace like it on vellum or ivory?' she asked.

'Vellum,' he told her. 'I intend to have it mounted in a locket. Master Holbein is designing one.' His painter, Master Holbein, was a genius – and so he ought to be, for her brother Lucas had tutored him.

Susanna laid down her black chalk. 'I have finished, Sir. Would you like to see it?' She took the sketch over to his chair, hoping the drawing was not too overtly flattering. She could not have borne to paint the King with brutal realism. Art should be a beautiful thing; it should raise the spirits and please the senses.

'Excellent, as usual,' Henry said admiringly. 'It will be a gift for my bride.'

It was just three days since the announcement of his coming marriage to the Princess of Kleef, and the court was still talking about it. Susanna was pleased for him. He had grieved terribly for the loss of Queen Jane, two years ago.

Susanna had been a gentlewoman to Jane, and sincerely hoped she would not be required to take up the same post in the new Queen's household. She had had to give up her art, and all it meant to her, for painters were artisans, equal in the minds of courtiers to merchants and master craftsmen, and it would not have done for a gentlewoman to the Queen to have earned her own living. She had been sorry for Jane Seymour's death in childbed, but relieved to be able to return to the first of her great passions in life. It had offered a panacea for her own grief at the death of her husband earlier that year, and stopped her feeling cast adrift after being anchored to John Parker for twelve years.

She had done well for herself, people said. John had been keeper of the Palace of Westminster, Yeoman of the King's Crossbows, and Yeoman of the King's Robes. Life had been good. She had divided her time between the court and her husband's houses at Fulham and King's Langley. He had even provided her with her own workshops, although she had continued to spend time in her father's atelier at court, where there were always too many commissions to be filled, and an extra pair of gifted hands was greatly appreciated.

The other great passion in her life was waiting downstairs for the King's sitting to end. He was the other reason why she did not want to return to the arid life of a royal gentlewoman, constrained always to subsume her own desires in social conventions, and live vicariously through her mistress. She wanted to spend her free time with John Gilman.

She had expected his Majesty to rise from his chair and leave, but, to her surprise, he stayed there, seeming unusually hesitant.

'I can trust you, Mistress Gilman, can I not?' he said at length.

'Of course, Sir,' she assured him, surprised.

'And you are a married woman, so I can talk freely to you.'

'Yes, Sir.' She could not imagine what this was all about.

'There are certain matters that are better handled by ladies than by ministers or ambassadors,' he said, his fair cheeks slightly flushed. 'Sit down, I pray you.'

Susanna sat on the stool, smoothing her paint-stained apron over her dove-grey skirts, completely baffled.

'The Princess of Cleves looks charming in Holbein's portrait,' the King said, 'and all the reports I have received praise her virtues and her demeanour. But I need to know more, to nourish love, if you take my meaning. I need to know who her friends are, and if . . .' He paused, seeming to be struggling for words. 'I have been told by my envoys that, some years ago, she was away from court for many months, suffering from a mysterious illness. I say mysterious because no one seems to know what it was, and I suspect it was some woman's ailment. And if that was the case, I need to know if it had any effect on her ability to bear children. That is where you can help.'

Susanna didn't like the way this was going. 'I, Sir?'

'Yes. You speak her language; you can also teach her English, and about English customs. Doing that, you would spend hours together, of necessity; it would be easy to gain her confidence.'

Susanna's heart had sunk. 'Does your Grace mean for me to do this when the Queen arrives in England?'

The King shook his head. 'No, Mistress Gilman. I want you to go to Cleves, be her mentor, and discover the things I need to know before I marry her.'

Susanna could not hide her dismay. 'Your Grace, I have been married but two weeks! I had not looked to leave my husband alone so soon.' *And I do not want to cross the sea again.* She had never forgotten the violent tempest that had blown her and her family to England when she was nineteen.

The King smiled at her. 'He may go with you, for I think you will be there for some weeks,' he said. 'I will pay his passage and expenses, and forty pounds to equip yourself.'

She gasped. It was more than she earned in three years. 'Oh, your

Grace! That is more than generous.' All the while, she was screwing up her apron in her distress. She had no excuses left now.

'It is a measure of my trust in you,' the King said.

When she and John got home to the house in Bride Lane, which John had rented because of its closeness to Fleet Street, where he traded as a vintner, Susanna had still said nothing about the King's command, for she wanted to come to terms with it in her own time. She went through to the workshop to cut a disc of vellum and grind the colours she would need, so that she could begin work on the King's miniature after supper. For this particular portrait, she would use gold paint for the jewels on his costume. The beauty would be in the detail.

As she stood at the bench, John came up behind her, cupped her breasts in his hands and nuzzled her ear.

'Come to bed, sweeting. This can wait!'

As usual, she could not resist him. She had never known such sweetness in her first marriage bed. And, for John too, the love that had burgeoned between them was a heady balm. He too had lost a spouse and known grief. They had first encountered each other when he was delivering wine to Whitehall Palace and saved Susanna from falling over a barrel. Their eyes had met, and a bond was sealed. They were of an age, both thirty-six, both successful in their careers. Susanna's first marriage had been childless, but she enjoyed being stepmother to John's little girl as much as she enjoyed being the wife of a freeman of the City of London, with all the privileges that brought with it.

Later, as John lay watching her dressing, she told him of the King's command that they visit Kleef.

'That's excellent news!' he declared. 'It will be an opportunity for me to sample the wines they grow in that region. And we can make a holiday of it, together.'

Susanna began to feel better about having to go. 'I may be there some weeks,' she said, fastening her bodice. 'They will fall in your busy Christmas period.'

'No matter, I can put Smith in charge.' Master Smith was John's journeyman vintner, a capable and affable man, utterly dependable.

* * *

The voyage was not quite as bad as Susanna had feared. It brought back vivid memories of the year her father had brought them all to England, at the invitation of the King. Gerard Horenbout had become famous for the exquisite miniatures he painted in manuscripts, and he and his gifted son Lucas had conceived the idea of painting miniature portraits. By a great chance of fortune, the King of France had sent one of these portraits to King Henry, and of course King Henry must have one of his own. In fact, he wanted miniature portraits of all his family, and some of those uniquely wonderful illuminated manuscripts. His offer had been irresistible. But Susanna also had memories of how strange it had felt to be catapulted into a foreign land where she could not understand anything anyone said. She still marvelled at how her father had risen to the challenge, and felt great sympathy for the Princess of Kleef, who had yet to face it.

She herself had coped well. It helped that she had inherited the family talent for artistry. At seventeen, she had begun working in her father's workshop in Ghent, where Gerard was court painter to Margaret of Austria, Regent of the Netherlands. At first, she had to do the routine tasks like making up paints, preparing panels and clearing up, while observing how the master worked. Allowed to try her own hand, she was soon completing commissions to his designs, and then began painting original miniatures and illuminations of her own.

At the Regent's court, where she was sent to deliver a commission, she had been received by one of Margaret's *filles d'honneur*, a dark-eyed young lady of great poise and charm, who introduced herself as Anne Boleyn. Years later, she had heard that name again, many times, when Anne had become the scandal of Europe, and had married Henry VIII. Anne had not recognised her when their paths crossed again at the English court, but when Susanna reminded her of that early meeting, she had been kind enough to say that yes, now, she did remember her. Susanna always felt sad when she thought of Anne, whose head and body now lay in the church in the Tower of London.

Within a year of starting at the workshop, Susanna's fame had spread. She had never forgotten the day when the great master Albrecht Dürer visited the atelier and bought her illumination of the *Salvator Mundi*.

He had smiled at her, and said, 'It is a great marvel that a woman should do so much.' It pleased her immeasurably to be highly regarded in a man's field.

As the English coastline receded, she marvelled anew at how quickly the commissions had flowed in after her father had set up his workshop in his adoptive land. There were all kinds of requests, not only for paintings, but for designs for vestments, tapestries and stained glass. His great talent encompassed them all.

It was Lucas who had painted most of the royal miniatures, but Susanna had worked on a goodly number, as well as on illuminations commissioned by the King. It was Lucas, though, who was paid a salary, and a high one at that. She felt no jealousy, for she was pleased to see her brother so successful; what mattered most to her was enjoying the King's favour. She had received gifts – gold plate or apostle spoons – from him every New Year, tangible proofs of her success. Five years ago, she and all her family had received a patent of denization, and anglicised their name to Hornebolt.

They arrived in Kleef in October. Susanna's arrival was expected, and in Düsseldorf she received a kindly welcome from Dr Wotton, the English ambassador, and a more formal one from Duke Wilhelm, who – she was to find out – was the soul of correctness, and something of a bore. A highly controlling bore. The princesses of Kleef, his sisters, seemed to spend their lives mostly in seclusion, guarded by their mother and their nurse, a plump, bustling martinet called Mother Lowe.

Susanna liked the Princess Anna on sight, although, privately, she had reservations that Anna had sufficient charm and accomplishments to inspire passion in the King. She was a humble soul, dignified and modest, with pleasing features (if you ignored the long nose), but without a clue how to please a man. And she was profoundly grateful to meet Susanna and have her for a gentlewoman. It was easy for Susanna to befriend her, for she was avid to learn all about the King and the

English court from someone acquainted with both. In fact, she seemed avid for any diversion, poor soul.

It irked Susanna to hear that, in Kleef, women were not allowed to sing, dance, play instruments, go hunting or even paint; all were frowned upon and seen as occasions of lightness. The more she heard about the English court, the more the Princess worried that she would be at a disadvantage.

Susanna did her best to reassure her that all would be well, and that the King was longing to greet her. She thought about saying that love would triumph over everything, but wasn't so sure about that.

The Dowager Duchess assigned them a splendid room for the English lessons. Anna struggled with them, but Susanna persisted, and her pupil began to make slow progress.

'I don't know how I'm going to report to the King on her friends,' Susanna confided to John one evening, over supper in the comfortable lodging they had been allocated. She had at last confided to him the true nature of her mission, reasoning that he was her husband and should know. 'She doesn't appear to have any friends. She seems to spend all her time with her mother, or her giggly sister, the Princess Amalia.'

'Then tell him that,' John said. 'It's the truth.'

'I fear she is becoming too attached to me,' Susanna went on. 'She speaks much of our special friendship, and she is fascinated by my painting. I've painted some miniatures of scriptural scenes for her. But it will not do for a queen to befriend one of her lowly attendants. And I feel it's all a bit one-sided. I like her, but I am friends with her because the King asked me to be.'

John raised an eyebrow. 'But aren't you supposed to be gaining her confidence? You're going about it the right way.'

'I suppose so.'

She was waiting for an opportunity to broach the subject of the Princess's long absence from court due to the mysterious complaint the King had mentioned. Dare she ask outright? And should she say it had come to the King's ears that Anna had been away from court at some point? Probably it was best to say she had heard one of the ladies mentioning it in Kleef.

She seized her moment two days later when the Princess spoke of the long illness of her late father, Duke Johann.

'I hear that your Highness also suffered a prolonged malady some years ago,' Susanna said.

Anna looked startled and, before she recovered herself, Susanna saw a flash of what was possibly fear in her eyes. Was there a secret to be uncovered?

'A long time ago,' Anna said. '*Many* years ago, in fact.'

'That must have been serious, and worrying for everyone. Your Highness is quite recovered now, I trust?'

'I was quite recovered by the time I returned from my convalescence,' Anna said, with unusual firmness.

Her refusal to discuss her illness seemed suspicious in itself. Susanna dared not press for further information, because it would now seem like an inquisition. No matter, she would be able to reassure the King that there were no ill effects of the illness – as far as she could tell. But what female ailment – for it had to have been that, otherwise there would have been no need for secrecy – could have caused her to be ill for many months?

There was an obvious answer to that, but Susanna could not credit it where Anna was concerned. The Princess was too innocent, too closely supervised. Yet she could think of nothing else.

Puzzling, she picked up her quill and wrote to the King, sealing the letter before she entrusted it to Dr Wotton.

In November, Susanna and John travelled in Anna's train to Schwanenburg, where Anna would bid farewell to her family and set off on her long journey to England. Much of Susanna's time was devoted to translating or teaching Anna English, in which she was making better progress than she had to begin with, and acquainting her with English customs.

The great hall of the castle was packed with courtiers and dignitaries, and there was an interminable ceremony in which those who had been chosen to accompany the Princess were presented to her. Susanna was standing behind her with the other gentlewomen, watching as the herald summoned each person to come up and kiss Anna's hand.

She was growing bored, when suddenly her attention was diverted by a handsome young man announced as Otho von Wylich. He bowed and took the Princess's hand, faultless in his demeanour, but Susanna could just see the flush blooming on Anna's cheek, and saw her hand clench on the arm of her chair. She was used to reading people's faces and mannerisms; it was important to put something of their character into their portraits. This, she thought, was odd; it bespoke a reaction beyond the normal. Meister von Wylich clearly aroused some emotion in the Princess. But he was a married man, and his pretty wife was there with him, curtseying. What opportunity would he ever have had for paying his addresses to the Princess? Had she lusted after him from afar?

The moment passed, and the next person came forward.

Susanna forgot about the incident with the excitement of passing through Flanders and seeing the once-familiar landscape again – and then, after a few days, with the tedium of the long journey. At first, accorded the privilege of riding with Anna and Mother Lowe in the great gold chariot, she was occupied with keeping the Princess cheerful, for she was sad at leaving her kinsfolk and her homeland, and nervous of what lay ahead in England. Later on, they were all trying to cheer each other, as they grew frustrated at the repeated delays in their progress.

It was not until they were staying at the English House in Antwerp that Susanna was reminded of what had happened at Schwanenburg.

At dusk, exhausted after receiving many visitors, the Princess escaped to the shadowed formal garden for some fresh air, and took Susanna with her, for it was unthinkable that she go out unattended. Wrapped in their cloaks, they encountered Dr Wotton on the way down, and Susanna had to explain the custom of *Brautstücke*, about which the King had enquired.

'It means "bride pieces",' she said. 'In Germany, on the morning after their marriage, a man of rank gives his wife a morning gift of money, land or jewels. He also gives *Brautstücke* to her gentlewomen, and to the men who serve her.'

'Mayhap his Majesty will give your Grace *Brautstücke* on your wedding morn!' Dr Wotton smiled, then took his leave.

Anna and Susanna continued their walk around the garden, where they met two giggling young maids of honour out by themselves. Anna bade Susanna escort them back to the house, lest Mother Lowe see them and administer a scolding.

When Susanna returned, she was dismayed to see Anna deep in conversation with Meister von Wylich. Her suspicions were aroused. Had he waylaid her there? Or had they planned a secret tryst?

Didn't Anna know that her reputation could be irrevocably tarnished by being alone with him? Was she that innocent? Susanna could not hear what they were saying, but there seemed to be some warm rapport between them. If this came to the ears of the King, or anyone else, for that matter, there could be trouble. Henry had had his second Queen beheaded for infidelity; he would not want another with loose morals. And if Anna got herself sent home, Duke Wilhelm was unlikely to be lenient. Susanna knew she had to put a stop to this. She hastened towards the couple.

Anna seemed slightly discountenanced to see her.

'Thank you, Sir,' she said to Otho von Wylich, as Susanna approached. 'I will consider your request, but I should warn you that there is no place at present for your wife among my ladies.'

Otho bowed. 'Thank you, Madam.'

Almost, Susanna felt relieved; had she not seen Anna's reaction to Master Wylich on that earlier occasion, she would have been completely convinced. 'A good-looking young man that,' she observed as they continued their walk.

'Indeed,' Anna agreed. 'He is a cousin of mine.'

Well, that might explain it. But still Susanna wondered.

They had a marvellous welcome in the English town of Calais, where they were delayed for days, waiting for a favourable wind to take them to England. At least the Channel was at its narrowest here; on a clear day, you could see the white cliffs of Dover across the sea. It would not, please God, be a long crossing.

Susanna took advantage of the lull to work with Anna on her English, and the Lord High Admiral diverted her by teaching her cards, for she was eager to learn how to please King Henry. Susanna cringed when Anna invited the Admiral and the other lords to sup with her. Queens did not ask gentlemen to dine with them in England! But the Admiral was courteous in explaining that, and relented when the Princess told him it was the custom in Kleef. Nevertheless, Susanna noted, he made it clear that he would inform the King of their evening's entertainment.

After Christmas, the wind finally blew up and they boarded the flagship of the great fleet that was to convey Anna to England. The Princess insisted on going out on deck, and there, to Susanna's dismay, struck up a conversation with Mary Stafford, the late Queen Anne's sister. It was no secret at court that Mary had once been the King's mistress, and Susanna, who was obliged to act as interpreter, did not think it fitting that Anna, who had no idea who she was, should be so familiar with her. She wondered what Mistress Stafford was doing here. The last she had heard was that Mary had made a scandalous marriage and been banished from court, some five or six years ago. Then Susanna heard her say that her husband was a soldier in the Calais garrison, and had obtained a place in the King's guard. She would warn Anna later about associating with the woman.

The sudden rolling of the ship made Susanna head for the cabin, all thought of Mary Stafford obliterated. She feared, with mounting dread, that it would be a bad voyage, and she was right. But Anna was brave. She looked green, but she did not complain. For hours, they were tossed by the winds, and Susanna could only lie on her bunk and pray for the torment to end. It was dark before they disembarked at Deal, and by then she had almost resigned herself to dying of seasickness. She had never been so thankful as when she stood again on English soil.

* * *

In slow stages, the Princess's long procession made its stately way through Kent, its ultimate destination the palace of Greenwich, where the King was waiting to welcome his bride. As they drew ever nearer, Susanna could sense Anna growing more tense. How daunting it must be, to be marrying a man you had never seen – and a king at that!

On the last day of the old year, they lodged at the Bishop's Palace in Rochester, where one of his Majesty's richest beds had been made ready for Anna's use. It did not feel like New Year, for there were none of the customary celebrations, but, on the following afternoon, a bull baiting was staged in the courtyard for the Princess's entertainment.

She was standing at her window, absorbed in it, when Sir Anthony Browne, one of the King's gentlemen, was announced. He told her that another gentleman of his Majesty's Privy Chamber would be arriving shortly with a New Year's gift from the King. She thanked him graciously, and turned back to the window.

Susanna was startled when eight gentlemen in marbled coats and hoods entered the chamber; at once, she recognised their leader as the King, who saw her and put a finger to his mouth.

'Madam,' she murmured urgently, 'there are some gentlemen here to see you.'

Reluctantly, Anna turned around, and the men bowed. The King rose and stared at Anna, then he stepped forward, embraced her, and kissed her full on the mouth, as was the English custom on greeting. It had taken Susanna a while to get used to it, but Anna's face was flushed in outrage. Of course, she did not know who he was!

Susanna watched, aghast, as she pulled away, bristling, and glared at the King. But he had turned to take a casket from one of the gentlemen, which he presented to her.

'A New Year's gift from his Majesty, Madam,' he said. When Anna opened the casket Susanna caught a glimpse of gold and precious stones.

'Pray thank his Majesty, Sir,' Anna said coldly. 'Tell him that I will treasure this beautiful jewel always.'

'I will tell his Grace,' the King said. Was he enjoying this? Susanna couldn't tell.

After the briefest of conversations, Anna said, 'Well, Sirs, I wish you a good journey back to Greenwich.' She returned to the window. The King watched her for a moment, his eyes narrowed, then left the room.

'Oh, what a rel—' Anna said as the door closed, but Susanna silenced her with a look, because the gentlemen were still standing there. There was an awkward pause as she stared at them, then the door was flung open. There stood the King, magnificent in royal purple. The gentlemen, and Susanna, fell to their knees.

Susanna felt deeply sorry for Anna; she could understand how humiliated she must be feeling. The look on the Princess's face was one of pure horror. She dropped to her knees, blushing a deep red, looking utterly thunderstruck. But the King seemed unperturbed. Again, he raised and kissed her, and spoke courteously to her, trying to put her at her ease.

Presently, Susanna followed them in to supper, to act as their interpreter and chaperone, sitting unobtrusively by the fire. The conversation was pleasant, and the King did apologise for surprising Anna, who was gulping down her wine rather too fast, but eating little – and looking visibly distressed. She started when he told her they were to be married in three days' time.

It was not a good beginning. Susanna feared that the King might be offended by his bride's evident reluctance, although, to be fair, the Princess never once defaulted in the courtesies due to him. But it was plain, too plain, that she was unhappy.

At the end of the evening, King Henry kissed her hand and bade her goodnight, with great courtesy, but little warmth. As soon as he had gone, she looked helplessly at Susanna, and threw herself into her arms.

'Oh, God!' she cried. 'Oh, God, help me!'

In the morning, Sir Anthony Browne arrived, laden with sumptuous furs.

'These are for your Grace, with his Majesty's compliments.'

Anna thanked him, showing humble gratitude, but at dinner she was again subdued, and the King was less affable, seeming preoccupied and testy, which made her even more nervous.

After dinner, when the King and his gentlemen had gone to make ready for their return to Greenwich, Susanna helped the German maids to pack the Princess's chests, ready for her departure on the morrow.

'Susanna, can you fetch my watch, please?' Anna asked. 'I left it in the dining chamber.'

It was there, on the table, but as Susanna picked it up she heard murmuring in the hall beyond, and saw that the door was slightly ajar. Immediately, she recognised the King's high-pitched tone.

'She is not so young as I expected, nor so beautiful as everyone affirmed.' His tone was plaintive. 'She looks about thirty, although I am assured she is twenty-four. And those German maids! They are inferior in beauty even to their mistress, and their dress is so unbecoming that you would think them ugly even if they were beautiful!'

'I am sorry to see your Grace so disappointed,' a man said, 'and that you mislike her person.'

'I am not contented!' rumbled the King. 'When I saw her for the first time, I was glad I had kept myself free from making any proxy marriage with her till I saw her myself; for I assure you, I liked her so ill, and found her so far contrary to how she was praised, that I regretted that ever she came into England. I have been deliberating with myself how to find some means to break the betrothal. I will never marry her!'

Susanna stifled a gasp. She had been aware of an awkwardness between the King and Anna, but had never dreamed he had conceived such an aversion for his bride. She dared not move, lest he heard her, for he was still ranting.

'I can never love this woman,' he declared. 'She is so different from her portrait. I see nothing in her as men report of her, and I marvel that wise men would make such reports. I like her not! Alas, whom shall men trust? I have been ill-used and deceived! Cromwell got me into this mess, and he must get me out of it! He'll smart for it if he doesn't.' He had worked himself into a rage, and Susanna quaked for Cromwell.

Quickly, she took the watch and tiptoed back to the Princess's lodging, where she found Anna in tears, being comforted by Mother Lowe. Her first thought was that Anna had somehow heard what the King had said, but then Anna asked her what she thought of his Majesty.

Susanna knew she could never repeat the King's words, but she could try to prepare the Princess for the disaster that would inevitably engulf her. 'Forgive me, your Highness, but I thought he played an unkind trick on you, putting you at a disadvantage. At dinner, he seemed to be holding back, and at times, I thought he was angry about something. Maybe some matter of state has displeased him.'

'Maybe it's me,' Anna sighed. 'He came specially to see me, yet he gave no sign that he was pleased with me, nor did he act like an eager bridegroom.'

'He *was* very courteous to you,' Susanna said.

'I was hoping for more than courtesy,' Anna sniffed. 'There has to be some liking, surely, and I'm not sure the King likes me. I know I'm not beautiful, but, in all modesty, I think I am seemly.'

'You are lovely,' Susanna said. 'And beauty is a matter of personal perception.'

Outside the town of Dartford, the household officers and ladies-in-waiting appointed by the King to serve Anna were waiting to receive her, buffeted by icy winds. Archbishop Cranmer and the Duke of Suffolk presented the thirty ladies and maids-of-honour who would from now on be waiting permanently on her, serving alongside her German attendants for the time being.

To her dismay, Susanna had been informed that she would be staying on in the post of gentlewoman, and Anna was pleased about that.

'You shall be the first of my gentlewomen!' she declared. Susanna cringed inwardly, wishing she liked Anna more, and envisaging the long years of servitude ahead – until she remembered what the King had said, and that there might be no marriage after all.

John comforted Susanna, reminding her that Anna loved watching her work, and that she could continue to paint.

'Yes, but I can't accept commissions,' she reminded him. 'Oh, I wish I could just go home!'

Instead, she found herself, as interpreter, riding behind Anna when the Princess descended Shooter's Hill, just outside London, for her formal welcome by the King. Huge crowds turned out for the occasion, as well, it seemed, as the entire nobility of England. King Henry played his part to perfection – you would never have guessed that he was planning to abandon his bride – and Anna conducted herself with grace and dignity.

Later, when the Princess had rested in her sumptuous apartments in Greenwich Palace, she unburdened herself to Susanna.

'I do not think I can ever love him,' she whispered. 'I am dreading my wedding night more than I can say.'

'There is nothing to fear,' Susanna said. 'There might be some pain at first, but it soon passes.'

Anna said nothing, and Susanna wondered if there was something more that was troubling her. What if she had been intimate with Otho von Wylich? That would be reason indeed to dread bedding with the King!

'All will be well, I am sure,' she said. She was about to say that Anna could confide any secret to her without fear of betrayal, but just then the English ladies came bustling in, and she never finished the sentence. Anna looked at her questioningly, but Susanna shook her head and smiled, glad that the moment had passed, for if Anna had confided some past misconduct or present dalliance, she would have been bound to tell the King.

6 January, 1540

Susanna was astonished when the King went through with the marriage. She could only conclude that he had come to terms with it, or found no way out. During the festivities that followed the early-morning ceremony, the new Queen bore herself handsomely with every eye upon her. Watching her dancing with the King, Susanna hoped that all would go well for her. She was a nice woman, and deserved to be happy.

When the dancing had ended, the King murmured something in Anna's ear. Susanna saw her flush as he signalled to Mother Lowe. 'Have the ladies attend the Queen to bed,' he commanded and stood up, bowing to Anna. The dancers halted, and everyone made low obeisances.

'Madam, I will see you presently,' he said, bowing. Followed by his lords and gentlemen, who were smirking and nudging each other, he departed.

When the King and Queen had been put to bed, the bed had been blessed and the guests had departed, Susanna and Mother Lowe returned to the hall, where they sat over their wine cups with some of the Queen's English ladies.

Lady Rochford was rather drunk. Susanna had heard unsavoury things about her, and it was well known that she had accused her own husband of incest with his sister, Queen Anne, for which he had lost his head.

'I thought the King seemed tense tonight,' Lady Baynton said.

'As well he might,' Lady Rochford replied. She leaned towards the others and lowered her voice. 'Queen Anne told my lord that he lacked vigour; he can be useless with a woman.'

Susanna bristled. 'Then how did he get a son on Queen Jane?'

Lady Rochford shrugged. 'I think he manages on occasion.'

Susanna turned away. Such talk was dangerous, and it was disrespectful.

The next morning, Mother Lowe told Susanna that Anne was tearful, as the King had not consummated the marriage.

'She was worrying that she'd offended him in some way. I told her what Lady Rochford said last night, and she felt better after that. I said that drink can also do that to a man, especially when he has much pain from a bad leg.'

The next day, Anna emerged from seclusion and walked in Greenwich Park with Susanna and her English ladies. They met, by chance, a party of her German gentlemen, among whom was Otho von Wylich, and Susanna, watching keenly, was aware of the Queen's face lighting up at the sight of him.

Should she warn her not to show her liking so openly? If she,

233

Susanna, could see it, others could too — and it was death to betray the King!

She was uncomfortably aware that her first loyalty was to the King, who had commissioned her to be his eyes and ears in Kleef; but she owed some loyalty to Anna too. For her sake alone, she could not allow this to go on. If it happened again, she resolved, she would say something.

When Susanna returned to the palace, a royal usher informed her that the King wished to see her. She followed him in trepidation, her heart like lead, her suspicions preying on her mind. Had he suspicions himself? Was he about to berate her for her failure to warn him? But when she was shown into the closet he used as a study, his Grace was most affable.

'Be seated, Mistress Gilman,' he bade her. 'I trust you enjoyed your time in Cleves.'

'I did, your Majesty,' she said, 'but it is good to be back in England.'

'I was grateful for your reports,' he said, fixing her with those piercing blue eyes. 'It did seem that there was no cause for concern. But now, alas, there is. What I wish to discuss is in the strictest confidence, do you understand?'

'I hope you know that you can trust me, Sir.'

He leaned back in his chair. 'Mistress Gilman, I am king enough to know that I must marry for the good of my realm. Yet, for the sake of ensuring the royal succession, it must be to a lady I can love. Do you take my meaning?'

'I do, Sir.'

He sighed. 'I find the Queen nowhere near as beautiful as I was told, and if I had known as much beforehand as I know now, I would not have married her. But it seems there is no remedy. My Lord Cromwell tells me so.' He sounded furious with Cromwell, and small wonder, for it was no secret that the minister had negotiated the marriage.

Susanna wondered what she was supposed to do to help.

'But,' the King continued, frowning, 'if I alienate the Germans, I will stand alone without allies, with France and the Empire hostile towards me. And if I reject the Queen and send her home, her brother might make war on me. But my nature abhors her!'

'Sir, if I might be so bold as to venture an opinion,' Susanna said, 'the Queen has done nothing wrong, so it would be wise to find some good and sound pretext for putting her away.'

The blue eyes narrowed. '*Has* she done nothing wrong? I have good reason to mistrust her virginity. Mistress Gilman, I have felt her belly and her breasts, and I can judge by their looseness and other tokens that she is no maid. It was this that so struck me to the heart that I had neither will nor courage to proceed any further.'

Susanna was taken aback, as much by his frankness as by what he was telling her, which resonated with her own suspicions. He had been married three times; he must know what he was talking about.

'Your Grace, I know not what these tokens might be,' she said.

'That is because you have not borne children,' he told her, at which she marvelled at the strangeness of this conversation; never had she dreamed that she would discuss such an intimate subject with the King.

'They are proof of her having been with child at some stage,' he said. 'Proof of dishonest and loose living.'

'But how, Sir? It's hard to imagine that she ever had the opportunity, for she has been brought up strictly at her mother's elbow.'

'Lusty swains will ever find a way,' he said, with a grimace. 'That is why women are to be ordered by men. In this case, someone was clearly negligent.'

Susanna thought she knew who the culprit might be. A cousin. Someone who might be considered safe company. But she dared not say anything, because the consequences for Anna could be terrible.

'If there was a child, Sir, where is it?' she asked, shaking her head.

'There are ways of concealing these things,' he told her. 'I keep thinking about that time she was away from court for months. Was her mystery illness a pregnancy?' She could see he had convinced himself, and she was close to believing it too.

'Yet what remedy have I?' the King asked. 'I could ask for her to be examined by a panel of matrons, but think of her brother's reaction! And a lack of virginity is no grounds for annulling a marriage.'

'How can I help, Sir?' Susanna asked, still wondering where she came into this.

'You can talk to her. You've gained her confidence; she loves you. See what you can find out. Mrs Gilman, I need a reason to set her aside. My ministers can only do so much. You can learn her heart, her mind, her inmost thoughts – her secrets.'

Susanna could have told him that Anna too would probably leap at the chance of her marriage being annulled. 'I think she will be ready to please your Grace and ease any doubts you have,' she said carefully, 'whatever it takes.'

'If it became known how I have been deceived,' he said, 'the way would be smoothed. No one would blame me for not consummating the marriage. I could be set free.'

For some days, Susanna went about with a heavy heart, feeling the burden of the impossible task the King had laid upon her. She had no idea how she was going to go about it. What could she say to Anna?

Did your Grace ever have a lover?

Has your Grace ever borne a child?

No! She needed something far more subtle, but she could not think of anything that wasn't intrusive or insulting.

She became aware that the courtiers were now whispering about the King's failure to consummate his marriage. So the matter had become common knowledge. It was even being said that the King thought himself able to do the marriage act with others, but not with the Queen. He had never even taken off his nightshirt, giggled the gossips.

It was as well that Anna spent most of her time in the seclusion of her apartments. Susanna hoped that she was unaware of what was being said, and did not realise that people were looking at her speculatively, perhaps conjecturing why her body was such that the King shrank from making love to her. How dreadfully humiliating it would be to hear such things. Yet Anna gave no sign that she was aware of the gossip, and the pretence was maintained that all was well between her and the King.

Susanna was aware that he came to Anna's bedchamber each night.

She wanted to shake her mistress, for she had no idea how to flirt or entice a man. Susanna wondered afresh if the King had been wrong about her past, and had mistaken the signs on Anna's body, for she seemed so naïve. Of course, naïvety could have played its part in her fall from grace. It was all too easy to imagine an innocent young princess being taken advantage of by some unscrupulous seducer – possibly one she had known and trusted.

And still Susanna had not dared broach the matter with her. Daily, she lived in fear that the King would summon her again and ask if she had discovered what he needed to know. And all the while, the court was abuzz with gossip. It was only a matter of time before the Queen heard it.

Susanna felt she should say something. It was better coming from her than Anna overhearing malicious tongues.

'Oh, Madam,' she said, dropping to her knees before her mistress one day, when she could bear the tension no longer. 'I hardly know how to tell you what people are saying in the court, but you should know. I only wish I wasn't the one to have to tell you.'

'*What* are they saying?' Anna cried.

Susanna swallowed. 'They are saying – forgive me, Madam – that the King has said he will never have any more children for the comfort of the realm, for, although he is able to do the act of procreation with others, he cannot do it with you. Some are saying he is impotent, but most – most of those I overheard think that the fault lies with your Grace.'

She had never seen Anna look so angry; she had not thought she had it in her.

'It lies with him!' Anna cried, unable to stop herself. 'I had resolved never to speak to any of his inability to consummate our marriage, yet now, it appears, he has blazoned it to all *and* laid the blame at my feet. And he thinks himself a man of honour! How dare he make me the scapegoat for his own inadequacy!'

Susanna was stunned. 'Madam, I had no idea . . .'

Anna was beside herself. 'No wonder people have been staring at me! Are they wondering what horrors are concealed under my royal robes, and what is so awful about me that the King cannot bring himself to make love to me? It is horrible, and utterly humiliating! How will I ever show my face outside my apartments again?'

'Madam, please calm yourself . . .'

'How can I? Something must be done to stop this scurrilous talk! Summon Lord Cromwell, now, at once!' the Queen commanded.

But Lord Cromwell didn't come. He sent his excuses.

The weeks were passing, and still the royal marriage remained unconsummated – and still Susanna had not pressed the Queen about what the King had said. Yet she must, *she must*, if she was to retain his favour.

She tried to approach the matter in a roundabout way. One March day, as they took a stroll in the Queen's garden, she sniffed the air and said, 'Oh, the coming of spring brings back memories of youth!'

Anna took her hand. 'It was a happy time for you?'

Susanna nodded. 'Very happy, Madam. My father was busy running the workshop, and my mother had long since given up hope of my learning the domestic virtues. I had a lot of freedom – but I did not use it well!' That was not strictly true, but she hoped it would prompt confidences.

'I cannot imagine you getting up to mischief,' Anna smiled.

'I assure your Grace I did. There were young men who pursued me, and I encouraged them. Oh, the thrill of it!'

Was she imagining it, or had a wariness come into Anna's eyes?

'I expect your Grace was too closely guarded to have such adventures,' she ventured.

Anna frowned. 'I trust you did not compromise yourself?'

'No, it was all innocent love play. But it could have got more serious. Thank Heaven it didn't! Did not your Grace ever love anyone before the King?'

Anna stared at her. 'Of course not. How could I? I had no opportunity. And it would not have been allowed.'

'Of course,' Susanna said, aware that she was overstepping the bounds of what was proper – yet the King was waiting for answers. 'But did you ever admire a young man from afar? I have seen some handsome German gentlemen in your train. There is a fair-haired one who is particularly charming.'

'I was taught custody of the eyes,' the Queen said coldly, 'like a nun. You do not let them look where they should not. And I do not know which gentleman you are referring to.'

Anna had never been so terse with her. Susanna knew she had gone too far. But at least she could tell the King what his wife had said.

They walked on in silence. Thereafter, although Anna remained friendly, Susanna sensed that a distance had opened up between them. And when the new ambassador of Kleef arrived at court and befriended the Queen, she felt herself ousted as a confidante.

She was not the only one in Anna's household who noticed that the King was paying court to one of the English maids-of-honour, Mistress Katheryn Howard, a pretty girl with a sweet nature. It had been going on for a month, and there was much speculation in the court as to whether Katheryn would surrender her virtue, or whether King Henry was bent on a new marriage. He and the Queen were now living virtually apart, aside from his observing the courtesies and dining with her, or having her at his side on the rare occasions protocol called for it. He stopped summoning Susanna and asking for information, and it was not hard to guess why. Most people thought it would be only a matter of time before he divorced the Queen. Yet Anna carried on as if all was well – until one night in May, when she asked Mother Lowe and Susanna to help her prepare for bed.

'I did not want my English ladies to be present,' she said, as soon as they were alone, turning to them with a worried face. 'What do you know of Katheryn Howard?'

Susanna blenched inwardly. 'She is a niece of the Duke of Norfolk,' she said. 'This is her first post at court, secured by her uncle, no doubt.'

'How old is she?' Anna asked.

'Twenty,' Mother Lowe replied. 'Poor as a peasant. Her father died last year, and she has no fortune.'

'I don't think she has much education,' Susanna added, beginning to unplait Anna's hair. 'But I like her. She's a good, honest girl, and very kind.'

'Why are you asking about her, Anna?' Mother Lowe wanted to know.

Anna sat down and they began to remove her shoes and stockings. 'It occurred to me that I have never paid her very much attention, and that I ought to know more about her. I am surprised that the Howards have not found her a husband.'

Susanna rather feared that they had. And that the Queen knew nothing about the King's interest in her maid-of-honour.

Gossip about the Queen became yesterday's news in June, when the court learned that Cromwell had been arrested on charges of treason and heresy. Susanna was not surprised. Like most people, she believed it was the Kleef marriage that had done for him. It was a dangerous matter, dabbling in the marriages of princes.

On the day Parliament condemned Cromwell to death, she came upon the Queen staring intently out of a window overlooking the gardens. Anna turned and beckoned Susanna to follow her into her closet.

'My good friend, tell me truly,' she said, 'has the King cast his fancy on Katheryn Howard?'

Susanna hesitated, but she knew her face had already given her away. 'There was gossip back in April,' she admitted. 'We did not want to upset you, as you had enough to contend with.'

'Who knew?' Anna asked, hurt turning to anger that anyone should have kept this from her.

'Nearly all your ladies, Madam.' Susanna feared to meet Anna's eye. 'We were hoping it was just a passing fancy.'

'From what I've just seen, and the time it has being going on, that is unlikely,' Anna snapped. 'Tell me what you know.'

Susanna felt very uncomfortable. 'Kate Carey overheard Katheryn boasting to the Duchess of Richmond that the King had made her a grant of land. This was some weeks ago, when first we came to Whitehall. He has given her jewels too; she told Lady Rochford, and

Lady Rochford – well, you know how she enjoys stirring things up – said she'd perceived his Grace was marvellously set on her, more than he had been on any woman in his life.'

'Are they lovers?' the Queen whispered.

Susanna swallowed. 'She hinted to Lady Rochford that he was laying siege to her virtue, as Lady Rochford took great pleasure in telling us, but she said she would not stain her family's honour by granting him favours. Madam, it is the same game Anne Boleyn played, and look where it got *her*.'

'It got her beheaded,' Anna cried, pacing up and down. 'These Howards, they are behind this. I know it.'

Susanna spread her hands helplessly. 'I fear you are right. I heard someone say in the court that Katheryn was alienating the King's affections from you.'

Anna glared at her. 'Who knows about this affair?' she asked sharply.

'I think it is common knowledge, Madam,' Susanna confessed.

'I will not have gossip about it in my household,' Anna declared. 'Will you make that clear, that I do not approve of it?'

'Yes, Madam,' Susanna said, dropping a curtsey as if they were on the most formal of terms, and feeling like a worm. She saw that there were tears in Anna's eyes.

'You may go,' Anna said, her tone hostile.

Susanna left, feeling as if her betrayal of her mistress was as bad as Katheryn Howard's – and knowing that she had lost a friend. For Anna, she admitted honestly, it was no great loss, for she had been a poor friend to her. She had spied on her and discussed her intimately with the King; she had kept from her important things she should have told her. And now that Anna was angry with her, and hurt, she realised that she should have valued that friendship while she could. What sort of friend kept something so vital to herself? She did not deserve Anna's kindness; she had never deserved it.

She did her best to win back Anna's confidence. She showed herself the most willing of all to perform the most mundane tasks; she took the

Queen's part in every issue; she tried to make her smile or engage in the kind of easy conversation they had once shared.

Susanna warned her not to listen to gossip. 'Pay no heed, Madam,' she said, 'it is just malicious talk. You do not need to hear what people are saying.'

'Yes, I do!' Anna flared. 'You kept too much from me before.'

Susanna fell silent. It seemed that she was not to be forgiven.

In bed with John at night, she wept with remorse. 'I have betrayed the kindest mistress who ever lived,' she sobbed.

'Now you are being dramatic,' he soothed. 'She will come round, you'll see.'

But she did not. When it was announced, in July, that the King's marriage had been dissolved, the news came as a shock to Susanna, for by then she had been consigned to the fringes of the Queen's circle. She soon discovered that other ladies had been taken into Anna's confidence, and knew she had been left out in the cold.

On the day the Queen's household was broken up, and all who had served her stood in line to say farewell, Susanna prayed that, on parting, Anna would show her some kindness and leave the door open to rebuilding their friendship. But when her turn came, and she searched the Queen's face for any sign of affection or regret, Anna merely inclined her head, and Susanna had perforce to walk away.

Had she hoped for a place in Anna's new establishment? Her mistress was now the King's dearest sister, with palaces of her own and a great income, but clearly she did not want Susanna in her life. The door was firmly closed to her.

What saved Susanna from guilt and despair was the growing certainty that she was with child. Her first son was born that Christmas, in the fine house John had taken for them at Twickenham, and the King himself stood godfather at the font, a signal honour. Beside him, all smiles, and cooing over the baby, stood his new Queen, Katheryn Howard. He had married her in the summer, on the very day Cromwell was beheaded.

Young Harry was barely out of leading reins when his sister arrived.

Susanna insisted on calling her Anne, in honour of her former mistress, but her letter to Anna announcing the birth went unanswered.

As soon as her children were weaned, Susanna engaged a nurse and took up her painting again. When John was appointed Gentleman Harbinger to the King, she went sometimes to court with him. By then, King Henry was married to his sixth wife, Katharine Parr, who showed an interest in Susanna's painting. Again, Susanna found herself pressed into serving a queen, but this Queen had enlightened views, and did not see why royal service should preclude an artist from working. Indeed, she patronised several painters, including another Flemish lady, Levina Teerlinc. Levina was ten years younger than Susanna, and there might have been rivalry between them, but Susanna liked the young woman, and knew herself to be the better painter. Levina somehow managed to make all her sitters look wizened, with stick-thin arms and bulbous features. For all that, both the King and Queen liked her work, and she was paid a salary.

It was more than Susanna got, but she had little time for painting now. With the demands of royal service and the children, her days were full. Her father had died in 1541, and Lucas had taken over his workshop, so commissions had come Susanna's way, but Lucas himself was now dead, as was Holbein, and a new generation of painters was rising at court. Susanna had wound up the workshop, disposed of the remaining works, and tried not to think back to the days when they were all working there, enjoying their sudden success and filling their days creating tiny masterpieces.

The old King died too, and Queen Katharine retired from court. Susanna went home to Twickenham. She wished she had in her the impetus to paint again, but inspiration seemed to have deserted her. She wondered what the Princess Anna was doing now. She had seen her at court from time to time in King Henry's last years, and been glad to see how well she and his Grace got on. They had become friends, despite everything.

Susanna had attempted to see the Princess on those occasions, hoping to be reconciled to her. But Anna was never to be found when she went looking for her. She did not blame her for eluding her. Anna's sense of betrayal must be as painful as her own sense of guilt. Yet there came a day when Susanna came face to face with her in a gallery, each going in the opposite direction – and Anna smiled. It was the balm Susanna had been seeking. They exchanged a few words, asking how the other was keeping, and then it was time for Susanna go – she had one of her rare sittings. She walked away on wings; they would be friends again. It was clear that Anna had forgiven and forgotten – and she seemed so much happier these days.

She never saw Anna again. For now there was a boy king on the throne, and no place for ladies at court. Anna had her own life elsewhere, and Susanna and John were preoccupied with wresting some of her first husband's estate from his heirs, which proved a lengthy and stressful business.

When Queen Mary ascended the throne in 1553, Susanna was fifty. She received her invitation to serve as a gentlewoman of the Privy Chamber to the Queen with mixed feelings. Part of her wanted to go to court again and be at the centre of things; the other part longed to stay at home with John and her growing family, for she knew herself to be unwell, and feared that her sickness was mortal. She had not told anyone about the pain in her womb, or the unnatural bleeding, but it was getting worse, and she knew she could not conceal it much longer.

John and their children must come first. With a heavy heart, she wrote to the Queen, thanking her for her good favour, and declining the post, confiding to her Majesty that her poor health prevented her from accepting.

She felt better after that, in every sense, and decided to accompany John on his next journey out of London. He made these trips from time to time, to deliver consignments of wine to merchants in provincial towns, and negotiate new sales, and this time he was going to Warwick and Stratford and Worcester.

The journey by jolting horse-litter was uncomfortable, for the roads were bad. It took a week to get to Worcester, and when they arrived, Susanna knew she could not go on. She pressed her hands to her womb and felt the hard lump.

'Husband, I am not well,' she breathed. John directed his groom to pull to the side of the road, and helped her out. She was almost bent double with the pain. They were by the entrance to the great cathedral, and John half carried her into the shelter of the porch, and thence to a bench in the nave.

'Twenty years ago, when this was a priory, they would have had an infirmarian,' he said, gazing down at her anxiously. 'I wonder if this man will know where I can find a physician.' He got up and spoke to an approaching canon. 'My wife is ill, good father. Is there a doctor nearby?'

But Susanna knew there would be no need for a doctor. John and the canon were a blur. The pain gripped her, more violently than ever before, taking her breath away. And there was a dove, coming towards her through the stream of light that shone from the great glittering windows at the far end of the nave.

Author's Note

I have based Susanna's story on the sparse records documenting her life. She did serve Anna of Kleve, and there has been some speculation that she was sent to Kleve as a spy. The story that unfolds from that, in my novella, is fiction.

She may have painted Henry VIII, but none of his portraits can be safely attributed to her.

We don't know when Susanna died, but she was dead before 1554, when John Gilman married his third wife. One account places Susanna's death in Worcester.

No known example of her work survives.

KATHERYN HOWARD

Timeline

1520–1
- Probable birthdate of Katheryn Howard

1533
- Marriage of Henry VIII and Anne Boleyn
- Coronation of Anne Boleyn (June)
- Birth of the Princess Elizabeth, daughter of Henry VIII and Anne Boleyn

1536
- Execution of Anne Boleyn
- Marriage of Henry VIII and Jane Seymour

1537
- Birth of Prince Edward, son of Henry VIII and Jane Seymour
- Death of Jane Seymour
- Katheryn Howard has an affair with Henry Manox

1538
- Katheryn Howard starts an affair with Francis Dereham

1539
- Henry VIII betrothed to Anna of Kleve
- Katheryn Howard appointed a maid-of-honour to Anna of Kleve

1540
- Marriage of Henry VIII and Anna of Kleve (6 January)
- Thomas Culpeper begins courting Katheryn Howard (spring)
- Henry VIII begins courting Katheryn Howard (April)
- Annulment of Henry VIII's marriage to Anna of Kleve (12 July)
- Execution of Thomas Cromwell (28 July)
- Marriage of Henry VIII and Katheryn Howard (28 July)

1541
- Thomas Culpeper resumes his courtship of Katheryn Howard (spring)
- Execution of Margaret Pole, Countess of Salisbury (27 May)
- Fall of Katheryn Howard (November)
- Dereham and Culpeper tried and condemned to death at the Guildhall (1 December)

- Dereham and Culpeper executed at Tyburn (10 December)

1542
- Royal assent given to the Act of Attainder condemning Katheryn Howard and Lady Rochford to death (9 February)
- Executions of Katheryn Howard and Lady Rochford (13 February)

THE
PRINCESS
OF
SCOTLAND

Margaret Douglas

Sometimes, I am amazed at how Fate has brought me to my twenty-seventh year. I have seen the rise and fall of queens and the temper and fury of kings, and have been a whisper from both the throne of England and the executioner's block . . .

As far back as I can remember, my Englishness was impressed upon me. My mother might have been queen of Scots and then the wife of a Scots nobleman, but she never forgot that she was first and foremost an English princess – and a Tudor one at that.

It was only chance that saw me born an English subject, just over the border in Northumberland, even though my father was Scots and a Douglas, which was almost as important as being royal. To Mother, though, our royal English blood was paramount. Born the eldest daughter of King Henry VII of England, she was thirteen when, to cement a peace, she was married to James IV, King of Scots. She had loved him, for all his lechery, and given him six children, though only my half-brother James survived infancy.

Mother liked to talk about her younger days, but she could barely bring herself to speak of the great battle that changed everything. Two years before my birth, King James was slain on the battlefield of Flodden, alongside the flower of the Scottish nobility. It was a terrible defeat for Scotland and a great victory for the English, and it left Scotland under the rule of my brother James V, a toddler in leading reins. Though the great lords were all hungry for power, my mother was named regent of Scotland during the minority of her son and awarded the guardianship of the young King. Her rule began well, until she became entangled with the Douglas clan and, in particular, with the Earl of Angus, my father, and secretly married him. It was not a politic marriage, but one based on lust, which very quickly burned out, and the secret was not kept for long. Then there was a mighty outcry indeed!

We Douglases can trace our ancestry back to the Emperor Charlemagne and the Sir James Douglas who carried King Robert the Bruce's heart to the Holy Land. We honour his memory with a crowned heart in our coat of arms. They say we are a violent clan, but we're a proud one too, even if few of my ancestors died in their beds. My father was no different, and he had charm and audacity in equal portions. My parents' marriage excited the jealousy of the Scottish nobles. They suspected Father – and with good reason – of planning to usurp the regency and rule Scotland. The country was divided and, as civil war broke out, my mother was ousted from office and locked up. Fearful for her life, she escaped into England and the protection of her brother, my uncle, King Henry VIII; she was so far gone in pregnancy that it's a wonder I wasn't born in the saddle.

Apparently, I wasn't expected to live, but thrive I did. 'You were a fair young lady,' Mother was fond of saying. As soon as I was old enough to understand about kings and queens and kingdoms, she never ceased reminding me that I was third in line to the English throne, King Henry having but the one daughter, Mary, and my mother herself being his next heir.

King Henry was very angry that Mother had been driven from Scotland and invited her south to London. But Father refused to go with her. He wanted to make peace with the lords and get his lands back, for they had been seized in the fighting.

'He never even took leave of me,' Mother recalled. 'He just rode away. You may imagine how aggrieved I felt – I, who had loved him!'

Of course, I was far too young to be aware at the time of the clouds that would overshadow my childhood. I do not remember our sojourn in England, although we were there for about a year and King Henry and Queen Katherine apparently made much of me. Mother had summoned her old nurse to look after me, which left her free to plan her triumphant return to Scotland as regent.

I was not two years old when I stepped on Scottish soil for the first time, near Berwick. Father was waiting to greet us, but it was clear, Mother recalled later, that he was there under sufferance. Nonetheless, they were reconciled. But, on arrival in Edinburgh, it was made clear to my mother that she would not be allowed a share in the government or access to the young King James.

For years, she fought to regain power and custody of her son, but in vain. Even Uncle Henry let her down, signing a truce with the Scots lords without insisting on redress for the wrongs she had suffered. There was no money, for the lords withheld her revenues.

Throughout this time, I saw relatively little of Mother, for she was preoccupied with these political affairs and wrangling for what she believed to be her due entitlements. I was looked after by nurses and servants, yet she did make time to tell me all about her illustrious past and her grievances and her difficulties. She could not hide the fact that she was more devoted to King James than to me, even though I was with her, and she was not allowed even to see my brother. But I suppose it was understandable. I grew up believing that a mother must naturally look chiefly to the interests of her sons and that daughters were relatively unimportant. I did feel some pangs of jealousy, and resentment against James, but I hardly knew him and there was never a close bond between us.

For all Mother's grumbles about poverty, I was brought up as a princess. We moved from palace to palace, like a small court. Scots was my first language, although Mother did teach me English. I was trained to virtue and grace, to obedience, truth and the fear of God. I tried very hard to do good and learn wisdom. And I suppose I was content – for a time.

I was five when Mother found out that Father had a mistress. There were vicious quarrels, which I heard all too clearly on occasion.

In her anguish and jealousy, Mother did not spare me. 'Your father has done me much evil!' she said to me, young as I was. 'I am minded to part with him, for I know well he loves me not, as he shows me daily!' I ended up feeling disloyal for just loving my Father, as the Commandments enjoined; and then I felt disloyal for thinking ill of him. I was cruelly torn. Looking back, I think I should have been protected from it all. But my parents were too far gone in hatred and acrimony to wonder about the effect their quarrels were having on me.

The Douglases, of course, sided with Father, and when Mother finally did leave him that December, Uncle Henry sided with him too, thinking it outrageous for a woman to desert her husband. But it was a relief to me that they were apart, even though I had to live with my mother's anger and bitterness. It is hardly surprising that I grew up with a jaundiced opinion of my father. And, really, he deserved it, for he seized her property and appropriated her revenues, obliging us to live a poor existence in Edinburgh.

'I will never allow him any share in the regency when I get it back!' Mother thundered, as if the regency was almost within her grasp, which it wasn't. Then she began to talk of divorce. She had to explain to me what that was. 'I have grounds!' she declared. 'My marriage is bigamous because King James was still alive when we wed.' Even I knew that to be a lie.

When Father continued to trespass on Mother's property, she allied herself with his enemies. He complained she had deserted him; she pretended she was having a love affair with the Regent, the Duke of Albany. Maybe she was behind Albany's attempt to arrest Father for treason, although, when he was sentenced to death in his absence, she did plead for his life and have his sentence commuted to exile. Father went to France and thence to England, where my uncle granted him asylum. Of course, he wanted something in return, and that was Father's agreement to form a party friendly to the English in Scotland.

I was nine when Albany was overthrown and Mother was made regent again. That was the state of affairs when Father returned to Scotland that year. Mother would have nothing to do with him; she believed he had been turned by the English and was now spying for them. She also feared he might snatch me from her. By then, she had fallen for the charms of Harry Stewart, a young, ambitious man eleven years her junior. Young as I was, I understood what adultery was, and shrank, humiliated, from the scandal. In truth, Mother was so blinded with folly that she didn't care.

Father was still involved with his mistress – talk about the pot and kettle – but he hated Harry Stewart and was outraged that I was being exposed to such an undesirable and immoral influence. More to the point, he wanted the regency. He stormed into Edinburgh, intending to force his way into Parliament – and take me away – but Mother ordered her soldiers to open fire on him, so he fled to his stronghold of Tantallon on the east coast and proceeded to rally many lords to his side.

I was torn. I was aware that Mother and Henry Stewart were doing their best to poison my mind against Father. Half of me was glad when Father staged a coup, occupying Edinburgh, summoning Parliament and seizing control of King James, who, having been under Mother's influence, regarded Father as something akin to the Antichrist. But, now that Father was in power, Mother was forced to establish a fragile accord with him – if only for James's sake. In private, however, she was still badgering him for a divorce.

Worn down, he agreed, and Mother petitioned the Pope on the grounds that, before their marriage, Father had entered into a precontract with his mistress.

'I have urged his Holiness to consider that I was ignorant of that and that neither you nor I should suffer any loss or damage,' she told me, greatly agitated.

'What loss or damage?' I asked, bewildered.

She put an arm around me, a rare gesture of affection. 'Often, when a marriage is annulled, the children are declared bastards; but if it was made in good faith, its issue can be deemed legitimate. Margaret, I entered into this marriage in good faith. You are trueborn, never doubt it!'

I only hoped that the Pope would agree. I knew how shameful it was to be a bastard, and how the word could be used abusively.

I was eleven when the Pope granted Mother's petition for an annulment. Heeding her wishes, he added a special declaration that I was legitimate and ought not to be disinherited. But still I became aware of gossip that told me I was openly reputed a bastard in Scotland; it was even said that King James spoke of me as his base sister, which I found, to my hurt, was the truth. As I never saw him, I could not take the insufferable little prig to task for it. So I held my head up. Such things were said covertly, never to my face. No one would have dared, for Father now enjoyed great power in Scotland; he even made himself Lord High Chancellor. Mother was lying low, muttering about how he was keeping my brother James a virtual prisoner, diverting him with women and dice from learning his kingly duties. But the Douglases were now supreme, and no one would say a word against them.

Then Mother revealed that she had secretly married Harry Stewart. No one was more furious than my uncle, King Henry, although I felt he was being somewhat hypocritical, given that he was then trying to divorce Queen Katherine so that he could marry Anne Boleyn. Yet I could not think too harshly of him since, at base, he was trying to protect my interests. I was, after all, still third in line to the English throne – second, if you counted the fact that no one in England would have wanted my tempestuous mother as queen. To my uncle, I was an innocent victim. He urged Mother to reconcile herself to Father, if she wanted to avoid eternal damnation as an adulterer. She should do this for my sake, he thundered, out of the natural love, tender pity and motherly kindness she should feel towards me. There was more in his letter about my beauty and my virtues mollifying a heart of steel, still less a maternal one, the implication being that Mother's heart was forged in that fashion and was anything but maternal.

Even the gentle Queen Katherine wrote and sorrowfully reminded my mother that she had committed the great sin of disparaging my legitimacy. Mother wrote back tersely that she had married Father in good faith, so that could not be in question.

Father had no time for legal niceties. I was nearly twelve when he came to our house in Edinburgh one day and demanded that I leave with him immediately.

'Your mother is not fit to have custody of you,' he grimaced.

Mother flew at him. 'And you are, rutting with your mistress as you do?'

He would not deign to answer that. He waited while my nurse packed my gear and put on my warm cloak. Mother was shrieking and swearing, but he heeded her not, and I shrank into a corner, just wanting it to end. I was not averse to going to live with Father. I was tired of Mother's tirades and her complaints about us being poor. I knew I would have a better life with Father. He, at least, was cheerful company.

'As your father and a peer of the realm, I have every right to have custody of you, child,' he said, as we rode up to Edinburgh Castle. 'Regrettably, your mother is a bad moral influence.'

I was too young to have to confront moral issues. It was hard for me to have to choose between my parents. I did miss Mother, more than I had expected, but I was even more upset that she made little effort to get me back. But, after witnessing one too many scenes between her and Father, I was grateful to be able to lead a more stable life – for a time, at least.

Father sent me to live at Tantallon Castle, his magnificent and forbidding fortress of red stone, spectacularly situated high on a rocky headland overlooking the sea. It was a Douglas stronghold, of course, built to withstand attacks by armies. Father placed me there to prevent Mother and her supporters spiriting me away. The sea was on one side, the ramparts and a huge ditch on the other. It was impregnable.

My rooms were in the Douglas Tower, which was seven storeys high. I loved to stand on the battlements and look far into the distance, imagining that I could see mermaids and sea monsters. Father saw to it that I had every comfort and was honourably housed and looked after, whatever my brother James said later about his not treating me as my birth merited. I did not see much of Father at first because he was often in Edinburgh, much occupied with ruling Scotland, but his influence was everywhere. He wanted me to grow up a true Douglas, rather than an English Tudor. Later, when we were thrown together more, an enduring bond was forged between us. Hurt by my mother's indifference, I turned to him. He was protective towards me and affectionate. He often told me I was the woman he loved most in all the world.

I had been at Tantallon for just a few months when, soon after his sixteenth birthday, James declared himself of age and asserted his royal authority as king. The first thing he did was throw off the constraints imposed on him by Father, which he found hateful, and escape to our mother at Stirling Castle. Before long, he had toppled Father from the regency and forbidden him and the Douglases, whom he loathed and feared, to come within seven miles of his royal person. Then he began ruling by the advice of Mother and Harry Stewart, whom he created Lord Methven.

Father came to Tantallon, seething yet willing to retire peacefully from politics, but James tried to force him and all the Douglases into exile. When they stayed firmly put, he threatened them with imprisonment. Father retaliated by refortifying Tantallon against attack by the royal forces. It was a tense time, but we both felt safe in the castle. It has long been said that to 'ding doon' Tantallon Castle is to achieve the impossible. Even so, the storm clouds gathered over our heads. James had Father attainted as a traitor, sentenced to lose his life and forfeit his property to the Crown. The same sentence was passed on my uncle, George Douglas, and Father's cousin, Archibald Douglas of Kilspindie. They both fled into exile. Father stayed where he was, but he was a marked man and so feared capture or assassination that he had his loyal lords keep watch, in full armour, at his chamber door each night.

Kilspindie's wife, Isobel Hoppar, sought refuge at Tantallon. Father appointed her my lady-in-waiting, for I was now thirteen and quite the great lady. She also served me as governess. Isobel was a strong, outspoken lady who had once enjoyed influence in high places. Cousin Archibald must have been in awe of her, as was Father. She was not a woman to be trifled with. Some thought her proud and haughty, but I liked her. She did a lot for me, ensuring that I was well educated. She encouraged me in my letters and inspired in me a love of verse. One day, I told myself, I would be a strong-minded, fearless lady in her mould.

As well as my lessons, I was learning what it meant to be in opposition to the King. When James besieged Tantallon in the summer of 1528, Father held it effortlessly. We heard that heralds had been galloping through the Scottish Borders, proclaiming that the King was offering a reward to anyone who could return his base sister – me! – to our mother, who could provide me with an establishment suitable to my rank. By then, I had no wish to return to her. I had girlish hopes of marrying one of the lords who had visited Father at Tantallon in his glory days, the Earl of Bothwell, who was sixteen, fair-haired and handsome, but Father's agents had warned that Mother meant to wed me to Harry Stewart's younger brother. I had no intention of letting that happen, and Father was incensed, especially when he found out that Mother meant to secure for her brother-in-law the confiscated estates of the earldom of Angus.

The Earl of Bothwell was – I was certain – a far better match. But this was no time for romancing. Father's priority was to get me away to a place of safety, far beyond my mother's reach. He resolved to spirit me into England, counting on my Uncle Henry welcoming me.

'You are of marriageable age,' he told me, 'and a highly desirable bride. You will be an asset to the King. He will find you a good husband.' Miserably, I thought of the Earl of Bothwell, now irrevocably lost to me. And I wept profusely at the prospect of being parted from Father. Yet I could see the sense in his plan.

In October, he stole away with me to Norham Castle, on the English side of the River Tweed. The Earl of Northumberland had offered me his protection and agreed that my beloved Isobel might seek refuge with me. Father would be welcome too, if things went badly for him in Scotland.

Norham was an ancient border stronghold standing on a rocky bluff high above the River Tweed near Berwick. But my lord of Northumberland's steward was concerned that it was not a suitable residence for the daughter of a queen. He was right. It had not one chamber fit to shelter anyone and, when it rained, water streamed in from the roof right down to the dungeons.

I did not care. I was miserable to be so far from Father and all that was familiar. Homesickness was my worst privation. Yet I had Isobel with me, and her brisk pragmatism fortified me. I was well guarded and the steward did his best to ensure that I was accommodated in as much comfort as possible.

Daily, I was expecting a summons to the English court, but none came. I know now that King Henry was preoccupied with his 'Great Matter', being determined to divorce Queen Katherine. It would not have been appropriate for me to go to his court at that time. So I rusticated at Norham for eight miserable months.

Father, meanwhile, had held out against King James's forces. Tantallon proved unconquerable. Father sued for peace, but the terms my brother offered made it plain that he meant to treat Father as a rebel and a traitor.

I was spending a bleak Christmas at Norham when King James and King Henry concluded a treaty, whereby James was to take the Douglas lands on condition that Father was permitted to seek asylum in England. In the spring, Father surrendered Tantallon in hope of a pardon that was never forthcoming, and fled into England. I was overjoyed to see him at Norham and hear him say that I was to go with him.

We rode eastwards along the border to Berwick, where we sought shelter in the castle with its custodian, Sir Thomas Strangeways, who was comptroller of the household of my godfather, Cardinal Wolsey. Berwick Castle proved a safe haven. Father left me there when he travelled south to my uncle's court. The Cardinal had sent orders that I was to be kept securely at Berwick and be well entertained; I was to have as much liberty and recreation as possible. Relieved that Father was safe, I was quite merry and content. I was sad to hear of the death of the Cardinal, who had failed to obtain the divorce the King wanted, fallen from favour and died of sorrow, but I felt glad on hearing that Father had been made welcome at the English court.

At last, I received a summons from King Henry. Sir Thomas Strangeways himself escorted me south to London. Isobel came with us, but only to see me safely to the south. She did not want to remain among the Heathen English, as she called them. It was spring when I arrived and I was delighted to find that my uncle had provided me with a whole new wardrobe – he had ordered gorgeous gowns of velvet, damask and satin, kirtles and partlets. I had never been so richly or grandly dressed.

I was much struck by the contrast between Scotland and England.

My uncle enjoyed widespread popularity, that was evident everywhere. England was at peace, not riven by strife between the King and the lords; its people were prosperous and law-abiding, its court magnificent, affording numerous pleasures. I was soon caught up in a whirl of pageants, masques, music, dancing and tournaments. In the spacious gardens that surrounded the royal palaces, there were bowling alleys, banqueting houses and tennis-plays. There was money a-plenty, and open-handedness. These delights came as a pleasant surprise after the comparative poverty of Scotland.

And yet . . . I was homesick. My uncle's court seemed a world away from the wild, rugged landscapes of Northumberland, the magnificent hills of the Scottish Lowlands and the stark, magnificent fastness of Tantallon.

In October 1530, I turned fifteen. My silver mirror showed me that I was blossoming into pretty womanhood; I had good features and the reddish-auburn hair of my mother's family. People paid tribute to my beauty, and it went to my head a little. The King openly admired my high spirits and laughed at my pert remarks. I think maybe he detected the inner strength and fearlessness in me and approved. I do believe that he dearly loved me. I will never forget his bounty and kindness, for all the harsh lessons he later taught me.

But his mood was not always sunny. I had escaped the tensions of a life overshadowed by feuding parents, only to arrive at a court riven by the Great Matter. The Pope had revoked the case to Rome and matters had reached a stalemate. Queen Katherine was still in residence in her apartments, Anne Boleyn in hers. I was not surprised to be told that it had been deemed best for me to go to live with my aunt, Mary Tudor, Queen Dowager of France and Duchess of Suffolk, my mother's younger sister.

They called her the French Queen, although she had left France some fifteen years earlier. She had not been to my uncle's court for three years. Thanks to the financial strain of paying the fine he had exacted as the price of her ill-advised marriage – for love, praise be! – to the Duke of Suffolk, she could rarely afford to go there. She wouldn't have gone anyway, as she vehemently disapproved of Anne Boleyn, who was now riding high at court, waiting impatiently to be made queen of England. My aunt confided to me that, when told that the Boleyn wanted to befriend me, she had instantly invited me to stay with her!

When I arrived at her great palace at Westhorpe in Suffolk, I found her listless and ailing. Her famous beauty had faded. She was lonely, for the Duke supported the King and was rarely at home. She was angry with him for favouring the Boleyn, and sad too, for there was now a great rift between them.

I spent my days wandering around the great house, the cloisters and the French-style gardens. There was a large statue of Hercules seated beside a lion in the courtyard, and I spent many an hour perched on the lion's back, reading books purloined from the library. But I was not solitary. I had the company of my cousins, Frances Brandon, my junior by twenty-one months, Eleanor, aged nine, and Henry, Earl of Lincoln, aged seven. I grew fond of them, and the Duke's ward, Katherine Willoughby, who was then eleven. And I grew to love my aunt, who was a warm and gentle lady, popular with all.

My idyll in the country did not last long. At Christmas, I was summoned to attend the Princess Mary as chief lady of her privy chamber. My role was to be her foremost companion. I was excited at the prospect, yet sad to be leaving my aunt. My sadness dissipated, I regret to say, when a cartload of wonderful gowns and other clothing arrived from Greenwich. The King had decided that, in consideration of my new role in the Princess Mary's household, I should be provided with a fitting wardrobe. How I preened in front of my mirror, trying on gowns of crimson velvet lined with cloth of gold over a kirtle of crimson velvet, a nightgown of satin furred with black coney, a black cloak with black satin vents . . . There were biliments for edging necklines or hoods, night shifts of lawn, kerchiefs, smocks, and two French hoods of black velvet. My uncle must have spent a fortune!

And so, grandly attired, I went to court for Christmas, weeping as I bade farewell to the French Queen and my cousins. I was soon swept up in the gaiety and revelry of the celebrations, enjoying my exalted status as the King's niece and basking in the admiration of the young gallants of the court, for I was fifteen now and ripe for wooing.

The new year saw grave matters afoot. The King demanded that Parliament and the clergy recognise him as Supreme Head of the Church of England. It was the first step towards breaking forever with the Pope. That summer, he separated from Queen Katherine and sent her away from court. By then, I had become fast friends with my new mistress, the Princess, who was only five months younger than me, and I had to comfort her increasingly often during those difficult months. You could never have hoped to meet a sweeter and kinder girl than Mary, and I grieved to see her so unhappy. We had much in common, for we both knew what it was to have warring parents, and both of us had been taken by our fathers from our mothers. We shared too a deep faith and prayed constantly that the King would be reconciled to the Pope. But there seemed even less hope of that as time went by.

In the autumn, my uncle sent me more lavish attire and Mary and I spent happy hours trying on my new gowns, although they were big on her, as she was small and too thin, thanks to all the anxiety she was suffering. I felt such sorrow for her and did all I could to cheer and reassure her. Privately, I could only deplore my uncle's treatment of the Queen. Yet, outwardly, I knew it was wise to keep a still tongue and not involve myself in controversial matters. I needed to keep the King's affection and high opinion. I was hoping he would arrange a good marriage for me.

That year, he sent Mary and me money so that we could both disport ourselves over Christmas. I was disappointed not to be invited to court, but it was probably for the best, as the Boleyn was queening it there and Mary loathed her with a passion. We spent our time playing hide-and-seek or cards and making music.

Mary was inconsolable when, the following spring, we learned that Thomas Cranmer, the new Archbishop of Canterbury, had declared her mother's marriage invalid and pronounced her, Mary, a bastard. She was even more horrified to hear that her father had married the Boleyn, who was pregnant. I was witness to the hours Mary spent wailing and weeping. I wept with her, and even more copiously when I was told that my aunt, the French Queen, was dead. Her death may have left me the second lady in the land after the Boleyn, but I was bereft.

In September 1533, Mary and I secretly rejoiced to hear that the Boleyn had borne, not the long-desired son and heir, but a daughter, Elizabeth. Mary had steadfastly refused to relinquish the title of princess, and she roundly declined to acknowledge Elizabeth as their father's heir, or her mother as Princess Dowager of Wales; nor would she concede that her mother's marriage was incestuous and unlawful. The King was furious with her and retaliated by reducing the size of her household. I was allowed to stay on, but not for long. By December, my uncle was so exasperated with what he called Mary's obstinacy that he dismissed all her servants and packed her off to Hatfield to wait on her new half-sister. I was told – as if some great favour was being conferred on me – that I could attend upon Elizabeth when she was brought to court. For that was where I was bound. The King had appointed me a lady of honour to the Boleyn.

Of course, I did not want to go, or serve that creature, who was the cause of all Mary's troubles. I knew that my loyalties would be cruelly divided. Yet I had no choice in the matter. I was dependent on my uncle's kindness and charity. I knew that, to retain his favour, I must show myself amenable to the new Queen. I could only pray that Mary would understand.

The Boleyn welcomed me coolly; she mistrusted me because of my former closeness to the Princess. Neither of us were very happy with the arrangement, but we both made the best of it. My uncle was gratified to see us getting along so amicably.

It eluded me, what he saw in the Boleyn. Close up, she was swarthy and no beauty. She had wit, I grant her that, and she was a terrible flirt. Yet it was clear that her wiles did not always have the effect she intended on her husband. Sometimes he responded with kisses and caresses; at others, he rebuffed her or coldly reminded her that such levity did not become a queen. She would laugh, but her eyes betrayed her. This was a frightened woman. It was imperative that she gave the King a son. It would bind him to her. She would be safe from her enemies. I'm sure she knew that, without the King's love, she was nothing.

I was treated like a queen's daughter and attended by my own train of servants. My mother remembered me for the first time in years, writing to the Boleyn to thank her for finding a place for me and saluting her as her dearest sister. I felt like puking. But I maintained the pretence of liking my mistress.

I was not unhappy at this time. At court, I could tell that I was liked, or even loved, by all. The Imperial ambassador addressed me as the Princess of Scotland, which made me smile, as I was neither a princess by birth, nor a Scottish one. But it was good to be so highly regarded.

From time to time, my uncle spoke of arranging a marriage for me. The Duke of Florence was mentioned as a potential husband, and the son of the King of France. Nothing came of either, even though the passing of an Act of Succession left me third in line to the throne after the Princess Elizabeth and my mother, but I knew myself to be a most desirable bride. It could not be long before I was wed.

Another Act of Parliament made my uncle Supreme Head on Earth of the Church of England, in place of the Pope. Everyone holding public office was required to swear an oath recognising his title and his marriage to the Boleyn.

These were turbulent times, but I strove not to get involved with the controversies that raged through the land. I took the oath. I avoided engaging with the reformist fervour of the Boleyns and their circle, but quietly went on observing my devotions in private. No one challenged me.

There was much pastime in the Boleyn's chamber. We played our lutes and sang, danced, joked, gambled on cards and dice, and flirted. With two of my friends, Mary Shelton, the Boleyn's cousin, and Mary Howard, who was married to the King's bastard son, my cousin, the Duke of Richmond, I wrote or collected poems. We transcribed them and bound them into a book, which we intended to circulate at court. I have it somewhere still.

The Boleyn had been queen for two years when I met her uncle, Lord Thomas Howard, at one of the gatherings in her chamber. He was twenty-three and I was twenty. He was the much younger brother of the powerful Duke of Norfolk. We came together through our shared love of poetry. Tom was a competent poet himself; he enjoyed plays on words and conundrums. He paused by the table where the two Marys and I were busily transcribing and picked up one of my poems. I was lost from that moment.

We were circumspect. Instinct told me that the King would not approve of my falling in love with a man he had not chosen for me. My marriage was in his gift. It would be made to his advantage, and England's. Thomas Howard, a younger son with no fortune, no prospects and no influence in any quarter, would not stand a chance. But I was young and headstrong, and my heart was heedless of policy. Even so, I retained enough sense to play hard to get. For a long time, Tom complained that I was disdainful, even though I was only being cautious.

'I love you!' he whispered, again and again, when we met in secret.

'I can only be your friend,' I kept telling him, fearing to entangle myself further. 'I value friendship as highly as love.'

'Friendship?' he echoed, one evening, when we were walking in a quiet corner of the gardens. 'If that is all you want from me, we might scarcely be acquainted!'

My cheeks burned. 'When I agreed to meet you here, I did not mean for you to declare such raging love for me. All I want is honest, friendly company.' It was not true. I wanted his love, but dared not say so.

'I love you exceedingly,' Tom declared, 'and yet you take it ill! Do you know how hurtful that is?'

'What hurt could honest friendship bring?' I asked.

'It's as good as banishing me!' he muttered. 'God, I pray for patience!'

He wrote me a poem after that, complaining of my coldness. Underneath, he drew two barbed arrows, showing me that Cupid's darts can have a sting in them.

After that, I grew warmer towards him. I could not help myself, I was so smitten with him. I was scared that someone would discover our love and report us to my uncle, but love blinded me increasingly to the reality of our situation. Yet I was not that far gone in folly that I had forgotten the need to preserve my honour. I took Mary Howard into my confidence and she said we could meet in her bedchamber and agreed to be present, as chaperone. There, we enjoyed many secret trysts. Thomas told me that I was his true love and kissed me hungrily, but he always behaved like a true gentleman. Although we shared passionate embraces, he never asked me to give myself to him. That could wait until we were wed. It was hopeless, and I think we both knew that there could be no future for us, but we deluded ourselves that there was. And thus we continued for a whole year.

We should have known that we were courting disaster. Whenever I picked up the book that my friends and I were compiling, I had a salutary warning before my eyes, on the very first page.

> Take heed betime lest ye be spied,
> Your loving ways you cannot hide;
> At last the truth will sure be tried,
> Therefore take heed!

1536 was a terrible year. In January, Queen Katherine died. Four months later, I was in attendance on the Boleyn at a May Day tournament when the King abruptly rose and departed with a face like thunder, leaving her nonplussed. We were still speculating on what this portended the next day when she was arrested at Greenwich and imprisoned in the Tower of London, charged with adultery with five men, one her own brother, and for conspiring to assassinate the King. Even I found that barely credible.

The court was in an uproar. We were all wondering who would be apprehended next. We ladies were all questioned, but I had seen nothing untoward in the Boleyn's behaviour and could not give any evidence, although I would have been willing to testify against her. I did not grieve for her when she was beheaded on a bright May morning, for I had hated all she stood for, although I was shocked at the speediness of her end.

I rejoiced when, only eleven days later, my uncle the King married her maid-of-honour, Jane Seymour, whom I knew and liked. Jane was a quiet pale blonde whom nobody thought very beautiful, yet I knew her to be a good Catholic who deplored the break with Rome, and that she was sympathetic towards Mary. I know Jane liked me too. She gave me a gift of beads soon after her marriage. It's a pity I was allowed so little time to enjoy that friendship.

While these momentous events were taking place, I had been living in my fool's paradise with Tom. I was so far gone in love with him that, when he asked me to marry him, I agreed. When the court moved to Whitehall Palace in June for the opening of Parliament, we plighted our troth to each other, vowing to wed in the future.

I could remember my parents' divorce. I knew what a precontract was and that, in plighting my troth, I had just entered into one. I knew that it was as binding as a marriage and could only be loosed by a church court. It was headstrong and reckless of me, but, by then, I was past caring about any consequences. Of course, both of us knew that my uncle would be wrathful if we were discovered. In our defence, I can only say that we were too far gone in love to care about consequences. There was no malice in us, no desire to anger anyone. How naïve we were! We should have known that secrets could not be kept long at court.

When King Henry rode with Queen Jane to Westminster on the feast of Corpus Christi, to open Parliament, I rode behind at the head of the Queen's ladies, for I had been appointed her chief lady of honour. In Westminster Abbey, I carried her train as she proceeded to High Mass. My prominent role in the procession reflected my new status. All the King's children had been declared or born bastards. My brother James was barred from the English succession because he was a foreigner, and my mother had now renounced her claim. As things stood, I was the next in line for the throne as my uncle's nearest heir. Everyone was treating me with the greatest respect.

Far from being overjoyed by my new importance, I was terrified, because it made what Tom and I had done even more reprehensible. I did not have long to fret, however. Someone betrayed us to the King. I'm not sure who it was, but they knew about our precontract. It could not have happened at a worse time because my uncle was not well disposed towards the Howards in the wake of the Boleyn's fall, and they were decidedly out of favour.

I still wonder if Mary Howard confided in her father, the Duke of Norfolk, and if it was he who betrayed us. Did he do so to demonstrate his loyalty to his sovereign? Mary had been my confidante and accomplice, and Norfolk would have wanted to deflect the King's wrath from her – and himself.

The King was much incensed by my folly and enraged at Tom's presumption. I imagine he was bitterly disappointed in me, having cherished such a high opinion of me. But that was the least of it. When I was being questioned, it became horrifyingly clear that the King suspected Tom of traitorously coveting the crown. It was believed that he had precontracted himself to me only to gain a throne. What hurt most was that my accusers kept referring to me as baseborn. My uncle was making it plain that there was now no question of my deserving a place in the English succession.

Looking back, I suppose he had good reason for suspecting Tom's motives, because our precontract was made after the Princess Elizabeth had been pronounced a bastard. Tom could have realised then that I had realistic hopes of the succession. He could also have seen our marriage as a means of restoring the Howards to power and reviving the Roman faith; the Howards, I might add, are Papists in all but name. I still sometimes wonder if these possibilities had occurred to Tom, but I doubt it. I know in my heart that our betrothal was founded upon love.

Tom was imprisoned in the Tower. I was hysterical when they told me. Only hours later, they came for me and, trembling with fright, I was conveyed along the Thames in a covered barge towards the brooding fortress where my lover lay. I grew quite light-headed worrying about what they would do to me. The fate of the Boleyn was at the forefront of my mind. I was shaking uncontrollably when I disembarked and was taken under guard to the royal apartments she had occupied.

There, I could not sleep. I saw ghosts in every corner. Every time the door opened, I thought my time had come. All I could do was lament my ill fortune and the loss of my love, and pray that my uncle would be lenient. He loved me, didn't he? Wasn't it evident in the comfort of my apartments and the privileges I was allowed? Surely he was just teaching me a lesson, one I would never forget.

I comforted myself with such thoughts, assuring myself that this luxurious confinement was the worst that would happen to me, so I was shocked when Sir William Kingston, the Constable of the Tower, informed me that an Act of Attainder had been passed, sentencing Tom to death for high treason. In the wake of our ill-considered betrothal, Parliament had declared it treason for a man to marry, deflower or contract himself to any of the King's female relatives without royal permission. To this Act, my uncle had given his consent.

'But the Act was not in force when we plighted our troth!' I protested vehemently, but to no avail.

'Madam, it is not my office to question the King's laws,' Sir William said frostily. 'And I would remind you that you stand in the greatest jeopardy. It is my painful duty to inform you that, because you consented to the precontract, you yourself will likewise incur pain of death.'

I could not believe what I was hearing. This could not be happening! My uncle would never go so far! Terror gripped me. I swayed and Sir William stepped forward to catch me, or I would have fallen.

I spent several dreadful days agonising over the prospect of dying a hideous death for the crime of having fallen in love. I was just twenty years old and I was nowhere near ready to die. I would have appealed to the King, to King James and to my parents, but I was not allowed to write letters. I was under no illusions as to what I was facing. I remembered that my uncle had sent his own wife to the scaffold, and that he had executed others of his own blood in the past. Why should he spare his niece? That he would send me to the block was all too believable. And he might do worse. The Boleyn had been sentenced to be burned or beheaded at his pleasure. Because she was queen, she was allowed the kinder death. Would the King be so merciful to me? I came near to screaming several times when I considered that he might not.

But then came my reprieve.

'You have been pardoned your life,' Sir William informed me, looking almost as relieved as I felt. 'This is on account of it having been established that there is no proof of a conspiracy and that you did not have carnal relations with Lord Thomas.'

Thank God, *thank God*! I sank to my knees.

Sir William looked at me with compassion. 'You will be relieved to know that Lord Thomas has been spared too. You will both remain in the Tower at the King's pleasure.'

Hope sprang in me. It was very rare for my uncle to reprieve a traitor who had been sentenced to death. He was just punishing us for our presumption! He might even let us marry after we had learned our lesson.

Well, I would be patient. I would live in hope.

I needed that patience. I was not allowed visitors. I was constrained to live modestly, given that the King was paying for my upkeep in the Tower. I pretended that I no longer cherished feelings for Tom. I was determined to be the model prisoner, so that my uncle would relent and let me out the sooner.

When winter drew in, it was hard to stay positive, for it was cold in the Queen's lodgings, despite the fires I was permitted, and the nights were long. Often, I lay awake, feeling despondent. Would my imprisonment never end? And then, on the last day of that terrible year, a package was brought to me. I unwrapped it eagerly to find lengths of costly silver and crimson silk fringe. Then a chair of crimson velvet with a fringe of Venice silk was carried in. All were gifts from my uncle. The message could not have been clearer. He had thawed towards me. I was well on the way to being forgiven. My spirits soared. I could look forward to the new year of 1537 with hope, for freedom was in my sights.

It was a blessing that I was now allowed writing materials in the Tower, for I found solace and release in composing poetry. I wondered if Tom was able to enjoy the same privilege. I did not even know where he was, although it was a comfort to know that he was not far away. My constant prayer was that he was being held in agreeable conditions; surely his family would have ensured that? If only I could have seen him. I longed for him so much it was painful.

Surely my parents had heard of my plight by now, even in Perthshire, where mother was living with Harry Stewart? And Father was at the English court; he must be aware of my sad situation. I had been hoping and praying that one or the other of them would have interceded for me. But I knew in my heart I could hope for little from Father. He would do nothing to antagonise King Henry, his benefactor.

My lodgings overlooked a walled garden in which I was permitted to take the air. One winter's day, I was padding around, my hands in my muffler, when the door in the wall was unlocked and a porter came in with a wheelbarrow. He doffed his hat to me.

'Morning, my lady. Thomas Shelton at your service,' he said.

Shelton? I stared at him in surprise.

'Are you acquainted with Mistress Mary Shelton?' I asked.

'I'm her brother,' he said, grinning.

I stared at him. 'What are you doing working here?'

'I need to eat! I am my father's youngest son and have no estate to look forward to. There is no dishonour in earning your living.' He lowered his voice. 'Mary asked me to tell you that Lord Thomas Howard asked that a book of poems be brought to him in the Tower. I was able to help. And I am willing to act as a go-between, if you want to pass a message to him. No one notices me. I come and go at will.'

'You would do that for me?' My heart was thumping. 'Oh, thank you, thank you, Mr Shelton!'

As I ran upstairs, I thought quickly. I would send Tom some verses, anonymously, so that, if he was caught with them, he could say he had written them himself. In poetry, I could express myself with more feeling than in a letter.

I sat down, trying to calm myself, and took up my pen, while Mr Shelton waited below, tidying the garden. The words flowed from me.

> Now may I mourn as one of late
> Driven by force from my delight,
> And cannot see my lonely mate
> To whom forever my heart is plight.

Alas! That ever prison strong
Should such two lovers separate,
Yet though our bodies suffereth wrong,
Our hearts should be of one estate.

I will not swerve, I you assure,
For gold nor yet for worldly fear,
But like as iron I will endure,
Such faithful love to you I bear.

On wings, I sped downstairs and gave the folded paper to Mr Shelton. Only when he had gone did I wonder he had sprung a trap on me. But why would anyone want to do that? I decided I would trust him.

By evening, I had a reply from Tom. I unfolded it with shaking hands and devoured his words. He had written in like vein.

With sorrowful sighs and wounds smart
My heart is pierced suddenly.
To mourn of right it is my part.
To weep, to fail full grievously.

The bitter tears doth me constrain,
Although that I would it eschew,
To wit, the reproach of them that doth disdain
Faithful lovers that be so true.

The one of us from the other they do absent,
Which unto us is a deadly wound,
Seeing we love in this intent:
In God's laws for to be bound.

He still loved me – and he still regarded us as bound to each other! His love had survived all the obstacles placed in its way. Not even imprisonment in the Tower or the threat of death, had shaken it. My heart was on wings.

Thus began our correspondence. Never did poets write verses so passionately. It was a joy to me to know that Tom was missing me as much as I was missing him, although I was sometimes unnerved by the bitterness in him. He did not hesitate to criticise our imprisonment and those who had separated us. If the poems had been discovered and brought to my uncle's notice, Tom would have been in serious trouble. It was never a wise idea to question or criticise the decisions of the King. But Tom was clearly an angry man. His vehemence was the measure of his love.

We both were still hoping that we had a future together, although Tom was at times despondent. Then I would encourage him, praising him for his devotion and constancy. Of course, I was the one with more cause for hope. The King loved me and had at times shown himself an indulgent uncle. He had stayed his hand at sending us to the block, and his displeasure could not last forever. Yes, we did have a future, and I told Tom in my verses that we must hold to that. One day soon, we would be freed.

But summer came, and still we were prisoners. With it came a change in Tom's poems. He dwelt too morosely on the hopelessness of his situation and became morbidly preoccupied with death. It made me wonder if he was keeping something from me. Had he been warned that he would never see me again? When he spoke of lovers being parted, I feared they had told him that I alone was to be sent away from the Tower. Whatever it was, he clearly felt there was nothing left for him in life but a speedy decline to the grave. I wept when I read his verses, longing to comfort and hearten him.

Even in the Tower there was rejoicing when Queen Jane bore a prince. I heard the church bells ringing and Sir William permitted me to share a toast with him. I think he had grown quite fond of me by then. I never gave him any trouble and did everything I was bid. I'm sure he never knew about the messages Mr Shelton conveyed for me.

The Prince's birth meant that I was no longer in the perilous position of being heir presumptive to the crown, or so important politically.

Immediately, in the joyous flush of new fatherhood, my uncle pardoned me and set me at liberty.

My bondage was past, my hope of freedom won! I prayed that Tom would be released too.

But I rejoiced too soon. Just as I was preparing to leave the Tower, I fell ill with a fever and lay tossing in my bed, not knowing if it was night or day. My uncle sent his own physician to attend me. That doctor told me that Tom was ill too, and that he would be visiting him next. By then, I was slowly coming to myself again, although I was weak as a kitten. However, the lust for liberty was strong in me, and I began to make a steady, if slow, recovery.

Then Sir William came to me. His face was grave. In words that seemed incomprehensible, he told me that Tom had died.

It had been an ague, but I was convinced that my beloved had suffered a broken heart, and that he had died because of me. How I wept and stormed at Fate, at those who had parted us and left him to decline in prison. With bitter tears I lamented his loss. It was as if I was frozen inside. I would never love again. I knew it in my bones. I was twenty-two.

My uncle gave orders for me to be moved to the healthy air of Syon Abbey, where the Abbess would look after me, and I could rest and recuperate. As my litter was borne away, I heard the bells of London tolling for the Queen, who had died in childbed. The King would be in mourning as I was, but at least he had been vouchsafed the freedom to love his chosen lady.

Tom's death had dealt me a body blow and sickened my soul. I was still ill when Easter came, although I was able to take walks through the cloisters and the abbey's orchards, or sit in the shade of its ancient mulberry trees. Thanks to the Abbess's care of me, I grew stronger daily, even if I was still deep in grief. I spent time in the famous library, seeking for books that could offer me spiritual solace. My life was ruled by the bells of the great church calling the community to the divine offices seven times a day. Often, I would pray with them, sending up fervent intercessions for Tom's soul.

I left Syon in April, still quite weak. There was no queen now, so I could not return to court. I was sent to stay with my old friend, the Lady Mary, who had been restored to favour at court, thanks to Queen Jane's good offices. Mary warmly welcomed me. To my relief, she assured me she had never resented my having served the Boleyn; she knew I had had no choice in the matter. And so we resumed our friendship.

My uncle bought me another new wardrobe and defrayed the expenses of my servants. By that, I knew that I was truly forgiven. Yet I could take little pleasure in his gifts. I was too listless even to try on the gowns.

One day, a package arrived for me. It contained the book of poems that Tom had had with him in the Tower and all our passionate poems to each other. There was no note. I suspected that Thomas Shelton had sent it. Reading over my beloved's verses, I wept all over again.

That summer, Mary Shelton wrote to me, saying there was gossip at court that the Earl of Wiltshire – the Boleyn's father, of all people! – was seeking my hand in marriage. No! I cried, in the solitude of my chamber. I would never agree to it! He was an old man, but that was the least of it. I would never marry one of that tribe. Fortunately, I heard no more of the matter, for which I was devoutly thankful.

But there was no doubt that my uncle was seeking to negotiate a marriage for me. He wrote to me himself, informing me that he was considering Cosimo de' Medici, Duke of Florence. For a time, I envisaged myself restored to health and living in Italy, revelling in its art and culture – and its warm, reviving weather. But of Duke Cosimo, I could not think. I was not ready, or well enough, to marry any man. My heart was still Tom's. I would rather have died and been reunited with him than go to Florence. My health was broken and I fully expected to go to an early grave. I welcomed the prospect, indeed, I had resolved to die. I felt so ill that year that I even summoned my father and my friends so that I could bid them farewell.

Father was then resident at the English court. He came galloping down to see me and told me I should rise from my couch and get some air; and he stood by to ensure that I did. Daily, he made me walk in the gardens, then he got me up on a horse again. I truly believe that I am still here today thanks to him.

I heard no more of the Italian marriage. It seemed I was not destined to have a husband and children. I was not sure whether I was happy or sad at the prospect. Restored in health I might have been, but not in spirits. I was quite happy to remain in the country. But, after a decent interval, my uncle took a fourth wife, the Lady Anna of Cleves, and I was brought back to court to serve as her chief lady of honour. I had not seen my uncle for three-and-a-half years, and I was shocked by the change in him. Then he had been a magnificent figure of a man; now, he was old before his time, massively fat and a virtual invalid. I marked that he was more maudlin, sanctimonious and tyrannical than ever. Everyone was wary of him, but he was affectionate enough to me. Clearly, all my transgressions were forgotten.

I was to be chief of the six great ladies of the Queen's household. We were presented to the Lady Anna when she arrived at Dartford after her long journey from Dover. The weather was atrocious, and she spoke almost no English, but she kept smiling all the time. I admired that. I admired her too, for her discretion when, soon after her marriage to the King, it became apparent that he did not love or even like her.

I was lucky. Unlike most of her other ladies, I had been assigned my own lodging in the palace, near the Lady Mary's, so I could escape from the tense atmosphere of the Queen's apartments in those weeks in which it seemed that a cauldron was about to bubble over. The King rarely visited Anna, and it was all over the court that he was impotent with her, but able to perform the marriage act with other ladies. The palaces were alive with rumours and gossip.

I felt sorry for Anna. I hoped she had not understood what people were saying about her. The poor lady led a retired life, pretending that all was well. I whiled away much of the time gambling with the Lady Mary and my other friends. None of us were surprised when, after six months the royal marriage was annulled and Anna, richer by a very handsome settlement, left court, the best of friends with the King.

By then, it was notorious that my uncle had fallen for the charms of a pretty maid-of-honour, Katheryn Howard, a cousin of the Boleyn. Less than three weeks after his divorce from Anna, he married her. In August, when the new Queen's household was formed, I was summoned again to be chief of her ladies.

I liked Katheryn. She was lively and kind, if a touch naïve. Once more, we ladies could enjoy dancing and making music and all our old pleasures in the Queen's chamber. Yet always, for me, the ghost of Tom was hovering. This was where we had fallen for each other.

In the summer of 1541, King Henry departed with the whole court on a great progress to York, to meet with his nephew. But King James never came, much to my, and my uncle's, annoyance. He was furious at James's perfidy. He would have been even more furious if he had known what was going on almost under his very nose.

I know now that, during the progress, and possibly before, Queen Katheryn was rashly carrying on a secret love affair with the connivance of Lady Rochford, one of my fellow ladies-in-waiting. I swear I knew nothing of it, nor saw anything that aroused my suspicions. But, if I had known, I would probably secretly have taken a sympathetic view, even though what Katheryn was doing was sheer folly.

For she was not the only one who was indulging in a clandestine liaison.

Late in October, I received news that my mother had passed away after suffering an apoplexy. I had not seen her for thirteen years, and we had not been close or corresponded often. I still resented the fact that she had always preferred my brother to me, although my uncle had told me that, when I was in the Tower, she had been greatly distressed and done her best to save me from my fate. For that alone, I mourned her. And when the King showed me a report that her thoughts were with me at the last and that she had desired King James to be good to me and make sure I received the jewels she had left me, I wept for her.

I never did receive that bequest. Later, I learned that James had given my jewels to his new wife, Queen Marie.

* * *

I ought to have learned a lesson from the tragic consequences of my love for Tom, but I didn't. How quickly the young forget. And how blind, foolish and unheeding love can be.

He was the Queen's brother and a gentleman of the King's Privy Chamber. His name was Charles and he was in high favour with my uncle. It began as a flirtation during the progress, but it was not long before I began to have feelings for him, although I never loved Charles as much as I loved Tom. And so it all began again, the snatched, secret meetings, the subterfuge, the coded poems. No wonder I did not notice the Queen's naughtiness: I was too preoccupied with my own, although *I* managed to preserve my honour. I should have known better, but I am like my mother, impulsive in affairs of the heart.

When we returned to Hampton Court, Charles and I continued to contrive trysts. Then, with no warning, came the Queen's arrest, which shocked him to the core. He too, had had no idea of what had been going on, and he was petrified for his sister, who was now confined to her rooms under guard. I consoled him as best I could, but he would not be comforted.

A week later, Charles did not come to our meeting place, a deserted banqueting house in the gardens. I waited ages, but in vain. In the end, I walked back to the palace in the November gloom, wondering if his absence had anything to do with the Queen. Had he learned the worst, which was what we were all expecting?

As I went indoors, I met Sir Anthony Browne, who had always been friendly towards me.

'My Lady Margaret,' he murmured, looking around to see if anyone was is earshot, 'I am glad to see you here. Mr Howard has been forbidden to enter the King's chamber. Be warned, there is trouble afoot.' He patted my arm and hurried off, leaving my brain whirling. What trouble? Had Charles and I been discovered? Or was this to do with the Queen?

I ran to Charles's lodging, but it was in darkness. In vain did I bang on the door. I knew he shared his rooms with his brother Henry, so I went looking for him.

'He's gone,' Henry told me, when I found him at the servery, rather drunk.

'Gone? Where?' I cried. 'Why?'

'I don't know for certain,' Henry said, slurring his words, 'but he told me before he left that he was banished from the court on account of you.'

So they knew! I began trembling.

'You mean, he has left me to retrieve my reputation all alone?' I could not believe it.

'He said he was making for France to try his luck at the tournaments there,' Henry said, looking at me with maudlin pity.

'I hope they kill him!' I snapped, and walked away, trying not to cry at my folly in trusting my heart to such a knave. I had sought the best and found the worst. This was where my foolish fancy had led me!

I lay on my bed, weeping salty tears and filled with remorse and grudges. I knew it was only a matter of time before they came for me. My head was filled with dark memories of the Tower, where I expected to be confined again before long.

I quaked when Archbishop Cranmer and a deputation of Privy Councillors called upon me. Cranmer looked at me severely.

'Madam, we are here to do the King's pleasure. His Highness knows how indiscreetly and ungratefully you have behaved yourself towards him, first with Lord Thomas Howard and now with Mr Charles Howard. He wishes me to censure you for your conduct and to warn you to beware the third time, and wholly apply yourself to please him and obey his will and command.'

I fell to my knees. 'I am very sorry to have offended his Highness,' I bleated.

'Think yourself lucky,' the Archbishop barked. 'The King is most vexed at having to be bothered with your misconduct at this time.'

'It was but a flirtation,' I cried.

'His Highness is aware of that, Madam. Nonetheless, you have been foolish. Your marriage is in his Majesty's gift and you may not dispose of yourself or indulge in illicit flirtations. Do I make myself understood?'

'Yes, my lord,' I said weakly. 'What is to happen to me?'

'The Queen's household is being broken up,' he informed me. That sounded ominous, but I was too preoccupied with my own fate to dwell on what might happen to Katheryn. 'The King's pleasure is that you be conducted to Kenninghall in Norfolk in the company of my lady of Richmond, if she and my lord her father are agreeable.'

It took me a moment to realise that this was to be the extent of my punishment. I was to go to the palatial Kenninghall, a house of which Mary Howard had often spoken proudly, and lodge with her, my dear friend and fellow poet. My spirits soared. It was not even banishment, for there was no place now for any lady at court.

Of course, the Duke of Norfolk agreed, and Mary and I left Hampton Court almost immediately. Fortunately, the weather was kind to us on our journey.

'My father is grateful to be of service to the King by offering you shelter under his roof,' Mary said, as we took the road to London, our small escort trailing behind. 'He was grieved to see the King so sad and feels responsible.'

'His Highness loved the Queen so much,' I said.

'We were all taken in by her,' Mary said, her lips pursed. 'My father said it was his misfortune to have two nieces offend the King. He feared the Queen's crimes would rebound on him. Several members of our family are in the Tower on her account.'

'Then I am glad that my uncle has looked kindly on him,' I said, reining in my steed to avoid a great puddle.

'It will be good to have you at Kenninghall,' Mary said, reaching over and squeezing my arm.

I found Kenninghall to be a magnificent brick house. There were fourteen tapestries in the great chamber alone, and numerous family portraits on display in the long gallery. Costly Turkey carpets adorned the tables and even the floors. I was given the best apartment, which was reserved for honoured guests. Now I sit here, in my window seat, looking out upon the wintry gardens, filled with a sense of having been very lucky, after reflecting on the extraordinary course of my life so far. If this was my punishment for involving myself with a scoundrel, it was by no means onerous. And it was far, far more lenient than what happened to poor Queen Katheryn.

A MAN OF GOD

One bright afternoon late in October 1541, Archbishop Cranmer sat at the desk in his closet at Hampton Court Palace staring into space. He was reflecting on how God had brought him to this place, when, at the turning point all those years ago, he had been looking forward to a very different existence. He had been an idealist back then, having embraced the forbidden tenets of Lutheranism while still at Cambridge, like so many of his fellow students. He smiled faintly as he recalled Black Joan, the barmaid he had impulsively wed back in his riotous days, as he thought of them. He had spent the ensuing months regretting it, knowing that marriage was an insuperable bar to the career in the Church he had been contemplating. His problem had been solved when Joan died in childbirth with her infant. He had taken holy orders and embarked on a lifetime of study at Cambridge – or so he anticipated.

His career had taken a remarkable turn twelve years back, while he was staying near Waltham Abbey at the height of the controversy about the King's Great Matter. A legatine court had just sat at Blackfriars to examine the legality of King Henry's marriage to Katharine of Aragon; Henry wanted an annulment, but Katherine was resisting. The legate sent by the Pope had referred the case back to Rome, much to the King's fury. The talk in the inns and taverns was of little else.

Cranmer was not even meant to have been staying at Waltham. He was on his way to Cambridge, but was warned not to go there because plague was rampant. At Waltham Abbey, he was offered a room in the guest house and there, to his good cheer, he found two old friends who had been with him at university – Stephen Gardiner and Edward Foxe.

287

It was a merry reunion and Cranmer had found himself being treated to a good dinner.

Both his friends had done well for themselves and were now in the King's service. They had just returned from an abortive mission to Rome and were gloomily perplexed as to how the Great Matter could be resolved. After dinner, over a flagon of ale, they asked for Cranmer's opinion.

'You always were sound at theology,' Foxe said.

'I haven't studied the matter in depth,' he told them, 'but, to my mind, this is not an issue for the Papal court; it should be judged by doctors of divinity in the universities. There is one truth in it, and the Scriptures will soon declare it if they are correctly interpreted by learned men trained for such a task. Taking this way, you might have made an end of the matter long since.' Fateful words, for it was at this point that his life had changed.

Foxe and Gardiner had regarded him keenly. 'You mean, Tom, that the case should be decided according to divine law, not canon law.'

'Yes. The Pope's intervention is not necessary. If the divines in the universities give it as their opinion that the King's marriage is invalid, then invalid it must be, and all that is required is an official pronouncement by the Archbishop of Canterbury to that effect, leaving the King free to remarry.'

'By God, his Grace must hear of this!' Gardiner declared. And before Cranmer knew it, he was being whisked before the King, who listened to his proposal as if it were glad tidings from Heaven, then clapped him on the shoulder. 'Dr Cranmer, you have the sow by the right ear!' he had bellowed.

So the universities had been canvassed and, Cranmer suspected, hefty bribes had changed hands. But opinion had been divided and old Archbishop Warham had been decidedly reluctant to make any pronouncements on the case without Papal sanction.

Like everyone else in the world, Cranmer had been aware that the King was desperate to marry his sweetheart, Anne Boleyn. He had had no great opinion of her until he was placed in her father's household as chaplain, at the King's behest. There, he had been struck from the first by Anne's zeal for reform. She and her family were passionate about it – so much so that he suspected that they were secret Lutherans like himself. A bond was formed between Cranmer and Anne: together, they would revolutionise religion in England.

When the King began the cumbersome and controversial process of severing the English Church from Rome, he relied heavily on Cranmer's support. Cranmer had been at the very centre of affairs, leading anything but a quiet life of study. Nearly ten years ago, he had been sent to Nuremberg on an embassy to the Holy Roman Emperor. There, he had enjoyed meeting fellow reformers. One, the pastor Andreas Osiander, had a niece called Margarete, with whom Cranmer had instantly been smitten.

'I would marry her, but I cannot, for I am in holy orders,' he'd confided to Osiander.

'Where in the Scriptures does it say that the clergy should be celibate?' his friend replied. Cranmer had seen the sense in that. He had married Margarete, knowing that her must keep her existence a secret in England, because King Henry was firmly against the idea of those in holy orders taking wives. Margarete had had to be smuggled into the country in a travelling chest. He smiled at the memory, but the smile soon faded. She was back in Germany now, having fled there with their children two years ago when the King had begun to enforce the laws on celibacy, and he missed her. Until then, they had been discreet and untroubled by officialdom; looking back, Cranmer was in little doubt that the King had been aware of his domestic arrangements, but had turned a blind eye until he could do so no longer.

Just after his marriage, Archbishop Warham had died and King Henry had wasted no time in appointing Cranmer to the See of Canterbury; it was the highest office in the English Church, but Cranmer had known that he would have to tread warily. He was devoted heart and soul to the Lutheran faith, and his greatest desire was to advance it in England, but he had had to keep his views to himself, for the King would have regarded them as heretical, and the penalty for heresy was death by burning.

Almost as soon as he had been consecrated, he had annulled the

King's union with Katherine and confirmed the secret marriage Henry had entered into with Anne after discovering that she was pregnant; then he had crowned Anne. Three years later, he had voiced his belief that she was innocent of the charges of adultery laid against her, until the Privy Council had warned him off. It had hurt to declare the marriage he had worked so hard to bring about null and void. And he had wept when, two days later, she had gone to the scaffold, mourning not only his patroness, but also the blow her fall had dealt the cause of reform.

Yet he had bounced back. The following year, the King had named him godfather to Prince Edward, the long-awaited royal heir. Then the short reign of the child's mother, Jane Seymour, the hope of the Catholics, had ended with her death in childbed. After that, Cranmer and his fellow reformers had steered the King towards an alliance with the Protestant German princess. That had been a disaster from the moment Henry set eyes on Anne of Cleves. Cranmer had had to break that marriage too, in the dismal knowledge that Norfolk and Gardiner, stout Catholics both, had pushed Norfolk's niece into Henry's path and the King had taken the bait. Not that Cranmer had anything against Katheryn Howard personally. She was a pretty, kind and virtuous young girl, even if queenship had gone somewhat to her head. It was what she represented that he deplored. While the conservatives were in the ascendant, the cause of reform could never be advanced.

He sighed. The King was veering ever closer towards traditional religion. Bishop Gardiner and his cronies had got to him. But now he was on progress in the north, receiving the submission of the multitudes who had rebelled against his reforms by rising in the Pilgrimage of Grace, which he had ruthlessly suppressed. Cranmer had been left behind with other Privy Councillors to deal with affairs of state in the King's absence. Most were ardent reformers, like himself. They had sat in council many times now and deplored the conservatives' attempts to put the clock back.

He glanced at the clock on the mantel. It would soon be time for them to meet again. He picked up his pen and signed the letter he had been writing before he'd begun reminiscing. At that moment, the door opened and his clerk came in.

'A gentleman is asking to see your Grace – a Mr Lascelles.'

Cranmer knew of John Lascelles. An ardent reformer, he served in the King's Privy Chamber and was spoken of as a man of principle. Cranmer had inwardly applauded last year when Lascelles had openly called Gardiner and Norfolk obstacles to further reform who were standing manifestly against God and their Prince.

'Send him in,' he said.

Lascelles was tall and lean-faced, and there was about him an air of zealotry. Cranmer greeted him with a smile and asked him to be seated, wondering what this was about.

'It's about the Queen, your Grace.'

Cranmer raised his eyebrows.

Lascelles looked him unwaveringly in the eyes. 'I feel it my duty to report something that has come to my knowledge. I have taken advice on this from a friend and we both think it would be high treason not to reveal such a matter immediately.'

Cranmer was suddenly riveted. What on earth was the man talking about?

'You have done well to come to me,' he said. 'Pray proceed.'

Lascelles barely drew breath. 'Before she married, my sister Mary was a servant of the old Duchess of Norfolk who brought up the Queen. Because she was an old acquaintance, I recommended her to seek service with her Grace when she married the King. She said she would not, but that she was very sorry for the Queen. I asked her why, and she told me that her Grace was of light morals.'

Something stirred in Cranmer, but he did not interrupt his visitor.

'She told me,' Lascelles continued, 'that one Francis Dereham, who was also a servant in my lady of Norfolk's house, had lain in bed with Mistress Katheryn Howard, as she then was, between the sheets, on a hundred nights, and there was such puffing and blowing between them that a maid who slept in the same dorter told Mistress Katheryn that she would never again share a bed with her because she knew not what marriage was.'

'Your sister is certain of these things?' Cranmer asked. 'She understands the seriousness of her allegations?'

'She is a godly woman and would never bear false witness. You can question her yourself.' Lascelles leaned forward. 'Dereham was not the Queen's only lover. My sister told me that one Manox, who taught her Grace music, knew a private mark on her body. Another maid told Mary that Manox was betrothed to Mistress Katheryn Howard, with whom he was much in love. It was commonly believed in the Duchess's household that Manox was troth-plight to her. My sister told me that she wondered at the King taking for his Queen one who had lived so wantonly before marriage. She said she was sorry for it and lamented that the King's Majesty had married Mistress Katheryn.'

Cranmer was thinking rapidly. Betrothed? Troth-plight? Was the King's marriage actually valid? Exhilaration was building in him. God truly did work in mysterious ways.

'Your sister never confided these things to you before?' he asked.

'No, your Grace.' Lascelles looked worried, as well he might. Concealing such matters might be construed as misprision of treason – if there was any treason. It might just be a simple case of annulling the marriage. Young people were often ignorant – and foolish.

'I wonder what prompted her to reveal these things to you now,' Cranmer said.

'She has been on the brink of saying something for a long time, but a lady in the Queen's household recently wrote to say that her Grace had accepted Dereham into her service, and Mary was worried about that. She felt she ought to say something.'

This was getting better and better. Cranmer saw instantly why the woman was worried. For what reason would the Queen employ her former lover, unless it was to rekindle their relations? In which case, it would not be just wantonness, but adultery – and adultery in a queen was treason. If that were the case, and Lascelles's sister had known of the earlier connection between them, she could be in very serious trouble indeed if she did not reveal what she knew.

'I am astonished to hear that her Grace is not a woman of such purity as is esteemed,' he said. 'This must be investigated further.' A great opportunity had just been delivered into his hands and he was determined to take full advantage or it. If there had been a precontract between the Queen and Manox, or with Dereham, it would be possible to unseat her and discredit the Catholic party. The way would then be clear for the King to marry a bride put forward by Cranmer and his fellow reformists, a bride who would hopefully be as energetic as Anne Boleyn in the cause of true religion. It was not mere luck that the councillors who had been left behind at Hampton Court were of the same persuasion as Cranmer: it was God's providence. They would know what needed to be done.

He thanked Lascelles for coming to see him and sent him away. Then he sat for a while, thinking deeply. He could find no reason to fault Mrs Hall's testimony. And he was duty-bound to report what he had heard.

Fornication before marriage was not a crime, but it argued a lightness of morals that might well alienate the King, who rejoiced in his wife's purity. Yet Cranmer knew he was treading on very dangerous ground. Henry was deeply in love with Katheryn Howard and likely to react violently to any implication that she was not as virtuous as he believed. Cranmer knew it would be wise to consult his fellow councillors, considering the weight and importance of the matter.

He sought out the Lord Chancellor and the Earl of Hertford and spoke to them in private. He watched as they took in the news, clearly aware of its gravity.

'This troubles me greatly,' the Lord Chancellor said, shaking his head.

'It leaves me much disquieted,' Hertford chimed in. 'What is your Grace's view?'

He had anticipated that they would bat the ball back in his court. 'My lords, I think I know the King well enough to predict that he will sacrifice his personal feelings in the interests of his realm. He will be devastated by this news, but he will not be made a fool of. And I know you will agree with me when I say that the wedded happiness of one man can weigh little against the salvation of millions of souls.'

'Your Grace has hit the nub of it,' Hertford observed.

The Lord Chancellor looked at Cranmer. 'I think that you should reveal this information to the King's Majesty.'

'I agree,' Hertford concurred.

'Leave it with me,' Cranmer said, and returned to his closet feeling sick with sorrow for the King, whose joy was about to be brutally extinguished. But, if there was a canker in the body politic, it must be rooted out. It was best to distance your emotions – and your finer self – from distasteful practicalities. Even so, he could not find in his heart to repeat that damning testimony to the King's face. So he wrote it in a letter, most sorrowfully, as he hoped he had made clear, and sealed it. Next to the seal, he added a note recommending that his Grace read it in private.

The next day was the feast of All Saints. During the celebration of Mass for the dead, when the King and Queen were offering at the altar, Cranmer crept into the royal pew and left the letter on his Majesty's chair. Then he returned to his chamber and waited, dread and excitement mounting within him.

THE
WICKED
WIFE

1520

As she rode away, Jane allowed herself one last look back at her family home. At the sight of her mother standing outside the door, waving to her, she almost turned back and begged to stay. But, young as she was, she was made of sterner stuff than that – and the court beckoned. She could not resist its call. She was going to be a great lady one day, one of the greatest in the land. She knew it in her bones. And this was the first step on the road to greatness.

She loved her parents, especially her learned, devout father. She was grateful that he was accompanying her on her journey and would be at her side when she entered the court. He knew it well and it was comforting that he would be there to guide her.

'Be brave,' he said to her. 'Think of this as a great adventure.'

She did – oh, she did! It felt like her natural right, going to court. She was the third and youngest daughter of Lord Morley and she was proud of the fact that her family had served the kings of England loyally and redoubtably for more than three hundred years. Although they owned other great estates in eastern England, they had made Hallingbury Hall in Essex their chief seat, but it stood empty now, for Jane's father, who'd inherited great wealth, had built a palatial house nearby, in the middle of a vast hunting park. It was known as Great Hallingbury, and Jane and her younger brother Henry had often played chase and hide-and-seek in its forty-five rooms. Now six-year-old Henry stood forlorn next to Mother, watching Jane and Father ride away. He would miss his playmate, Jane thought with a pang. Their sister Margaret was now twenty, quite the lady and too old to romp about with him. There had been another brother and sister, but they had died young and Jane had only the dimmest memories of them. Her mother, however, spent much time praying at the family tomb in St Giles' Church, where they lay, asleep in Christ.

Through her mother, Alice St John, Jane was great-niece to the King's late grandmother, the Lady Margaret Beaufort, Countess of Richmond and Derby. It was the Lady Margaret who had arranged Alice's marriage to the debonair Henry Parker, who had been brought up in her household. The Lady Margaret had now been dead for more than ten years, but Father still spoke often of her with warmth and devotion.

'She was a most remarkable woman,' he had told Jane, who loved to hear tales about royalty. 'She paid for me to be schooled at Oxford and it's thanks to her that I have this love of learning that will last me all my life.'

When not at court, Father spent his days in his study, working on his translations of the works of Boccaccio and Petrarch and other Italian writers, which he liked to present as New Year gifts to the King himself, the Princess Mary and others whom he wished to please. Always, they were well received. Lord Morley's love of learning had ensured that his daughters were as well educated as his son. Jane was leaving Great Hallingbury literate and well read; she had even studied the works of Cicero, Seneca and Plutarch, her father's favourites. She was equipped, he assured her, to serve Queen Katherine, who was known to be an erudite woman, and to mingle with all ranks at court. She could be confident of receiving a warm welcome, for the Parkers were held in honour in the King's household. Lord Morley's presence was commanded at every ceremonial occasion, as now, when he too was to attend the Queen at the coming meeting of the kings of England and France.

The road to London took Jane and her father through Epping Forest and past the priory at Stratford-atte-Bow before swinging south to Greenwich Palace. Jane was impressed by the splendour of Greenwich, which was crowded with eager courtiers preparing for the coming venture to Calais and beyond. She was expecting Queen Katherine to be a beauteous lady, like the Guinevere of legend, and was trembling in awe by the time she was announced. She was disappointed, therefore, to find her older than she had expected and no beauty. Yet she would soon come to realise that there was a luminosity about her that came from a pure heart and a deep faith. It shone forth brighter than ever when the little Princess Mary joined them. It was clear to anyone that mother and daughter adored each other.

Katherine extended a kind welcome to Jane and her father. She sent Jane off with the Mother of the Maids, who told her quite firmly that she was to be courteous, obedient, discreet and, above all, virtuous. Jane's heart sank. As the days passed, however, she found, to her delight, that life was anything but dull in the Queen's household. Young men of the King's chamber or Cardinal Wolsey's household were encouraged to visit and socialise with the maids-of-honour. There was much merriment, music and dancing. She did so love to show off to such admiring company – and, apart from seeing him because she wanted to, she had been in no need of her father's advice.

'The Queen's Grace has your future in her hands,' the Mother of the Maids had told her. 'Your parents will be hoping that she will arrange a good marriage for you.'

Jane was thrilled to hear that. Many young lords had been sent by their families to make their way upwards in the King's service or the Cardinal's, the Cardinal being the chief power in the land after the King. Among them were the heirs to earldoms or dukedoms. She was twelve years old, old enough to be a wife – old beyond her years, her mother had said – and some of the heirs to peerages were in want of a wife. Her dream of greatness might come true sooner than she could ever have hoped.

She took to poring over her silver mirror, gazing at her reflection. Her features and her figure were delicate, her eyes wide set; her face tapered down to a pointed chin and her lips were full. There was much there for a man to admire, she told herself. Until her great lord came along, she would flaunt her charms to advantage and enjoy herself.

* * *

France was wonderful! Never had she seen such splendour and opulence as when the French and English courts came together in open countryside between the towns of Guisnes and Ardres. The maids-of-honour had a wonderful time and Jane found herself swept up in the little group that surrounded pretty Mary Carey, the just-married daughter of Sir Thomas Boleyn. Mary had lived in France before her marriage and served at the French court; they all loved hearing her racy tales about it. Jane liked Mary, but not her younger sister, Anne, with whom Mary had been reunited, for Anne had followed her to the French court. Jane thought her conceited and flippant.

Two days earlier, vast crowds had gathered and she had stood with the English maids under the stern eye of the Mother of the Maids – whose supervision they were always trying to elude – watching, rapt, as King Henry, a tall, glittering, powerfully built, god-like figure, greeted King Francis. This meeting was meant to bring about peace between England and France, those two ancient enemies, but, as Jane watched the two monarchs posturing and competing with each other, and witnessed King Henry's anger when King Francis threw him to the ground in a wrestling match, she did not hold out much hope for the desired conclusion. But no matter. For two whole weeks, being required only for light duties by the Queen, she was able to throw herself with passion into the revelry, dancing, feasting and flirting, watching the jousts – and snatching forbidden kisses from her admirers. But that was as far as it went. Nothing must be allowed to compromise her chances of snaring a noble husband.

Back in England, however, the noble husband showed no sign of materialising. Months went by and, with each one that passed, Jane's confidence wavered. She watched the lordly gallants dallying with her fellow maids-of-honour, trying to damp down her jealousy and curb her frustration. It would happen soon, she told herself. She had only to wait.

Jane twirled around in her white satin gown. She could barely contain herself. Tonight, she and seven other maids and ladies were to dance in a pageant before the King himself! Some nobleman was bound to notice her! She knew she looked beautiful in her bonnet of gold encrusted with jewels and embroidered with the name of her character, Constancy.

She glanced at the other ladies in the attiring room. One was the King's sister, who had been Queen of France; she was a tall, red-haired beauty, and all went in awe of her. Mistress Carey was lacing her gown, assisted by her obnoxious sister Anne, who had just joined Queen Katherine's household after returning from France when war loomed. Mistress Anne Boleyn was elegant and poised, not beautiful, but possessed of vast confidence, which irritated Jane. Try as she might, she could not like the newcomer and the dark-eyed Anne did not seem overly fond of her. Already there was an unspoken rivalry between them.

It was time. They all took their places inside a big model castle called 'Le Château Vert', and it was wheeled into the great hall of York Place, the Cardinal's London residence. On cue, they leapt out and engaged in a mock battle with eight masked lords who were pretending to storm the fortress. There had been speculation that the King would be among them, and Jane thought she knew which one, for he stood out in stature and ebullience above the rest. Laughing as she and the other ladies pelted the lords with comfits and doused them with rose water, ducking the fruit they were throwing in retaliation, she joined them for their inevitable surrender to the men and passed from partner to partner in the ensuing dance. But the man she thought was the King seemed interested in dancing only with Mary Carey and no other gallant paid particular attention to Jane.

She might now be one of the court's young stars, but she had no prospects to speak of. When, the following year, Anne Boleyn was forbidden to marry the Earl of Northumberland's heir – God only knew how she had snared him – Jane secretly gloated. She could not have borne to see Anne elevated so high.

That year, she was present at the wedding of her brother Henry to mousy little Grace Newport and could not help but think that he could have done better for himself. She also bade farewell to her father, who was being sent to Nuremburg as ambassador to present the Order of the Garter to the Emperor's brother. He wrote excitedly from there to say that his portrait had been drawn by the great artist, Albrecht Dürer. He also wrote of his despair at seeing the heretical ideas of Martin Luther so widely accepted in Germany. 'I thank God that will never happen in England, with our sovereign lord so zealous a champion of the Church,' he added.

1524–5

When Father returned to England and arrived at court to report back to the King, he came to see Jane.

'It is time I found you a husband,' he told her.

Her first instinct was to say, *Not someone insignificant like Grace Newport*, but she held her tongue.

'I will talk to your mother and put out some feelers,' he said. And with that she had to be content.

She was horrified when, that summer, he wrote to inform her that he had reached an agreement with Sir Thomas Boleyn. She was to be married to Boleyn's heir, George – Anne's brother. He wasn't even a knight! And she disliked the Boleyns. They were too full of themselves. George might be handsome in a saturnine way, but he had a terrible reputation. People spoke about his exploits in whispers, and she wished now that she had not listened. He was not chaste, and rumour had it that his living was bestial. It was even said that he had forced widows and maidens to do his will, sparing none at all. But the King approved of the marriage, and graciously presented George and Jane with the manor of Grimston, Norfolk, as a wedding gift.

Her dreams turned to dust, Jane knew there was now no hope of a reprieve. George Boleyn came a-courting – no doubt his father had told him to – and she tried her best to smile and find something to admire in his dissolute good looks. But it was easy to see that he was as lukewarm about their marriage as she was. On her wedding day, which fell in a week of bleak November weather, she felt as if she was going to her doom.

'Cheer up!' her mother said, as she fixed the chaplet of flowers on Jane's head. 'The Boleyns are going up in the world. This is a good marriage.'

But her mother was not there later to see what happened when George got into bed with Jane without having uttered one word of love or encouragement. It was so vile, so painful, and so different from what she had expected that she lay there afterwards in shock, knowing she could never speak of it to anyone. The horror was that she was George's wife now, his to do as he pleased with. There could be no redress.

There was no hope for either of them. They were locked in a marriage from which there was no escape. Jane dreaded her nightly ordeals. George was relentless, unable to resist his vile, unlawful inclinations. There was no tenderness in him, no sense of remorse. Even when he left her sore and weeping, he said no word of comfort or apology. It was easy to believe what rumour said of him. He was evil, evil!

In public, he was witty and charming; in private, when he was not tormenting her, he was morose and moody. Jane found herself longing to be back at Great Hallingbury. The court held no joys for her now. It had become an alien place and she had come to see her youthful ambitions as empty and frivolous.

Yet, ironically, it seemed that they might yet be fulfilled, for the Boleyns were indeed going up in the world, and that was all thanks to Anne.

1526–30

Jane never could understand what the King saw in Anne Boleyn. Anne was too sallow, too spiky, too full of herself – and no Venus. But there he was, besotted, enthralled, bewitched, some said, and willing to be led a merry dance.

At first, it did not seem a matter of great significance. Anne confided in her father and George – thick as thieves they were, those three – that King Henry was hot in pursuit of her, but she was adamant that she would never be his mistress. She would not go the way of her sister Mary, who had allowed herself to be caught and been abandoned when she became pregnant. It had all been very hush-hush – the King prided himself on his discretion in such matters – and Jane still had no idea whether Mary's husband believed the child to be his.

All this Jane learned from George. Anne never spoke of it to her. But then there was a subtle shift in the affair. The King was talking about marriage; Anne was going about with a secret smile on her face.

Soon, the court was abuzz with rumours.

'Is it true that his Grace means to put away the Queen?' Jane asked one day, when George joined her for dinner.

His eyes were alight with excitement. 'Yes,' he told her. 'He has asked the Pope for an annulment. Our sister will be queen soon!'

The secret was a secret no more. People began to take sides. Jane's sympathies were with poor, forsaken Queen Katherine, who was showing heroic dignity and courage in public, yet must be dying inside. Jane could have wept for the Princess Mary, who was being forced to endure what no child should endure, the infamy, the divided loyalties, the heartbreak of her parents separating.

Soon, the King's Great Matter, as everyone was calling it, was notorious throughout Christendom. Jane hid her opinions from the Boleyns; they had no truck with anyone who opposed the divorce. They were cocksure, belligerent and insufferable.

And yet, they came near to disaster. The sweating sickness, that terrible plague that visited England every few years and scythed down so many victims, scourged the land in the summer of 1528 and nearly carried Anne and George off. A royal physician came hurrying to Hever, his horse in a lather, and Jane shut herself in a guest chamber, well away from her stricken husband. Wicked as she knew it was, she prayed that God would see fit to take him and release her from her miserable marriage. But God deemed otherwise. George and Anne recovered. The King, Jane knew, would be delirious with relief.

When they were all back at court, and Jane was feeling at a low ebb, Anne got her alone and pressed her to tell her what was wrong between her and George. And she had blurted it all out, which she now regretted. Because Anne had done nothing; in her eyes, George could do no wrong. Jane felt that she had exposed her misery unnecessarily. For that, she hated Anne even more.

Two years passed, and still the Pope had not spoken. It seemed that he was deliberately prolonging the agony. King Henry was becoming more angry and frustrated by the day, and Anne was bemoaning her passing youth. Hopes were raised when his Holiness sent a legate into England to try the case, but dashed again when, after weeks of anticipation, he revoked the case to Rome. That was the end of the great Cardinal Wolsey, who had failed to make the legate grant the King his heart's desire. Anne saw to it that Wolsey would never enjoy influence again.

After that, King Henry grew more determined than ever to make Anne queen. He created Thomas Boleyn Earl of Wiltshire, whereupon George took his father's subsidiary title and became Viscount Rochford, and Jane, at last, found herself a peeress. George was now one of the most powerful men at court, loaded with offices and wealth, and outwardly Jane enjoyed a life of luxury and privilege. Privately, she still lived in what she had come to view as her private hell – when George bestirred himself to make demands on her, that was. After five years of marriage, he was no longer as interested in using her for his filthy practices. If he was going elsewhere, that was all to the good. She could not have cared less.

She wondered if anyone in his family other than Anne had any inkling of his leanings. Had they ever wondered why she had borne no children? You might have expected Thomas Boleyn to want grandsons to inherit his new title. He was a shallow man for whom self-interest was everything. Like George and Anne, he was consumed with insufferable pride. But he was not interested in Jane. All his ambitions were vested in Anne.

George had a bastard son; it was no secret, but openly spoken of in the family. Jane had never met the child or his mother; she did not even know who the mother was or if the affair was still going on. Had George loved her? Sometimes Jane wondered if he was incapable of love. And yet he was devoted to Anne. He lavished on Anne all the love that should have been reserved for his wife. Every day, he was in her chamber, dancing attendance on her – and it was not just because Anne was going to be queen one day. It went far deeper than that. Jane had even begun to think that George was too close to Anne. And yet even he would surely stop at incest – wouldn't he? And wouldn't Anne?

She knew he hated being married as much as she did. They had been wed two years when she had found a book he'd left lying around, a cynical satire on women and wedlock. Having read the first paragraphs, she had to read on, appalled to find that the French author had written of the torments he had suffered since the day he wed. There was no doubting why the book appealed to George; it probably reflected his own views on her and their marriage.

Well, he was not alone! And henceforth, she resolved, without respect of any wifely obedience or dread of God, that she would waste her youth no longer. She was twenty-one, still beautiful, and surely some man must desire her. She would follow her lust and find pleasure where she would!

She was discreet; the Boleyns would not have brooked any public betrayal. She had nothing to lose now, neither her virginity nor her chance of making a good marriage. Somehow, by covert looks and gestures, at table or in the dance, or in the fashionable gatherings in Anne's chamber, she managed to convey that she was available – and men seemed to sense it. She had far more offers than when she was awaiting a marriage proposal – although these were not, of course, honourable ones. And so she indulged her fancies, congratulating herself – even as a paramour heaved above her – on paying George back.

She liked the idea of it – but she did not enjoy it. The horrors of her marriage bed had killed something in her. She could feel lust, she could fantasise about lovemaking, and thinking about others doing it excited her – yet she did not like doing it herself. It left her cold. Soon, she realised that all she was indulging herself for was revenge. Revenge on George for his cruelties, and revenge on the Boleyns for being so dismissive of her. They suffered her to be part of their circle only because she was George's wife.

In time, she tired of having her revenge. She was not enjoying herself, she lived in dread of becoming pregnant, and she was aware that she was gaining a reputation. No doubt some men had bragged of their conquests. It had to end.

1533–36

Anne was queen! There was equal excitement and dismay when the news was bruited around the court. As Anne processed to the Easter Mass, decked out in royal robes and bowing to right and left at the crowds of open-mouthed courtiers lining the galleries, Jane walked behind with the other ladies-in-waiting, burning with indignation. The King had not even waited to have his marriage to Queen Katherine decently annulled by his new, pliant Archbishop of Canterbury. And it was plain to see why! Anne was with child. Should it prove the son Henry had desired all his adult life, England would have its heir and his momentous break with the Pope would be justified. And the Boleyns would be even more insufferable!

By the time Anne was crowned at the beginning of June, her belly was enormous, yet still she wore virginal white. Jane was secretly pleased to see that the crowds did not cheer for her. Their sympathies lay with the banished Katherine, who had been deprived of her crown, her title and the company of her daughter. Jane's heart went out to both ladies. She knew her father felt the same. When he came to London for the coronation, his disgust was obvious.

'The Lady Margaret would be turning in her grave,' he muttered. 'She was overjoyed when the King married the Lady Katherine. It was such a royal match, allying the might of Spain with that of England.

And now . . .' His voice tailed off. 'We are none of us supposed to say a word against what has been done.'

Jane looked nervously about her, but there was no one in the gallery to hear them.

'I dare say I ought to be grateful that Henry has been made a Knight of the Bath in the coronation honours,' Father went on. 'I just wish he could have received the accolade in different circumstances. What an *annus terribilis*!'

Jane nodded. 'But it's not all been terrible, surely? Henry and Grace's son is a blessing.'

'Aye,' Father smiled. 'A future Lord Morley. He's a bonny boy. And you, Jane? How fares life with you?'

Jane had long resisted the temptation to confide in him the truth about her marriage. She had put on a brave countenance and pretended that all was well.

Father gave her a long look. 'You know where I am if you ever want to talk to me.'

For a moment, she felt her mask slip. 'There is nothing to talk about,' she said quickly, feeling tears threatening.

'Even so.'

There was a pause, then Father took her arm and began walking towards the end of the gallery.

'I see you are become friendly with Master Cromwell,' Jane said, as brightly as she could. Master Cromwell had slipped almost effortlessly into Wolsey's shoes and was now the most powerful man in the kingdom after King Henry. But Cromwell was no Wolsey: he was a fierce gospeller, hot for reform and change.

'Against my better inclinations, I am,' Father smiled. 'We have many interests in common. He is a cultivated man and has spent time in Italy.' It was the land of Father's dreams. 'I have sent him some of my translations. And yet, there are some matters on which we cannot agree. We have an unspoken agreement not to touch upon them.'

'But you have accepted the break with Rome?'

'I am a pragmatist, Jane. Some would say I bend with the wind. I just want to be left unmolested. There are those who are brave enough to make their disapproval known. My old friend, Bishop Fisher is one of them. As is Sir Thomas More, who resigned as Lord Chancellor rather than compromise his principles. John Fisher is zealous for Queen Katherine. But kings will be obeyed. It is folly to resist.'

'We are all making compromises,' Jane said. 'It is dangerous to have strong principles.'

Anne's child was a girl. All that fuss and upheaval, the break with Rome, the misery of Katherine and Mary – all for this! But, if the King was disappointed, he did not show it. Jane saw his face as he peered over the cradle, saw it light up when he looked upon the infant Elizabeth, heard him say that, by God's grace, boys would follow.

Anne emerged from her confinement in a bullish mood. It would be a son next time, she assured everyone. Within a few weeks, she was pregnant again. It ended the following summer in blood and tragedy. Jane watched, appalled, as the midwife covered the tiny dead face of the King's son and hurried away with him. This time, there was no announcement, no public churching of the Queen. A veil was drawn over this momentous loss; no one was to speak of it.

Anne was no longer so bullish. She lay there listlessly, weeping or complaining that the King had been unfaithful. It wasn't the first time he had strayed. And the young lady he was bedding was Joan Ashley, one of Anne's maids-of-honour. Only George could bring a wan smile to Anne's face, but not for long. He sat by her bed for hours, consoling her as only he knew how – and God knew how, Jane wondered.

When her confinement ended, Anne sat in her chamber, weeping. Her women looked at each other, not knowing what to say about Henry's flirtation, for it was dangerous to criticise the King. Jane was sure that Anne had overheard her gossiping about the King's affair.

Anne's eyes bored into her. 'I want to get rid of Joan Ashley,' she said. 'I need a pretext to send her away. Maybe we could contrive an urgent summons home?'

'Far better if she merited dismissal!' Jane said.

'She certainly does,' Anne agreed. 'If it could be put about that she is making herself available to all and sundry, then I would have every justification – and the King would be angry with her for sharing her favours. He will brook no rival. Jane, you know all the latest gossip. Who better to spread the word?'

'I'll do it,' Jane said reluctantly.

'You would do that for me?' Anne asked, surprised.

'Why not? It spares your Grace the bother – and the blame. I'll see off the little cow,' Jane said, and began her whispering campaign.

Why was she doing this? she asked herself. It was not without risk. In her heart, she knew she wanted to show that she was stronger than Anne, that Parker blood was stouter than Boleyn blood.

Anne dismissed the girl with a few choice withering remarks. When the pert minx opened her mouth to protest, she shooed her away and sent her packing.

The very next day, Jane was hauled, shaking with indignation, before Master Cromwell.

'Lady Rochford,' he said, dragging his eyes from the papers before him and looking up at her. 'I hear you have been telling stories about one of the Queen's maids. Several people have testified that you made them up to give the Queen a pretext to dismiss her. That was very wrong of you. Mistress Ashley is blameless in this matter.'

Jane dared not refute that. She did not doubt that this rebuke came from the King himself.

'You are dismissed from your post and must go home without delay,' Cromwell said. 'Good day to you.'

She went raging to Anne. 'I have been banished from the court!' she cried. 'I am to leave at once, and it's all your fault!'

'On what grounds?' Anne asked.

'For spreading gossip!'

Jane told Anne what Cromwell had said, spitting out the words. 'I wish I had never helped you in your foolhardy scheme!' she hissed. Then, omitting her curtsey, she flounced off to her lodging to pack. No doubt George would be glad to see the back of her. Certainly, he raised no voice in protest and Anne lifted no finger to save her. So much for gratitude!

George had told her to go to Hever, but she had refused. Go to the Boleyns' country house? Never! She was finished with them, and told him so. He just laughed, derisively, and said she should go to Grimston instead, or as far away as possible. Well, that would suit her, but first she was visiting Great Hallingbury, where her parents would welcome her. Calmer now, she was relieved to be leaving George and the court.

She was not the only one to suffer banishment. The Boleyns took no prisoners. She was almost gleeful when she heard that Anne's sister Mary, whom they had tried to make invisible because of her affair with the King, had suddenly appeared at court in an advanced stage of pregnancy with a penniless husband in tow. Anne had been incandescent and Mary was soon packed off to the country, having been warned never to show her face at court. Jane could not resist smiling, imagining Anne's discomfiture.

It was not long before she had even more reason to be grateful for having been dismissed. Some brave souls yet remained openly opposed to the King's divorce and would not acknowledge Anne as queen or the King as head of the Church of England. One was the saintly John Fisher, Bishop of Rochester, her father's old friend; they had met years ago in the household of the Lady Margaret Beaufort, to whom they had both been devoted. John Fisher had been her confessor. Father often recalled how he had been present when she died during a Mass celebrated by his friend. The Bishop had since been a frequent guest at Great Hallingbury and everyone in the family loved him.

A few years back, there had been an attempt to poison him that had, thankfully, failed. Jane was in no doubt that the Boleyns had been behind it. Their vindictiveness knew no bounds, for, since then, the Bishop had been imprisoned in the Tower for denying the royal supremacy, and Father was deeply concerned because just after Jane had left court, the King ordered the execution of a nun from Kent and her accomplices, all of whom had spoken out for Queen Katherine. Those executions had shocked everyone. It was the first time that blood had been shed in the Queen's cause. No one had expected the King to go so far.

Jane did not believe that he would execute Bishop Fisher – not that holy old man. But Father was very worried. He even went to London and bribed his way into the Tower.

'I felt that someone should be with him at such a perilous time, to strengthen him,' he said afterwards. 'He is so good a man and so divine a clergyman – and so resolute in his principles. But I found him aged and sick – I fear he is not long for this world.'

His words were prophetic, but not in the way he meant them. In late June, news arrived that Bishop Fisher had been beheaded for refusing to acknowledge the King as supreme head of the Church of England and his marriage to Anne Boleyn.

Father shed bitter tears of anger and grief. His usual caution deserted him. 'It is the Boleyns who have done this!' he raged. 'I pray that God will make them pay for it. Jane, I want you to have nothing more to do with them.'

Jane wanted nothing more to do with them either. They were wicked, evil – and the cause of all the terrible upheavals in the realm.

'We must all place our hopes in the Princess Mary,' Father declared, giving her the title that had been cruelly taken from her. 'She is the true heir to this kingdom and a model of virtue and learning. She should be restored to the succession! I will make sure she knows she has my allegiance.'

'Hush!' Mother hissed. 'You'll have us all in the Tower if anyone hears you.'

In October, word came that the King and Queen were gone on a progress and that the Lady Mary was at Greenwich. Jane determined to go there in the hope of seeing Mary and letting her know that she had friends ready to support her who were sorry for the way she had been treated.

Father agreed to her going and sent two grooms to escort her the thirty-odd miles to Greenwich. When she got there, she was astonished to find a vast crowd of women outside the palace. As she reined in her horse, she glimpsed a small procession approaching through the excited throng. Their ranks parted to reveal the Lady Mary, looking utterly overwhelmed as weeping women fell to their knees before her.

'Your Grace is our true princess!' they cried out.

Mary seemed frozen in her litter. She made no reply, but stared at them like a rat caught in a trap.

'God save the true Princess!' Jane yelled, above the hubbub. Immediately, a guard from Mary's escort grabbed her bridle. She was shocked.

''Tis treason to say that, lady,' he growled. 'You must come with me.' He led her through the crowd, and she could see that other women were being rounded up and taken prisoner. One she recognised as Lady William Howard, Anne's aunt by marriage. What was she doing here? Could it be that Jane was not the only one who had abandoned the Boleyns?

She was terrified when she realised that they were taking her to the Tower. It dawned on her that she really had uttered treasonable words in a public place and that the punishment might be severe. What would they do to her? She began envisaging all kinds of dreadful things.

She was praying that the grooms of her escort, who had vanished into thin air when the guard apprehended her, had gone winging back to Essex to tell Father what had happened to her. It was her only hope.

They locked her in a room in one of the towers, after asking if she had any money with her. Fortunately, she had, and they took it to pay for food, firewood and warmer bedding. The room was small, but adequately furnished, yet she barely noticed. She could only pace up and down, wringing her hands.

It was a very long, lonely night. It was impossible to sleep. When the door was unlocked, dawn was breaking. She jumped, fearful of what might happen next, but broke into tears of relief when she saw the Constable of the Tower with her father.

'You are to come home with me, Daughter,' Father said in a stern voice. 'George and I are sworn to stand surety for your good behaviour and conformableness to the King's laws. We have agreed it is best that I take you to Great Hallingbury.'

Jane's knees nearly buckled under her, but she managed to walk out of the room, barely able to believe that she was free to leave. She knew she would never forget the last awful hours and that she had had a very lucky deliverance.

Once they were out of the Tower and in the waiting litter, Father gave her a hug.

'Your loyalty to the Lady Mary is commendable,' he said, 'but, in future, use a little discretion and stay out of trouble.'

She resolved to stay at home and never go to court or involve herself in public affairs again. It was months before that resolve wavered and that was when the Morleys received a visit from no less a personage than Thomas Cromwell, now the King's Principal Secretary.

They had had warning. Master Secretary was coming to dine with his friend, Lord Morley. Mother, Jane, Henry and Grace were present, but through all the lively and erudite conversation that flowed over the meal, Jane kept wondering if this was purely a social visit. She was aware that Master Cromwell's shrewd, piggy eyes kept straying in her direction. It made her feel nervous.

After dinner, Father was closeted with Master Cromwell for a time. Jane escaped into the garden, making herself scarce. She was quite dismayed to see Master Secretary walking towards her, and to realise that they were quite alone.

'Lady Rochford,' he said, smiling. 'Your father said you might be here. What a pleasant spot this is.'

'You like gardens, Sir?' she asked nervously.

'I do, but I rarely have time to appreciate them,' he grinned. Then the smile faded. 'Shall we walk together?' He offered her his arm and steered her along the gravel path by the flower beds.

There was a pause before he spoke. 'Madam, I am investigating a delicate matter touching the Queen. Please think carefully. Have you ever had cause to suspect her of any misconduct?'

Jane was astonished – and strangely excited. What delicate matter? And what did he mean by misconduct?

'I'm not sure that I take your meaning, Sir,' she said.

'I have reason to believe that she has betrayed her marriage vows,' Cromwell revealed. 'It seems she has taken lovers.'

Jane was tart. 'I find that hard to believe. There's only one man she really loves and that's my husband!'

Cromwell's eyes glittered. 'Indeed. And is this love the normal kind between brother and sister – or is it an abominable sin?'

Too late, Jane realised what she had said. She hesitated. Was this a God-given opportunity to bring down Anne and the hated Boleyns? Had she been chosen as the instrument through which their fall would be achieved? It was barely believable.

Cromwell halted. 'I understand your reluctance to answer me, my lady. Am I right in thinking that you bear no love to your husband's kin?'

Jane thought of all the horrors of her marriage bed, of George's complete indifference to her misery, and of poor Bishop Fisher, Queen Katherine, the Princess Mary . . . She thought of Father raging that he would make the Boleyns pay for their wickedness. Her duty was clear.

She took a deep breath. 'If you must know, Master Secretary, I have had my suspicions for a long time. They are too close, those two. Don't think I speak from jealousy. There are things I could tell you about my marriage that would make the Devil blench.' She found her voice breaking.

Cromwell was frowning. 'Sit down here, my lady.' He indicated a stone bench. 'Are you telling me that you have proof of incest.'

'I have the proof of my own eyes!' she cried. 'They are all to each other! They have often been alone in her bedchamber – it's the truth. I once saw him kiss her as she lay abed. They look at each other like lovers. She told him, before she told the King, that she was with child.'

'Did she?' Cromwell interjected. 'And did that lead you to suspect that the child was his?'

Jane clapped her hand to her mouth. 'I never thought of it,' she faltered. 'I just think that they are unnaturally close for a brother and sister.'

'Would you be prepared to sign a statement to that effect?'

Jane hesitated again, then remembered what a service she would be doing herself, her family and all those who had suffered injury because

315

of the Boleyns. And it seemed that they were on a headlong course to disaster anyway; it would be politic to dissociate herself from them. 'I would,' she said.

When she heard that the Queen had been taken to the Tower and that several men had been arrested with her, she began trembling. It was because of her that this had happened. No, it couldn't be – she had only spoken to Cromwell of George. Then something occurred to her. What if Cromwell had cozened others to give evidence against the Queen? Well, what if he had? There was no smoke without fire!

To salve her conscience, she wrote immediately to George, asking how he was faring in the Tower and promising to make suit to the King for him – which she had not the slightest intention of doing. She sent her letter to Master Cromwell, saying it would look suspicious if she did not write to her husband, and that she did not want George suspecting that she had testified against him; she asked if it would be possible to pass on her missive. Cromwell informed her, almost by return, that the King himself had authorised him to do so. Jane wondered if she was receiving special treatment because of her willingness to give evidence against George and Anne – or if they were hoping to obtain further incriminating evidence from George's reply. But reply there was none.

Father was summoned to London as one of the peers who were to sit in judgement on the accused. He went willingly, zealous in his determination to see justice done.

'Do not think I am unaware of what that knave has done to you,' he told Jane. 'Sir Francis Bryan tells me that Rochford's particular vices are well known at court. Be assured, he shall pay for it.' His voice was gruff with righteous outrage.

When he came home, all was over. He had declared George and Anne guilty without a qualm. Jane learned that it was not her evidence alone that had brought down Anne – and several courtiers with her. She had not testified to Anne taking four other lovers or plotting the King's death. But it was her deposition that condemned George. She could feel neither pity nor remorse, not even when Father told her that all the accused had been beheaded. It was shocking, but all she could feel was a heady sense of freedom.

'I watched Rochford die,' Father said. 'He prayed that he might be forgiven by all whom he had injured. He said he deserved to die for he was a wretched sinner and had sinned shamefully. He said he had known no man so evil. Well, we all know that.'

'Amen,' Mother said, tight-lipped. 'This world is well rid of him.'

1536–9

Jane donned black, for form's sake. Officers of the King came to seize George's goods, which were now forfeit to the Crown. They even took Jane's rich court gowns. Since her husband's landed property had been confiscated, and his offices vacated, she found herself deprived of an income – and facing poverty. Had it not been for her father, she would have been destitute. Was this how she was to be repaid for helping to rid the realm of traitors?

She wrote to Master Cromwell, begging for help. Give him his due, he and the King acted at once, and she was informed that his Majesty had commanded Thomas Boleyn to pay her an income. Boleyn would be spitting with rage at that! And Father was rewarded for his loyal service with lucrative offices at the nearby royal manor of Hatfield Regis.

'I notice that my revered father-in-law has omitted to offer me a home at Hever,' Jane observed.

'Not that you would want it!' Mother muttered.

'Your home is here,' Father assured Jane.

That summer, she went with her parents to visit the Princess Mary at Hunsdon, six miles from Great Hallingbury. In going there, Father was risking the wrath of King Henry, as it was unwise to show sympathy for one under the cloud of royal displeasure. But it was worth it to see Mary's eyes light up with pleasure when she saw him. No mention was made of recent events, but somehow Father conveyed to Mary that his first loyalty, his love and his truth, were to her, as the King's lawful heir. There could be no other, since Elizabeth had been declared a bastard.

Jane returned to Great Hallingbury and the gentle domestic round her mother daily observed. It was what she needed after the nightmare years of her marriage and the high dramas of the past months.

She was unprepared for the summons to court. She was to serve the King's new wife, Jane Seymour, as lady-in-waiting. It was a reward, she knew, for her cooperation in toppling the Boleyns.

'I knew Jane Seymour at court,' she recalled. 'She was very quiet, but devoted to the Lady Mary. I shall enjoy serving her.'

Father provided new gowns and Jane soon found herself back at Greenwich. She was delighted to find the Princess Mary back in favour, thanks to the good intercessions of the gentle Queen Jane. Those were happy months, especially after the Queen found herself with child. It was a boy, a long-awaited heir for the King, and Jane was swept up in the celebrations. Father came to Hampton Court for the christening and had the honour of carrying the Lady Elizabeth in his arms. Only weeks later, though, he was one of those holding aloft a canopy over Queen Jane's bier at her funeral. Afterwards, an exhausted Jane returned home with him, having spent long hours in vigil beside the coffin for the past fortnight.

For the next two years, Jane stayed at Great Hallingbury, enjoying the peace of the Essex countryside – when she wasn't chasing Thomas Boleyn for her dower, the income George had settled on her when they wed. Boleyn had grudgingly paid her allowance, as the King had ordered, but he kept insisting that it was in lieu of her dower. Losing patience, Jane complained to Lord Cromwell, as he now was, and was astonished when Parliament passed an Act confirming her dower and protecting her interest in some manors owned by Boleyn. She was even more astounded to learn that the Act was passed after its three readings were rushed through on the same day – and that it was signed by the King himself. On top of this, his Majesty granted her two manors in Warwickshire. It was, she realised, further evidence of how grateful he was to her for helping him to rid himself of the Boleyns.

Basking in royal favour, Jane returned to court in December 1539 to serve King Henry's fourth Queen, Anna of Cleves. She would be serving alongside the King's niece, Lady Margaret Douglas, and many other ladies she knew. She was particularly taken by a new maid-of-honour, Mistress Katheryn Howard, niece of the Duke of Norfolk. Katheryn was young, pretty and naïve, with an air of vulnerability about her. Her parents were dead and her step-grandmother, in whose household she had grown up, appeared to have neglected her. Jane took the girl under her wing and acted as her mentor, showing her how things were done at court and writing letters for her, having noticed that Katheryn struggled with literacy. Soon, the pair of them were fast friends. In some ways, for Jane, who was now past thirty-one, Katheryn was the daughter she had never had.

1540–42

Father came to Greenwich to walk in the procession of gentlemen who preceded the King when he formally welcomed Anna of Cleves to England at a great state reception on Blackheath. The word at court was that his Majesty had met his new Queen already and been unimpressed, but there was no faulting his courtesy in public. However, it was soon obvious that all was not well in the royal marriage. When the wedding festivities were over, the placid Anna was relegated to her apartments – and Jane was not the only one left bored by such a dull existence. *We are parrots in a gilded cage*, she thought.

She continued to take a genuine interest in Katheryn Howard's affairs. Two young gentlemen of the King's Privy Chamber were pursuing her: Thomas Paston and Thomas Culpeper. Culpeper was beautiful, ambitious, wealthy and of good birth. Jane was smitten too. She would have liked him for herself; he was the only man for whom she had ever felt desire, and for that she would have died for him, because she had thought herself spoiled for ever by George and incapable of wanting any man. Yet Culpeper never looked upon her in that way; to him, she was just a good friend. He had eyes only for Katheryn.

By the spring, it was obvious that the couple were in love. Jane was happy for them; she liked to imagine them together and helped to arrange their secret trysts. They had to be secret because the King himself was pursuing Katheryn.

In the summer, the royal marriage was annulled and Anna of Cleves cheerfully left court, laden with a substantial settlement and four great houses. Immediately, it became clear who the next Queen would be.

Culpeper was heartbroken when Katheryn told him they must stop seeing each other. He wept on Jane's shoulder. When the King married Katheryn, Culpeper was physically ill. Jane could not bear to see him so low, but there was nothing she could do to comfort him. If only he had let her, she would have made him forget, but the moment never came.

Six months later, Jane found herself serving Queen Katheryn, and willingly too. She couldn't blame Katheryn for Culpeper's misery. The girl had had no choice. Besides, what nineteen-year-old wanted to marry a sick, fat, prematurely aged man of nearly fifty? For the King was no longer the chivalrous, sporting prince Jane remembered from his younger days, but a bloated mass of wasted muscle and diseased legs. No, Jane pitied Katheryn and admired her fortitude, and the charming way she behaved to Henry.

1541

'The King is near death,' Culpeper whispered after Jane collided with him on the stairs on a cold day in February and he stopped her. They were easy with each other now, good friends and confidants. She looked around nervously, but there was no one to see.

'He is ill again?' she murmured.

Culpeper beckoned her to follow him up to the next landing and led her into a lumber room, closing the door behind them.

'Yes, and not likely to survive, the doctors say.' His eyes were dark with portent. 'Lady Rochford, we face the prospect of a regency. The Prince is not four years old. The Queen may find herself in a position of great influence – and her friends stand to benefit.' He bent to her ear and she thought she would swoon with the nearness of him and the vista he was opening up before her eyes. 'We must make the most of our opportunities,' he said. 'We must make ourselves indispensable to her Grace.'

'The Queen is our good friend,' Jane said, fired up by his words.

'And must be more! You know how much I love her. His Grace has no idea! He sets me to keep her company and entertain her whenever he is indisposed. She says she loves him, but I think she dissembles. Lady Rochford, if you could encourage her to permit me to be her servant, neither of us will ever forget it.'

Jane wavered for a heartbeat. 'You mean to marry her when she is free?'

'I do. I mean to be her husband and her chief counsellor. Through her, I could rule this realm. And you would be first in our favour. I beg you – tell her that I am dying of love for her. Think of what could come of it!'

Jane could not resist. She agreed wholeheartedly to do as he wished. A glorious future was opening out before her.

Katheryn would not listen. She would not be unfaithful to the King, she said. It took weeks of subtle persuasion before her resolve began to waver. By then, Henry had recovered, but still Culpeper was bent on laying his plans. It could only be a matter of time, he said.

At length, Katheryn did agree to receive him – but only to put an end to his designs, she insisted. He was jubilant when he heard. 'Give me an hour with her and she will be mine!' he declared.

It was Jane who arranged their meeting, who concealed Culpeper in her own bedchamber one midnight so that Katheryn could go to him there, and who kept watch in the gallery. And all for nothing! The silly girl wanted no more to do with him. She even became distant towards Jane.

And then Katheryn suffered a miscarriage and the King's passion for her cooled. She was in fear that he would discard her. It drove her into Tom's arms.

Now Jane found herself busily acting as go-between, carrying letters, contriving secret meetings and, all the time, keeping watch, for this was one secret that must never come to light. All through the summer the affair went on, and throughout the King's great progress to the North. At every house where the court stayed, Jane would be seeking out places where the lovers could meet; sometimes, Katheryn did that herself, so eager was she to be with Culpeper. Once or twice, there was no suitable trysting place, so the two of them had to meet in the Queen's privy.

Culpeper's motive in reviving their affair had seemed mercenary at the time, although Jane had never blamed him for that, for she herself was hoping to profit from it – and it was keeping Katheryn happy. Yet she believed that Culpeper genuinely loved the Queen – and there was no doubt that his love was reciprocated. She did not think the pair were actually lovers; Katheryn might be naïve, but she was not that silly. But they were certainly indulging in some fleshly joys. Jane's heart beat faster when she imagined what these might be.

She knew that others in the household had become aware that something was going on. It was impossible to manage the logistics of the liaison without help, but Jane took care to ensure that Katheryn's maids and chamberers knew nothing of the true nature of their errands. They were merely there to fetch, carry or keep watch. And woe betide them if they asked questions!

It was a strain – sometimes, she had to admit it to herself. The long nights without sleep, the fear of discovery, the knowledge that the King was once more the doting husband and could at any moment take it upon himself to visit Katheryn. There had been one heart-stopping minute when Jane had managed to spirit Culpeper away just in time – and another when Katheryn thought the King had set a watch on her. Yet Jane was sure it would all be worth it in the long run.

When they were in Yorkshire, an overbearing knave called Francis Dereham joined the Queen's household and began throwing his weight about. Before long, he was dropping hints that he and Katheryn had once meant more to each other than was seemly, and this aroused Culpeper's anger. Suddenly, the two were rivals, to Jane's dismay. Dereham would ruin all, she feared.

By All Souls Day, they were back at Hampton Court. At Mass, the King publicly gave thanks to God for sending him such a virtuous and loving wife – a rose without a thorn. Standing in the nave, Jane flushed and bowed her head lower, not daring to think how Katheryn, in the royal pew above, was keeping her composure. But Katheryn seemed unbothered when she emerged from the chapel, smiling.

The following afternoon, Jane was in the Queen's chamber playing cards with Katheryn and some of the other ladies when the door was flung open and the Lord Chancellor and a deputation of Privy Councillors strode in, attended by four of the King's guards.

'Katheryn, Queen of England, you are under arrest!' the Lord Chancellor announced. He held out a warrant.

Jane began trembling. Were they all betrayed? Or was this about some other matter? She wished she could believe it. Katheryn looked stricken.

'Ladies, you may leave us,' the Lord Chancellor commanded, and Jane had no choice but to walk out of the apartment with the other women. Behind them, the guards took up their places outside the door and crossed their halberds in front of it, leaving Jane in no doubt that this was serious.

She was desperate to know what was being said behind that door. She wondered if Culpeper had been arrested too. If he had, there was no hope for Katheryn – or for her. She dared not let herself think about what that might mean. She forced herself not to look back on the terrible events of 1536, when another Queen had been brought down.

Common sense came to her rescue. If they knew about Katheryn and Culpeper, surely she, Jane, would have been arrested too. And she was proved right because, when the ladies were allowed back to tend to an inconsolable, petrified Katheryn, Katheryn managed to tell them that she was accused of misconduct before her marriage. Jane knew it was imperative that she impress on her mistress the need to keep silent about what had happened after it. That was a far more serious matter.

The Lord Chancellor had warned them all not to discuss the charges with the Queen. But Jane cared nothing for that. She followed Katheryn to the privy.

'Have you heard anything from Tom?' Katheryn asked her.

Jane had not, and could not risk searching him out today, even to quell their shared terror.

Katheryn's eyes were dark with dread. 'If the matter doesn't come out, there is nothing to fear,' she said. 'I will never confess it, and, if you love me, you will deny it utterly.' Jane felt Katheryn's despair, even as she insisted, 'Remember, if you confess, you will undo both yourself and others.'

'I will never confess it, even if I am torn apart with wild horses,' Jane promised. She could hear her voice growing shrill. 'Would I really sign my own death warrant?'

She was shaking again, painfully aware of the danger in which she stood. Fear was washing over her in great waves.

Fortunately, the ladies were allowed out into the court, provided they told the guards where they were going and why. Jane took it upon herself to go out daily, on the pretext of visiting the servery. In fact, she was looking for Culpeper, just to reassure herself and Katheryn that he was still at liberty. Katheryn kept asking her to go. Neither of them could stand the strain of not knowing.

In her worst moments, Jane tried to imagine what it was like to be beheaded. She'd heard it had taken three chops of the axe to kill George. She did not think she could bear to live much longer with this terrible fear. She wondered if God was punishing her for laying evidence against her husband. Once, she fell apart in front of Katheryn, clawing her neck and mouthing wordless cries. Katheryn spoke sharply to her. 'Peace be!' she hissed. 'You don't want anyone to hear you or see you like this. They will suspect something.'

Jane just stared at her. Much more of this, and she would go mad. She could feel herself fragmenting inside.

Four days had elapsed before Archbishop Cranmer came to question the Queen. They were closeted together for hours. In the next room, the ladies could hear Katheryn crying pitifully. Jane tried to breathe slowly. Her fear was like a solid lump in her chest.

When Katheryn finally staggered out into her bedchamber, she looked drained and ill, yet she would not tell them what had passed between her and the Archbishop. Jane could only pray that she had kept her resolve not to talk about Culpeper. Had he even been mentioned? She had no way of knowing. Terror was like a cloak enveloping her.

The days dragged on. Nothing happened, and there was no news. The suspense was so nerve-racking that Jane thought she would end up climbing the walls. And yet Culpeper was still free. She allowed herself to hope – just a little.

Then, one day, she could not find him. And no one would tell her where he was.

Katheryn gaped at her, horrified.

They knew. The words lay unspoken between them.

'Say nothing, remember!' Katheryn begged.

Jane went about light-headed and unable to concentrate on anything. If something awful befell Culpeper, she did not know how she would go on, because it would be as much her fault as his. Every day she looked for him, but he was not there, and she dared not keep asking after him lest she aroused people's suspicions. She was living in hell, terrified that it was only a matter of time before they came for her.

The King had left Hampton Court, abandoning Katheryn to her fate. Wandering through the deserted palace, Jane knew she now had no hope of establishing Culpeper's whereabouts.

Then came a dreadful Friday afternoon, nine days after Katheryn's arrest, when Sir Thomas Wriothesley, one of the King's councillors, arrived in the Queen's chamber and brusquely informed her that he wished to speak to her about Thomas Culpeper. Jane had withdrawn a little distance with the other women, but her ears pricked up when she heard Culpeper's name and she almost cried out. She could not hear what Wriothesley was saying to Katheryn, but their exchange was brief. After he had left, Katheryn hurried into her bedchamber and Jane followed.

'I denied everything,' Katheryn said. 'I said I did not know what he was talking about. If they ask you, you must say the same, for both our sakes.'

Jane began crying. 'Oh, God, they know! It is only a matter of time now.' Hysteria threatened to overwhelm her.

Late that evening, Archbishop Cranmer informed Katheryn that she was to remove to Syon Abbey with a greatly reduced household. She asked if Jane could go with her, and her request was granted, which gave Jane cause to hope that all was not lost.

They were to leave on Monday. Jane sagged with relief. But it was short-lived because the very next day, the Archbishop returned with the Lord Chancellor and other councillors.

'We have come to examine your Grace touching Culpeper,' Cranmer said, and Jane, seated at her embroidery among the other ladies, felt icy dread clutch at her heart.

They questioned Katheryn in private. Afterwards, she would not look Jane in the eye. She became hysterical again, and they had all to do to calm her down. She was thrashing about on her bed, threatening to kill herself and spare the executioner the trouble.

'They will kill me anyway if the suspicion of adultery is proved, so why should I give them the pleasure?' she wailed.

Jane froze when she heard that.

The next day, Sir Thomas Wriothesley returned and broke up the Queen's household. Everyone was sent home, apart from the few ladies and gentlemen who were going to Syon. It did not augur well for Katheryn's future.

At Syon, life was relatively frugal. It was like being in a nunnery. The nuns had gone, of course, when the abbey was dissolved, but there was still a conventual atmosphere about the place, abandoned as it was. They were even accommodated in some of the cells around the cloister. Katheryn was made to wear only plain black gowns with little jewellery. All her gorgeous court gowns had been left behind.

Jane wondered if there was any room for hope. After all, they were not yet in the Tower. And, if the Council had uncovered evidence of treason, they surely would be.

She could not believe she had come to such a sorry pass, nor could she stop weeping. Her life had been awful, and she had known little real happiness. One day, the strain became all too much.

'None of this is my fault!' she cried wildly. 'I come of good parentage, but I was brought up in the court, unbridled, and let to follow my filthy pleasure!'

Katheryn put her arms around her. 'What do you mean?'

Jane could contain herself no longer. 'I had lovers enough, to my shame. I could have had my pick of anyone, but I had to marry George Boleyn. To say we were unhappy would be an understatement. When George abused me, I looked elsewhere. I had no respect for virtue; I did not dread God. And when my beauty began to be spent, I grew bitter. It was I, I who accused George and Anne of incest! I sent them to the scaffold!' She knew she was becoming hysterical, but she could not help it, could not stop herself laughing. 'And I did it to be rid of him! I had no grounds for saying it.'

Katheryn looked appalled.

'I think we're all a little overwrought,' Lady Baynton said briskly, and Jane felt her hand on her shoulder. 'Now, let's have no more of this wild talk.'

For a few blissful hours, Jane slept. She was too exhausted to do anything else. But, when she awoke, the misery of her situation came flooding back. There was no escape from it.

Two days later, Sir Edward Baynton entered the Queen's bedchamber, where her ladies were sewing. 'My Lady Rochford,' he said, 'you are summoned to Whitehall. The Council wishes to question you.'

Jane could not speak. The thing she had dreaded was upon her. Then something gave way within her and she began laughing uncontrollably as the tears poured down her cheeks. The laughter turned to screaming. If she screamed loudly enough, someone would help her.

Sir Edward was remonstrating with her, but she could not comprehend what he was saying. In the end, he gave up, and armed guards took hold of her and dragged her, still screaming and laughing, along the path to the river, where, they bundled her into a barge and told her roughly to shut up.

By the time she was brought before the grim-faced men of the Council, Jane was calmer, but still agitated. She had recovered her reason sufficiently to know that she must now fight for her life.

'The Queen has deposed that you encouraged and abetted her in criminal conversation with Master Thomas Culpeper,' she was informed. 'Others assert that you were the principal cause of her folly.'

So Katheryn had broken her promise and thrown her to the wolves. For a moment Jane knew disgust, but then she collected herself. Well, two could play at that game.

'That is not true,' she said breathlessly. 'I merely acted as go-between at the Queen's command. I dared not refuse.'

'You knew what was going on?'

'I had my suspicions. I was never privy to what her Grace and Culpeper did when they were together, except I know they talked a lot, but . . .' She allowed her voice to tail off.

'But what?' Wriothesley barked.

'I thought they were discussing politics; they spent a lot of time talking, but I think now that Culpeper has known the Queen carnally, considering all the things I have heard and seen between them.'

'You would be prepared to testify to that?'

Jane hesitated. 'Yes,' she said, knowing she was probably signing Katheryn's death warrant.

'When did this abominable treason begin?'

'In the spring,' she said. 'Master Culpeper made the first advances. At first, they were not welcome. But he persisted and eventually the Queen admitted him privately to her chamber.'

'Did they ever meet in your rooms?'

What was the point in lying? They probably knew the answer anyway. 'Yes. I stood guard in case the King came.'

The questioning went on and on until she thought she would start screaming again. It took all her resolve to portray her role in the affair as passive; she took pains to point out that she was only obeying orders.

328

'And you did not think you had a duty to report this treason?'

'I did not know for certain what was going on!' she cried. 'How then could I accuse her Grace? She is the Queen. What if I had accused her falsely?'

'Do you think the Queen was aware of the risks she was taking?'

'I do.'

'And you are aware that you may be charged with misprision of treason, for which the penalty is imprisonment?'

She sank to her knees. 'I intended no harm to his Majesty.'

They were looking at her with contempt. When they called for the guards, she started to cry.

'Take her to the Tower!' the Lord Chancellor ordered.

She started screaming again when the Tower of London loomed up above her and the barge turned in towards the water gate.

'Quiet!' snapped Wriothesley. But she could not stop herself. In the end, he shook her to her senses until she fell silent. Her knees felt as if they would give way when she climbed the steps and was handed over into the custody of the Constable of the Tower. He led her to a lodging in the royal palace. It was well-furnished and comfortable, yet it was still a prison. When the door closed, she curled up in a ball on the floor and lay there whimpering.

For three days, she retreated into herself to a place where no one could touch her. The Constable was not unkind, but he had no idea how to deal with her. At length, he summoned a physician. The concern on the man's face penetrated Jane's stupor and broke her. Sinking to the floor again, she beat her breast and screamed and screamed.

They gave her poppy syrup, which made her sleep. She was barely aware of being carried into a barge, or of arriving at a fine house on the Strand. When she came to herself again, she found herself in a pretty bedchamber, lying on a soft feather bed. For a moment, she thought she had died and gone to Heaven. Then an old lady seated beside the bed told her briskly that she had been transferred to the care of Lady Russell, wife to the Lord Admiral, because she was brainsick, and that the King was sending his own physicians to see her.

She could not take this in. Why would the King show such concern for one he had cause to destroy?

She puzzled over that as she lay there, marvelling that she was feeling herself again, albeit weak and nervy. And then she heard voices outside her door.

'The King's doctor is coming this afternoon.' It was a man speaking. 'He desires her recovery so that he may have her executed as an example and warning to others.'

Jane was seized with a fit of trembling as hysteria rose in her again. *Executed.* Sweet Mother of God, that could not be true. She had not even been tried in court.

'Why treat her if he means to have her put to death?' a woman asked.

'Because insanity is a defence in law. If she is truly insane, she cannot be executed. She will be imprisoned until the King pardons her – or she may escape justice altogether.'

The voices faded, but Jane had heard enough. She knew what she had to do. She opened her mouth and began screaming. It was not all pretence.

Lady Russell was solicitous, if distant, towards her – to begin with. She only grew exasperated when all efforts to stop Jane wailing and shrieking had failed.

'Stop this now!' she commanded, but Jane was past hearing her. Terror had possessed her.

Her ladyship stood by as the doctors examined Jane, trying to reason with her. They too gave up. 'There is no hope for her,' they said. 'She has lost her mind.'

In the dark place where she had retreated, Jane heard them, as if from a long way off. Safe, she thought. *Safe.*

She lay in the pretty bedroom for weeks, affecting not to be aware of what was going on around her. The hysteria was always fizzing beneath the surface, especially when she thought of what they might do to her if they thought her sane. Lady Russell and Brigid, the old woman who

330

tended her, seemed to be scrutinising her all the time. She took care not to respond to them; she knew her very life depended on it.

Christmas came and went. She heard the sounds of revelry in the house and could have wept. Would she ever celebrate a Christmas again?

In January, Lady Russell came to her. 'Lady Rochford, Parliament is to determine the matter of your abetting the Queen in her treasonable offences. Do you understand me?'

Jane lay rigid with terror, not daring to move and staring straight ahead as if she had not heard Lady Russell.

'Lady Rochford? Oh, Brigid, it's no use! She is either in a trance or a frenzy. I fear she has lapsed into a madness from which she can never recover.'

Jane heard the door close behind her ladyship.

'You don't fool me!' muttered Brigid. Jane ignored her.

Weeks passed with no news. She wondered constantly what had befallen Katheryn and Culpeper. Of course, she could not ask. February came in; Jane heard Lady Russell order Brigid to buy extra candles for the chapel for Candlemas.

Some days later, there was a commotion below and the sound of heavy boots on the stairs. The door to her bedroom opened and there stood Sir Thomas Wriothesley and another gentleman.

'Lady Rochford, you have been, by authority of this Parliament, convicted and attainted of high treason, and shall suffer pains of death and the forfeiture of all your property to the Crown. You must arise and come with us.'

Jane began shaking uncontrollably.

'Sirs, she is mad and cannot understand you,' Lady Russell protested. 'She is insane!'

'Madam, Parliament has also passed an Act decreeing that, if a person, being *compos mentis*, commits high treason, and afterwards falls into madness, they may be tried in their absence,' the Lord Chancellor explained. 'If found guilty, they should suffer death, as if they were of perfect memory.'

At that moment, a great calmness came over Jane. The worst she had feared had happened – and she found, to her utter astonishment, that she had been given the strength to face it.

She struggled to sit up. 'I do understand you, Sirs,' she said. Lady Russell stared at her, nonplussed. 'If I am helped to dress, I will come with you.'

Very weak after her months in bed, she was assisted down the stairs and into a covered barge. Down the Thames it took her, to the Tower. She was astonished at how calm she still was. It was as if confronting her worst fears had shown her that she had the courage to face them.

She was accommodated, though not in the palace – that was full, the Constable told her, full of those who had offended with the Queen, who was herself condemned to die. She gasped when she heard that, yet she was not really surprised. Even so, the thought of that silly girl dying so young, and the knowledge that she herself had helped to bring her to her death, almost had her sinking to her knees. Somehow, she forced herself to follow the Constable to his own lodging, which was newly rebuilt. The room assigned her was finely furnished and there was a prayer desk. Jane sank to her knees and prayed that her fortitude would endure until she had made a good end. It would reflect well on her. Beyond that, she was incapable of prayer. She wondered if Katheryn was here too and how she was bearing up.

She could hardly bear to think of her family, especially her father, whom she loved and revered. What would they all think of her but the worst? She had done terrible things and deserved to die, and she was terrified that her crimes would rebound on them. She wanted to write a letter, explaining everything, but did not know where to begin. In the end, she could only scrawl a short note, with a shaking hand, begging their forgiveness.

She had been in the Lieutenant's lodging for four days when, on a cold Sunday evening, the Constable came and told her to prepare for death on the morrow, when she and the Queen would be beheaded. The executions would be carried out in private, within the Tower precincts. Her resolve wavered then, and she felt the hysteria rising again, but managed to control it. If she could just hold on to her composure for a few more hours . . .

She asked for the chaplain and confessed her sins. It took her much soul searching and a long time. Afterwards, she felt lighter. She could face this. She would be brave.

Her window did not face Tower Green, so she was unprepared for the crowd that awaited her early on Monday morning. She looked for Katheryn, but saw no sign of her. Slipping on the frosty path, she walked with the Constable and her guards to the scaffold that stood opposite the White Tower and mounted the steps, conscious that all eyes were upon her. Then she stopped dead.

The black cloth covering the scaffold was soaked; the block and the straw surrounding it were wet. The water that had pooled on the ground was pink. It was blood, she was sure, and whose could it be but Katheryn's? It brought home to her the barbarity of what they were about to do to her.

Shrinking with horror, Jane forced herself to stand on the scaffold. She had been told that she might address those who had come to watch her die, but she could barely speak.

'I confess my offences,' she faltered. 'I die repentant. Profit from my example; amend your ungodly lives, and gladly obey the King in all things, for whose preservation I do heartily pray. And now I commend my soul to God and call upon Him for mercy.'

It was all over. There was nothing more to be done but kneel to meet her end. Dear God, this could not be happening!

She looked about her wildly. The executioner nodded in the direction of the block, but she could not move. Her teeth were chattering. The Constable touched her arm, but she flung his hand away. 'Help me, help me!' she was whimpering. 'No, no, no, please, don't hurt me!'

'Madam, you must kneel and submit to the law,' the Constable murmured in her ear. She stared at him as if he had spoken in some strange language. He placed his hand firmly on her shoulder and forced her to her knees. She was gabbling incoherently, frozen in fear. Then someone pushed her forward across the damp block.

'No, no!' she squealed, trying to rise, but those same hands constrained her. Frenzy seized her, but she was powerless.

'Keep still!' The executioner's rough voice was sharp. 'It will go worse for you if you move.'

Her breath coming in short pants, Jane lay rigid, bracing herself for the blow. Her last thought before the axe fell was that she had deserved this. It was her punishment.

KATHARINE PARR

Timeline

1512
- Birth of Katharine Parr (August)

1513
- Birth of William Parr, Katharine's brother

1515
- Birth of Anne Parr, Katharine's sister

1517
- Death of Sir Thomas Parr, Katharine's father

1527
- Marriage of William Parr and Anne Bourchier

1529
- Marriage of Katharine Parr and Edward Burgh

1531
- Death of Maud Green, Lady Parr, Katharine's mother

1533
- Death of Edward Burgh

1534
- Marriage of Katharine Parr and John Neville, Lord Latimer

1536-7
- Pilgrimage of Grace

1538
- Marriage of Anne Parr and Sir William Herbert

1543
- Death of John Neville, Lord Latimer (February)
- Annulment of the marriage of William Parr and Anne Bourchier
- Marriage of Henry VIII and Katharine Parr (July)
- William Parr created Earl of Essex

1547
- Death of Henry VIII (28 January) and accession of Edward VI
- William Parr created Marquess of Northampton
- Marriage of Katharine Parr and Thomas, Lord Seymour
- Death of William Parr, Lord Horton, Katharine's uncle

1548

- Marriage of William Parr and Elizabeth Brooke
- Birth of Mary Seymour, daughter of Katharine Parr and Thomas, Lord Seymour (August)
- Death of Katharine Parr (September)

THE QUEEN'S CHILD

September 1548

I have tears in my eyes as I look down on her, dear little soul, sleeping all unheeding in her vast gold cradle, snuggly swaddled and replete with her nurse's milk. She does not know that her mother has just been taken by God and that her father is like a man lost. It's all very well to be lying in this rich nursery with its costly tapestries and gold plate, but that is as nothing compared to a mother's love – and Queen Katharine did love her baby. She adored her – and she entrusted her to me because she knew I would put her needs before all else. I am the only mother Mary has now.

There's a horrible hush in this castle, as there always is following a death. Everywhere, even here in the nursery, there are black hangings, which only add to the gloom. And to think that, just over a week ago, we were all rejoicing over little Mary's birth and toasting her health and that of the Queen. Her Grace came through the birth without any mishap; it was only afterwards that childbed fever set in. How she raved in her delirium, poor soul. My Lady Tyrwhitt told me that she said such things to my lord that she could scarce believe them. I pressed her to tell me what they were, but she would not, and I felt hurt that she would not confide in me, for I have served her Grace for five years and was as close to her as any.

This establishment has been a house of secrets from the first. When her Grace married my Lord Admiral soon after the late King Henry's death left her a widow, they kept their marriage secret for some time. The King died in January last year and they were supposed to have been wed in May, but gossip had it that they were joined in wedlock much sooner – indecently sooner, some would say. But I saw for myself how difficult my mistress's years as queen were, and I knew how much she wanted a child. And here that child is, but her Grace is not. Forgive me, I am going to start weeping again.

'Bess,' the Queen said to me, 'I want you to be lady mistress to my child. I can think of no one fitter to whom I can entrust my little one.'

I miss her so much. She was a strong, feisty lady, well educated and deeply devoted to the Protestant faith; and I shall see to it that Mistress Mary is brought up with a reverence for the Gospel and for learning, as her mother would have wished.

My lord will want that for her too. He comes to the nursery from time to time, and he once came to see his daughter when we were walking with her in the gardens, but he is distracted, and no wonder. He's not been a good husband – and therein lies another secret. We all breathed a sigh of relief when the late King's daughter, the Lady Elizabeth, left this household in June. We thought she was coming to Sudeley Castle with us, but there was a last-minute change of plan. I think that matters had somehow come to a head.

Those morning romps – the whole household was talking about them. And the Queen, God bless her, living in blissful ignorance. That girl was bad news. Mrs Ashley, who had charge of her, told us that the Admiral had made a bid for her before he wed the Queen, but that the Privy Council said no. Elizabeth, I have no doubt, would have said yes – she wanted him, you could see it. Oh, it was all meant to be good fun, all perfectly open and above-board, and so the Queen saw it, poor, deluded soul. I am sure that something happened to make her think again, which was why my Lady Elizabeth left and why my lord was always dancing attention on his good wife afterwards. He has to live with his conscience now.

I wonder if he will marry the Lady Elizabeth. After a decent interval, of course – but we all know he isn't given to decent intervals.

I have sat down to write to my brother Hugh in Cumberland, but I can't concentrate. I wish he was here. When we were at court and he was clerk of the Queen's council, I could always go to him for advice. I know he will be deeply saddened to hear of our mistress's passing.

Sometimes, during this past week, I have wished myself back at Newbiggin Hall – or Jerusalem, as we Aglionbys have long called it. The name was given to one of its towers by the Crackenthorpes, who owned Newbiggin before us. It would be so good to be at home, living a peaceful life with the only excitement being a trip into Penrith – but I could never leave my little lady, not when she needs me so much.

They are burying her Grace tomorrow in the castle chapel. She's still lying in her privy chamber, in her coffin. The weather being warm, they embalmed and cered her immediately. My lord has been in there quite a lot, and poor young Lady Jane Grey, who loved her so much, weeps ceaselessly. She is the Admiral's ward and will perhaps go home soon, since there is no lady of rank here to look after her.

The Queen was buried this morning, amid great pageantry. The chapel was hung with black cloth, even the altar rails, and the coffin was carried in procession to the altar, preceded by gentlemen, knights, officers of the household carrying their white staves of office and Somerset Herald wearing his tabard. Six gentlemen in black gowns and hoods bore the body, with torchbearers at either side. Lady Jane Grey followed, looking very small and wan in her black dress with her train borne by a young maid, and behind her came ladies, gentlemen and lesser folk. The Admiral, of course, did not attend. He stayed in seclusion in the castle; he is a heavy man for the loss of the Queen.

As my late mistress would have wanted, the service was conducted in English, according to Protestant rites. Watching the coffin being lowered into a vault beneath the altar pavement, the choir all the while singing the *Te Deum*, I could not stop the tears and had to pull my voluminous mourning hood over my face, noticing that other ladies were doing likewise. After the service, I did not join the guests for the funeral feast because I had to get back to my charge. I don't know the nursery maids and rockers well enough to trust them with the care of her for too long, although I am sure they are quite capable and well meaning.

I wonder if the Lady Elizabeth is grieving for her stepmother, or if she now sees the way clear to having her heart's desire. We shall see. I know that the Lady Mary, the late King's elder daughter, will mourn the Queen, as will his Majesty. She was a loving stepmother to them all and kept them as close as she could as a family – no mean feat when they were all born of mothers who had been deadly rivals. I pray that closeness continues.

There has long been bitter rivalry too between the Admiral and his brother, the Lord Protector – much of it the fault of the latter's wife, the Duchess of Somerset. She hated the Queen, being jealous of her, of which she made no secret. Now that death has taken her Grace, we may see a patching up of that rift, but I'll wager it will not put an end to my lord's envy of the Protector. That accounts for more of the secrets this house holds, for I am certain, from things the Queen said, that the Admiral has done nothing but plot against his brother. He is determined to have the rule of the realm and the young King for himself.

I doubt we will stay much longer at Sudeley. My lord will want to return to the world of men and affairs, which means moving back to Chelsea or Hanworth or even Seymour Place in London. He has his choice of houses, for the Queen left him everything, including her property, in her will. I was present when she dictated it. So he's a rich man now. Yet some can never be contented with what the good Lord has given them, and I doubt he will be.

I wish we could stay here. I love Sudeley: it's the most beautiful house. The gardens are delightful – her Grace took great pride in them – and the countryside hereabouts is glorious. It's a wonderful place to rear a child. Maybe we will be allowed to stay here while my lord goes to court. He has kept on the Queen's ladies, which might be a good sign. It might also mean that he is thinking of taking another wife – and we all know who that might be.

September 1548

Another good sign. My lord informed me today that his mother, old Lady Seymour, is coming from Wulfhall to take charge of the household and Lady Jane Grey. That means we must be staying on here, for now at least.

My little lady is feeding well, God be praised. She's a contented babe, for all that the world is new and strange to her, and gives us little trouble.

October 1548

The Admiral has gone to London with Lady Jane. He has decided that Lady Seymour shall look after her at Seymour Place. We are to remain at Sudeley. My lord agrees with me that country air is best for his child.

It's peaceful here without his booming voice echoing all over the castle and the bustle of a great household, although an aura of sadness overshadows us all. The ladies are still with us and do their best to make merry company. I have got my little lady into a good routine. The nurse gives suck when she needs it. Morning and afternoon, I take her into the gardens and walk her up and down or lay her in a basket and sit beside her, reading or singing to her. She likes looking at the flowers or the birds that wing and dive in the sky above us. I wish this beautiful weather could last, but already the evenings are drawing in. When my little lady is abed, I often go out again for an hour, and sometimes the ladies join me for a glass of cordial or something from my lord's cellar. He would not mind. He was ever open-handed.

November 1548

Even here, in remote Sudeley, there are rumours that the Admiral will marry my Lady Elizabeth. Some travellers were talking about it in a tavern in Winchcombe and the news was all over the castle in five minutes. The ladies are especially exercised, anticipating that they will soon be serving another royal mistress. I'll believe it when I see it.

But they act as if it is a certainty.

'How could she resist him? He is so handsome,' one says, as we sit by the fire late one evening. 'And he is the noblest unmarried man in this land.'

'I'd have him myself,' Mary Odell laughs.

'He aims high again,' I say.

'If he was good enough for the Queen, he's good enough for the Lady Elizabeth! Mark you, we will see some changes here.'

There is no quelling their excitement. But I wonder if the Lord Protector will consent to such a marriage – or his wife!

November 1548

Not long now until Christmas. Of a certainty, we will be keeping it here at Sudeley.

My little lady will be almost four months old by then. Already she is smiling and taking notice. I think she will absorb something of the magic of Christmas. I only wish her dear mother could be there to see it.

The Admiral is still in London and the rumours about him and the Lady Elizabeth persist. We get very little news down here, only what we hear in letters from our families, or from the talk in taverns and from travellers who occasionally beg hospitality here. But no one knows what is really happening behind the closed doors of the court.

December 1548

Christmas was beautiful, even if it was overshadowed by sadness. My little lady loved the evergreens with which we decorated the castle, the carols we sang and the silver rattle my lord sent her. I gave her a bonnet I had embroidered myself and a cloth dog for when she is bigger. Her curls are growing now and are the same rosy gold colour as her mother's hair was.

There is good news from London. Mary Odell had it in a letter. The Catholic Mass has been banned and we are to have a new Book of Common Prayer. How my late mistress would have rejoiced! Still, her little one will grow up in this kingdom that has been reclaimed for God, and she herself had no small influence in that, I believe.

January 1549

I am still in a state of shock. The Lord Admiral has been arrested for treason and is in the Tower. We found out today when a troop of horsemen wearing the Lord Protector's livery arrived at Sudeley with orders to escort my Lady Mary to Syon, where we are to join the Protector's household; being her uncle, he evidently feels responsible for her. He's likely responsible too for the arrest of his brother, so he has a moral obligation. But I know nothing of what my Lord Admiral is supposed to have done, so I will reserve judgement on that. We asked the captain if he knew my lord's offence, but he couldn't – or wouldn't – tell us.

I rushed upstairs to make ready. Seeing my little lady lying in her cradle, my heart gave a great lurch and I picked her up and rocked her, tears falling down my face as it dawned on me that she might soon be an orphan. How terrible to be deprived of both mother and father when you are not yet five months old.

But there has been little time for weeping. We've had all to do, getting packed up for the move and loading everything onto carts and sumpter mules. They want us to leave this afternoon so that we can reach Stow-on-the-Wold by evening. They have commandeered rooms for us at an inn there. There are a dozen of us – my little lady, myself, the nurse, two maids, two rockers, two chamberers, two grooms, a laundress and three stable boys. The ladies are all most upset because, having expected soon to be serving a royal mistress, they are being sent home.

I wish I knew what was happening and how bad the situation really is.

January 1549

We are now ensconced at Syon. It was an abbey until King Henry closed it down, and the house follows the layout of the cloister. It's like a palace now and is very impressive, for my Lord Protector has remodelled it in the Italian style with spacious apartments and beautiful gardens; although they look bare now, I am assured that they are botanical gardens, a new fantasy of the Duke's. He is not here, of course, being busy with state business in London, which is a dozen miles away, but his Duchess is in residence. We haven't seen her yet, but I know of her by repute. The late Queen hated her and there was a feud between them over some jewels that were never returned to my lady. But I will tread carefully. I have to live under this woman's roof, perhaps on sufferance and certainly on her charity.

There is no one here I can ask about my Lord Admiral. The steward showed us to the nursery lodgings where we found the Duchess's own children being very noisy indeed. There was no opportunity for questions, even had I dared to approach such a forbidding man.

My little lady is grizzly today because of the long journey and the changes to her routine and surroundings, and she is in no mood for the hurly burly of this nursery. I had not realised that the Duke and Duchess had so many children – I counted seven of them and was told that another is on the way – or that my little lady was to share a lodging with them. They have but one lady mistress and a tutor for the older boys, as well as the usual servants, so it is rather crowded. I've already worked out that, while the tutor is strict, the lady mistress lets the children run wild when he departs. But she does impose her rule when it is needful.

I thank God that Mary will be sharing a bedchamber with Edward, the baby, and Catherine, who is a year old. I have my own chamber adjoining, a very pleasant apartment with a comfortable bed. Meals are taken in the nursery parlour with the older children and the food is very good. Everything is clean and the children are made to tidy up before they go to bed. I dare say they are all scared of their mother.

January 1549

We have been here for two days and, until this afternoon, I was none the wiser as to what is going to happen to my Lord Admiral, or what he has done. But, after dinner, the Lord Protector arrived with two of his fellows from the Privy Council and summoned me before them.

I had seen my lord before when he visited Chelsea, where the Queen and the Lord Admiral used to live. I thought him proud then, although friendly in an aloof way, but today he was coldly efficient. He has a bushy red beard, like his brother, but there the similarity ends. One is a prig, the other is a swaggerer.

'Pray be seated, Mistress Aglionby,' he invited, and I sat on the stool facing the table, from behind which my lord and the councillors were regarding me sternly. What had I done wrong? I began to tremble.

The Protector spoke. 'We are examining all who are known to have associated with my Lord Admiral. Does the name Sharington mean anything to you?'

Somewhat relieved, I told him that Sir William Sharington had sometimes been a guest of the Queen and my Lord Admiral. No, I had not been privy to their conversations.

'You did not know that they were dabbling in forgery?'

'No, my lord!' As if they would have confided in me.

'Did you know that my Lord Admiral regularly obtained stolen goods from pirates operating under his protection in the English

Channel, and that some of those goods came from English ships?'

'I know nothing of that, my lord,' I replied, wondering if I should tell them about the many treasures my lord had been steadily accumulating, which are stored away in all his houses.

'Very well, Mistress Aglionby. Were you aware that the Admiral was doing his best to poison his Majesty's mind against me, the Lord Protector, and was plotting to kidnap him?'

I could not stifle a gasp at that. My surprise was so evident that they had their answer. I just shook my head.

'So you know nothing about the counterfeit keys made for the gates to the King's privy garden and apartments or the forged stamp of his Majesty's signature that the Admiral had made?'

'I'm sorry, I don't.'

'Were you aware that the Admiral intended to marry the Lady Jane Grey to the King?'

'No, my lord.'

The Protector stroked his beard. 'Did you ever see any store of weapons at Sudeley Castle?'

'No, my lord.' I had been aware of horses and carts arriving at the castle in the middle of the night in the weeks before Christmas, but I was resolved not to say anything that might be incriminating. I have my little lady to think of, and she needs her father.

The Protector was regarding me shrewdly. I think he knew I wasn't telling him everything. 'We have reason to believe that my Lord Admiral has fomented rebellion, amongst other offences,' he divulged. 'If true, it were better for him if he had never been born.' His icy tone chilled me. This was his brother he was talking about. 'You think I am overreacting, Mistress Aglionby,' he went on. 'We believe that the Lord Admiral has committed high treason, great falsehoods and marvellous heinous misdemeanours against the King's Majesty and the Crown. You should know that, not a week ago, he used his forged key to enter his Majesty's lodging at Hampton Court, intending to kidnap him. But, when he opened the door to the King's bedchamber, his Grace's dog leapt at him, barking loudly, so he drew his gun and shot it dead. The report brought the Yeomen of the Guard running, fearing, quite rightly, that the King was in mortal danger.' The fool, the fool, I was thinking. But he must have acted on impulse.

My Lord Protector was regarding me as severely as if *I* had shot the poor dog. 'When asked to explain his presence, armed, outside his Majesty's bedchamber,' he continued, 'the Admiral said he had come to prove how well the King was guarded and that he killed the dog in self-defence. His Majesty was most distressed and quite shaken. It could have been he who was shot. Because of the danger, we, the Privy Councillors, decided to commit the Admiral to prison in the Tower of London. Now, is there anything you wish to add to your testimony?'

I froze. This was indeed a serious matter, yet I was puzzled. Clearly, my Lord Admiral had embroiled himself in several shady practices, but what would he have had to gain by murdering the King?

'You hesitate, Mistress,' one of the councillors said.

'I am trying to think of anything that might have been untoward, Sir,' I told him, still resolved to keep silent about matters that might be entirely unrelated. 'I was never in my lord's confidence, only the Queen's. And he went to London soon after her death. We never saw him again at Sudeley.'

The lords nodded. Then the Protector spoke again. 'Did you ever hear the Admiral speak of marrying my Lady Elizabeth?'

'Never,' I said, truthfully, determined not to elaborate on what I did know about what had passed between them, or to let on that we had all speculated that he might marry her.

'One last question. I must ask you this. Was there any suspicion that the Admiral murdered the late Queen?'

'What?' I was aghast. It was so absurd that I could have laughed, except this was no laughing matter. 'Absolutely not,' I declared.

'Very well, that is all, Mistress Aglionby,' the Protector said. 'You may go.'

I got up to leave and, as I neared the door, he spoke again. 'How is my niece?'

'She is well, my lord, and a very happy child, for all that she has no mother. I pray that no other tragedy will blight her life.'

I could not believe my own boldness; I had not meant to speak so plainly. But I had seen my opportunity to appeal to his better nature and seized it.

He gave me a strange look, but merely nodded. 'I will visit her when I am next at Syon.'

When I closed the door behind me, I was trembling so much that I had to lean against the wall for support. I could feel only relief that I had not contributed to my Lord Admiral's downfall. Pray God the Council takes a lenient view. Goodness knows what my late mistress must think of these proceedings, looking down from Heaven.

March 1549

There has been no trial. My Lord Admiral has been adjudged guilty by Parliament and condemned by Act of Attainder to lose his life and possessions. My lady the Duchess came to the nursery today and informed us of this. She's a hard woman and a demanding mistress, but I thought I detected a tear when she picked up my little lady and held her, gazing into those innocent eyes.

'Your Grace, what is to happen to my lady – and to us?' I asked, realising, to my utter dismay, that the child was now penniless.

'I'm afraid I don't know, Mistress Aglionby,' she said. 'I am awaiting my lord's instructions.' That was rich, when all the world knows that he does as she says.

When she had gone, the maids and I looked at each other, all thinking the same thing. The thought of being parted from my little lady is devastating. I have grown to love her so much that she could be my own flesh and blood. And, if she is left destitute, we could be too, and out of a job, although that would be by far the lesser evil.

March 1549

My lady is here again. 'Alas, I bring heavy news,' she says. 'His Majesty has ordered that the Admiral's execution proceed according to law. My lord, naturally, was reluctant to sign the death warrant, but my lord of Warwick and the Council forced him to it.'

'When is it to be, your Grace?' I ask, appalled.

'Five days hence. His Majesty has graciously commuted the sentence to decapitation.' That is bad enough, but at least my lord is to be spared the agony of hanging, drawing and quartering.

'The Admiral wants to see the child,' she says. 'Permission has been granted. Tomorrow, Mistress Aglionby, you will be taken by barge from here to the Tower, where the Constable will conduct you to the Admiral.'

I draw in a breath. How can I face this man who is condemned to death? How will I bear to see him say a final farewell to his precious daughter? But I have no choice. Better me than anyone else.

It's chilly this morning. Mary looks so pretty in her embroidered bonnet, with her plump rosy cheeks, her pouting lips and her blue eyes. She's sitting here on my lap in the barge, happily babbling to herself, unaware of the terrible tragedy that is about to befall her. She's beginning to say words now and called me 'Beh'. I've been trying to teach her to say 'Papa', but with no success until this morning, when she uttered 'Pah' with great pride. I pray she says it to my lord.

The grim walls of the Tower are looming ahead and I am filled with dread, thinking of the poor souls who have been imprisoned or beheaded here. I can see the public scaffold on Tower Hill, where my lord will suffer in four days' time. It is a terrible thought. He's a big man, larger than life and filled with vitality – how shall such a one just be snuffed out? I never knew him well, but I have not been impervious to his charm, and can see why the Queen risked all for him. I know little of what he is supposed to have done, or of his motives, but I cannot believe that he is a truly bad man. She would never have married him if he was.

The barge pulls in at the Court Gate, where the stately Sir John Gage, the Constable of the Tower, helps me alight and escorts me up the stairs and along the outer ward to my Lord Admiral's lodging. I notice him looking with compassion on the child, who is casting her eyes about her and taking notice.

'A sad business,' Sir John observes. 'It's the innocent who suffer most.'

He should know. He was here when Katheryn Howard was put to death. He has seen suffering in many of its forms.

He unlocks the door to the Garden Tower and ushers us into a small chamber, quite adequately furnished with a chair, a table, two stools, red curtains and rush matting. There are books on the table. My lord springs to his feet, gazing at Mary in wonder.

'Mistress Aglionby, a thousand thanks!' He reaches for the child and I place her in his arms. 'My, how you have grown, my little one!' he exclaims. And then the tears come coursing down his face as he presses his cheek to those golden curls and Mary starts squirming. She hates being held too tightly. 'Oh, God,' he says. 'Oh, dear God.'

I let him weep. I have no words to comfort him.

When Mary starts grizzling, he sits down, pulls himself together and dandles her on his lap.

'Sit down, Mistress Aglionby,' he says, and I take a stool.

'You know why I am here?' he quizzes me.

'I know hardly anything, my lord. The Lord Protector and the councillors examined me, but they gave little away.'

He snorts. 'They wouldn't. They'd be trying to trip you up. Mistress Aglionby, yours might be the last kind face I shall ever see. I know my late wife liked and trusted you, and I need to trust you now because I want you to ensure that Mary grows up knowing the truth about me.'

'Of course you can trust me, my lord. I would do anything to help you and my little lady.'

He nods. 'I thank you. You should know that my brother believes that I devised a secret marriage between myself and the Lady Elizabeth, so that I might easily seize the person of the King's Majesty and dispose of the entire Council. It is all lies. No poor knave was ever truer to his prince. I meant him no harm; I sought to make life easier for him.'

He gets up, hands Mary to me, and starts pacing the room. 'I was denied a trial. I said I would not answer the charges brought against me until I could do so in open court and air my grievances to the world. But they would not heed me.' He smashes his fist into his other hand, greatly agitated now. 'Thirty-three counts of treason they brought against me! They accused me of plotting to usurp the throne, like Richard the Third, when nothing was further from my mind. I did wish to marry the Lady Elizabeth, but not for any nefarious purpose. They said I had turned my mind against the Lord Protector, but it was his lady who turned his mind against me. They even accused me of murdering the Queen, who was very dear to me. It's the malice of my brother and his wife that has done for me.'

He slumps back in his chair. 'After the attainder was passed, I did speak out. I denied that I had ever meant to usurp my brother's position or kidnap the King. I admitted that I had looked for certain precedents dividing power fairly between regents during a royal minority, but I had become ashamed of what I was doing and left off my search. I do have some fraternal feeling – unlike some people.'

What can I say to him? I am not qualified to pronounce on these matters and I do not wish to delve too deep because I want to be able to tell Mary good things about her father when she is old enough to hear them.

'I am sorry that you have been so mistreated, my lord,' I say. 'You may rest assured that I will tell my little lady what you have said and that she will be brought up to think well of you and honour your memory.'

'I thank you, from the bottom of my heart, Mistress Aglionby,' he says. 'It is comforting to know that there are good people in this miserable world.' His face darkens. 'I do not want Mary to be brought up by my brother and his wife. I have asked for her to be given into the charge of my lady of Suffolk, who was one of the Queen's closest friends.'

I nod. I know the Duchess of Suffolk, a firebrand of a woman, zealous for the Gospel and never afraid to speak her mind. 'A fitting choice, my lord.'

'And you will see that Mary is treated like the Queen's daughter she is?'

'I will, I promise.'

'They will surely not seize her nursery stuff along with my other goods,' he mutters. 'See that she keeps it, I beg of you.'

'She has it all with her at Syon, my lord. I do not think they will take it from her now.'

'Good, good,' he says distractedly. He takes the child again, and kisses her, ever so tenderly, and gives her his blessing.

'Go now,' he bids me. 'Go before I unman myself.'

I leave, tears blinding my eyes. As I knock for the door to be opened, Mary fixes her gaze on her father and says, 'Pah!'

March 1549

It is to be this morning. There is a palpable sense of tension and dread hanging over Syon House. I have said my prayers, winging my lord's soul on its way to Heaven, and now I am sitting here in the nursery as Mary plays contentedly on the floor, unaware that she is about to be made an orphan.

The Duchess has gone to Somerset House to be with the Protector. I imagine he needs all the moral support he can get, for he must have much on his conscience. He has made no pronouncement on Mary's future, and I do not like to ask, but it is horrible living in limbo and not knowing what is to happen to us.

I keep looking to see if it is nine o'clock. The hand is there now. The Admiral's hour has come. I can barely breathe.

I sit here, hardly able to move. The time seems endless.

Half an hour has gone by. It must be over now. That restless soul is at peace.

'Oh, my darling!' I swoop Mary up into my arms and rock her. 'Oh, my sweet one, I am so sorry, so very sorry. I'll look after you, I swear it. You will never want for love.'

March 1549

My lady the Duchess is back. She is wearing mourning, which seems to me a little hypocritical, although maybe she wishes people to think that she and her husband never wanted to make an end of the Admiral.

She has come to the nursery to see Mary.

'Poor mite,' she says, ruffling the golden curls. 'Poor little mite.'

'Did the Admiral die bravely, your Grace?' I dare to ask.

'He died very dangerously, irksomely, horribly,' she says cryptically, and I am left to imagine the worst. 'God had obviously forsaken him,' she continues. 'Whether he be saved or no, I leave it to Him, but surely he was a wicked man, and the realm is well rid of him.' Assuredly, she is wearing those weeds for show only.

Who was I to believe? I so want to believe my late lord; he had seemed so exercised by the injustices done him. It was surely a nonsense that he had plotted to murder the Queen, so the rest of it might be a nonsense too.

'Some have got off lightly,' the Duchess says, and I know she is referring to my Lady Elizabeth. Whatever her sins, she had feelings for the Admiral – I am in no doubt of that, for I saw them together – so she must be much grieved at his death. And she is just fifteen, a highly impressionable age. In her short lifetime, she has seen her mother and a stepmother executed and two stepmothers die in childbed. It would not surprise me if all that has put her off marriage for good.

'Mary is to remain here for the short term,' the Duchess informs us, 'and my lord and I wish you all to stay on to look after her; your wages will be paid. The servants remaining at Sudeley have been dismissed, so think yourselves fortunate.'

'We are most grateful, your Grace,' I say quickly, wondering what 'the short term' means.

March 1549

Again, my lady comes to see us. She takes Mary on her lap as her own children cluster around.

'Sit down,' she tells them, and they obey, like lambs. She addresses me. 'Parliament has passed an Act disinheriting this poor child. She is penniless and destitute, but for the charity of my lord and myself. Her late father asked for her to be brought up by the Duchess of Suffolk, who, for the late Queen's sake, has agreed to take her in and is willing for you all to accompany her.'

She sounds relieved and I realise she will be glad to say farewell to my little lady, this living reminder of the wrongs done to her father. For my part, I shall be glad to get out of this house, where I have never felt that we are welcome. Maybe my opinion of the Duchess of Somerset is coloured by the late Queen's antagonism towards her, but anyone can see that she is a strident, proud woman – and well I know how her jealousy of my dear mistress led to much unkindness.

The Duchess of Suffolk is strident too, but in a different way. She has a sense of humour and natural warmth. I think we shall get along well together.

'My Lord Protector will be paying the Duchess an allowance for Mary's upkeep from the Admiral's confiscated properties,' her Grace tells me. 'There will be no need to worry about money.'

April 1549

My instructions have come. We are to travel to the Duchess of Suffolk's country seat, Grimsthorpe Castle in Lincolnshire. She is sending a litter for me and Mary and a baggage cart. And therein lies the first of my problems.

My lord wanted Mary to be royally attended and housed, as the daughter of a queen. She has a lot of nursery stuff, much of which has had to be stored in the old nunnery cellars at Syon. There are beds down there and hangings and goodness knows what else – and we have the one cart to convey everything to Grimsthorpe. Moreover, one litter will not carry me, Mary, the nurse, two maids, two chamberers, a laundress, two grooms and three stablemen, although the latter will ride.

Marshalling my courage, I find my lady of Somerset and explain the problem. She does not look pleased.

'How many carts and litters will you need?' she barks.

'At least three carts and two more litters, if your Grace pleases.'

'I am not pleased, but you shall have what you ask for. I will never have it said that my lord and I did not do the right thing by our niece.'

I thank her profusely, find a groom and hasten down to the cellars to organise the packing of my little lady's stuff. I hope that Grimsthorpe is a spacious house and that my lady of Suffolk realises just how much we are bringing with us. She seems to be generously inclined. Money has been sent for our lodgings and refreshment on the journey. It seems we have a long ride ahead of us.

April 1549

It has been a very long journey, especially with a small child who does not want to be cooped up in a litter for mile upon mile. Mary has fretted and wriggled her way to Grimsthorpe, and repeatedly refused to take suck, even after screaming with hunger. What a contrary little madam she is!

But we are here now, praise God. Our little cavalcade is moving up the drive and ahead I can see a magnificent mansion. All around us stretch acres of parkland. This is a beautiful place. I think I will like living here very much indeed.

When we have alighted before the imposing entrance, the grooms lead us to the great hall, where the Duchess is waiting for us, seated in a high-backed chair by the fire. She is wearing a furred black robe and a French hood, and her beloved dog, Gardiner, is at her feet. Mischievously, she named him after the Bishop of Winchester, whom she loathes.

'Poor little Mistress Mary,' she says, taking the child from me and kissing her. 'How big she is – and how like her mother. I trust you are well, Mistress Aglionby?'

'Very well, I thank your Grace, and very grateful to you for taking my little lady in.'

She is eyeing the nursery staff who stand behind me. 'I did not realise that there would be so many of you.'

'Your Grace, my Lord Admiral wanted Mary to be attended and served as a queen's child.'

'Queen's child she may be, but she is a pauper who must now live on charity. But I welcome her with a good heart, for the Queen was my friend.'

I am puzzled. 'My lady of Somerset said there was to be an allowance from the Lord Protector.'

'So I was told,' the Duchess replies with a tight smile. 'The Privy Council has granted Mary five hundred pounds for her maintenance for the next eighteen months, to be paid by the Court of Wards. It is to cover her servants' diets and wages, but I have not received it yet and, until I do, this child will be living at my expense.'

'I see,' I say, seeing all too clearly the precariousness of my situation. I too am living on charity.

'Madam, there are three cartloads of stuff outside,' one of the grooms says.

'Three cartloads?' The smile slips. 'Mistress Aglionby, how can this be?'

'It is the stuff from the nursery at Sudeley, your Grace.'

She looks vexed. 'I have twelve other orphans in my care here. I had not expected to maintain Mary in state. But, Mistress Aglionby, for the late Queen's sake, you may have three chambers. Watkins, please see that the stuff is taken to King John's Tower. The second-floor chambers.'

'Thank you, your Grace.' Feeling somewhat downcast, I take Mary from her new guardian and follow Watkins to what must be the oldest part of the castle. There is no grand staircase here, only a spiral stair that leads up to the rooms we have been allocated. They are spacious and whitewashed with rush matting on the floors. There is a great chamber for the day nursery, a bedchamber for me and Mary, and a larger one we can use as a dorter for everyone else.

There is just room in the bedchamber to fit the cradle and the gilded tester bed, which Mary will use when she is older. In the meantime, I will use it and sleep in splendour, for it has embroidered hangings of scarlet and a matching counterpane. The servants will have to make do with the two large feather beds we have brought, while the nurse has her pallet bed with another embroidered counterpane and the men will sleep over the stables.

Watkins brings some men to help put up the hangings depicting the months of the year, as the rest of us unwrap the wrought stools, set the cushions on the chair upholstered in cloth of gold, and stow away the silver pots, goblets, salt cellar, spoons and porringer in the wooden cupboard her Grace is persuaded to lend us. On top, we place the two pewter milch beasts for the nurse's expressed milk and the lute that once belonged to Queen Katharine; it's the only thing of her mother that Mary has. I can play it, and my gentle strumming helps lull my little lady to sleep.

While Mary has her afternoon nap, the Duchess shows me the kitchens and the dorter where the orphans sleep – and where she had clearly expected Mary to sleep too. The older girls are in the still room now, being taught how to make preserves, the little ones out for a walk with their nurses. I can see them through the window, toddling along the garden paths, sombre in their identical grey gowns, all of them wearing white caps and aprons.

'They are the children of my relations or dependents,' her Grace explains. 'They are learning the skills that will enable them to find positions in noble households. One or two have dowries, so can be found husbands.'

'What does your Grace think of Mary's prospects?' I venture.

My lady sighs. 'Not brilliant, I fear. She might be a queen's child, but her father was a traitor. Mind you, the saying goes that all the best families have at least one traitor in their pedigree.' She smiles wryly. 'Even so, without a dowry, it will be hard to find her a husband. We shall have to hope that she grows up to be beautiful – that might compensate.'

She insists on coming upstairs to see how we have arranged the rooms.

'Such marks of high estate!' she exclaims. 'Those hangings are worthy of Hampton Court.' She does not look best pleased about it. 'Are you planning on serving Mary's meals here?'

'Yes, your Grace.' I open the cupboard and show her all the silverware.

She nods. 'When she is older, she might join the other orphans at table.'

I say nothing, knowing that the Queen would not have liked that arrangement.

'Mistress Aglionby,' her Grace says, 'we are remote from society here at Grimsthorpe. Up here in this tower, there is no need to stand on such ceremony for so small a child.'

'It is what her parents both wanted, Madam.'

'Yes, but neither of them is here to dictate it now. Mary does not need all these servants. You and a nursery maid would be sufficient, especially since there is no money to fund a larger establishment.'

I feel chilled, aware of the other servants watching us, ears pricked up, looking worried.

'We will try to practise economies as far as possible,' I promise.

'That would be as well,' she says. 'I am not made of money.'

July 1549

It is abundantly clear now that we are here on sufferance. My lady makes her resentment obvious at every opportunity. Doubtless, if I had agreed to Mary being with the other orphans, she would be more amenable, but I am trying to keep my promise to the Admiral and to see that she is brought up as he and the Queen would have wished. It is at some cost to myself and the others who serve in the nursery, for none of us have seen a penny in wages. We do not like to be suitors to the Duchess, but we have no choice but to keep asking her if we might have some remuneration, however small. Begrudgingly, she gives us a pittance from time to time, but her answer, always, is that we must wait on payment of the maintenance ordered by the Council for the rest.

She is ten months old now, my little lady, and hauls herself up to her feet, clinging to the furniture, but she has not taken steps on her own yet. She has a growing vocabulary and enjoys nursery rhymes.

She is a joyous soul, happy and contented, and very pretty.

But my lady the Duchess cannot take pleasure in her, it seems. She is more concerned with economies – she, who must be a very rich woman. She makes out that she is much put upon by this responsibility for the Queen's child. She is quite frank with me.

'I wrote to Mary's uncle, my Lord Marquess of Northampton, asking if he would have the child, because she is, after all, his niece, and he has replied that he would be willing if the Duke of Somerset pays him the allowance promised to me for her upkeep. But Mary has been here for nearly four months now, and I have not received a penny of it, so how can I persuade my Lord Marquess to take her?' She looks at me, shaking her head, very agitated. 'This burden is all falling on me. It is too onerous, since the child has to be provided with all the service and trappings suitable to her rank, and these are expensive. My Lord Protector should know that!'

I don't think she bears any personal resentment towards me. In fact, I think she quite likes me, which is why I feel able to speak my mind to her. I know that she has sent many complaints to the Duke and Duchess of Somerset and is unlikely to obtain any satisfaction there.

'Your Grace, is it worth appealing to the Council?' I quite fancy the idea of taking Mary to live with her uncle. He's an amiable man and I have always liked him.

'That's exactly what is in my mind!' the Duchess tells me. 'I will write today and send Bertie with the letter.'

Richard Bertie is her master of horse. It's an open secret that something is going on between them and Cook wagers that they will marry before long. I say it's unlikely that a duchess, and a baroness in her own right, will stoop to a man of so low a rank, but stranger things have happened.

'I've sent a letter to William Cecil,' the Duchess tells me, after dinner. 'He acts as secretary to the Protector and, unlike his master, he gets things done. He loved the late Queen, so he will be all the more willing to use his influence.' She gives me an exasperated smile. 'I have utterly wearied myself with letters to my Lord Protector and his wife. I've told him that I cannot clear my debts this year if I have to keep bearing this heavy expense.'

'I pray that Master Cecil can help your Grace,' I say, finding it hard to believe that such a great lady could ever plead poverty.

'So do I, Mistress Aglionby, so do I!'

August 1549

'Read this!' the Duchess squawks, bursting into the nursery and thrusting a letter into my hands. I check that Mary is not crawling into any danger and read it, as my lady stands there seething, her face puce.

It is from the Duchess of Somerset, and it is the strangest letter. She merely says that she will be forwarding some nursery plate for her niece and, in return, she wishes to see an inventory of all the valuables in use in the nursery, so that she can decide for herself what pension is needful.

My lady looks fit to explode. 'What pension is needful? The council assigned the child five hundred pounds! What I want to know is, where is it? I will write again to Cecil and tell him what a beggar I am, and that Mary Seymour is like a sickness that increases mightily upon me. My lady of Somerset must know that she is lying here in my house, with her company, wholly at my charge. It is up to my good Cecil now to afford me all the help he can. Mistress Aglionby, could you kindly draw up that inventory if I send you a clerk? I'd like it today.'

'Very good, your Grace,' I say, resenting her referring to my precious child as a sickness, but aware of the need to cooperate with her. 'Might I be so bold as to suggest that I write you a letter begging you to pay my wages and those of the nursery servants, so that you can enclose it with your letter to Master Cecil as ammunition for your plea?'

She looks at me with respect. 'That is an excellent idea. I will tell him that my ears can hardly bear the clamour of your voices, and my coffers still worse.'

She whirls away to write her letter and I fetch writing materials and begin listing the nursery plate, unable to believe that my lady is a beggar. She has no understanding of what the word really means. She can afford to keep Mary in state; she just doesn't want the responsibility of her.

'No, sweeting!' I wrestle a spoon from my little lady's chubby fist. 'Play with Puppy.' It's the name we have given to the stuffed cloth toy I made her, which she carries everywhere. 'With any luck,' I tell her, 'we'll be going to live with Uncle William. You'll like that, won't you?'

October 1549

My lady is at the end of her tether. Cecil forwarded the inventory to the Duchess of Somerset, but not even one piece of plate has been forthcoming. And we have just learned why. The Lord Protector, the mighty Duke of Somerset, has been overthrown. What his unfortunate brother failed to do has been accomplished by the Earl of Warwick. Somerset is in the Tower, the Seymours are in disgrace, and God only knows what will become of my little lady. I look at her, playing happily with not a care in the world, and wonder how God can have inflicted so many tragedies on an innocent. But one can hardly blame God, of course. It is the wickedness and envy of men – and one woman – that have blighted her life.

My lady of Suffolk is in no doubt as to the reasons for the Protector's fall. She stands there in the nursery, half seething, half triumphant, watching Mary moving around in her wheeled walking frame. 'He pursued that costly war with Scotland that has won us nothing! He let them spirit away their Queen to France. He has bankrupted the Crown and we see riots and rebellion everywhere. He cannot govern. He has not the wit or the stomach for it. I'm glad to see him gone. The question is, will my lord of Warwick be sympathetic to my request for Mary's allowance to be paid? For surely, I will be sending him one, this very day!'

I won't say that I think she is wasting her time. Warwick will surely have too much on his hands dealing with the consequences of Somerset's misgovernment to look to the welfare of the disgraced Duke's orphaned niece.

January 1550

I was wrong. It had obviously not been at the top of Warwick's list of priorities, but we did not have to wait long for a response to my lady's plea. After Christmas, an application was made in the House of Commons for Mary's restitution to her inheritance. Today, we have just heard that Parliament has passed an Act restoring her in blood to all her father's lands and property, although not his titles.

The Duchess shows me Master Cecil's letter. 'This Act enables Mary to inherit any property of her father's that has not been returned to the Crown. But – and it's a big but – nearly all the lands owned by her parents and forfeited by her father have been sold off, so she will receive very little – or nothing at all. But, at least, I have received the five hundred pounds in maintenance granted by the Council.'

That is something. For one glorious moment, I had glimpsed a bright future for my little lady, a dowry, a fine marriage. Now I feel deeply sad that she is to inherit nothing.

'Will your Grace send Mary to her uncle?' I ask.

'I will write to him and see what he says,' she tells me. Can I detect a certain reluctance? I have sensed of late that she is growing fond of the child. Who could not? She is a winning little soul. She's toddling now and I have to keep a tight grip on her leading reins, or tether them to the table, as she tends to wander off. She hates being restrained and has a good temper on her, just like her father. I can see tantrums in the months ahead as she tries to assert her independence more and more. I like to see that spirit in her!

June 1550

My little lady has a cold. It started this morning with a runny nose, but she took her food and played on the floor with her toys, just as normal.

I am worried. Mary is burning up with an ague now and I have put her to bed. She lies there, listless, as we stand around, watching helplessly. I have made an infusion of peppermint, but we cannot get her to take it. It dribbles out of her mouth. The fever is rising, I fear, and nothing we do seems to make any difference. She is in the hands of God now. I have never prayed so hard in my life.

The Duchess has shown her mettle, sending at once for her physician, as we sponge down the child and try to spoon a syrup of feverfew into her mouth. She has also summoned Dr Parkhurst, who has been chaplain both to her and the Queen and had written to let her know that he was staying in Norwich.

'Queen Katharine would have wanted him to minister to her daughter,' her Grace told me. We both knew what that might mean.

The doctor arrives and tests Mary's urine, then bleeds her. It does her no good; in fact, I fear it weakens her. She no longer knows us, and her breathing is laboured. Sitting beside her, holding her small hand, I pour my whole being into beseeching God to make her well, reciting every prayer I can think of. And yet He, of His fathomless mercy, seems bent on gathering her into His arms.

I have not stopped crying. I keep saying to myself, as if to make it real, my little lady is dead; she is gone from us. She is dead.

She left us this morning with scarcely a whimper, and now she lies on her bed, all dressed in white, looking like an angel.

She was not quite two years old, and a sweeter child the world never saw. My empty arms ache for her. She was born under an unlucky star and, truly, I think she was too good for this world.

June 1550

My little lady was buried today in the church at Edenham, not far from Grimsthorpe. The Duchess's family have lived here since time immemorial and she is lady of the manor of Edenham. She thought it fitting that Mary be laid to rest in the church, a little angel to join the carved and painted angels that adorn its roof. How I got through the funeral I do not know. It was one of the most searing experiences of my life.

Dr Parkhurst is here. The Duchess is planning a memorial stone and he has composed an epitaph. I think it is beautiful, but reading it brings tears to my eyes. I have it by heart now. It goes:

> I whom, at the cost
> Of her own life,
> My queenly mother
> Bore with the pangs of labour
> Sleep under this marble,
> An unfit traveller.
> If Death had given me to live longer
> That virtue, that modesty,
> That obedience of my excellent Mother
> That Heavenly courageous nature
> Would have lived again in me.
> Now, whoever
> You are, fare thee well.
> Because I cannot speak any more, this stone
> Is a memorial to my brief life.

All too brief. Yes, Mary proved an unfit traveller. And that sweet child had all the virtues of her mother. She brought so much joy to those whose lives she touched. Mine, I know, will never be the same without her.

Sleep well, little one. God bless you.

Author's Note

There is no record of Mary Seymour's death. All the evidence suggests that she died in infancy. I have found new evidence to support that, and to show that she did not grow up and marry, as Agnes Strickland, the Victorian author of *The Lives of the Queens of England*, suggested. The evidence I found will be published separately.

IN THIS
NEW
SEPULCHRE

1549

Mary Odell gazed down at the fine new alabaster tomb, still barely able to credit that her kinswoman, the vital and attractive Queen Katharine, lay beneath. It had been eight months now and sometimes, during the last weeks, Mary could only feel relief that her kind mistress had been taken before she could witness the ruin of her husband. The Lord Admiral would never lie here beside her now. His body, minus its head, was scarcely cold in its shameful grave in the Tower of London. He had been adjudged a traitor and died as one. And little Mary Seymour, eight months old, would never know either of her parents. Tragedy upon tragedy. Who would have thought it this time last year, when the Queen and the Admiral were riding high, with everything to look forward to?

At least the Lord Admiral had lived long enough to erect this lovely tomb to his wife's memory.

Mary dragged her eyes away from the sepulchre, walked across the chancel of the chapel and sat down in the Queen's pew opposite the tomb, where a squint gave a view of the altar. She allowed herself a few tears – heaven knew, she had shed more than enough these past months – and bent her head in prayer and reflection.

Some time later, she rose and returned to the monument, to pray by it one last time and say farewell. Sudeley Castle had been seized by the Crown on the Admiral's execution, and his household had been ordered to leave. Mary stared down at the Latin epitaph chiselled around the monument. It had been composed by the Queen's chaplain, Dr

Parkhurst. Mary could not read Latin, but he had translated it for her and she had it by heart now. *In this new sepulchre the royal Katharine lies . . .*

Sighing, and almost blinded by tears, Mary bowed before the tomb for the final time, then turned and walked through the side chapel, past the Queen's pew, and through the door that led to the covered gallery linking the chapel to the castle; it had been Katharine's private way to her apartments.

Mary turned around for a final view of the chapel, with its squat tower, tall windows and twin rows of soaring pinnacles. How beautiful this place was. It was comforting to think that the Queen would lie here peacefully for eternity.

1642–4

On this occasion, Fear-the-Lord Jenkins did not want to obey orders. When Sudeley Castle had fallen to the besieging Parliamentary forces, he had been jubilant, thinking, *Another stronghold vanquished for the cause, another ungodly aristocrat ruined.* He had stood with the company offering up prayers of thanksgiving for the victory vouchsafed them by the Almighty. It was the reward of virtue. And he *had* led a godly life, unlike Lord Chandos and his ilk.

But, when his captain ordered Fear-the-Lord and his companions in arms to break up the chapel, he baulked. Whatever its unholy ornaments, it was still the consecrated house of God, and there were in his heart vestiges of loyalty to the Anglican religion he had been taught in infancy, before his Puritan tutor had shown him the light. It was then that he had abandoned his given name, William, and taken on the identity of a true pilgrim.

Reluctantly, he took an axe and accompanied his fellows, who were in a bullish mood, raring to smash up a temple of idolatry where Popish practices had polluted the purity of the Christian faith. On their way, they hacked down the rotting timbers of a covered walkway that led from the battered castle to the chapel, then kicked open the door.

Inside, there was a smell of damp stonework and decay. The windows were cracked or broken and the floor strewn with leaves and twigs. The chapel looked unloved and uncared for. Apart from a threadbare altar cloth and a few items of tarnished or dented plate, there was nothing of value. What did draw the eye was a handsome chest tomb on the north side of the altar.

'We'll start with that!' Ensign Oates declared.

Fear-the-Lord was about to protest, for there was a beauty about the tomb that made its imminent destruction seem like desecration. But he took one look at the fervour-filled faces of his fellow soldiers and shut his mouth, wincing inwardly as the axes rained down on the tomb.

He could not stand here daydreaming. He must show his zeal for the cause. Wars were not won by faintheartedness. He swung his axe with the rest. Soon, as the dust fell, the despoiling of the chapel was complete. Graves had been opened and desecrated, and the bones of their occupants thrown into a pile outside. Fear-the-Lord wondered if the Almighty approved of such zeal in His name. Surely, He would be pleased that centuries of superstition and idolatry were being swept away?

Within two days, the troop had turned the chapel into stables and cordoned off the east end, where the altar was now being put to use as a butcher's block. Presently, the soldiers departed and the Great Rebellion continued its bloody course. Before a cannonball took off his head at the Battle of Naseby, Fear-the-Lord heard, when campaigning in the west, that Lord Chandos had re-taken Sudeley, but not for long enough to repair it. The forces of Parliament had placed it under siege again, and it had suffered a heavy bombardment. Fear-the-Lord spared a thought for the beautiful chapel he had helped to smash up and pillage. Was it still standing?

After King Charles had been beheaded and the war ended, Parliament imposed on Lord Chandos such a crippling fine that he could not afford to repair Sudeley Castle. And anyway, the Council of State was determined that no royalist should keep a stronghold that might be used against the new regime. They ordered that, like so many castles in England, it be slighted and rendered useless for any military operations.

Sudeley was reduced to a ruin. The roofs of the castle and the chapel were demolished, ensuring that nature could do its worst with what was left.

As the dead Queen slumbered unheeding in the earth beneath where her tomb had stood, the vicar of nearby Winchcombe began holding fortnightly services in the side chapel where she had worshipped. The land was rented out to tenant farmers, while the remains of the castle and the roofless chapel fell further and further into decay.

1782

Julia Bockett devoured books. It was fortunate that she was the daughter of Mr Brookes, steward to Lord Rivers of Stratfield Saye, the owner of Sudeley Castle. Her indulgent father, saddened to see her left a widow at twenty – her late husband had died after a fall from his horse five years ago – was glad of her interest in history, which had provided an admirable distraction from her grief, and pleased to keep her well supplied with the historical and antiquarian books she loved. She was lucky to have been born at a time when romanticism was flowering, for she was naturally fascinated by ruins, folklore, hidden places and the macabre in general. She had read *The Castle of Otranto* and *The Mysteries of Udolpho*, amongst other works of Gothic fiction, and been deliciously scared.

Lord Rivers did not live at Sudeley, for it was too ruinous, but he visited from time to time, staying at a house in nearby Winchcombe and taking his steward and other servants with him. On this occasion, in the spring of 1782, having heard from Mr Brookes of Julia's passion for the past, he had invited her to visit him there so that she could explore the remains of the ancient castle. She was more than excited. Sudeley, for her, was a beckoning paradise, a feast for the imagination.

The invitation was serendipitous because, a week beforehand, Mr Barlow, a personable Reading solicitor who had paid her compliments and shared her taste for all things weird and romantic, had called to pay his respects and brought her three gifts, which her mother said she might accept because they were books – quite a proper present from a gentleman to a young widow.

As soon as Mr Barlow had gone, having been pressed by Mrs Brookes to return for dinner that evening, Julia opened her parcel. To her delight, her admirer had given her George Ballard's *Memoirs of Several Ladies of Great Britain*, which she had long coveted. Beneath it was a printed pamphlet on the opening in 1777 of the tomb of Katherine of Aragon, the frightful Henry VIII's unfortunate first consort. Fascinated, Julia was just about to delve into it, when she saw what lay below. It was a heavy tome, clearly newly published. On the flyleaf, Mr Barlow had written: 'To dear Mrs Bockett, hoping that you will especially enjoy the account of Sudeley Castle contained herein. Your devoted admirer, Septimus Barlow.'

The book, written by one Samuel Rudder, was entitled *A New History of Gloucestershire*. It was 800 pages long and the price tag of two guineas was still affixed, an oversight by her beloved (for that was what he was, and she had high hopes in that direction).

After much debating with herself on which of her gifts to begin with, Julia settled down on a window seat to read the pamphlet and was soon deeply absorbed. From the sketchy evidence available, it seemed that Queen Katherine had been buried beneath a black marble table tomb near the high altar of Peterborough Cathedral, but that the gilding, the hearse and the small altar it enclosed had disappeared during the Civil War. The tomb itself was dismantled at that time and the marble used to floor one of the Dean's houses.

Julia frowned. What wanton desecration! As if the poor Queen had not suffered enough in life, losing all those babies and then being divorced and exiled from the court – and dying alone and abandoned by her dreadful husband. About sixty years ago, one of the canons had taken pity on her and had a brass plate with her name and dates inserted in the floor where the tomb had stood.

But now she was coming to the interesting part! Queen Katherine had had a devoted Spanish lady-in-waiting, Maria de Salinas, Lady Willoughby, and it had long been thought that she had been laid to rest in the same tomb as her late mistress. Seven years ago, in order to establish the truth of this, the tomb had been opened, but only one coffin lay within. It had been very strongly fastened and, to Julia's disappointment, no one had attempted to open it, for it had been adjudged a sacrilegious act to disturb the ashes of the dead for the sake of unveiling the secrets of the grave. But a verger, who was also somewhat of an antiquary, took it upon himself to bore a hole with a gimlet and introduce a long wire into the coffin, with which he drew out a fragment of black and silver brocade. Julia was transfixed. That must have been the fabric of the Queen's funeral robes. How she wished she could have seen it – something that one of King Henry's wives had worn. But it had been damp and had mouldered away when exposed to the air, whereupon the tomb was sealed.

Julia laid down the pamphlet, sad that there was no more to discover.

After luncheon, she curled up on the brocade sofa and made a start on Samuel Rudder's book on Gloucestershire. Cheating a little, she turned first to the section on Sudeley Castle and stared, entranced, at an engraving of the castle and chapel in ruins. Queen Katharine Parr, Henry VIII's sixth and last wife, had lived and died there, and been buried in that chapel. Julia wondered if there was anything left of her tomb. How she wished she could go to Sudeley and find out. If she had her way, she would visit all the tombs of the King's wives, but two were buried in the Tower of London, where they had lost their heads, and visitors were not permitted – unless you knew the right people, which Julia didn't. It was the same at Windsor, she believed. She had visited Westminster Abbey, where she had, with some difficulty and the help of a chorister, located the tomb of the unfortunate Anne of Cleves, but she would dearly have loved to have seen the last resting places of tragic Anne Boleyn and Katheryn Howard – innocent victims, she believed, of the tyrant they married.

And then Lord Rivers' invitation arrived, sending her into transports of joy. She would be seeing Sudeley – next week!

That night, she dreamed of Katherine of Aragon's tomb at Peterborough. There was the plaque and a portrait of the Queen. High above, on either side, hung banners bearing the royal arms of England and Spain. Some workmen came with picks and axes to open the tomb, but, just as they were about to do so, Julia woke up, the dream leaving a vivid impression in her mind. It was strange, but the pamphlet had said nothing about banners adorning the tomb; it had only mentioned the plaque and slabs of masonry that had been placed against the wall. It was remarkable what the imagination could do. It would be right and just if Queen Katherine was accorded in death the honours of which she had been so cruelly deprived in life.

Julia spent the next day writing an account of the queens' burial places in her journal. She only had Katharine Parr's to add, which she would do next week when she was staying at Winchcombe.

Two days later, however, she was reading *Memoirs of Several Ladies of Great Britain* in which Mr Ballard stated that the burial place of Katharine Parr was unknown – a circumstance somewhat extraordinary, he observed. Never one to be daunted, Julia wondered if she might find some trace of it in the chapel. It would be her mission to find even a fragment.

Samuel Rudder's description of the chapel at Sudeley had been accurate. There was nothing remaining of the church but the outer walls; the roof had long gone, leaving the interior exposed to the elements, but there was enough to show that it had been a beautiful building adorned with battlements and pinnacles; the only intact part was a small side chapel where, Julia was informed, divine service was performed once a fortnight.

She was accompanied to the ruins by the Honourable Marcia Pitt, Lord Rivers' youngest daughter, and Marcia's friend, Miss Caroline Wesley. Julia found her companions most congenial. The three young women were much of an age and shared an interest in ancient monuments, and, after she had told them of her desire to find Katharine Parr's tomb, they were fired up with enthusiasm for their expedition But, when they got to the chapel, there was something about it that repelled her. Shrouded in ivy, it looked forbidding, eerie. But she swallowed her unease and followed the others up what had once been the nave.

Almost at once, she noticed a large block of alabaster fixed to the north wall.

'What's that?' she murmured, walking over to examine it. 'I do believe it might be the back of an old sepulchral monument that once stood here. Mr Rudder mentions it in his book.'

'You don't think, Mrs Bockett, that it could once have formed part of the tomb of Katharine Parr?' the Honourable Marcia Pitt asked, her eyes brightening at the thought.

'That is exactly what I am thinking!' Julia replied, anticipation mounting in her breast. She looked down at the broken floor, through which a profusion of weeds had sprouted, and then, through a ruined window, espied some farm labourers working in a field beyond the chapel.

'Would your father mind if we asked those men to dig here to see if there is a grave below the surface?' she asked Marcia.

Caroline looked fearful. 'We shouldn't disturb a grave, Mrs Bockett!'

'But what if Katharine Parr is lying down there? If we find her, his lordship might erect some decent memorial.'

'I suppose so.' Caroline looked dubious.

'I don't think my father would mind us searching for her in the slightest,' Marcia beamed. 'It's not right that the grave of so admirable a queen is lost.'

'Maybe we should ask the tenant who farms this land,' Caroline suggested.

'Mr Lucas does not farm inside the chapel!' Marcia pointed out. 'Let's call those men over and ask them to dig here.'

The labourers came willingly when she called them, tugging their forelocks when they saw who she was. And they fetched their spades when she told them where she wanted them to dig. 'Just there, by the wall.'

Julia watched, transfixed, as the men moved what remained of the pavement and began to shovel away the earth beneath. She was holding her breath, praying that they would find Queen Katharine.

They had dug to a depth of about two feet when they found something grey and discoloured. Soon, excavating with greater care, they uncovered a lead coffin, of the envelope type that was moulded to the body. It was quite whole.

Julia could barely speak. 'There's an inscription on the lid,' she whispered.

Caroline had stepped back squeamishly, but Marcia had no such scruples.

Kneeling down, she peered into the grave. 'There is an inscription, but it's barely legible.' She leaned forward, brushed off some earth and rubbed the letters with her handkerchief. 'Oh, gracious me! It says, *Here lieth Queen Katharine*. We've found her! God be praised, we've found her.'

Julia was trembling with excitement. She had not forgotten that missed opportunity to view the corpse of Katherine of Aragon, and she would not be cheated this time. 'We have to see her!' she cried. Falling to her knees beside Marcia, she helped her lift the coffin lid, which came away quite easily to reveal a human form wrapped in cerecloth. Bursting with curiosity, she took her little gold scissors from her reticule and, reaching into the grave, cut open the layers that covered the face. Pulling them back, like a flap, she gasped, for staring up at her was the face of Katharine Parr herself, exposed to view after more than two hundred and thirty years. It was, miraculously, in a perfect state of preservation. The Queen lay there, her bright eyes wide open, her red-gold hair curling around her face. She had a firm chin and well-defined eyebrows. In life, she had clearly been comely.

The three young women stared at her, hardly able to believe what they were seeing. She looked as if life had only just left her. But then, after only a few moments, to their horror, the eyes dulled and sank into their sockets and the face began to turn grey and purple. A horrible stink filled the air.

'Cover it up!' Caroline cried, backing away. Julia and Marcia scrambled hastily to their feet, all thoughts of a memorial now forgotten.

'Fill in the grave, now!' Marcia urged the labourers, who had been watching from a respectable distance and were now holding checked kerchiefs to their noses. They hastened forward and began shovelling in the earth. Too late, Julia realised that they had forgotten to cover up the face. But she could not bring herself to look upon those decaying features again, so she left them to it.

Much later, when she had stopped trembling, she was able to take pleasure in remembering that she had this day been vouchsafed a glimpse of the face of a famous, long-dead queen.

1782

When John Lucas, the tenant farmer who occupied the land on which the ruins of the chapel stood, heard from his farmhands of the discovery in the chapel, his curiosity was piqued. He wished he had been there to see the coffin opened. It galled him to think that the Queen's face had been exposed in a perfect state of preservation for a few moments, and that he had not been there.

It was high summer before he resolved to dig down and open up the coffin himself. He did not think that his lordship would have any objection; after all, he must have sanctioned the search made by the young ladies.

Farming hours were long in summertime, and it was dusk before Lucas took his lantern and made his way to the chapel. Probably, after being exposed to the air, the body would have decomposed by now. But he might see something of interest.

When he had dug down to a depth of a foot and more, he found the lead coffin and ripped off the top of it. There lay, not the skeleton he had anticipated seeing, but, to his great surprise, an entire, human-shaped body wrapped in layers of linen cerecloth and looking as if it was uncorrupted. Even the face was preserved, although the features had sunk and were discoloured.

Keen to see what was under the cerecloth, Lucas took his knife and cut through the layers that covered one of the arms. He was pleased to find the flesh white and moist and that the weight of the hand and arm were as those of a living body.

His reverie was interrupted by a shout. 'Ho, Lucas, what are you doing?' It was his lordship, out for his evening perambulation; he sometimes came this way, and his footsteps were quickening now.

'By what right did you disturb this grave?' he barked, as soon as he saw what the farmer had done.

'My lord, I wished to see the features of the Queen, of which I had heard much,' Lucas replied, shaken by the appearance of his angry landlord.

'You took it upon yourself to open this coffin out of pure unwarrantable curiosity? Surely, it would have been quite sufficient to have found it and then to have made a report of it to Mr Brookes or myself? I am most displeased.'

'I meant no harm, my lord,' Lucas protested. 'I thought that, as the young ladies had opened the grave, your lordship would not object. I beg pardon if I have given offence.' Hastily, he replaced the coffin lid.

'Hmm.' Lord Rivers was peering down at the grave. 'I see there's an inscription.' He took out his kerchief and rubbed off the dirt. 'It reads: "K. P. Here lieth Queen Katharine, VIth wife to King Henry the VIII. And after the wife of Thomas, Lord of Sudeley, High Admiral of England and uncle to King Edward VI. She died September MCCCCCXLVIII." That's 1548. Lucas, you had best fill in the grave.'

He stood by, to see that his instructions were complied with.

'And now we will let good Queen Katharine rest in peace.'

1783

In the summer, his lordship's business made it necessary for Mr Brookes and his son William to be at Sudeley Castle. On being told by Lucas what he had seen when he investigated the Queen's grave the year before, the steward was seized with a similar curiosity to see the body and asked Lord Rivers if he might open the grave in the interests of writing an account of the exhumations for an antiquarian journal.

Armed with his lordship's permission, he went to the chapel with his son and directed that the earth be once more removed. All was as Lucas had described it, the coffin and corpse being just as he had represented them, only he had not mentioned the dreadful smell. The flesh where the farmer had made his incision was no longer white and moist, but brown and putrefied.

Hastily, Brookes stood up, feeling horribly nauseous. William began copying the inscription, but soon started retching and ended up vomiting on the broken flagstones. Brookes bade him cease his labours, but the young man insisted on completing the transcription and departed for Winchcombe looking quite green. Having ordered two grooms to seal the coffin and cover it with earth, Brookes came hurrying after him.

'I will recommend to his lordship that a stone slab be placed over the grave to prevent any future improper inspection,' he declared.

'Amen to that,' replied William, wishing he had never gone to the chapel.

When Brookes reported back to his lordship and mentioned the stone slab, Lord Rivers nodded in the way he had that told you the matter would be shelved indefinitely. And so it was.

1784

Hester Wigginshall was an old woman, but her forceful character was undimmed. When, one May afternoon, she and her husband were touring the ruins of Sudeley and entered the deserted chapel, she immediately set about locating Katharine Parr's grave. She had read of the previous excavations and was determined to see for herself whatever there was to be seen.

'Dig there!' she instructed her mouse of a husband, who had once dared to contradict her and learned very quickly that life would be much more pleasant if he kept his mouth shut. She had made him bring a spade and he dug, as ordered, presently uncovering the lead coffin his wife was seeking.

'Open it!' demanded that redoubtable lady. So he did and, at her instance, he cut away the cerecloth from the corpse, wrinkling his nose.

'My word!' exclaimed Hester. 'I thought to find her in a shroud, but look at that gown! Have you ever seen anything so rich and costly?'

'No, dearest,' George Wigginshall said meekly.

'And look at the shoes! What small feet she had!'

Hester scrutinised the body. The Queen's proportions were extremely delicate, and she particularly noticed that traces of beauty were still perceptible in the countenance, of which the features were almost perfect, except for the livid colours of the flesh. Her long hair was of burnished gold.

Hester never understood what possessed George, who suddenly lifted the corpse into a sitting position, with the head flopping forward.

'What are you doing?' she cried, but it was too late. By such injurious treatment and exposure to the air, the process of decay rapidly accelerated. Hester was about to vent her fury on George, but the Reverend Roberts, vicar of Winchcombe, chose that moment to walk into the chapel to prepare for Sunday's service. As he stared at the guilty pair, George dropped the body.

'By Heaven!' the shocked clergyman exclaimed. 'What are you doing?'

Hester, undaunted, explained that they had come to view the body of Katharine Parr – as if doing so was her God-given right.

'I'm sorry, Madam, but this is entirely unacceptable conduct,' Roberts protested. 'The dead deserve to be treated with reverence and respect. You, Sir, must close the coffin and fill in that grave at once.'

George hastened to obey, knowing that the wrath of Hester would descend on him once they were away from here. He replaced the cerecloth, so neatly that no one would ever know it had been cut open, and laid the lid on the coffin. All the time, the vicar stood watching him.

'I trust you will reflect on your deeds today and repent,' he said icily as they left. Hester sailed past him, head held high like a queen.

1786

The Reverend Treadway Russell Nash was in his element. He had just obtained permission from Lord Rivers to examine the chapel at Sudeley.

Like most antiquarians, he had read Samuel Rudder's book and was fired up by the description of the ruins therein. What Rudder had done for Gloucestershire, Nash had done for Worcestershire, being a historian of high reputation and a fellow of the Society of Antiquaries of London. He was educated, landed and well-travelled, having obtained his doctorate of divinity from Oxford, and also managed to find time to carry out his duties as vicar of Eynsham.

On an appointed day in the middle of October, Nash found himself gazing up at the chapel, which was a beautiful miniature of that belonging to Eton College. He and his friends, the Honourable J. Sommers Cocks and Mr John Skipp, both local antiquaries, examined the ruined interior, trying to envisage what it had looked like before the depredations of time and the Civil War.

The Reverend Nash was planning to write an account of the chapel for *Archaeologia*, but what he had really come to find was the burial place of Katharine Parr. He and his colleagues had read reports of the previous exhumations and been horrified at the lack of respect and care shown to the remains. Because of that, he doubted there would be much left to see now. And he was right.

On opening the ground and tearing up the lead, the three men found the face of the Queen totally decayed; most of the teeth, which were sound, had fallen out of their sockets.

'At least the body looks perfect,' Nash observed, 'as we would expect of a virtuous Protestant queen. It is clear that it has never been unwrapped, so it would be indelicate and indecent to uncover it.' The others agreed.

'The left hand is exposed,' Mr Skipp pointed out. 'We could unwrap that entirely, surely?'

They agreed that this would be permissible, and found the hand and nails perfect, but of a brownish colour.

'She must have been of low stature,' Nash said. 'Look, the coffin cannot be more than five feet four inches long.'

'I find it remarkable,' said the Honourable J. Sommers Cocks, 'that she should be buried in such a shallow grave.'

'My dear fellow,' said Nash, 'the pavement would have been higher when she was first laid to rest.' He seated himself on a folding stool and began to sketch the body. When he had finished, he transcribed the inscription on the coffin, which was hard to decipher because it was so dirty. It was no easy task as there were pesky rabbits everywhere; they had colonised the chapel and kept leaping into the grave and scratching very irreverently about the royal corpse. Repeatedly, Nash's friends had to haul them out.

Anger was building in him. 'I could heartily wish that more respect had been paid to the remains of this amiable queen,' he muttered. 'I would willingly, with proper leave, have them wrapped in another sheet of lead and decently interred in another place, that at last her body might rest in peace. It's intolerable that this chapel is used for the keeping of rabbits. I will be making representations to Lord Rivers.'

Nash went to see his lordship when he returned to Winchcombe later that day, but, for all his pains, received a lukewarm response to his plans for moving the Queen's body to a new sepulchre elsewhere. In the end, he gave up and went back to the chapel, where, dejectedly, he set about filling in the grave, not just with earth, but also with rubble, to deter anyone who might try to open it again.

The next day, his lordship being away on business, Nash took Mrs Cox, the housekeeper who looked after the residence at Winchcombe, to see the grave in the chapel, she having expressed a wish to do so. 'This is where Queen Katharine lies,' he said. 'Please thank his lordship for allowing us to examine the chapel. Tell him I will send him a copy of my article.'

'Very good, Sir,' Mrs Cox replied. She was a pleasant woman, far more friendly than her master. 'I think she should be left to rest in peace,' she said, looking sadly at the grave.

'Pray God she will now,' Nash replied fervently.

1792

When the Reverend Treadway Nash again perambulated Gloucestershire in the spring of 1792, he made a detour to Sudeley to satisfy himself that Katharine Parr's grave had not been disturbed again – and almost wished he hadn't.

Before he made his way to the chapel, he called on the excellent Mrs Cox, only to find her in a state of distress.

'It is Providence that has sent you to us!' she cried, wringing her hands. 'Only yesterday, some rough men opened the grave and – oh Lord, Reverend, I can hardly bear to tell you. They took out the body in a most disrespectful manner and even danced with it, flinging it about. And they have left it exposed on a heap of rubbish. His lordship being away, I have informed the vicar.'

'This is appalling!' Nash exclaimed. 'I will see what I can do.' Clapping his hat back on his head, he hastened off to the chapel, where he saw, lying on a pile of masonry and refuse, the Queen's skeletal remains, looking very forlorn, and only recognisable from the strands of long golden hair that were still attached to the skull. Richard Roberts, the vicar of Winchcombe was standing there, shaking his head.

'Good day, Reverend,' Nash said. 'What a terrible business. Mrs Cox told me about it.'

The vicar grimaced. 'I've asked Lucas to send a couple of his men to put the body back in the grave, then I shall say a few words over it. Perhaps you would like to do so too, Reverend?'

'I should indeed,' Nash agreed. 'Prayer will give some sense of decency to the proceedings.'

The two clergymen watched as Lucas's labourers returned the body to the grave, closed the coffin and replaced the earth and the rubble. Then they spoke the words of committal and prayed for the repose of the faithful departed.

'Do you know who was responsible?' Nash asked, as they walked back to the village.

'Yes. It was probably some of Mr Cantly's labourers. He farms the land adjoining Lucas's and keeps a very lax hand on his men. They're a wild bunch, up for any prank, and this smacks of them. Mr Brookes has been informed and is going to have a word with Cantly.'

Evidently, he had not done so, or Cantly had not acted on it, or the hands concerned were in no mind to pay heed to him. The very next day, Mr Lucas called upon the Reverend Treadway Nash as he was having breakfast at the White Hart Inn, where he was lodging.

'One of Cantly's boys has been seen prowling around near the chapel,' he said, holding his hat. 'Two of my neighbours saw him and warned me that that gang might be plotting some new outrage against the poor Queen. Jock Hunter fears they might try to steal her body. They think I should have it moved to a new grave and make that secure. Vicar agrees.'

'That's probably a very wise idea,' Nash said, finishing his devilled kidneys and dabbing his napkin to his mouth. 'It's best to bury her with the least trace possible, and leave a note of the location with Mrs Cox for his lordship.'

'Yes, Reverend.' Lucas looked uneasy. 'The thing is, my men don't relish this kind of work. They've been asked to open and close that grave several times now and, the last time, they had to handle the body. It ain't a pleasant task. I'm having them dig a plot much deeper than the one it's in now, and it's been agreed that they'll move her one night in Whitsun week. To sweeten their labours, I'm standing them a dinner in my barn beforehand, and I'm inviting several neighbours and the vicar. If you're still here, Reverend, you'd be most welcome – to see that everything's done right and proper, like.'

'That is most generous,' Nash said. 'I'd be happy to accept.' Bidding Lucas farewell, he hastened off to tell his landlord that he would be prolonging his stay.

It was a good dinner and the evening, fortunately, was warm. The food was hearty and plentiful, and the ale potent. Being an abstemious man, Nash sipped his, making it last. He noticed that the vicar was quaffing with the rest and that the labourers who were to move the body were becoming increasingly drunk. Lucas alone was looking at them nervously; his neighbours were all tipsy themselves and had probably not noticed.

When the dessert plates had been removed and fortifying glasses of brandy downed in record time, the company proceeded – or rather lurched and swayed – to the chapel. As Nash watched from the ruined chancel, the labourers stumbled over to the old grave, which they had already opened up, reached down and took up the body.

'What a hedge-whore we have here!' slurred one, wrinkling his nose at the smell.

'Show some respect, man!' Nash barked.

'Shut up, you great gollumpus,' the farmhand responded, in a most offensive fashion.

Before Nash could think of a suitable riposte, another labourer pulled off some hair from the skull. 'A souvenir for my missus,' he crowed.

A third man knocked out the remaining teeth and pocketed them. 'These could be worth something.'

Another man ripped off pieces of the tattered gown in which the bones were still clad. 'I could sell these too!'

Nash was so horrified he was speechless. He looked around for Lucas, expecting him to control his men, but he was nowhere to be seen. The neighbours seemed too drunk to care and the vicar had passed out and was lying on the ground, propped up against a large chunk of masonry. Nash was disgusted.

'You will treat those remains with respect!' he commanded the men at the grave.

'What business is it of yours?' one retorted. 'Why should you care for some old queen? Strikes me those Frenchies across the Channel have got the right idea about curbing the power of royalty. They just bleed the likes of us dry. Old Harry the Eighth, he was the worst. From what I've heard, he would have cut off her head, given the chance.'

'But we'll do it for him!' his friend crowed and swung his spade high.

'No!' Nash shouted. But it was too late. The blow severed the head, which rolled away. Then the men brutally pulled off the arms and one, wielding an iron crowbar, stabbed the skeleton repeatedly, breaking it up.

'You will burn in hell for this,' Nash warned, tears of impotent rage threatening. In truth, he was very frightened, all too aware of what these men might do with their spades and a crowbar. But they were done with their sport. Ignoring him, they picked up the various parts of the skeleton, crammed them into the coffin, nailed it shut and tipped it into the new grave, which they proceeded to fill in, whilst bawling out bawdy songs.

Nash walked away, unable to bear any more. He would come back in the morning to check that the new plot was properly disguised and could not be detected. And he would speak to the vicar and remind him of what a reprehensible example he had set his flock.

Back at the White Hart, still shaking with rage, he took out his pocket-book to write an account of what he had just witnessed, but soon laid down his pen. He could not bring himself to revisit such truly shocking events. He would write only that the remains of the Queen were again exhumed, this time by a set of Bacchanalians, who had perpetrated outrages so disgraceful that a veil must be drawn over them.

1817

The Reverend John Lates laid down the book that his patron, the Marquess of Buckingham had lent him. It had been fascinating to read about the discovery, four years past, of the body of the unfortunate King Charles I in a vault in St George's Chapel at Windsor. Even more intriguing had been the account of the remains of King Henry VIII, who was buried in that same vault with his third wife, Jane Seymour, whose small coffin had been left undisturbed. But that of the Tudor King, which measured six feet two inches in length, had been much decayed and appeared somehow to have been forcibly beaten in about the middle, exposing his Majesty's skeleton. Some of his red beard remained upon the jaw.

John Lates wondered how the coffin had become so badly damaged. Was it knocked about when the Parliamentarians deposited Charles I in the vault? Or had gases from the body caused it? There was an old tale he had read somewhere about the coffin exploding when it lay in state in Syon House. Maybe that had been true, although he had not quite believed it when he read it.

Lates had been vicar of Winchcombe for twenty-three years now, having replaced Richard Roberts. He was a conscientious man who served his flock well, which had led to his being appointed rector of Sudeley Chapel this very year. He did not mind the extra duties, for he loved the chapel, and his lordship, Sudeley's new owner, had enthusiastically sanctioned his proposal that it be restored, putting him in charge of the project. Hence his interest in royal burials, for he knew that somewhere in the chapel lay the remains of Katharine Parr. But where?

Well, he would concern himself with that later. For now, his interest was chiefly focused on the discovery of a fine stone vault in the little side chapel that had been used for services for the best part of two centuries. The workmen he had engaged had found it when excavating the floor and he was eager to see it. When he arrived that day with Mr Browne, the Winchcombe antiquary who was assisting in the restoration, the men opened up the vault, revealing only one skeleton inside and an empty coffin, with a plate stating that it belonged to Lord Chandos, who had owned and defended Sudeley during the Civil War. As the workmen replaced the bones in the coffin, Lates noted that the vault was sound. He was aware of the sorry and scandalous history of Katharine Parr's remains, and it occurred to him that it would be a good idea to recover them and place them securely in the vault before it was sealed up and the new floor laid. Mr Browne heartily agreed, as did his lordship when he was consulted.

Lates knew who might be able to tell him where the Queen was buried, and hastened away to the neat little cottage where lived Mrs Cox, the former housekeeper to the late Lord Rivers, who had sold the castle to Lord Buckingham.

At sixty-seven, Mrs Cox was still as bright as a button and pleased to see him. She insisted on serving him tea and her best seed cake and ratafia biscuits. He accepted them gratefully and listened politely as his hostess told him, not for the first time, how she had once thrown her substantial person across the bottom of a ruined staircase in Sudeley Castle's Octagon Tower to break the fall of King George, who had insisted on climbing the ruinous tower and tripped on the way up.

'You probably saved his Majesty's life,' Lates told her.

'He was ever so grateful,' she said. 'He gave my William a commission in the Guards. But you didn't come here to hear all that. To what do I owe the pleasure, Vicar?'

The Reverend Lates told her about the vault and his plan to place the Queen's remains in it.

'But I don't know where she is buried,' he ended. 'Mr Browne and I have searched all over the chapel. I was hoping that you could help me.'

'I can show you, Vicar. Finish your tea and I'll walk up there with you.'

When they arrived, Mrs Cox went straight to a spot near the altar. 'She's here.'

Lates asked the workmen to dig down. It was a tricky job because the grave had been lined with masonry.

'We've found something,' the foreman said.

Lates and Browne peered into the cavity. 'By Jove, she's been buried upside down!' Lates exclaimed. 'Who would do such a thing.'

'Lucas's drunken farmhands,' Browne said disapprovingly.

The coffin was lifted and laid on the ground the right way up. Lates and Browne had brought cloths, with which they cleaned the lid before opening it. To their great disappointment, they could not find the inscription described by the Reverend Nash in his scholarly article, so they proceeded to examine the body. It lay in a great profusion of ivy, which had invaded the lead and wound itself into a green coronet around the Queen's brow. Alas, all that remained of her was a heap of bones, to which adhered a few pieces of cerecloth. Under the skull, there was a dark-coloured mass. When dipped in a bucket of water, it was found to be a small quantity of hair, which exactly corresponded with some Lates already owned – taken, he suspected, during the desecration of 1792. But he had come by it honestly, having bought it from a gentleman in Cheltenham some years earlier.

'I think,' Browne said, 'that, as the inscription cannot be found, for the benefit of future antiquarians, it would be well, before the vault is closed, to engrave upon it the inscription given by the Reverend Nash.'

'A capital idea,' Lates replied. 'Would you be happy to do it?' He handed Browne a bent piece of lead that had covered the breast. Browne was about to hammer it flat to facilitate the engraving, when he saw the words *Thomas Lord* and *Sewdley* with some others. 'Look, Lates! This must be the original inscription!'

They worked on it for hours, carefully cleaning it and removing the grime, until it was perfectly visible. Then Browne took some impressions in thin paper.

Lates said a prayer as the body was moved into the vault in the small chapel adjoining. On his instructions, the workmen had firmly nailed the different pieces of lead together, so that they resembled the original form of the coffin. It was then laid on two large flat stones next to that of Lord Chandos. Lates measured the coffin and found it to be five feet ten inches in length. Nash had been wrong, Queen Katharine had been a tall woman.

The original inscription was replaced on the coffin and the vault was very carefully and securely closed.

'I pray that her late Majesty will not be disturbed again,' Lates said fervently.

1854–62

Emma Dent would have liked the chapel to be left as a romantic ruin, a poignant monument to Queen Katharine Parr, in front of whose memorial tablet, in the long years of her engagement to John Coucher Dent, she had erected an ironwork screen to deter souvenir hunters. But John's uncles, who had bought Sudeley Castle and the adjoining estate in 1837, the year of Queen Victoria's accession, had been adamant. They were wealthy men, glovemakers from Worcester, and were now determined to be landed gentry. Which meant, of course, restoring the castle and making it a fit abode for them. They had taken one look at the ivy-shrouded ruins of the chapel and decided that must be restored too. They had even brought in the renowned architect, Sir George Gilbert Scott, to plan and oversee the works, which began in 1854, two years after Emma and John were married.

And so the ruinous desecrated chapel was transformed into one of the most exquisite gems of ecclesiastical architecture. A new vault was prepared for the Queen's remains, to the left of the chancel window.

The Dent uncles died within a year, leaving no children, and Sudeley was inherited by John Coucher Dent. Emma came into her own, throwing herself indefatigably into the life of the castle and the village of Winchcombe, overseeing the ongoing restorations and making Sudeley a beautiful habitation, as it would have been in Queen Katharine's day.

She stood watching with tears in her eyes when, one April day in 1861, the Chandos vault was opened in readiness for the relics of Queen Katharine to be collected with pious care. When the coffin was opened, though, all there was to see was a little brown dust. Emma gazed at it, thinking of the portraits of the Queen and of how sad it was that a human life could be reduced to this. But her spirit was with God – that was what mattered.

The coffin was lifted up and then placed in the new vault. Above it, in the months that followed, was built a beautiful canopied tomb in the gothic style, designed by Sir George Gilbert Scott and adorned with the coats of arms of the Queen's four husbands. Sir George had unearthed a woodcut of the original sepulchre in a curious old work, *The Seven Lamps of Virginity*, and had also identified some sculpted masonry in the north wall as having once belonged to that monument. It gave him inspiration for the ornamentation of the new tomb.

Working from portraits of Katharine Parr, he designed a life-size effigy to lay on the tomb and engaged Mr Philip, with whom he had worked on the memorial to the late Prince Consort in Kensington Gardens, to make it in white marble.

Emma Dent rejoiced to see the effigy laid on the finished tomb in 1862. To mark the occasion, she hosted a ball in Katharine's honour, to which everyone came in Tudor dress. She ordered that a plate with an engraving of the inscription from the coffin be placed on a pillar nearby. She designed stained-glass windows in jewel colours depicting Katherine Parr with Henry VIII and Thomas Seymour and had them made by a Worcester firm of glaziers and installed in the chapel.

When all was done, she stood back and admired the finished works. She was glad now that her protests about the restoration had been overridden. She and her uncles had created a beautiful shrine to a much-loved queen. At last, after all the mishaps that had befallen them, Katharine Parr's remains were finally at rest.

2020

The historian stepped into the chapel and was pleased to find it empty. Good. She wanted some time alone here for reflection.

She could not quite believe that she had finished the series already. Six books. It had seemed a mammoth undertaking six years ago, although it had been her own idea. She had been passionately excited about the project, as were the publishers who had, to her great surprise, commissioned it. And, mammoth project though it indeed proved to be, she had loved every minute of it. It had been a joy to build on her earlier research and achieve new insights on these six Tudor queens.

But now, the series was completed. She had delivered the book about the sixth wife – who was buried just ahead of her, to the left of the altar. And she felt strangely bereft.

She walked up the nave and rested her eyes on the serene white effigy with its lovely face and hands joined in prayer – Katharine Parr as the Victorians had seen her: the pious Protestant heroine and the embodiment of all the feminine virtues. But she had been so much more than that.

'Pray God I have done you justice,' she whispered. She had sent up this prayer on completion of each other book in the series. They were novels, but they were based on living human beings, and she felt she had a responsibility there, a duty to portray her heroines as authentically as possible. She thought back on the hours she had spent crafting author's notes, explaining what was fact and what was fiction, and why she had followed certain storylines. If she had taken creative leaps of the imagination, she had only done so where there was evidence, however slender, to support them. The historian in her could never be stifled!

She said another short prayer by the tomb and stood there for a few moments more, reflecting on the extraordinary afterlife and miraculous survival of the Queen's remains, and of the story of her life that had unravelled over these past months. It had drawn her back here; she had felt a need to visit Sudeley. Much altered it might be, but this was where you came to find Katharine Parr.

She became aware of the faint sweet scent of apples. She looked around, but there was nothing to account for it. Probably it was whatever they used for cleaning the chapel.

She turned around and walked back down the nave towards the open door and the sunlight beyond. She did not see the tall lady dressed in a green gown and a Tudor headdress who watched her, smiling, from the shadows.

THE TUDORS

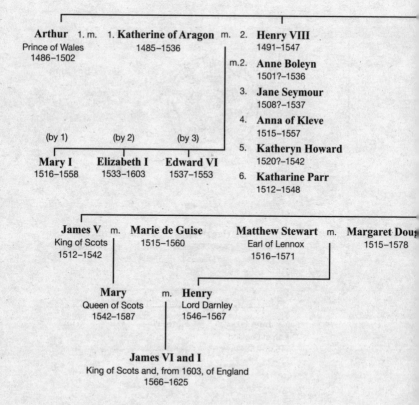

Arthur 1. m. 1. **Katherine of Aragon** m. 2. **Henry VIII**
Prince of Wales   1485–1536   1491–1547
1486–1502

     m.2. **Anne Boleyn**
        1501?–1536

     3. **Jane Seymour**
      1508?–1537

     4. **Anna of Kleve**
      1515–1557

(by 1)   (by 2)   (by 3)   5. **Katheryn Howard**
      1520?–1542

Mary I   **Elizabeth I**   **Edward VI**   6. **Katharine Parr**
1516–1558   1533–1603   1537–1553   1512–1548

James V m. **Marie de Guise**   **Matthew Stewart** m. **Margaret Doug**
King of Scots   1515–1560   Earl of Lennox   1515–1578
1512–1542   1516–1571

Mary   m. **Henry**
Queen of Scots   Lord Darnley
1542–1587   1546–1567

James VI and I
King of Scots and, from 1603, of England
1566–1625

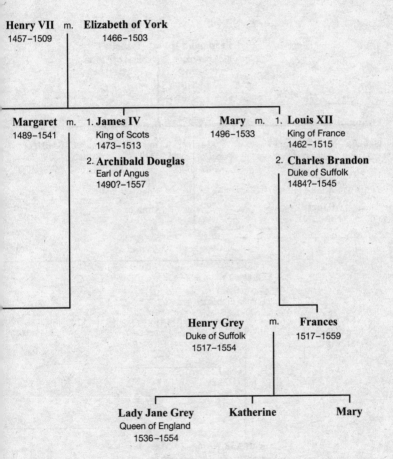

Henry VII m. **Elizabeth of York**
1457–1509   1466–1503

Margaret m. 1. **James IV**
1489–1541   King of Scots
             1473–1513

          2. **Archibald Douglas**
             Earl of Angus
             1490?–1557

Mary m. 1. **Louis XII**
1496–1533   King of France
             1462–1515

          2. **Charles Brandon**
             Duke of Suffolk
             1484?–1545

Henry Grey m. **Frances**
Duke of Suffolk   1517–1559
1517–1554

Lady Jane Grey   **Katherine**   **Mary**
Queen of England
1536–1554

THE ROYAL HOUSES

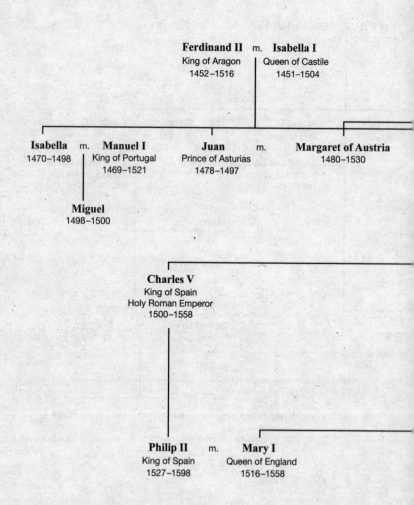

Ferdinand II m. **Isabella I**
King of Aragon | Queen of Castile
1452–1516 | 1451–1504

Isabella m. **Manuel I**
1470–1498 | King of Portugal
1469–1521

Juan m. **Margaret of Austria**
Prince of Asturias | 1480–1530
1478–1497

Miguel
1498–1500

Charles V
King of Spain
Holy Roman Emperor
1500–1558

Philip II m. **Mary I**
King of Spain | Queen of England
1527–1598 | 1516–1558

OF TRASTAMARA
AND HABSBURG

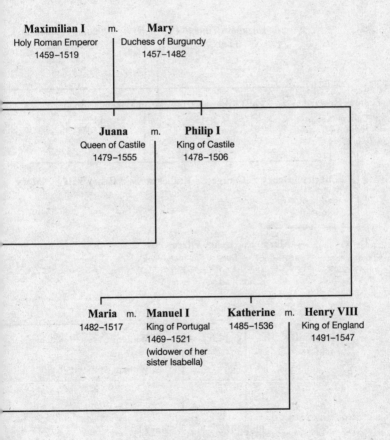

Maximilian I m. **Mary**
Holy Roman Emperor   Duchess of Burgundy
1459–1519   1457–1482

Juana m. **Philip I**
Queen of Castile   King of Castile
1479–1555   1478–1506

Maria m. **Manuel I**   **Katherine** m. **Henry VIII**
1482–1517   King of Portugal   1485–1536   King of England
1469–1521   1491–1547
(widower of her
sister Isabella)

The Howards
and The Boleyns

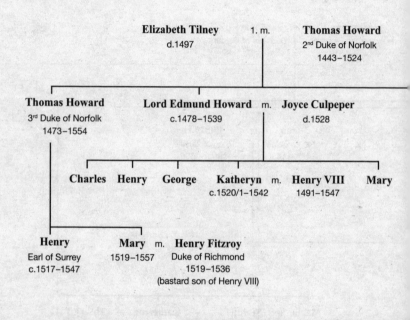

Elizabeth Tilney
d.1497

1. m.

Thomas Howard
2nd Duke of Norfolk
1443–1524

Thomas Howard
3rd Duke of Norfolk
1473–1554

Lord Edmund Howard
c.1478–1539

m.

Joyce Culpeper
d.1528

Charles **Henry** **George** **Katheryn**
c.1520/1–1542

m.

Henry VIII
1491–1547

Mary

Henry
Earl of Surrey
c.1517–1547

Mary
1519–1557

m.

Henry Fitzroy
Duke of Richmond
1519–1536
(bastard son of Henry VIII)

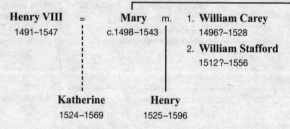

Henry VIII
1491–1547

=

Mary
c.1498–1543

m.

1. **William Carey**
1496?–1528

2. **William Stafford**
1512?–1556

Katherine
1524–1569

Henry
1525–1596

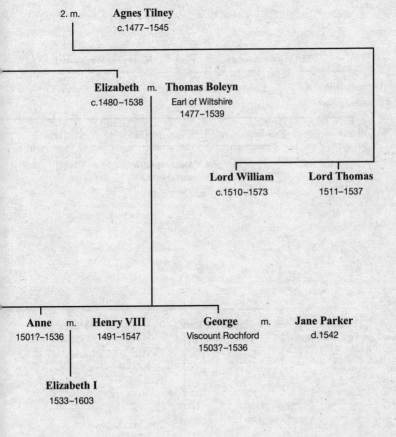

2. m. **Agnes Tilney**
c.1477–1545

Elizabeth m. **Thomas Boleyn**
c.1480–1538   Earl of Wiltshire
1477–1539

Lord William   **Lord Thomas**
c.1510–1573   1511–1537

Anne m. **Henry VIII**   **George** m. **Jane Parker**
1501?–1536   1491–1547   Viscount Rochford   d.1542
1503?–1536

Elizabeth I
1533–1603

THE SEYMOURS

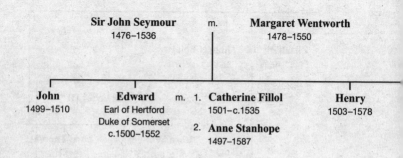

Sir John Seymour m. Margaret Wentworth
1476–1536 1478–1550

John   Edward   m.   1. Catherine Fillol   Henry
1499–1510   Earl of Hertford   1501–c.1535   1503–1578
        Duke of Somerset
        c.1500–1552   2. Anne Stanhope
                             1497–1587

Thomas   m.   Katharine Parr   Margery
Lord Seymour of Sudeley   (widow of Henry VIII)   d.1528
c.1508–1549   1512–1548

Mary
1548–1550?

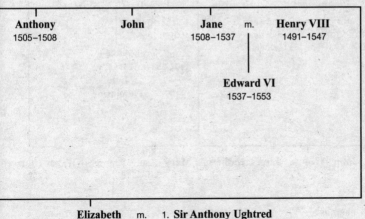

Anthony	John	Jane	m.	Henry VIII
1505–1508		1508–1537		1491–1547

Edward VI
1537–1553

Elizabeth m. 1. **Sir Anthony Ughtred**
c.1518–1568   1478–1534

            2. **Gregory, Lord Cromwell**
            1520–1551

            3. **John Paulet**
            Marquess of Winchester
            c.1483–1572

THE BASSETTS AND THE HUNGERFORDS

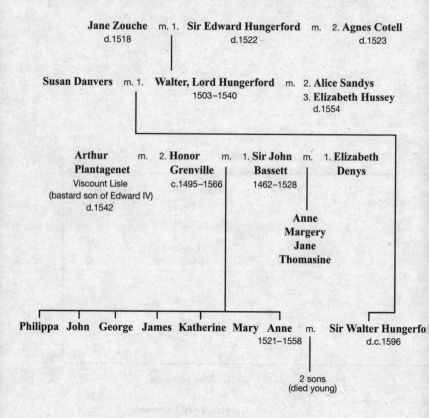

Jane Zouche   m. 1.   **Sir Edward Hungerford**   m.   2. **Agnes Cotell**
d.1518   d.1522   d.1523

Susan Danvers   m. 1.   **Walter, Lord Hungerford**   m.   2. **Alice Sandys**
1503–1540   3. **Elizabeth Hussey**
d.1554

Arthur   m.   2. **Honor**   m.   1. **Sir John**   m.   1. **Elizabeth**
Plantagenet   **Grenville**   **Bassett**   **Denys**
Viscount Lisle   c.1495–1566   1462–1528
(bastard son of Edward IV)
d.1542

Anne
Margery
Jane
Thomasine

Philippa   **John**   **George**   **James**   **Katherine**   **Mary**   **Anne**   m.   **Sir Walter Hungerfo**
1521–1558   d.c.1596

2 sons
(died young)

THE DUCAL HOUSE OF KLEVE

Johann III m. **Maria of Jülich-Berg**
Duke of Kleve   1491–1543
1490–1539

Sybilla m. **Johann Friedrich**   **Anna** m. **Henry VIII**
1512–1554   Elector of Saxony   1515–1557   King of England
          1503–1554   1491–1547

Wilhelm m. 1. **Jeanne d'Albret**   **Amalia**
Duke of Kleve   1528–1572 (annulled)   1517–1586
1516–1592   2. **Mary of Austria**
               1531–1581

The Parrs

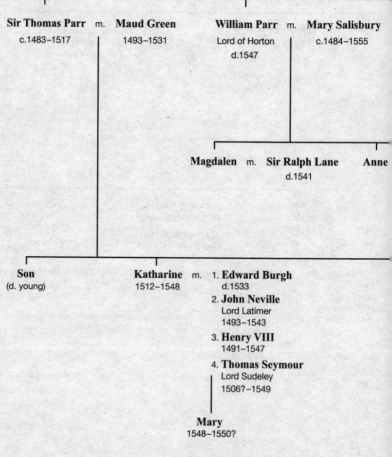

Sir Thomas Parr m. **Maud Green**
c.1483–1517   1493–1531

William Parr m. **Mary Salisbury**
Lord of Horton   c.1484–1555
d.1547

Magdalen m. **Sir Ralph Lane**   **Anne**
d.1541

Son   **Katharine** m. 1. **Edward Burgh**
(d. young)   1512–1548   d.1533

2. **John Neville**
Lord Latimer
1493–1543

3. **Henry VIII**
1491–1547

4. **Thomas Seymour**
Lord Sudeley
1506?–1549

Mary
1548–1550?

Anne Parr m. **Sir Thomas Cheyney**
d.1513   1449–1514

Thomas m. **Elizabeth**
Lord Vaux   1505–1556
1509–1556

Elizabeth m. **Sir Nicholas Odell**   **Mary**   **Margery**
         (or Woodhull)

Mary Odell

William m. 1. **Elizabeth Bourchier**   **Anne** m. **William Herbert**
Earl of Essex   d.1571 (divorced)   1515–1552   Earl of Pembroke
Marquess of   2. **Elizabeth Brooke**   c.1501–1570
Northampton   1526–1565
1513–1571

Acknowledgements

I owe a huge debt of gratitude to the fabulous team at Headline, especially Mari Evans, with warm thanks for commissioning the Six Tudor Queens series and these related stories; Flora Rees, for her brilliant and sensitive editing; Frances Edwards, for being a fantastic editor; Jo Liddiard, for her amazing, creative marketing; Caitlin Raynor, for being the best publicist ever; Katie Sunley, for her excellent administrative support; Hannah Cawse for the audio and Rebecca Bader, Chris Keith-Wright and the rest of the sales team, all unsung heros; and Patrick Insole and Siobhan Hooper for the gorgeous cover design. It has been the greatest pleasure to work with you all on this series.

I cannot sufficiently express my thanks to my agent Julian Alexander for bringing me and Headline together, and for all his support throughout the past seven years. And to Rankin, my husband, for being there for me. That means everything.